# Mischief & Manors

# Mischief & Manors

*For Angela~*
*The coolest pal! Thank*
*you for being awesome* :)
*♡, Ashtyn*

## ASHTYN NEWBOLD

SWEETWATER
BOOKS

An Imprint of Cedar Fort, Inc.
Springville, Utah

ISBN 13: 978-1-4621-1937-0

Published by Sweetwater Books, an imprint of Cedar Fort, Inc., 2373 W. 700 S., Springville, UT 84663
Distributed by Cedar Fort, Inc., www.cedarfort.com

LIBRARY OF CONGRESS CATALOGING-IN-PUBLICATION DATA
Names: Newbold, Ashtyn, 1998- author.
Title: Mischief and manors / Ashtyn Newbold.
Description: Springville, Utah : Sweetwater Books, An imprint of Cedar Fort, Inc., [2016]
Identifiers: LCCN 2016030677 (print) | LCCN 2016032895 (ebook) | ISBN 9781462119370 (perfect bound : alk. paper) | ISBN 9781462127139 (epub, pdf, mobi)
Subjects: LCSH: Orphans--Fiction. | Nineteenth century, setting. | GSAFD: Regency fiction. | LCGFT: Romance fiction.
Classification: LCC PS3614.E568 M57 2016 (print) | LCC PS3614.E568 (ebook) | DDC 813/.6--dc23
LC record available at https://lccn.loc.gov/2016030677

Cover design by Priscilla Chaves
Cover design © 2016 by Cedar Fort, Inc.
Edited and typeset by Jessica Romrell

Printed in the United States of America

10 9 8 7 6 5 4 3 2 1

Printed on acid-free paper

*To mischief-makers, matchmakers, and romantics everywhere.*
*And Mom, who is all three.*

# Chapter 1

*Maidstone, England 1818*

*B*roken fingernails and tattered lace were the cause of problems for many young ladies. A missing invitation to a ball could start a revolt. Surely the snub of a handsome gentleman would be enough to retrieve the smelling salts.

But today, much like every day, it wasn't any of these things that were causing me trouble. It was my younger brothers.

I hadn't noticed them leave my side. The clear shop window had been too great a distraction. So I hurried down the path, scolding myself for letting them out of my sight and for letting my imagination convince me I could afford a single item in that shop. Pretty ribbons and jewelry were not beyond the attentions of my admiring eye—just the coins that jangled in my reticule.

"Peter! Charles!" I called out, darting between laughing faces and rolling carriages. I stopped around a bend to scan the area, focusing my gaze on a man with whom I was regretfully acquainted. Although I could see only his balding head, I continued forward, sensing I had discovered my brothers' location.

As predicted, a closer view revealed two little heads, one covered in blond curls, the other in dark brown, standing beside the pie man. I released a huffed breath as I moved toward them. Not again.

Peter and Charles had a history of mischief, some of which centered on this man, Mr. Coburn. He sold pies in the village each week and my brothers grew increasingly clever in their efforts to steal from him. I had earnestly tried to engrave on their minds that stealing was bad, but they always needed to be reminded.

When I was twenty feet from where they stood near a bakery on the side of the road, I caught Charles's eye. His gaze froze on mine and then flickered to the small pie he held in his hand. I arched an eyebrow at him, tapping my foot and shaking my head. It seemed my stance had the opposite effect of what I intended, for Charles slapped a hand over his mouth, stifling sudden giggles. Peter was watching me too, a look of defeat on his face. It appeared that their latest strategy was to have Peter engage the pie man in conversation while Charles sneaked behind him and captured the pies. It amazed me that two little boys of seven and five could concoct such a devious plan.

As I came closer, Charles dropped the pie grudgingly into the pie man's basket, sharing a scowl with his older brother. I couldn't help but smile. They looked so much alike. Aside from Peter's darker hair and two inches of extra height, they could be twins.

I took a deep breath of relief and walked across the gravel to stand beside Peter. Mr. Coburn glanced in my direction with a grin that was more smirk than smile. "Good afternoon, Miss Downing." He bowed with mock civility. "I see you have left your brothers unattended yet again. How surprising."

I tried not to look too closely at his eyes. They were, in a word, revolting. They were a color most closely resembling bath water, and were pooling with a substance I could not name. Their miniscule size left them on the brink of existence. I held back a gag. "And to you," I greeted, ignoring his second remark.

He frowned, giving my brothers a sharp look. "I do not appreciate their company. They are ruffians." He cleared his throat and eyed me with a warning. "I do not take pleasure in associating with *ruffians.*"

I rolled my eyes inwardly. *Ruffians?* There were hundreds of things I could have said, and would have enjoyed saying, but containing my spite for the moment, I settled for, "I am sorry. It will not happen again."

Mr. Coburn seemed far from satisfied. I could see his beady eyes examining my face. A sardonic smile tipped his lips and I predicted his words before he spoke them. "Spending too much time in the sun, are we now?"

He was referring to my sunburnt face and, impossibly, I felt it burn hotter. "I misplaced my bonnet," I replied.

"What a daft thing to do. Perhaps the outcome was deserved." He grunted in disapproval and smoothed his hair over the bald patch on the top of his head.

My pride bristled.

"May I inquire after your age, Miss Downing?" he asked after a pause.

"I am nineteen."

The tremendous snort that followed made me jump. "Each of my daughters was married before the age of seventeen, and my youngest is soon to be married . . . if she recovers from her illness." For a moment his face flashed with sadness, but as soon as I noticed it, it was gone, replaced by his egotistical smirk. "At any rate, if you ever hope to be married, I suggest you stop spending so much time out of doors and more time tending to your appearance. With no dowry or connections, your appearance is all you are left with." He shook his head, giving me a disparaging look. "You are not ugly, but there is certainly work to be done."

I kept my mouth shut, afraid of what I would say if I chose to respond. My words could not be trusted when I had such fire racing through my veins. The man was absurd, and the biggest hypocrite alive.

"These two could use some assistance as well." He glanced at my brothers with a look of disgust. "Their behavior is completely unsatisfactory."

I followed his gaze behind me where Peter and Charles had now engaged themselves in the task of crafting very unflattering pictures in the dirt of who could only be Mr. Coburn, dragging their index fingers in the shape of hunched shoulders, a large belly, and the tail of his ridiculous coat.

I quickly pulled them to their feet and wiped the dirt from the seats of their trousers, making them giggle. My face burned with embarrassment, but part of me hoped the pie man would recognize his image in the dirt. It would probably do him some good, as his depiction of himself must have been equal to that of a Greek god at the very least.

He cleared his throat once my brothers were at my side again. "As I was saying . . . their behavior. Mrs. Filbee is far too elegant to allow such misconduct, so it must be your doing." He paused to dab at his eyes with a handkerchief. "I am not surprised."

My fists clenched at my sides. What an arrogant, odious man!

"And what, pray tell, is that horrendous creature they attempted to make a drawing of? Yes, drawing is primarily a woman's pastime, but a basic understanding of the craft should certainly be taught at an early age. If, of course, such simple minds could embrace the talent. Unlikely," he mumbled.

I took a steadying breath, but it was futile. I think it was safe to assume that Mr. Coburn needed to hear some humbling words. So I released the reins on my anger and allowed it to charge at him, full speed. But not without a bit of amusement, of course.

I walked a few steps closer, leaned toward him slightly, and squinted my eyes. "Mr. Coburn!" I gasped. "It appears your eyes have become even smaller since I saw you last. And what is that substance leaking from them?" I shuddered. "Perhaps you should see a physician about that."

"And you should stop eating so many pies for a while," Charles added with a thoughtful glance at Mr. Coburn's middle.

I nodded, nearly bursting from suppressed laughter. Somehow I managed to keep my smile in check. "He would be very wise to address some of his own issues before he begins fretting about ours."

Mr. Coburn glared at me through the horrifying substance.

Before I could lose my nerve, I took my brothers by their hands and smiled. "I thank you for your hypocrisy, Mr. Coburn. Good day." We turned swiftly and moved down the path, my heart racing in my chest. I ignored the feeling of the pie man's gaze on my back as we walked.

How long had it been since I had stood up for myself and my brothers? Until now, I had always remained silent, accepting the criticism. I felt strong, and strong was how I liked to feel. It was not easy, but silence was not how I wanted to live any longer. Silence was the sound of the sky at night, of the dead in the ground, of flowers as they bloomed. Not of me.

Peter and Charles erupted into giggles as soon as we were out of Mr. Coburn's sight. A little smile curved my lips as I watched them.

"Annette! I can't believe you said that!" Peter managed, turning his blue eyes up to me.

I grinned, grateful that I had won their admiration. "Yes, you can," I said teasingly. "But do you know what I cannot believe? I cannot believe that you two tried to steal from him again."

Charles clasped his hands together with a shy smile. "We almost got one."

I shook my head, my expression turning to a gentle rebuke. "Stealing is wrong. We must pay with money for the things that we want. We cannot just have them. We must pay for the things we want. Repeat it to me so I know you understand."

"We must pay for the things we want," they said together.

I smiled, content that they understood. For now, at least.

We walked in silence for a while as we passed the tall trees that separated the village from Oak Cottage. It was only three miles from the village, and it was a lovely day, so I did not object to the walk. The heat today was mild for summer, but my sunburnt face still burned uncomfortably under the sunlight.

It wasn't long until Charles started giggling again, sharing secret smiles with Peter. They both looked up at me, the tell-tale mischievous twinkle in both sets of blue eyes.

"What?" I asked with suspicion.

They snickered again, covering their mouths in an attempt to muffle the sound. "I know where your bonnet is," Charles said between giggles.

I stopped my steps. "Where did you put it?"

More laughter. I waited, folding my arms. I did not like where this was going.

"We put it with—with Aunt Ruth's . . . ," Peter fell into a fit of giggles before finishing, but Charles finished for him.

" . . . Underthings!"

I squeezed my eyes shut, shaking my head. I should have known my brothers were the culprits of my disappearing bonnet. But they hid it with Aunt Ruth's underthings? Ruth Filbee was not a woman to be trifled with, and my brothers knew that better than anyone.

They must have noticed my lack of amusement, because their giggles had fallen silent. "Is she going to be angry?" Charles asked, his face all seriousness now.

My heart melted in an instant. "She has called upon a friend this afternoon, so if you remove my bonnet from her . . . underthings, as soon as we return, she will never know. Not to worry. But you must be careful, do you understand?"

They nodded, squeezing my hands a little tighter.

As soon as the point of Oak Cottage peeked above the hill, my brothers were running, racing to the door as they always did. In the five years that we had lived here—nearly Charles's entire lifetime—I had never been able to call this place home. A home was a place of peace, security, refuge. Oak Cottage was none of those things. It was beautiful to the outside eye—I had heard it dubbed "fashionably quaint"—but I had trouble finding beauty in the place where I'd felt so much misery. It was hard to see beauty in Oak Cottage when I'd known true beauty once.

The house was positioned at the peak of a hill, appropriately named for the multitude of oak trees surrounding it on all sides. The facade was grey stone, carved with precision but with enough artistry to give it character. The plot of land set so far above level ground was not envied, mostly because of traveling inconvenience, so Aunt Ruth had received it for a very inexpensive price. But the price, I knew, was not the only thing that enticed her to purchase the home. Living on a hill would allow her to do what she loved most: put as many people beneath her as possible.

When I reached the top of the hill, I placed my hand on the door handle and turned it, but the door would not open. I pushed a little harder, opening a crack between the door and frame to reveal the glowing faces of my brothers, assuming themselves completely jocular, holding the door shut.

"You two are atrocious, do you know that?" I teased.

"Yes, we know that!" Peter and Charles exclaimed in unison, erupting yet again into high-pitched giggles.

I curled the corners of my mouth into a smirk. "Very well, boys, if you must be atrocious, then I must be atrocious right back." A series of shrieks followed my words.

Smiling, I stepped away a small number of steps, turned my shoulder to the door, and came at it with full force. I turned the handle at the perfect moment and the door swung open—causing my brothers to be knocked to their backsides several feet behind the threshold.

"Was that atrocious enough?" I asked, faking sincerity.

"Yes!" they shrieked.

I walked a few steps closer and arched an eyebrow questionably, at each of them in turn. "Are you quite sure?" My voice was all mischief.

Charles moved away from me, scooting backward on the wooden floor. "Yes, yes we're sure!" he screeched, eyes widening. Peter began to follow Charles's representation of what he thought to be a good way of escape, scooting backward beside him.

I paused, as if considering their response. "I don't think so." I lunged forward and my fingers landed first on Peter. I tickled all over his stomach and ribs—definitely his weakest point when it came to tickling. He released a sound somewhere between laughter and screaming as he thrashed and kicked on the ground. I gave him a break and moved on to Charles, who was still attempting his escape. I grasped his arm and tickled beneath his chin on his neck.

"No!" He giggled hysterically and pressed his chin down, trapping my fingers and eliminating passage for me to tickle him any further.

"Very well," I sighed, "I suppose we are even." I grinned wickedly and caught my breath, helping my giggling brothers to their feet. "Now hurry and retrieve my bonnet. It won't be long until Aunt Ruth returns." At the mention of our aunt, they hurried from the room without a sound.

As soon as they were down the hall, I turned to the small mirror resting on the wall beside me, examining the damage of my sunburn. The red seemed to have intensified, contrasting starkly with my dull green eyes and bronze hair. Another day in the sun had darkened the scarlet at least one shade.

I sighed. It was times like these that I was grateful I did not hold beauty to the importance and priority that most young ladies did. I had more important matters to attend to. And why should I care? Even if Mr. Coburn was right that all I had was my appearance, I did not plan on marrying. As soon as I was able, I would find a family to take me on as a governess. Until then, my brothers needed me to protect them and look after them and love them always. And I was to do it myself. There was no man in the world that could ever steal the place in my heart reserved especially for my brothers.

With these firm thoughts in mind, I turned away from the mirror. The moment I did, I heard the door slide open behind me and felt the rush of warm air at my back.

I whirled around. Aunt Ruth stood in the doorway, her silver-streaked hair pulled back tightly, her eyes turned on me. My breath stopped in my lungs. She was home early and my brothers were still in her bedchamber. Panic crept methodically into my stomach.

I didn't know if it was her hard, grey eyes, or her strong, thick arms that used to frighten me more. She was large for a woman. Large for a man, even. It had taken five years, but I could finally speak to her without cringing or dropping my gaze. *Do not make her angry*, I told myself. As long as she was in a cheerful mood, all would be fine.

I smiled in greeting as she stepped inside and closed the door. After achieving a clear look at her face, it did not take long for me to realize that she did not require provocation. She was already very angry.

She stomped into the room until she was several paces ahead of me and then turned, giving me a look that I knew meant danger. "I crossed paths with Mr. Coburn on my way here." Her voice was quiet, shaking with rage. "Your brothers attempted to steal from him again!"

Impulsively, I took a step back, toward the wall. "I apologized to him. Please do not be angry." My voice was steady, which I was quite proud of.

She lunged forward and gripped my upper arm so tightly I felt my pulse against her thick hand. I bit the inside of my cheek to keep from crying out. "Control those little thieving scoundrels or I will do it my own way."

Anger flushed my cheeks. "They are not scoundrels!" I jerked my arm from her grasp, daring myself to keep a lifted chin.

The look in her eyes brought the feeling of sore bruises to my mind, and wounds of fear that would never heal. She was silent for too long; I could hear my heart pounding in my ears. But before she could say another word, the sound of giggles and running footsteps split the air.

"Aunt Ruth's underthings were on top of it!" Peter yelled with disgust as he ran out of the hall, bonnet in hand. The moment his eyes fell upon the scene, he froze. Charles ran up beside him, his giggles fading instantly. Their gazes jumped to me frantically. Fear and urgency flashed in their eyes.

I hurried around Aunt Ruth, taking their hands and pulling them behind me. I turned to face our aunt, resolute to keep my brothers safe. As I did, Charles buried his face in my skirts, hiding from the one person that ever managed to break his laughter.

Aunt Ruth stood fuming, clenching her fists at her sides. Her voice was chilling as she said, "I will be back in a moment." She walked forward and stomped around us, moving with purpose in the direction of her bedchamber.

Releasing the breath I had been holding, I led my brothers across the room, closer to the door, where we could face her when she returned. I smoothed my hand over Peter's hair and wrapped my arm around Charles. "It will be all right. Just keep quiet." I didn't have to look at their faces to know they understood.

After several minutes of waiting, Aunt Ruth was back, clutching a wrinkled paper in her hand. I saw the black curve of writing.

"I am finished with their behavior!" she seethed, waving the paper in the air in a violent fashion. "I wonder why I ever invested in the lot of you. In return I have received *nothing*. Nothing! Nothing but two maddening children and a pathetic, undignified girl that is growing into precisely the same sort of woman." She stepped toward me and lifted her nose, examining my face through narrowed eyes. "One who has an obvious lack of charge for her complexion."

My eyes flickered back to the parchment in her fist. Aunt Ruth noted it.

"Ah. You wonder at the meaning of this?" She lifted the folded paper and swiped it quickly and forcefully across my face. I felt the slice of the edge as it cut through the skin at the side of my face near my ear. I heard Charles squeal and felt him bury his face into the side of my skirts. Peter squeezed my left hand even as I lifted my right to the new cut on my cheek. It was small, but I could tell it ran fairly deep, considering that a sheet of paper was the weapon. I withdrew my fingers and stared at the two droplets of blood there.

"What is another blemish?" Aunt Ruth said dismissively. "What matters is that I will be rid of you soon and shall not be forced to look upon it."

My stomach tightened. "What do you mean?"

"I'm sending you away, simpleton! If the boys do not return with significant improvement, then I will have no other choice but to punish them. And my punishments will be most . . . severe. Do you understand?"

"Punishments?" My heart pounded with dread.

"There is an orphanage in Scotland I believe will suit them quite well."

I took a step back, dread pouring through me with a new sense of urgency. "No." I was shaking my head. "You cannot do that."

"I can, and I will if my requirements are not met." Aunt Ruth held up the paper again, a short length of the edge now laced with my blood. She chuckled deeply. "You may calm yourself. I am not sending you to a hell as you may be imagining. I am sending the three of you to Kellaway Manor by an invitation of sorts. I trust you have heard of the place? Your parents were dashedly fond of the family."

*Kellaway Manor?* The name rang in my ears with familiarity. I had been there once before. Kellaway Manor was in Dover, I remembered that much from my single visit there. I remembered how much Mama and Papa loved to visit the Kellaways. And it was the place my parents were returning from when they died.

My mind tugged me back to a time that I still hoped for things. A time that was awakened by the sound of those two words: *Kellaway Manor.* But that memory also brought back the day my parents didn't return. It was the day that reminded me that hope is a very dangerous thing. Promises were made that day that mustn't ever be broken, and my heart had been schooled to uphold them.

"Read the letter!" Aunt Ruth barked, pulling me from my thoughts. She threw the paper in my direction, letting it fall slowly to the ground. "I will order the carriage tomorrow morning. You will stay there for the remainder of the summer." Then she marched from the room, mumbling very unladylike curses under her breath.

I didn't waste a second, bending over to pick up the letter with shaky hands. The date inscribed at the top read nearly five years ago. The seal had already been broken, so smoothing the wrinkles from the parchment, I read to myself.

*Dear Miss Downing,*

*I am deeply sorry to hear of the loss of your dear mother and father. I cannot imagine the grief you are inevitably feeling, and the new burdens that you must undertake. Your parents were among my closest friends and I was saddened profoundly to hear of their accident. I admit that I feel somewhat to blame. I invited them to visit my home, and had I not, I daresay they may still be alive. I am deeply sorry. I would like to express my utmost condolences and invite you, along with your brothers, to visit my home, Kellaway Manor, in Dover anytime you would like. I trust that your aunt will see to the arrangements. I hope to see you again soon.*

*Sincerely and with a heavy heart,*

*Mrs. Catherine Kellaway*

My heart leapt within my chest, diminishing my unrest to a faint memory. Kellaway Manor. Something about clean, bright stone, and lush, green grounds flashed in my mind.

But the letter had been written five years ago. Surely Mrs. Kellaway was not even remotely expecting us now. How rude of Aunt Ruth not to inform her! What if she decided to turn us away?

It had been years since the letter was sent! I held the paper close and reread it slowly.

My thoughts focused on one particular sentence: *I admit that I feel somewhat to blame for the death of your parents.* My heart sunk upon reading the words again. Mrs. Kellaway had felt that guilt for the past five years, and for no reason at all. I certainly did not blame her for their death. How could she blame herself?

I studied the letter a final time. She stated that we were welcome *anytime,* so surely she wouldn't turn us away. Still, my conscience burned with unconformity. How embarrassing it would be to drop ourselves on her doorstep! I forced my whirlwind of thoughts to decelerate and took a deep breath, and then another, holding the letter to my heart. In less than one day's time my brothers and I would be released from our tedious confines and free from our wretched aunt!

I folded the letter gently, surprised to see how tremulous my hands were. I turned to face my brothers, an eager smile pulling at my lips.

"What does it say?" Peter asked, attempting to pull the paper from my grasp.

I lifted the letter out of his reach and reiterated the contents to them briefly. As I did, I could see excitement shining in their eyes like little rays of sunshine that warmed my heart.

My rapturous spirits dropped as I recollected Aunt Ruth's intentions for this visit. My brothers were required to become perfect little gentlemen, to return well-behaved or else be sent to Scotland. My heart ached at the thought. I could not break any promises now. Not ever.

But Peter and Charles did not even know what a gentleman was like! They had never had the example of a good man to influence them. The only man they ever interacted with was Mr. Coburn, and he was not a man in whose footsteps I desired them to follow.

"You must be on your best behavior," I told my brothers seriously. "I will not have you enduring Aunt Ruth's horrid punishments. Do you understand? I will not have you sent away to an orphanage."

They nodded with solemn expressions, but I could see smiles tugging at their lips. They were expecting an adventure. I squeezed

Charles's cheek affectionately and ruffled Peter's hair. Then I took a deep breath and smiled. "Shall we go pack our things?"

The day was new and the sun was bright as I stood at the window of my bedchamber, staring out at the road beyond the hill where the coach was prepared to take us away. My heart skittered with something resembling excitement. The last time I had taken a carriage, or even left Maidstone, was years ago.

I threw the drapes back over the window. "Charles, Peter! It's time to leave!" I yelled across the house as I grabbed my traveling trunk and ran to assist my brothers with theirs. By the time I found them, they were already standing at the front door, speaking excitedly in hushed tones.

With Aunt Ruth nearly pushing us out the door, we made our way across the path and down the hill leading out to the carriage. Peter and Charles had never ridden in a carriage before, nor to their memory had they been outside this town. No doubt that was why they appeared to be running as fast as their legs could carry them. A laugh bubbled within me, and I hoped for their sake that there would be a great deal of fun and adventure awaiting them. They were much deprived of both.

After stepping inside the carriage, I cringed as my eyes fell upon the interior. The cushions were pink. I sighed as I sat down, shunning the admiration I felt at seeing the color. Although it was a beautiful shade, I couldn't allow myself to think such nonsensical things. Pink was just another thing that had changed in my eyes on the same day hope did.

My brothers giggled with anticipation as the carriage began to roll forward. I turned my gaze out my window, watching Oak Cottage until it was out of sight, assuring myself that it was true— that we were really leaving it behind. My brothers had their faces pressed against the glass of their windows, watching with awe at what lay ahead of us.

The ride was expected to be half a day's journey, so I sat back and willed myself to relax. Worry over what Mrs. Kellaway would say when we arrived crept back into my mind, but I pushed it away. There was no need to fret about that just yet. I watched with amusement the complete thrill that my brothers were exhibiting. Apparently they were enjoying the ride every bit as much as I expected.

Satisfied, I slipped lower in my seat. My eyelids were heavy, as if my lashes weighed tons. My rest the previous night had not been near sufficient, so I lay my head back on the plush cushions and before long, I had fallen into a deep sleep.

I awoke to Peter shaking my arm urgently. "Annette! Annette!" A slight tone of panic raised his voice.

I sat up quickly, the steady sway of the ride reminding me of my location. How long had I slept? One hour? Two? More? My half-sleeping gaze darted around frantically, not finding the problem. "What is it? What's wrong?"

Before Peter could answer my question, I saw Charles on the floor of the carriage just in front of me, looking quite green, on his hands and knees. He was leaning over a grotesque puddle of vomit.

Shocked, I jumped from my seat and knelt beside him. "Charles!"

He glanced up at me and a tear leaked from the corner of his eye. I placed a hand on his forehead, smoothing back his blond curls. His skin was cold and sweaty, and I could see his hands shaking as they pressed against the floor.

Dread and worry dropped in my stomach at once. "It must be the carriage," I muttered, taking him by the arm. "Can you stand?"

"I don't know." His voice wavered, then turned into a choked sob.

"Let us try."

He nodded and I pulled up on his arm gently, helping him to his feet. The moment he stood, his face turned a sickly yellow and he doubled over and vomited again, this time all over the front of my dress. He slumped back down to the floor, his chin quivering as it always did when he was in pain but trying to be strong. I sat down beside him, resting my back against the seats and holding his head in my lap.

"You will be just fine, Charles." I stroked my fingers across his forehead. He closed his eyes, his face beginning to sweat profusely, his arms beginning to tremble. "You are being so brave," I said in a whisper. And it was true. This little boy knew what it was to be afraid, to clutch onto his strength with firm hands. So that was why today, he did not cry. That was why everyday I did not cry.

Once I concluded that it was indeed the carriage that was making Charles ill, I alerted the coachman to stop driving. What Charles needed was fresh air and steady, motionless ground.

After we took several turns around the coach and through the meadow grass beside the road, we stepped back into the carriage. My gown and the floor were still painted in vomit when we started moving again, but what mattered was the pink flush returning to Charles's cheeks. I hoped it would last.

In the hours that followed, Charles slowly lost color again, and whatever remained of his breakfast found a home on my boots. The road was awfully uneven, and it made me dread the ride back to Oak Cottage even more. Maybe a tiny part of me dared to wish that it would stay bumpy forever, perhaps even become too bumpy to travel by. I wished that we would never have to go back on that road that led to fear and painful memories.

"Is that it?" Peter asked from beside me, peering out the window with wide eyes.

I craned my neck to look over his shoulder. It was Kellaway Manor. I could see it now, rising ahead of us beside the road. Dozens of windows covered its golden facade, and the bright green grass ahead of it stretched wide and short and smooth. "Yes," I answered with a smile.

It had been ten years since I had visited Kellaway Manor, but I remembered it as a beautiful place. I remembered the adventure and the smell of flowers and sunshine and secrets. My parents loved it there, so I did too. We had only stayed for a day or two, and everything had been perfect.

Well, except one thing, or person, rather . . .

The carriage slowed as it turned up the drive, coming to a gradual halt. Without waiting for assistance, I pulled Charles into my arms, stepped down, and moved my feet across the neatly trimmed lawn. My hair was in my face, and my hands were occupied with Charles, so I struggled to see through the thick strands covering my eyes. I placed Charles gently on his feet beside me and steadied him on my arm. As I did, a small gust of wind cleared the hair from my face as I approached the house, bringing its beauty into full, unobscured view. I stared in awe, lifting my hand to my head to keep my bonnet from tumbling.

It was surely more sizeable than I remembered, but the color of the stone was the same. It reminded me of a loaf of golden brown bread, fresh from the oven. It stood large and grand among the flourishing gardens surrounding it.

I felt a small bloom of excitement unfold within me as I gazed upon it, born from a childhood memory of walking to this very door on my father's arm. Even so, there was an unmistakable flutter of nervousness in my stomach. The Kellaways would not recognize me. Mrs. Kellaway had likely forgotten about her letter a long time ago. And this was not a pleasure trip. The task of turning my brothers into perfectly behaved children was on the table, and it could not be ignored.

I walked up the front steps, taking a deep breath. My heart pounded. Before I could lose my nerve, I took hold of the brass knocker and hit it three times—much more forcefully than I intended—against the strike plate. I cringed at the large echo the sound created. *Relax*, I commanded myself. *These were Mama and Papa's friends. They will be welcoming.*

We waited in stretched silence for several seconds, and when I heard the turn of a lock, my heart threatened to burst through my chest. Not a second later, the door swung open at the hands of the butler, who greeted us with a warm smile. That smile fell as he spotted Charles moaning in my arms. Then, as if from nowhere, a middle-aged woman appeared beside him, a confused look clouding her delicate features.

"Are you Mrs. Kellaway?" I stammered, even though I knew she was. Her hair was a striking, thick auburn, not easily forgotten. Her face had hardly aged in the ten years since I had met her.

"Yes," she answered, smiling with question.

My words spilled out quickly. "I am very sorry, but our aunt just gave your letter to me yesterday. It was extremely rude of her not to inform you, but she sent us on your invitation from five years ago." I watched carefully for her reaction. Her brow furrowed with consternation as her gaze settled on Charles.

"Oh! And Charles became ill on the drive here," I added, looking again at her expression. She was still confused. How could I have been so foolish as to think that she wouldn't be? After a moment of staring at her blinking eyes, I realized that I had not even given our introductions. Scolding myself for my stupidity and lack of manners, I said, "My name is Miss Annette Downing and these are my brothers, Peter and Charles."

Her face instantly softened and she gasped, bringing a hand to her lips. "Heavens, is it really you?"

I nodded, uncomfortable under her searching gaze.

She shook her head in awe. "It is indeed you. I am glad you came! It has been so very long!" She laced her fingers together and her smile grew. I noticed how her top lip nearly disappeared when she smiled, and her nose wrinkled on the bridge. She had a very friendly face, the details of which I had forgotten. "Come in, come in! I will find my son to attend to Charles."

"Thank you," I said, feeling a deep weight of anxiety fall from my shoulders. Something about her genteel air seemed to make all my worry melt away.

"Here," Mrs. Kellaway said, gesturing to the drawing room at the right, "have a seat and be comfortable. I shall return shortly."

I stepped through the doorway and immediately felt myself shrink. The entry hall ceiling stretched up and up, ending in a dome. The floor was marble, and an intimidating spiral staircase stood just ahead. Several footmen, the butler, and the housekeeper discreetly stepped into position. They had obviously not been expecting guests.

I swallowed and gripped my skirts. The inside of Kellaway Manor seemed much larger and grander than I recalled it being. I wondered what else had changed. Excitement fluttered in my stomach. There was much to be discovered here, and I wanted to see it all.

My eyes returned to Mrs. Kellaway. She was staring with masked dismay at my vomit-tarnished gown. "Did you come with a maid, dear?"

Chagrin flushed my cheeks. "I did not." I knew that for a young lady to travel without a maid was improper, but Aunt Ruth didn't care that I was proper. She cared only that she didn't have to sacrifice a servant upon sending us away.

To my surprise, I didn't receive the censuring look I was expecting. Instead, Mrs. Kellaway's inviting smile didn't falter for a moment. "Oh, that is quite all right. I will send one of my maids to fetch a clean gown from your trunk." Then she smiled again and disappeared around the corner.

Exhaling a sigh of relief, I set Charles down gently and took his hand to guide him under the golden archway that led to the drawing room. I lifted him onto a settee and sat down beside him. I removed my bonnet, set it on the cushion beside me, and ran my hand along the smooth cream fabric. Afternoon sunlight filtered in through the large windows, causing the crystal chandelier hanging at the center of the room to shine brilliantly. A tea table sat just in front of us with a great variety of books resting atop its smooth surface. I picked one up and examined the cover briefly.

I had just begun flipping through the pages when Mrs. Kellaway came striding into the room accompanied by a maid with dark hair and kind brown eyes, her round cheeks giving her a youthful appearance. She seemed to be close to my age. With a cheerful smile, she handed me a clean blue gown.

"Here you are, miss," she said, dropping a curtsy.

"Thank you." I took the gown and held it in my lap. It felt strange to be waited upon, even for such a paltry task. The servants at Oak Cottage knew that I preferred to accomplish things on my own. Independent was how I had learned to be.

Mrs. Kellaway stepped closer and addressed Charles with genuine concern, taking his hand in hers. "How are you feeling?"

Charles shook his head in silent response, his face still pale.

"Oh dear." She released his hand, moving her gaze to me. "My son is a wonderful physician. He completed medical school at Oxford and has been in practice for several months now."

It struck me as odd that a young man bred in such grandeur would have opted for a medical profession rather than the military or clergy. But that he had an occupation at all meant that he was likely Mrs. Kellaway's younger son. A memory pricked in my mind with distaste.

"You have met, I believe, when you visited years ago." She laughed lightly. "His behavior has mended itself since then, I assure you. Little Charles is in quite capable hands. He will be here shortly to assist him. Would you like Lizzie to show you and Peter to your rooms?"

I glanced at the maid who was still smiling. She must be Lizzie. I returned her smile. "No, thank you. I will stay just until I see that Charles is feeling well again."

"Yes, of course." Her thin lips curled into a smile that made her eyes twinkle. "I really am awfully glad that you came to visit. The last time I saw you, you were so small! You have become such a beautiful young lady." Her eyes flickered over my face with a hint of sadness, but her smile returned before I could wonder what it meant. "We shall chat later, but for now I have some things I must attend to." She took the dress from my lap and handed it to Lizzie. "Take this to the second floor and prepare a room for Miss Downing." Then she turned and with a swish of fabric from her gown, she was gone.

I stared at the door for several seconds before pulling my gaze back to Charles. He was looking much better already. He didn't seem to need attention from a doctor. And the doctor was Mrs. Kellaway's son. Oh, yes. How could I have forgotten about *him*? His mischievous smile and infuriating words and . . .

Just then the door to the drawing room opened again, and a young man, no longer a boy stepped into the room. I choked on a breath.

And his eyes . . .

# Chapter 2

*Ten Years Before*

*I* clung to Mama's sleeve as we entered the vast entry hall. My boots clacked against its marble floors. The walls stretched higher than I had ever imagined walls could be, and my eyes followed them upward until they finally met matter again as they touched the lofty ceiling. Straight ahead was a magnificent spiral staircase, winding up and up, like a coiled snake ready to strike. To the right was a tall archway, spanning the entry to a drawing room with a beautiful chandelier. My nose took in the scents of the home—it smelled big, open, fresh, and full of secrets. I wondered what those secrets might be.

I caught a glimpse of Papa's head over my shoulder, following my gaze where it roamed. "Do you like it?" he asked, his voice suppressed, curious.

I turned my head up to him, smiling. "I love it." In fact, Kellaway Manor was already much more than I had expected it to be. And I was excited to meet the friends that Mama and Papa had told me so much about.

Just then, a woman came swiftly down the staircase, a man trailing behind her. They both wore wide smiles and eyes full of memories and laughter. Papa stepped out from behind me to greet them, and Mama prodded me forward gently as she moved to greet them as well. Then she introduced me to Mr. and Mrs. Kellaway. They smiled a lot and Mr. Kellaway gave me a candy.

I decided I might like them.

"Where are your children?" I heard Mama ask.

*"Oh, I hardly know."* Mrs. Kellaway glanced around with a light laugh. *"I understand that Edmond is off playing with the neighbors a mile down the road, and Owen and Alice should be here somewhere…"*

I clicked my boots against the floor, enjoying the echo it created. I was eager to explore the place. I wanted to see what was up those winding stairs, and what was beyond the golden archway.

*"Hmm. How are they? Is Owen as mischievous as ever?"*

A laugh. *"Oh, perhaps even more so."*

I clicked my boots faster, bored with the languid conversation above me. I looked again to the archway, hoping to get a peek at the chandelier in the room beyond. But beneath the arch, stood a boy.

He looked to be a few years older than me, maybe twelve or thirteen. His hair was as golden as the archway and his eyes sparked with interest. *"Are you speaking of me?"* he asked, stepping forward with raised brows.

Mrs. Kellaway jumped a little, then laughed, waving him toward her. *"Do you remember the Downings?"*

He nodded, his gaze jumping to me. His nod froze. *"I don't remember her."*

I adjusted the pink ribbon in my hair and gave a little close-lipped smile. *"I'm Annette."*

*"This is my son, Owen,"* Mrs. Kellaway said, putting a hand on the boy's shoulder.

He smiled. I noticed a dimple in one cheek. *"Good to meet you."* Then he turned, as if to walk away.

*"Owen, where are you going?"* his mother asked, her brow furrowed.

He paused, turning back around. *"Outside."*

*"Take Miss Annette with you. She will be far too bored in here with us."*

Owen's gaze shifted to me, then back to his mother, a pleading look on his face that made me scowl.

*"Take her with you,"* she asserted.

He sighed, as if very annoyed, and looked at me again. *"Well, come on, then."*

I scowled harder. I did not like him. Not one bit. But with a nudge from Mama, I followed him reluctantly around the left of the staircase where a hall led to a back door.

"I am only coming with you if you apologize," I said as he stepped outside.

He turned, a surprised look on his face, half inside the door, half out. "I have no reason to apologize to a seven-year-old girl."

I gasped and jerked my hands to my hips. "First of all, I am nine, and second of all, yes, you do."

His lips pressed together. They twitched. "If you do not wish to come along, then you may stay here." Then he turned and walked the rest of the way through the door. It swung shut behind him.

I scowled after his retreating figure. This boy was atrocious and I did not like him one bit. But I followed him out the door anyway, curiosity winning the war as it always did. The grounds were much too inviting to pass up. I had to run to catch up to him.

When he looked down at me, I was surprised to see him grinning. "I knew you would not be able to resist. But you must know, what I am about to do is no activity for a little girl."

My eyes widened, but I quickly made them normal again, trying to conceal my excitement. "What are we going to do?"

"We?" He shook his head. "No. You are going to hide and watch."

I scowled at him again, lifting my chin. "I did not come along just to watch." My eye level came just below his shoulder, so I had to tip my head back to look straight in his eyes. They were very blue. Not ordinary blue, but the kind of blue that seemed to see everything from the outside straight to the inside.

He rolled those eyes. "You came along because my mother made me bring you along. So you do as I say."

"You are not in charge of me. I am not just going to watch."

He stopped walking, and looked down at me through narrowed eyes. I held his gaze with all the defiance and malice I could muster out of my small frame.

Owen's voice dropped to a chilling whisper. "Very well, if it will keep you quiet. But I don't think you should have spoken so soon. You don't even know what you just agreed to do."

A little nervous flutter settled in my stomach, born from the raw foreboding in his voice. "What did I agree to do?"

He turned his gaze to the woods at the edge of the wide lawn. "Just follow me."

When we reached the border between neat grass and gnarled trees, Owen stepped forward, and I followed tentatively. It was early spring, so the air was still crisp and chilling. The sun was close to setting, for the sky shone shades of pink and orange and every color in between.

"Where are we going?" I asked as I tried to keep up, running under dry, bare branches. "Owen! Where are we going?"

He didn't look back, but I heard him answer, "To climb a tree."

I almost stopped, my heart flipping in my chest. "But—but my mama will be angry if I climb a tree."

He either ignored me, or did not hear, because he continued forward in silence. I scowled to myself, heart pounding. Trees were not for climbing. That's what Mama said. That was what all mamas said. But I knew by the mischief in his smile that Owen was not the sort of boy who commonly obeyed his mama. Despite the qualms I felt, I continued cautiously forward behind him, mostly because I did not know the way back to the house, and partly because something adventurous inside me wanted to climb a tree. It wanted to do something daring. Something exciting and adventurous. Something that would make others like Owen see me as brave instead of as just a little girl.

At a narrow path breaking through the trees, Owen stopped beside a large, thick tree trunk, resting a hand against it and peering up through its branches.

"This is the one," he said. Then he bent over to a small pile of sticks, moved them aside, and scooped up a dark burlap sack.

I hurried over, eager to look inside. "What is in there?"

"Acorns," he replied in a whispered voice, widening the opening so I could peer inside. The sack was full nearly to the top with tiny acorns, bronze in the setting sunlight.

"What are we going to do with them?"

He smiled, mischief meeting his eyes with a twinkle. "You will see. But first we must hurry and climb the tree."

I looked up slowly, inching my eyes along the trunk, to the branches and the newborn leaves. The tree seemed to touch the orange sky where dark birds cut through the air without a sound. I swallowed my nerves. Mama would never know if I climbed it. As long as I did not tear my gown, she would never know.

It was settled then. I grasped onto that adventurous, wild thing within me with anxious hands.

Owen climbed first, and I watched where he stepped and where his hands clasped the branches and knots in the bark. He climbed so effortlessly, it was as if he had done so dozens of times. He was at the top. It was my turn.

Starting slowly, I made my way upward, realizing why this was the tree he chose. There were so many places to step, to place my hands, that I was at the top without much of a struggle at all. My pride soared like the birds above us. They were so much closer now—I felt as though I could fly too. And maybe I could. I had climbed a tree, after all. How much more difficult could flying be?

Owen rummaged with the sack, opening it and positioning it directly above the path. He held a finger to his lips, warning me to be silent.

That was when I heard the footfalls and lazy humming approaching from down the path. My eyes widened as I predicted Owen's plan. A woman who appeared to be the same age as Mama came into view below us. Before I could so much as gasp, Owen had capsized the sack, showering the woman in acorns.

The woman gasped enough for both of us, swatting at the air above her head as more acorns rained down on her like little hailstones. Owen was laughing as he pulled me back against the tree to a place where we couldn't be seen past the new leaves and tangled wood.

"Owen Kellaway, if that is you, I am going to inform your mother of what you have done!" she shrieked from below.

He covered his mouth to keep from laughing.

After a final huffed breath, the woman stomped off, mumbling something about mischief under her breath. I did not know what to say as I watched Owen laughing. This boy was certainly the most atrocious boy I had ever met.

"She is my mother's friend," he managed through a laugh. "She wants her silly girl to marry my brother one day. But I don't like her or her daughter."

"But that is no way to treat a lady," I snapped, folding my arms.

He shrugged and started down the tree without a word. I watched him with renewed fear in my stomach. Climbing down seemed much worse than climbing up. Once his feet touched the ground, he glanced up at me, a question written on his face.

"Are you coming?"

Tears stung my eyes as I looked down at him, at the ground that felt so much farther from me than the sky. I didn't want him to see my fear though, so I nodded and turned to my stomach, searching with my feet for a place to step. I found a place, a branch that was much too thin. The moment I released my grip, the branch snapped under my foot.

Flying proved to be much more difficult than I anticipated. So I fell. The ground rushed up at me, two arms reached for me, and then everything went dark.

# Chapter 3

*Present Day*

I felt my brow furrow into a scowl. After I had fallen from the tree I recovered quickly, but it was not among my fondest memories. Owen Kellaway did not exist among my fondest memories. After the tree incident, I avoided him for the remainder of our visit, keeping to my room with a book or my dolls, trying to forget about that odious boy.

But seeing him now, ten years later, I knew that I must have never forgotten his face, because I could identify all the things that had changed. His hair was slightly darker than the golden of my memory, but still lighter than brown. His smile was not mischievous, but kind as he looked from across the room at Charles. His jaw was much more solid, his brows and lashes dark, framing his piercing eyes.

His eyes had not changed. My heart leapt and I scolded it for doing so. Yes, he was very handsome. But that did not mean he was not still very infuriating.

He walked farther into the room and pulled a chair close to Charles. His gaze roamed Charles's pale face, and he methodically felt for his pulse. I sat silently, wondering why he had not acknowledged me yet. *Because he is atrocious*, I reminded myself. My eyes narrowed as I watched him lift Charles's head and bring a glass of liquid to his lips.

"What is that?" I inquired, unable to prevent a slight edge of distrust from creeping into my voice.

He turned his head abruptly. My heart faltered a bit as his eyes settled on my face. Did he recognize me? Had Mrs. Kellaway told him already who I was? It did not seem likely considering how quickly he had arrived.

He folded his arms across his broad chest, a small smile twisting his lips. "I can assure you that it is not poisoned." His voice was deep and rich and carried a faint hint of amusement.

Was I amusing to him? Well, then. I gathered my wits and looked him straight in the eye. "I don't recall asking you if it was *poisoned*. I only want to know what it is that you are about to feed him."

He raised one eyebrow. "Considering that we just met a moment ago, I don't understand what I have done to lose your trust so quickly."

"I don't understand why you refuse to tell me what is in that glass." I felt my own eyebrow rise to match his.

A smile fought his cool expression. "I don't understand why we are speaking when we have not been properly introduced."

My cheeks tingled with heat. After my governess had been removed, my manners had been embarrassingly inept. "Well, since the bounds of discreet propriety have already been ignored, then I see no reason that you shouldn't tell me what is in that glass. Is it a secret of sorts?"

He pressed his lips together in an effort not to smile. "Oh, yes. It is a secret. Even to myself." He brought the glass to his face and squinted at it closely. "I am fairly certain that it isn't lethal. Although, madness is a great possibility."

My eyes widened.

With his mischievous grin he moved the glass to Charles. "Let us find out."

Before I knew what I was doing, I had jumped from my seat beside Peter, reaching helplessly for the glass, trying to snatch it from Owen's hand. A sharp, cutting pain reached my ribs at my sudden movement and I bit my lip to keep from crying out. It was an old injury that still caused me problems.

Owen chuckled, a low, musical sound, effortlessly dancing the glass from my reach. "It's water," he said through his laughter.

I withdrew my hand and scowled at him. I growled inside. My cheeks burned with the chagrin of his tease. What an abhorrent, loathsome man! Nefarious, even! He had not changed a bit. In fact, he may have become worse than before.

"I'm sorry," he sighed. "That was a cruel joke. But now, if you please, would you allow me to tend to this poor boy?" His eyes were dancing with amusement.

I hardened my scowl and stared directly at him, trying to intimidate him somehow. I wished he could hear how frightening my inner growling sounded. *That* would have terrified him, I was sure of it.

But clearly, my glare wasn't enough to stop him. He raised a hand in defense and said, "I am terribly sorry, but you cannot have all my attention. I know you desire it, but your brother is ill here and I really must assist him."

I gasped, giving him my sharpest scowl yet.

His mischievous smile fell from his face at that scowl and he cast me a quizzical look. His eyes flickered over my face with recognition. Then only a second later, he shook his head as if to clear it, chuckling once more. "I am sorry. My manners are gone from me today."

I was shocked to see that he looked truly apologetic. I wondered what his quizzical look meant.

Then he smiled, broadly and without mischief, causing a dimple to dent one of his cheeks. That was another thing that had not changed. "Forgive me. It was as if I were thirteen years old again."

I barely caught his wink.

My heart pounded a little harder. Did he remember me? I tried to shoot him a quizzical look of my own, but he had turned to Charles again and was helping him sit up, instructing him to slowly drink the water. I waited patiently for him to turn to me again. When he did, he crossed his arms, watching me with a knowing smile.

"Tell me . . . have you ever climbed a tree?"

So. He did remember. But he wasn't absolutely sure. I decided to make him wonder a little longer. "A woman climbing a tree? What an absurd scenario. Of course I have not." I tried to look absolutely appalled by the idea, shaking my head and scrunching my brows.

It seemed to work, for his knowing smile faltered, the change almost unperceivable. But he was still watching me. His eyes were penetrating straight into my mind. I just knew it. He could tell I was lying. Finally he spoke again, changing the subject. "We have not given our introductions, have we?"

"We have not," I responded coolly.

"We could wait for my mother to return to introduce us, but since the bounds of propriety have already been breached . . . ," He stood, moving in front of me at the settee. "Might I make *myself* known to you. Dr. Kellaway. A physician and second son of a *third* son of a baron." He grinned in such a way that I almost found myself laughing. "But you might remember me by my Christian name, Owen." He smiled, searching my face for clues.

I put on a confused expression. "Remember you? I do not believe we have met, Dr. Kellaway."

His head was tipped to the side, his gaze searching my face. There was a faint smile on his lips that told me he was not entirely convinced. I held perfectly still, hoping he could not see in my eyes the same little girl that fell from the tree.

"What is your name?" he asked in a smooth voice.

This question should have caught me off guard, but I had pre-pared myself. "Miss Milba Durbin," I replied casually, daring him with a look to question it. Out of the corner of my eye I saw Peter jerk his head to me. I begged him silently to keep quiet.

Owen's smile grew and he reclaimed his seat beside Charles. "That is not your name."

"I find it awfully presumptuous that you claim to know better than me what my own name is."

He pressed his lips together, his eyes brimming with laughter. He looked down at his boots. "I apologize, Miss *Durbin*."

I crossed my arms, fighting another wayward urge to laugh. I maintained my cool demeanor. "That is much better."

Charles reached out a finger and tapped Owen on the shoulder. "Dr. Kell-today, you said her name wrong."

My stomach dropped.

Owen tipped his head back with a laugh, lifting an eyebrow in my direction. "Did I?"

Charles gave a quick nod before I could stop him. Peter nodded in agreement. "Her name is not Milba," he said before snorting into giggles.

Now both Owen's eyebrows were raised. "Hmm. How interesting."

My face was hot under his gaze.

"I did not think you looked like a Milba Durbin." He shook his head with a wide smile.

I scolded myself for noticing how his smile moved him from handsome to devastating. It was not wise for me to continue thinking about his looks.

"Do you wish to disclose to me your actual name?"

"No, thank you." I smoothed my hands over my gown, noticing the vomit that still stained around the lower part of my skirts.

"You do seem much too old to be playing pretend."

I glanced up sharply. "You do seem much too old to be pestering a woman you only just met about her name if she does not wish to tell it." I leaned my elbow over the side of my chair so I could face him more fully.

He gave an exasperated sigh that made me smile. "Why *do* you refuse to tell me?"

I shrugged one shoulder, shifting my gaze to Charles who was looking much improved, sitting with a dimpled grin and wide eyes. It took all my concentration to maintain my act and not break into laughter.

"You cannot conceal your name from me forever," he countered.

It was true, and I hated that he was right. But because it bothered him so much, I was going to conceal my identity for as long as possible.

He sighed again, as if giving up for the moment, and turned his attention to my brothers. "And what is your relation to 'Miss Milba'? Are you nephews, or . . . ," His words faded as he prompted them to answer.

I couldn't stop my sardonic comment. "I am afraid my age would deny that I have two children if that is what you were thinking on."

Owen smiled lazily. "I did not think on that for a moment. Not remotely." His eyes sparked with amusement. "You do seem far too old to have children of such youth."

My face pulled tight with indignation. Owen Kellaway was not lacking in wit, and I did not appreciate that fact.

"A sister perhaps?" he asked Peter.

He gave a shy nod of his head.

"Since I cannot know your sister's name, may I ask your names?"

I noticed Peter sit up a little straighter. "My name is Peter and this is my brother Charles."

"Peter!" Charles whined, his light brows drawing together. "I wanted to say my name!"

Owen laughed softly before saying, "Peter, Charles, it is a pleasure to meet you both."

They stared at Owen with quiet awe on their faces. Of course they were going to admire him. He was one of the only men they had ever spoken to. But I didn't fancy the idea of this man becoming their idol.

"And since we are friends now, you may call me Owen." He patted Charles's head and gave them each a warm smile. The gentleness in his eyes tugged at my heartstrings, reminding me of the way my father looked at me. Distracted by this as I was, my thoughts were not clear when Owen turned to me and said, "And you may call me Owen too. After all, it is what you called me before."

I shook my head, my words spilling out before I could plan them. "We were children, I couldn't possibly—" I stopped myself, realizing my mistake too late.

Owen grinned in victory. "I knew it was you."

I squeezed my eyes shut, blocking out his grin. I wanted to cover my ears too, because he was laughing, and his laugh was too infectious and endearing.

"I am sincerely sorry about the tree . . . ,"

My eyes flew open. "I cannot believe you forced me to do that! I was only nine years old! I could have broken an arm or a leg or—"

"But you didn't," he said through a laugh. "Remind me . . . what was it we were doing in that tree?" He threw me a wink that made me gasp and sent a blush to my cheeks.

"*You* were throwing acorns at a woman passing below us."

He gave a hard laugh. "Ah, yes, that was it." He smiled at me teasingly, a sight that I sensed I would see more than once during our visit.

"You're atrocious," I said with a half-hearted glare.

"I'm atrocious too!" Charles exclaimed.

Peter pointed at himself with a serious look. "But I am most atrocious of all, I think."

Owen laughed again and widened his eyes. "Well, if you two are atrocious, then it must be a very fine thing to be. Well done."

These three would get along quite well, I knew it already. But I doubted that Owen could help improve their behavior. His own behavior was still in need of improvement.

I realized then that I was smiling at him. Straight into his blue eyes that smiled back. I looked away immediately, feigning interest in the books on the tea table. Were his eyes truly that striking when we met before? A heart would have to be as guarded as the walls of Newgate to be unaffected by eyes like his. I counted myself fortunate that mine most certainly was.

I hadn't even noticed Mrs. Kellaway enter the room again, Lizzie beside her near the doorway. I straightened myself on the settee and tried to appear more content than I felt. Mrs. Kellaway hurried forward just after I noticed her. "How is he?" she asked Owen.

"He seems to be feeling much better."

Charles smiled and nodded in affirmation.

"Wonderful! Come now, darling. I will show you to your room." She took Charles by the arm and pulled him up from his place on the settee. She waved a hand for Peter to join them. "Lizzie, show Miss Downing to her room as well, please. And take her trunk."

The maid nodded submissively and walked out the door to the entry hall to pick up my trunk. "Follow me," Lizzie said with a smile, heading toward the staircase.

I hurried to catch up to her. A small bloom of anxiety pushed me forward. "I can carry my trunk."

"No, no, miss, I will carry it for you." She hardly glanced my way, but I saw a fleet of surprise in her profile.

I grasped her shoulder gently, stopping her at the foot of the staircase. "I appreciate your willingness to assist me, but may I carry it, please?"

She looked at me hesitantly. "Are you certain, miss?"

"Yes."

She handed me the trunk. "If you insist."

"Thank you, Lizzie." I felt much better with the weight of my traveling trunk under my arm. She looked nervous, but I smiled to reassure her that I was fine. She smiled back lightly and we started up the staircase. About halfway to the top, I felt a hand on my shoulder, making me jump a little. I turned my head to see Owen standing behind me.

"Oh." I relaxed only slightly. "May I help you, Dr. Kellaway?"

He frowned. "We already had this discussion. I would prefer that you call me Owen." He grinned and leaned casually against the banister as if amused about something.

"What?" I snapped.

He scrunched his face in disgust. Then he sniffed the air around me. "Something smells awful."

I gaped at him. How bold! He must have noticed my complete shock, because he pointed at the large stain that Charles had inflicted on my dress. My mood immediately lightened and I laughed in masked embarrassment. "Yes, I suppose I should change . . ."

"That must be where all of Charles's vomit went. He was completely clean." He chuckled. "But don't worry, that is not the *only* reason I followed you up here. There are three reasons, actually."

I raised my eyebrows, inviting, or rather, daring him to continue.

"The first reason, of course, was to inform you of the vomit of which you were abashedly unaware." His eyes danced teasingly. "The second reason was because I couldn't help my curiosity about something. I noticed that you took your trunk from Lizzie. Why?"

I shrugged. I hadn't been asked that question before, and I wasn't certain that I even knew the answer. The best response I could come up with was, "I like to do things on my own."

Owen stared at me for several seconds in silence, an intent look in his eye. I shifted uncomfortably, suddenly very aware of how close he stood. On the step directly below me, he was much closer to my height, and I could see more clearly the details of his overwhelming face.

"You are not like any other lady I have met. Not in the slightest," he said finally. The hint of admiration in his voice moved me to avert my eyes. I felt a light blush creep onto my cheeks and tingle on the tips of my ears. I glanced up to find his gaze still fixed on me. Was there something on my face? Oh, yes. My sunburn. I had nearly forgotten. The realization only made my face burn hotter.

"I know you must be curious about my sunburnt face, so I will just tell you. My brothers hid my bonnet as a joke, and I was out of doors far too long without it. That is all. Now, I would greatly appreciate it if you stopped staring."

He looked surprised by what I said, but he still didn't look away. "You shouldn't be ashamed, you know. I see nothing wrong with a young lady enjoying a bit of sunshine every now and then."

My eyes fell to my boots. "Most people see *many* things wrong with that."

"Well, I suppose that is what makes the two of us alike, then. We are not like most people. And I hope you never try to be."

I couldn't hear any teasing in his voice, so I sneaked a careful glance up at him. I wasn't expecting to see the kind twist to his smile and the warm look that was in his eyes. I couldn't help but smile back.

"While we are on the topic . . ." He pulled his hand out from behind his back and extended my bonnet. "My third reason. Unless your brothers have a taste for female fashion, I believe this is yours."

"Oh . . ." I reached forward and took my bonnet from his hand. I remembered leaving it on the cushion beside me in the drawing room. "I seem to misplace that often." I smiled an inch. "Thank you."

He laughed then looked at me sincerely. "If the burn gives you discomfort, I have something that can help."

I tried to think of a reason why I should accept further assistance from him, but I couldn't. "No, I will be fine. But thank you. And I want to thank you for helping Charles."

He waved off my words with his hand. "I did nothing that warrants gratitude. Being out of the carriage was a cure in itself. But if he feels ill again during any part of your visit, please inform me so I may be of assistance."

I nodded, not knowing what else to say.

"Well, *Miss Milba Durbin*, it was a pleasure to meet you." He had a teasing look in his eyes.

I was suddenly unable to prevent a smile from lifting my lips. "My real name is Miss Annette Downing."

He tipped his head closer to me, and in a soft voice, asked, "Will you permit me to call you Annette?"

I was shocked by his familiarity. Yes, we had met before but that was a long time ago. And we certainly were not friends. "Miss Downing would be just fine." Then I flashed a quick smile and turned to continue up the stairs, eager to escape his unsettling gaze. He had certainly grown too handsome for the good of anyone.

"I bid you farewell . . . Annette."

I turned to him in sudden outrage. If he thought his disrespect to be amusing, he was very mistaken. Prepared to deliver a witty diatribe, I was annoyed further to see him laughing, sauntering down the staircase without a glance back. He was insufferable.

# Chapter 4

After lingering for a few frustrated moments in my place on the staircase, I stepped—or rather stomped—up to where Lizzie stood waiting for me on the second floor.

"Is everything well, miss?"

"Yes," I said curtly, my mind muddled with confusion. One second he was kind and thoughtful, and the next he was entirely atrocious! My brothers were not going to have anything to do with that man if I could help it.

Lizzie must have read my thoughts because she said, "He really isn't as horrid as he seems."

I was surprised by her chosen description of "horrid" for a member of the family she worked for. If Aunt Ruth had ever caught wind of one of her servants using a single ill word to describe her (which I had witnessed on many occasions) they would have been dismissed in a heartbeat.

Recognizing her folly, Lizzie redeemed herself by saying, "Believe me, miss. He is actually quite the gentleman." Her round eyes widened in sincerity.

I cast her a skeptical look. "I have yet to see that side of him."

"You will."

"Doubtful," I mumbled under my breath as I watched her begin walking down the wide hallway. I shifted my trunk in my arms and followed her to a room on the right.

"Your bedchamber, miss." She threw the doors open and stepped aside, allowing me to lead through the doorway. I walked inside, letting my gaze sweep over the interior of the room. It was beautiful and large, and I gaped in amazement at the window draped in satin curtains with intricate embroidery. The lofty window framed a breathtaking prospect of the grounds and thick woods behind the home. On the wall beside it was a mirror and ivory chair, and a comfortable-looking bed sat elegantly at the opposite side of the room with a writing desk beside it.

"Lizzie," I turned around, stunned, "I cannot possibly—"

She flashed a reassuring smile. "Yes, you can. I was instructed to prepare the best rooms in the home for you and your brothers."

I looked around again, overwhelmed by the luxury of my surroundings. My room at Oak Cottage was not half this size. I moved slowly toward the bed and sat down, laying my trunk and clean gown beside me. I decided to unearth my gracious attitude and accept the accommodations. I lowered my gaze to my hands. "Please send my gratitude to Mrs. Kellaway."

"There will be no need for that."

My eyes flew up at the sound of Mrs. Kellaway's voice. She stood in front of Lizzie at the doorway, her posture straight and her speech eloquent. My spine straightened without consulting me.

"It is the very least I can do." She walked over to the writing desk and moved its chair so that it rested across from me, then sat down and smiled warmly.

"Mrs. Kellaway, this room certainly is beautiful, but my brothers and I are quite accustomed to—lesser accommodations. This is hardly necessary."

She shook her head. "I must insist that you have this room. Even if it is not necessary, it is certainly well deserved."

I looked down at my lap. I was not used to such treatment. That must have been why it was so difficult to accept. "Well, I thank you."

"Oh, you are very welcome." She smoothed her auburn hair then clasped her hands together and leaned forward eagerly. "Now tell me, what brings you here after so many years? I assumed that my invitation had been ignored or rejected, so you can imagine my delight in seeing you arrive here today."

I took a deep breath. "My aunt sent us. She insisted that we see a new piece of England, experience a change of scenery. It was very kind of her." I smiled with as much cheer as I could manage. It was not a complete lie. I did not want to tell her the true purpose for Aunt Ruth sending us here. There was no reason that Mrs. Kellaway should have to fret about unnecessary matters. It was my problem to resolve.

"Remind me, what is your aunt's name?" she asked.

"Mrs. Ruth Filbee, a widow. My father's sister."

"Oh, yes. We have met." Her face fell into confusion. "You say she sent you here as an act of kindness?"

I nodded, upholding my smile with effort.

"Hmm. How . . . uncharacteristic of her."

I decided it would be best to ignore that. So I just continued smiling like a ninny until I noticed Mrs. Kellaway's expression turn solemn. She looked down at her hands and wrung them together, turning her knuckles white. Her sudden change of mood surprised me.

"I do want to apologize sincerely for inviting your parents to visit that day." She swiped a tear from her lower lashes before it could spill. "Had I not, they might not be . . . ," she struggled to finish her sentence.

I remembered what she had written in her letter about feeling responsible for the accident. A pocket of compassion opened within me. "No, Mrs. Kellaway, you don't need to apologize; it is not your fault. Please, do not blame yourself."

I didn't know who to blame, and it was something that bothered me everyday. There had to be someone to blame besides my parents. There had to be. They were keen on adventure and unwary of danger and it had taken its toll. I could blame their carelessness, but I could never blame them. And I certainly could not blame Mrs. Kellaway.

She looked up, seeking reassurance in my eyes. "You don't blame me?"

"Of course not."

She relaxed visibly, as if a tremendous weight had been lifted from her shoulders. "I cannot convey to you how much those words mean to me." She exhaled sharply and wiped a stray tear from her cheek. "Oh, forgive me. I do not normally have tears so readily available."

I smiled. There was another reason for me to like her.

"Do you enjoy living with your aunt?" she asked.

I hated lying to her, but she was too kind, and I knew she would worry if she knew just how awful it was. I lied only partially once again. "It isn't home, but it is sufficient. We have what we need."

It seemed that she was unable to hide the look of pity she placed on me. "Please know that you and your brothers are welcome to stay here as long as you would like."

In all honesty, I wanted to stay forever. This place was beautiful and Mrs. Kellaway was very kind. But my ears captured a slight hint of obligation in her voice. Did she feel obligated to invite us here just because she and my parents were dear friends? "I don't want to be a burden," I said in a quiet voice.

She shook her head. "No, Annette, believe me, I have been hoping that you would come for so long! I *wanted* you to come."

I sighed with relief.

"How long do you plan on staying?"

I wasn't sure how to answer. "That is . . . undecided at this point. But my aunt will be sure to send word when she wants us to return. It will likely be a month or two before she calls for us, if that is all right. I do not wish to trespass on your hospitality any longer than necessary."

"That is wonderful! And you could not trespass even if you wanted to, dear. There is much around here that I am sure you and your brothers will find entertainment in." She nodded with reassurance. "We have been rather starved for guests around here. We have my parents staying with us for a few weeks, but they are in the village today and won't be returning until this evening. My husband is away with my eldest son, Edmond, and my daughter, Alice, is visiting a friend at her family's estate. They should all be returning in a fortnight or so. In the meantime, you and your brothers should get to know the house, the grounds! You will love it here, I am sure of it. Please, don't hesitate to ask for anything you need."

I thanked her with a genuine smile. This visit may be everything my imagination dared to hope for.

"I have assigned Lizzie to be your maid during your stay," she said, throwing a glance in Lizzie's direction.

I found the thought of having my own maid quite disconcerting. I did not need assistance with every little thing I attempted to do. But it was proper, and if I was going to spend the weeks to come living in this elegant home, I ought to make an attempt at being elegant myself, no matter how excruciating.

I threw a kind smile in Lizzie's direction just as a screech split the air from the main floor. I jumped. The screeching carried up the stairs as if the perpetrator of the sound was just outside the room. Mrs. Kellaway leapt to her feet and looked to the door.

"What was that?" I asked, my voice panicked. Images of my brothers working mischief led by Owen filled my mind.

"I don't know." She cast me a worried glance. "Come with me." She hurried from the room and I followed, praying that Peter and Charles didn't have anything to do with it.

We raced through the hall and down the stairs. The shrieking continued and I cringed as the sounds of mischievous giggling traveled into earshot. Of course. What had they done this time? And on our first day here? I raced ahead of Mrs. Kellaway and followed the sounds. I rounded a corner and found that the giggles were coming from what appeared to be the kitchen.

I placed my hand on the door handle and heard a particularly loud, wicked giggle followed by a horrified screech. Oh, my. Even I had not comprehended that Charles was capable of sounding *that* evil.

I burst through the door, hoping that my interference would tame whatever mischievous rant my brothers were in. If Owen Kellaway had something to do with this, so help me—

But as soon as I stepped into the room, I stopped in complete perplexity, staring at the scene before me. A short, plump woman— I assumed she was the cook—stood backed into a corner. Peter and Charles stood in front of her, confining her against the wall, each holding a steaming hot pan. Owen was nowhere in sight.

"We want food!" Peter pleaded. Charles giggled beside him in his wicked way. The cook looked absolutely terrified, pressing a hand against her heaving chest.

"Now!" Peter ordered, bringing the scalding pan closer to her face. The woman shrieked and Charles giggled.

I pulled myself from my state of paralysis and ran through the door, apologizing frantically to the woman as I snatched the pans from my brothers' hands. They turned around, surprised.

"What are you doing? You cannot do that!" I was trying my hardest to keep my voice below a shout.

Peter looked down shamefully. "But we're hungry."

"That does not give you reason to torment this woman." I lowered my voice only slightly. "If you act this way while you are here, Aunt Ruth will see that your behavior has not improved and she will punish you. Do you understand? I do not want that to happen, so you are going to apologize right now." I turned to set the pans down and saw Mrs. Kellaway and Owen standing in the doorway. They both wore looks of complete surprise.

"I am very sorry," I said, feeling my face grow hot. "I should have told you about their . . . possible behavior. It usually isn't this awful." I glanced at the cook who was clutching her chest and leaning against the wall in relief. I turned to Peter and Charles. "Apologize to her."

Charles bunched his sleeves into his hands as he did when he was nervous, and followed Peter to the corner. Peter's cheeks were ruddy and he hung his head bashfully. I found it amazing that they could go from so mischievous to so shameful this quickly.

"I'm sorry," they said together, glancing back at me for approval. I nodded and gestured for them to come to me.

"Now apologize to Mrs. Kellaway for tormenting her cook."

"We are sorry for tormenting your cook," Peter said quietly.

She stepped forward, stunned. I cringed. If there was anything that could make her reconsider allowing us to stay, it was this. To my surprise, she mustered up a smile. "I forgive you, but please do not do it again."

Charles nodded, then after a pause, said, "Do we still get food?" His question earned a laugh from both Owen and Mrs. Kellaway.

"I thought you were unwell," Owen teased.

Charles patted his belly, his lips upturned in a smile. "I got better."

Owen laughed, his eyes sparkling with amusement. "Yes, it appears you did. Let us give Cook a break and I will find something for you boys to eat."

"No," I protested, bringing Owen's gaze to me. "I will do it."

He came a step closer with a grin. "I believe I was the first to claim the honor."

I glared at him. Why did he have to give me so many reasons to glare?

Mrs. Kellaway interrupted before I could respond. "Owen." She stared at him harshly. "Allow Miss Downing to prepare their food if that is what she wishes. She is our guest."

"Why not a compromise? We could do it together," he suggested, throwing me a cajoling smile. "It is such a difficult task, after all."

"That sounds like a wonderful idea," his mother said, shifting her eyes to me.

There was no polite way to refuse, so I mumbled, "Very well," in a tone that I was sure gave Owen satisfaction. I wanted to scrape the grin off his face.

Owen was talking to my brothers, but Mrs. Kellaway pulled my attention from them, grasping my arm gently. Her voice was just a whisper. "I heard you mention something concerning your aunt."

So she had heard me. Should I confide in her? I liked her immensely, and it seemed that she would do all she could to improve my brothers' behavior. Perhaps telling her would be a thing of positive consequence.

I took a slow breath. "I told you a bit of a lie upstairs," I confessed. "The true reason our aunt sent us here is because she was overwhelmed with my brothers' behavior. She told me if they did not return well-behaved she would send them to an orphanage in Scotland." The words tasted bitter in my mouth.

"Oh dear." Mrs. Kellaway's face twisted with concern. "I daresay I have plenty of experience in the matter of improving impish behavior." I thought I saw her eyes flicker to Owen. "We can certainly sort this out. Not to worry. We will not have them falling short to endure the heartache of an orphanage." She shook her head swiftly. "I always knew there was something off in that woman's head. But Peter and Charles will meet her requirements before you leave here. Somehow."

"They must," I agreed glumly. "And I am going to do everything I can to ensure that they do."

She was looking heavenward as if searching for an idea. Then suddenly, her face lit up and she turned abruptly. "Owen, come here!" She waved him over and turned to me excitedly. "I know precisely what they need. They need a gentleman to guide them. Your father was a great man and it is a shame they didn't have the privilege of knowing him. But, he is their father, so within your brothers there must be great men—boys—too. They need only a bit of assistance from a gentleman to bring those good, well-behaved boys to light."

I did not like where this was going.

Mrs. Kellaway spoke again, this time to her son. "Owen, I need to ask you a favor. I need you to allot a portion of your time to assisting Peter and Charles in becoming little gentlemen. It should not be very difficult; they seem to adore you already. Your example alone should be enough, but please take this seriously."

I winced. I certainly did not like where this was going.

Owen surprised me by keeping a serious expression. "Of course. But their behavior is not so unheard of, is it?"

"Well, there is a reason for improvement Miss Downing may reveal to you if she wishes," Mrs. Kellaway said.

I hardly heard her. Why had I not kept this to myself? Now I had burdened Owen and he would likely torture me ceaselessly for it. I very nearly threw him a glare right in front of Mrs. Kellaway. He must have a motive that was undisclosed. Surely he was not agreeing to help only out of the goodness of his heart.

"I will do everything I can," Owen said in a firm voice.

"Wonderful!"

I frowned and decided that Mrs. Kellaway said *wonderful* far too much.

"I'll leave the matter in your hands then, Owen. Treat it as you will." Then she turned to leave the room, but stopped to speak a last time. "Dinner will be in two hours, so prepare just a small portion for the boys. Do so quickly; the servants will need to begin dinner preparations. My parents will be returning shortly, so change for dinner and meet in the drawing room as soon as you are finished here."

I watched helplessly as the door swung shut behind Mrs. Kellaway. I spied Owen out of the corner of my eye. He had turned around and was walking to a table to join my brothers.

"Come now, Annette. I thought you were the one who insisted on doing this," I heard him say, feigning impatience in his teasing way.

In all likelihood, any other lady would have melted under his teasing, and that was probably what he expected. He had already told me that I was unlike any other lady, so I planned to prove that in the best way I knew how.

I whirled around. "Call me Miss Downing," I snapped. "And first, I want to know how you plan on assisting my brothers with improving their behavior."

He leaned against the table and folded his arms. "I plan to keep them on two very short leashes and bring them with me everywhere I go, letting them bask continuously in the glory of my presence."

I rolled my eyes. Could he ever be serious? I walked over and stood behind my brothers, giving Owen an exasperated look. "What do you plan on doing?" I repeated, unamused.

He chuckled. "What? Can you not imagine me pulling them along on leashes?"

I considered his wry grin. "Actually, I can."

"Then you must have some I can borrow."

I cast him a pointed glance. "No, whether you believe it or not, I am not that barbaric."

He laughed before finally responding seriously. "Why is their behavior in such desperate need of improvement?"

My lips pressed together. I knew he would attempt to breach that subject. I shrugged. "Our aunt wishes that they become well-behaved."

He watched me carefully and folded his arms across his chest. "Is that why she sent you here?"

I dropped my gaze. "Well—yes. But they can do it. I am sure of it." I glanced up at him again, carefully.

He appeared to be deep in thought, but didn't pry any further. Instead he asked, "How are their dinner manners?"

"Quite awful, actually." I looked down at my brothers who were grinning at each other, sharing quiet giggles.

"Then we can begin tonight at dinner," he said in a nonchalant voice. Before I could speak again, he returned his attention to my brothers. "What are you hungry for?" He turned to rummage in

44

the cupboard behind him. "Bread, pears, oranges, and oh . . . ," he grinned slyly, "sweet biscuits."

"Yes!" they exclaimed in unison, both sets of blue eyes lit brightly.

"I thought so." Owen grabbed the bag the biscuits were stored in. He looked at me expectantly with that teasing glint in his eye. "Are you going to help me?"

Again, I rolled my eyes. I walked over and snatched the bag from him. "It is a terrible shame that you cannot open a bag without assistance," I said, tearing the top open, pulling two biscuits from inside, and handing them to Peter and Charles.

Owen grinned at me and took the bag, removing a biscuit for himself, then extended the bag to me. "Would you like one?"

At his offer I realized that I hadn't eaten anything since early that morning. They did look delicious. I was about to accept, but then my stomach growled loudly in its own response.

Owen's eyes widened in a mixture of surprise and amusement. "I will assume that you want one." He chuckled, taking a biscuit from the bag. My face burned with embarrassment. He handed it to me and then paused, staring with concern at my face. "What's wrong? You seem disappointed."

I looked up in confusion. What would I have to be disappointed about?

He spoke again and I sensed his mischievous side returning with full force. "Oh, I see." He nodded in realization. "You wished for me to feed it to you."

I gasped in protest.

"I'm sorry, Annette, but that would be a bit strange in front of your brothers, would it not? Please, don't misunderstand, I would love to feed you, but let us save it for another time." He grinned mischievously.

Surely he expected a blush, but my face remained cool, which I was quite proud of. "No. Let us not."

His face contorted to such a look of complete—and rather false—disappointment at my rejection that an unwelcome laugh escaped me. I immediately regretted it.

"Finally I have earned a laugh!" he exclaimed, pumping his fist in the air as if it was the greatest accomplishment he could have made.

I wiped the smile from my face. "Do not let your pride be elevated too severely. We Downings have a slight propensity to laugh very easily." I raised my eyebrows at Peter and Charles, who had begun to giggle in affirmation of my claim. They had finished their biscuits, so I looked again to Owen, and was surprised to see him staring at me again with that intent look in his penetrating eyes. Why did he always do that? I found it completely unnerving. I shifted uncomfortably under his gaze, eager to escape it. "Is that all?"

The intensity of his eyes softened along with my tenseness. "Almost. I have only one question.

"What?"

His amused smile returned. "Tell me, Annette—why are you still covered in vomit?"

My gaze shot down to my dress and I laughed, realizing to my dismay that I still hadn't changed. Owen laughed too, and it was then that I noticed just how much I liked the sound. His laugh was low and musical, contagiously delightful. It was then too that I realized, no matter how atrocious he was, that I didn't mind him calling me by my Christian name.

# Chapter 5

I stood in front of the mirror in my room, smoothing my hands over the clean blue gown I now wore. In comparison to Mrs. Kellaway's lovely dress, it looked dull and plain. Not to mention that my hair was falling from its knot, and my face looked every bit as red as it had this morning. Dinner was soon, and I was struggling immensely with my appearance, whether I wanted to admit it or not.

I walked closer to the mirror, pulled the pins from my hair, and ran my fingers through it, attempting to make myself somewhat presentable. It was always a futile effort, but tonight I needed to look nice. It was the best I could manage. A knock sounded at the door, pulling my attention from my task.

"Yes?" I turned toward the doorway.

Lizzie's high, friendly voice echoed through the hallway. "May I enter?"

I faced the mirror again. "You may."

I saw Lizzie's reflection as she walked through the door. She stopped dead in her tracks, her jaw dropping to her collar. "What are you doing?" she gasped.

My hands froze. "Making myself presentable for dinner."

She shook her head and hands in a fluster. "No, no, no. *No.* Please excuse me, I will return shortly." Then she turned and ran from the room, letting the door swing shut behind her.

I scowled at my reflection. What was that about? I shrugged and pulled hard on my hair, loosening a thick tangle.

A few minutes later, after my many attempts to tame my hair, Lizzie burst through the door, wielding a heavy hairbrush and a box of other items like decorative pins and cosmetics. She walked behind me and waved the hairbrush in the air. "Allow me."

"No, Lizzie, you don't have to," I protested quickly. But she was already pulling a chair up behind me and pressing down on my shoulders for me to sit down.

She clucked her tongue in disapproval. "Good heavens, why didn't you allow me to help you dress? This gown is too plain for dinner." She stared into the mirror at my reflection. "I am going to make you look beautiful!"

It had been so long since I had even considered beauty a possibility for me. Or since I had cared. But a girlish excitement lit up inside me at the thought. Then I remembered. "I don't have a prettier gown than this one."

She smiled at me. "Then I will have to make your hair breathtaking enough to outshine it."

I saw my eyes spark with excitement in the mirror the moment Lizzie's did. She nearly jumped with joy and set to work brushing through my hair. She smiled as if it was her favorite thing in the world to do. Then she froze, lifting the brush from my head. "Oh! Wait a moment. We must turn your chair around."

"Why?" I asked.

"Because facing the mirror will ruin the surprise."

"Oh." I nodded and turned my chair obligingly, and she immediately set to work again. I cringed as she untangled an exceptionally large knot.

"You will absolutely love Mr. and Mrs. Everard. They are completely darling," she said giddily.

"Mr. and Mrs. Everard?"

"They're Mrs. Kellaway's parents. She informed you of their arrival, yes? They are expected to arrive very soon."

"Oh, yes, she told me." I felt extremely relieved that there would be other guests staying here as well. This way, my brothers and I would not have to be the very center of attention. My heart sunk as I realized that I had let Peter and Charles out of my sight again. How had I been so daft? I should have kept them under constant watch after the incident in the kitchen.

I whipped my head around, cringing as the movement caused my hair to snag in the hairbrush. "Lizzie, do you know where my brothers have gone?"

She continued calmly brushing my hair. "They wished to go out and explore the grounds. Is that all right?"

My heart fell. "Is someone watching them?"

"Yes . . . yes, I think so."

I relaxed only slightly. "Perhaps I should go check on them."

"No, no, miss! I am almost finished. Your hair is already smooth, and I will have it arranged in ten minutes."

Almost finished? She had barely started. Lizzie gave me a wide, reassuring smile and set to work pulling strands up and pinning them, her movements faster than before.

Several minutes passed and I grew impatient. I had begun wringing my hands together, feeling pins scrape against my head as Lizzie worked quickly and skillfully.

"There." She stepped back to admire her work. "You look lovely. Now only a bit of cosmetics to make the red of your face less intense, and you will be breathtaking."

I sat patiently as she applied a thin layer of what she called her "own concoction" (which frightened me a bit) then clapped her hands together gleefully and released a dramatic sigh. "Yes, yes, not a soul will even bat an eye at the gown."

I stood and turned tentatively to the mirror. My hair was pulled up loosely, with intricate twists and braids trailing to a bun. My face was no longer bright scarlet, but appeared to be in a constant pink blush. But mostly, the glint of confidence in my eyes was what surprised me. Now I needed only to be able to act as elegant as I felt. Surely I could unearth my manners from the days that my parents regularly exposed me to society.

"Thank you, Lizzie," I said, smiling.

"Oh!" she gasped. "Yes. Keep it."

My brow furrowed. "Keep what?"

"The smile, of course! Dr. Kellaway will be unable to stop staring." She gave me a little grin.

I shot a warning glance at her. She knew that I did not desire Owen's attentions more than I did Aunt Ruth's. She put a hand to her mouth. "Forgive me." I could tell she was hiding a grin behind that hand. "Come, I will show you to the drawing room."

We reached the bottom of the staircase and I hurried to the window, looking for any sign of my brothers. My gaze swept over the grounds behind the home, taking in a huge expanse of land. The neatly trimmed grass stretched far and wide, framed with lush and beautifully tended gardens and topiary. I could see a set of stables and an orchard. But despite the beauty they beheld, my eyes were still missing what they sought. Peter and Charles were nowhere in sight.

"Lizzie, I don't see them."

She rushed to the window and took a look for herself. Her eyes squinted to small slits. "They must have come in already."

I shot her a worried glance before following her under the golden archway and to the door of the drawing room. Distracted, I nearly collided with her. She stood with her ear pressed against the door. "Oh, my! It sounds like the Everards are already here!" She opened the door and gave me a slight nudge. "Go on."

I stepped through the doorway and immediately saw Peter and Charles, both wearing giddy expressions, standing beside a wispy-haired old man who was sitting in a chair on the right side of the room. I sighed with relief. At least they hadn't indulged in any further mischief.

I lingered where I stood and observed an elderly woman sitting near my brothers, with Mrs. Kellaway beside her, and Owen—looking quite handsome—lounging on the sofa in the corner of the room. Just as my gaze found place on his face, his eyes flickered up to meet mine. Something flashed quickly across his features. Was it admiration? I quickly banished the thought and stepped farther into the room.

Mrs. Kellaway stood and rushed toward me. "Annette! You look absolutely stunning!" She admired my hair. "Was this Lizzie's doing?"

"Yes." I looked down demurely. I wasn't exactly one to ravish in having extra attention on myself, so when I noticed that all eyes in the room were on me, especially the pair of intense blue eyes in the corner, I felt a cursed blush burn slowly up my cheeks.

"Come, come, meet my parents." Mrs. Kellaway waved me forward. She held her hand out to the stout old woman who sat with great posture on the recamier. "This is my mother, Mrs. Harriet Everard. And Mother, meet Miss Annette Downing."

The woman smiled buoyantly. "Aren't you *darling!*" Her extremely high-pitched, friendly voice shocked me. "It is a pleasure to meet you, Miss Downing. I have already met your brothers. They are quite darling themselves." Her hazel eyes widened when she spoke, as if she was constantly engulfed in rapturous surprise.

I gave my most gracious smile. "I must warn you, their faces can be somewhat deceitful . . . they usually prove to be quite disastrous."

She threw her hand out in disagreement. "Nonsense. No young boy is truly himself if he doesn't prove to be disastrous every now and then. I am sure they will remain every bit as darling." She winked.

I smiled. I liked this woman immensely. "Well, it is a pleasure to meet you, Mrs. Everard."

She held up her hands in objection. "Please, call me Grandmother."

My heart warmed at her request. I had never known any of my own grandparents, and Mrs. Everard seemed to be the very epitome of what I would want my grandmother to be like. I nodded in silent acceptance of her request and followed Mrs. Kellaway to stand before the old man to whom my brothers had been speaking. She introduced me to him as she had to her mother, then introduced the man to me.

"This is my father, Mr. Hugh Everard."

I curtsied politely. "It is nice to meet you, Mr. Everard." His response consisted merely of a curt nod of his head, the movement making his thin, wispy, white hair sway.

His wife, Grandmother, leaned over the edge of the recamier and remarked, "Hugh. That rough exterior is not fooling a soul." She turned her gaze on me. "You may call him Grandfather."

I laughed softly and politely, the way I remembered hearing my mother laugh in social settings. "Very well." I gave Peter and Charles a questioning look, grateful to have them so near as a diversion from polite conversation—a skill I had never possessed. "What have you two been doing?"

"We played outside and then we came inside and talked to Grandfather," Peter said. "He taught us a trick."

I raised my eyebrows. "Really? May I see it?"

Peter looked uncertainly at Charles, then back at me. "Grandfather should show you, he's the best at it."

Grandfather chuckled lightly. "No, no, I will allow you to show her." His voice was low and soft, a surprising match to his gruff appearance.

Peter and Charles clasped their hands together in pleading gestures. Charles stuck out his lower lip. "Please, please, please, show her?"

I could tell that Grandfather was considering it, his mouth twisted in thought. "Oh, very well," he said, giving in. He pointed a blaming finger at my brothers. "How could I possibly say no to those eyes?"

"It is horribly difficult," I agreed.

Grandfather sat up in his chair and looked at my brothers in silence for several seconds, building the suspense in their eyes. "I shall begin."

I glanced up to see Owen hurrying over to stand beside me. "Wait, Grandfather, I want to see this too." He rubbed his hands together and let his gaze settle on my face. "It never fails to amaze me."

I pressed down my smile before it could form. He was utterly ridiculous.

"Does anyone else wish to join us before I begin?" Grandfather asked impatiently.

His wife waved her hand dismissively. "We can see you well enough from here."

He took that as leave to start, turning in his chair to face his audience. I watched as he held up two fingers, pinched together. "This is my invisible needle and thread. Grandmother over there gave it to me as a gift for my birthday. She is always insisting that I learn to sew." He smiled wryly, letting a pause precede his words, "And learn to sew I did."

Peter and Charles giggled, their eyes lit bright with excitement.

"I am going to sew my mouth right shut." Grandfather took his pinched fingers to his upper lip and poked the right side of it.

"Oh!" he gasped, feigning the pain that would come from the poke of a needle.

A smile crept onto my face as I watched the hilarity of his facial expressions. He pulled his invisible needle up through his lip, pulling it up and down, up and down. As he did, the corner of his lip moved as if truly suspended by a strand of thread.

Peter and Charles gaped in amazement. Owen shook his head as if completely bewildered. "Amazing. Absolutely amazing," he whispered, giving me a grin that I saw from the corner of my eye.

Grandfather repeated the mime with all four corners of his lips, then pretended to knot the end of the thread. His eyes widened in fear as he attempted—but failed—to open his mouth. "Mmph mmm mmph!"

My brothers burst into giggles and clapped their hands. I laughed and against my conscious will, turned my head to Owen, who was laughing too. I looked away quickly. He was only seconds away from saying something that would make me angry, I was sure of it.

Grandmother, Grandfather, and Mrs. Kellaway were already sitting—Grandmother and Mrs. Kellaway on the recamier and Grandfather in the chair in front of me. Owen went to the corner to reclaim his seat on the sofa, and my brothers took their seats on the settee beside Grandfather. I could already tell that the three of them would be fast friends.

I surveyed the room for a place to sit, standing awkwardly as I did so. And, of course, the only place available was beside Owen, who sat wiggling his eyebrows and patting the cushion beside him. I glanced around one last time, searching desperately for an alternative. There were none, so I reluctantly walked over and joined him on the sofa, sitting as far from him as possible.

He greeted me with an amused smile. "It looked as if you wanted to flee from the room when you realized the only place to sit was beside me." He regarded me in a serious way that I had not seen before now. "If I have done anything to offend you, I apologize. Everything was only meant in joking."

I sneaked a speculative glance at his face. He seemed sincere. Almost. But something about the way his lips were curled up at the corners made me feel like I was *still* being teased. I did not like it. Not at all.

"I do not wish for your apology. I'm not easily offended." My voice came out sharper than I intended.

Apparently, to Owen, the sharpness of my voice belied my claim. "It sounds to me that you were offended. So please, accept my apology."

"No, thank you, I would rather not," I said, taking a passive glance around the room.

He groaned and rubbed the back of his neck. "You are very stubborn."

A small smile curved my lips. I thoroughly enjoyed my outward state of defiance—and the frustrated expression on Owen's face. In fact, I felt oddly close to releasing a wicked laugh that would challenge even Charles's display.

In the midst of my self-celebration, I hadn't noticed Owen shift to where he sat only inches from me. My heart gave a wayward leap at his closeness. I had been quick to learn that he did not live strictly within the bounds of propriety. He leaned in my direction to speak softly in my ear. "Would it help if I told you how beautiful you look?" Then he raised a questioning eyebrow and smiled crookedly, making that dimple appear again.

My face blushed furiously and I looked around, hoping that no one had seen or heard him. What nerve, thinking he could woo me into accepting his apology with a compliment! And an ingenuine one at that. I pulled away quickly and scowled at him. "No, it would not."

He gave an exasperated sigh. "So you are offended by compliments. Hmm, is there anything that does not offend you? If so, I would love to hear it."

I glared at him, ready to snap a diatribe that would wipe away his maddening smile, erase that infuriating dimple. But before I could speak, Mrs. Kellaway's voice pierced the tense silence. "Is everything well over there?" She gave Owen a stern glance.

She must have noticed my glare. How embarrassing it would be if I were to admit that the only reason Owen was receiving my glare, was because he offered an apology and a compliment. So as quickly as possible, I said, "Yes, everything is fine."

I was grateful to see the door swing open just after I spoke, revealing the butler standing in the doorway. "Dinner is served."

Mrs. Kellaway stood and walked to him. "Thank you, Wilson." Then she turned around and waved us forward. "Come, everyone. Follow me."

The walk to the dining room required decorum, so I grudgingly took Owen's arm. In the dining room, Mrs. Kellaway was seated at the head of the table, with Grandfather in the seat of honor to her right, and Grandmother to her left.

"Come, come, take a seat!" she said, her smile warm. I walked to the table, which was set for seven, but could easily accommodate at least twelve, and took a chair beside Grandmother. Charles sat down beside me, and Peter beside him. Owen took the remaining seat directly across from me.

Frustration bubbled in my stomach. It would be nearly impossible to avoid his eyes with him sitting straight across from me. He seemed to recognize my dilemma, because just as I looked across to him, he flashed a smile in my direction.

I glowered at my plate. Why did he seem to relish in my discomfort? Charles tapped my arm. "What's wrong, Annette?"

I forced a smile for his sake. "Nothing." I sneaked a glare through my lashes at Owen.

The food was brought in and everything looked delicious. Some sort of cream soup was served first with bread, and was followed by a vast array of beef, roasted duck, vegetables, and fruits.

Peter and Charles gaped in wonder as the food was placed on the table. Their expressions made my heart sink as I remembered our early months at Oak Cottage. My damaged ribs ached as if the pain was provoked by memory. While I had enjoyed many meals of this grandeur before my parents died, my brothers had never enjoyed food of this quality. I felt a sudden pang of guilt and inferiority at the thought that I couldn't provide this splendor for them. When Aunt Ruth had grand meals made, she never shared.

The food was served and everyone dug in. My brothers quite literally dug in. To my dismay, they surpassed even their utensils, sipping their soup straight from their bowls. They picked up large chunks of meat and tore at them hungrily with their teeth, making juice dribble down their chins.

Mrs. Kellaway looked appalled. Owen was laughing secretively. "I suppose you truly meant it when you said their table manners were awful."

I was tempted to put my face in my hands and keep it there for the rest of my life.

"Peter, Charles," Owen said. They looked up for a moment, soup dripping from their faces. "Did you forget your spoons?"

Peter and Charles each offered a bashful grin. "Oh, yes. I forgot," Peter said, lifting his arm to quickly wipe his chin.

Owen chuckled. "And your napkins?"

I laughed, embarrassed, and grabbed my own napkin, using it to clean Charles's food-covered face. I shook my head as he broke into giggles.

Owen took his napkin, reached across the table, and began cleaning the rest of the soup from Peter's chin. At the sight, I was struck by the memory of a time when my father had done that very thing, with the same warm look in his eye. I tore my gaze away. No. It wasn't possible that he could have the same warm look as my father. My father was too kind and Owen was too . . . I actually didn't know what Owen was.

"There," he said, leaning back in his chair. "Try to eat slowly and use your silver. I know it is difficult to remember when you're hungry." He gave them a broad smile that melted my heart a little.

When dessert was brought in, my brothers stared with unblinking eyes at the trays circling the table. I was about to offer Charles a pudding when he began squirming in his chair. "Georgie! Be quiet," I heard him say in a hushed voice.

I gave him a puzzled look. "Who's Georgie?" I followed his gaze as it traveled slowly down to the pocket of his trousers. A small, round lump sat quivering over his leg. Dread began creeping up my stomach and into my chest. "Charles. Who *is* Georgie?"

In answer, he reached his hand inside his pocket. Before I could stop him, he had removed Georgie from his pocket and was holding him high in the air.

To my complete distress, my suspicions were confirmed— Georgie was a mouse. A small grey mouse, who happened to have a very slick tail. For as soon as Charles pulled Georgie from his pocket, he slipped his tail right from between Charles's fingers and scurried across the table. Charles stared after him with an adoring grin. "He is very quick, isn't he?"

I very nearly dove across the table. The mouse stopped just in front of Grandmother, as if to take a look around.

I could have never imagined what chaos such a small creature would ensue.

Mrs. Kellaway pointed a shaking finger at the mouse and let out a scream that could have shattered the windows. She nearly tipped the table as she leapt from her seat. With a bloodcurdling shriek, Grandmother flew from her chair and ran across the room, clutching her chest in panic.

I also would have never imagined that Grandmother could move so quickly.

I looked around frantically, only to see Peter and Charles giggling hysterically at the riot their beloved new pet was causing. Jumping into action, I grabbed my empty glass and slammed the open end over the mouse, trapping it inside.

"Don't hurt him!" Charles screamed, tugging on my skirts.

I twisted to look at him. My face flushed with embarrassment. "Take him outside."

Charles quickly obeyed, snatching Georgie and hurrying to the door. Peter accompanied him. I could hear their secretive giggles as they left the room.

I sat back in my chair and put my face in my hands. How embarrassing! I was completely wrong to assume that they hadn't been working mischief while they were out of doors unsupervised! Surely Mrs. Kellaway would not allow us to stay any longer. Two incidents in one day? Even I hadn't expected their behavior to be this horrible.

I took a deep breath. Then another. "I am very sorry." I did not dare look up, for fear of what their expressions would entail. Anger? Disapproval? After a long stretch of silence, the temptation was too great. I glanced up.

Owen was looking at me, his lips quivering in an apparent effort not to laugh. Grandfather sat rigid, his wrinkled face completely expressionless. Grandmother stood across the room, attempting to steady her breath, and Mrs. Kellaway had returned to her chair, but still looked extremely stunned.

I rotated in my chair and faced her shamefully. "I truly am very sorry." It was all I could manage. How many apologies had been uttered within the walls of this house today? It seemed like thousands.

She drew a shaky breath and put on a smile. "Don't worry, the fault is not your own."

I nodded silently. But of course the fault was mine. My brothers were so young, and it was now obvious to me that I had not taught them well enough. After a long moment of silence, everyone carried on with the meal except Grandmother, who was still catching her breath in the corner.

My heart beat hard with shame. I looked across the table at Owen. He leaned forward and said in a hushed voice, "It would seem that the mouse was a rabid wolf by the way they reacted." He pointed his gaze at his mother and Grandmother.

I allowed myself a small smile. "I'm surprised you were able to keep your wits. That thing was entirely terrifying."

He laughed. "Entirely."

Looking upon his smiling face, I was struck by a pang of guilt about not accepting his apology. He had meant it in earnest, and I had refused it. Although he was an unyielding, mischievous tease who could never be serious, I was fairly certain that his intentions weren't all bad.

My thoughts were interrupted by a flustered sigh from Grandmother as she reclaimed her seat at the table. She shook her head then patted her hair tentatively. "Those boys ought to be kept on leashes."

My eyes flew of their own accord to Owen. We looked at each other, as if to see who could hold out longer without laughing. His eyes widened and his shoulders shook. My lips pressed together and my chin quivered. Then, as if calling a truce, we both burst into laughter. I was reminded of just how infectious and delightful his laugh was.

Grandmother looked at us with confusion. "Am I truly that funny?"

Owen and I laughed until tears pooled in our eyes. Why Grandmother's unknowing agreement with Owen on his absurd idea about leashes gave me such a keen urge to laugh, I knew not. I only knew that I hadn't laughed this hard in years. Perhaps it wasn't only Grandmother's comment, but the look on Owen's face that brought me to such a state. I sighed as my laughter subsided, feeling much lighter than I had felt only moments before.

Everyone else had resumed their own conversations and didn't seem to notice Owen lean across the table. "Will you please accept my apology?" he asked, displaying his playful grin.

I looked at him appraisingly, for I did not want him to know just how relieved I was that he had asked again. "Yes," I said with an unconstrained smile.

He sat back, relief apparent in his eyes. "Now that you are in a cheerful mood, will you also accept me as your friend?"

The question rang loud in my ears, pulling at my heart. When was the last time I had considered anyone I knew as a friend? After moving to Maidstone, I knew no one. Grief was aching fresh within me and I had no intention of making friends. I had taken on the role of a mother to my brothers and that was the sole purpose of my life. I made a promise.

"At least something better than an enemy?"

Owen's voice brought my mind back to the present. My lips curled slowly into a smile. Something within me yearned for friendship with fresh longing. So, leaning toward him, I answered, "Yes."

As I lay in bed that night, I was surprised by how easily sleep was eluding me. With the contributions of both a long, eventful day, and the new comfort of this bed, I expected that I would fall asleep the moment my head hit the pillow. But that was not so, for the opposing emotions within me were much too strong. Embarrassment, worry, and excitement all played their part in my inability to sleep, and my thoughts refused to dispel their thick clouds of unanswerable questions.

How did Mrs. Kellaway truly feel about us staying here? What did she think of Peter and Charles's awful behavior? Would they ever learn to be well-behaved? And one question, that repeated itself, each time with renewed vigor, demanding an answer: what was it about Owen that made me feel so vulnerable?

Finally, after several hours of drowning in thought, my mind grew weary. I blamed my inability to answer these questions on the sleep that had begun blanketing my clear thought, carrying me down further and further into its depths until, at last, it swallowed me whole.

# Chapter 6

The sun was already shining bright through my window when I awoke. I flew out of bed the moment I saw it. How long had I slept? Clearly much longer than I had planned. I wanted to get an early start, to be able to explore the home and grounds at my own leisure.

I raced into a gown and checked my reflection quickly. The upper part of my arm where Aunt Ruth had gripped so tightly the other day was turning green and yellow with a fresh bruise. I wished for some of Lizzie's cosmetic concoction to cover it, but I certainly wasn't going to bother her with such a silly thing. Praying that it would go unnoticed, I raced down the hall to Peter and Charles's bedchamber.

I threw open the door and found only two empty, neatly made beds. Where could they be now? The only reliable explanation that came to mind was that they were at breakfast. However, noting their behavior the day before, they could be anywhere, doing *anything*.

I hurried down the stairs and stopped outside the dining room, leaning my ear against the door. I could hear Grandfather's soft voice intermingled with familiar giggles. Easing the door open, I stepped inside, finding Grandmother, Grandfather, and my brothers all seated at the table. I leaned against the doorframe in relief.

Grandmother looked up from her plate. "Oh, Miss Downing! Have a seat!" she exclaimed around a mouthful of food.

I walked around the table and took a chair beside Peter. "I suppose I got off to a late start this morning."

61

Grandmother threw out her hand. "No matter, dear, you had a very eventful day yesterday."

I nodded in agreement then asked, "Where are the others?"

"Hmm. I seem to have forgotten." She scrunched her brow. "But I can tell you that they were here at breakfast only minutes ago."

"Oh." I felt a small pinch of disappointment. I had planned on asking Mrs. Kellaway for a tour of the home. I looked to my brothers. "And how did you sleep?"

Their faces lit up and they both began rambling on at once. "The beds were so comfortable!" Peter exclaimed.

"And so bouncy!" Charles added.

Grandmother and Grandfather laughed heartily. "Why don't you boys come with us to the library?" Grandfather suggested. "If that is fine with your sister."

I eyed my brothers carefully, not knowing if I should allow them this excursion. They had behaved horribly the day before, so it could be unwise to let them out of my sight again. Grandmother and Grandfather seemed trustworthy enough, and they had proved to be kind. Even so, I had no doubt that they were both capable of delivering a good scolding if necessary. So I nodded and said, "Yes, that would be wonderful. I was actually planning on exploring around a bit myself."

"Perfect. We would be more than delighted to take them off your hands anytime. They are so darling," Grandmother raved.

Apparently she had forgiven them for the disaster at dinner. "Well, thank you." I stood and leaned over my brothers. "Promise me that you will be on your best behavior." I raised my eyebrows at them.

"We promise!" Peter answered before they jumped from their chairs.

I laughed and placed my hand on Grandmother's shoulder. "I won't be gone for long. Thank you very much."

She reached up a withered hand and patted mine. "Anytime, my dear."

With one last glance at my brothers, I left the room in a hurry, eager to begin exploring. I never fully claimed the opportunity to see the grounds in detail the first time I came here. I had been avoiding a certain boy by keeping to my room.

Remembering my bonnet, I raced up the stairs and swiped it quickly from my trunk. I made a mental note to unpack later. Oh, how I despised wearing my bonnet. It itched my neck and blocked my sight. But, for the purpose of preventing further damage to my already disfigured complexion, I put it on, and tying the ribbon as loosely as possible, I hurried down the stairs and out the door.

I was welcomed by a warm breeze that carried all the smells I loved: freshly cut grass, flourishing gardens, and sunshine—I knew sunshine must have a smell for how delightful it is. I walked out behind the home and stopped to admire a beautiful bed of flowers. Yellow, purple, white, and red met my eyes. I sighed. Flowers had always been a love of mine.

As I was bending over to examine more closely a hollyhock plant that had caught my admiring eye, the sound of nearby foot-falls startled me immensely.

I jumped a little, then turned quickly to discover who was approaching. Just as I did, the wind caught hold of my bonnet in a vicious gust, making it fall flat over my face. I stumbled blindly backward, being pushed by the sudden wind. In my wild attempt to adjust my bonnet, I fell over backward, landing rather hard and painfully on my backside.

Much to my dismay, whoever had been approaching now knelt beside me on the grass. And much to my even greater dismay, I heard his low and amused chuckle.

*Owen.*

What greater opportunity was there than this for him to tease me? I was mortified. What could I do? I racked my brain in a flurry for options. I could stand up boldly and walk away, or I could laugh at myself, or I could tell him that I fell over on purpose.

I berated myself for my stupidity and chose to leave my bonnet where it sat, shielding my face from the teasing expression that I would undoubtedly see if I were to adjust it.

Apparently Owen couldn't even leave me with the solace found in the concealment of my face. He took my bonnet, lifted it gently, and tipped his head to peer at my face beneath it. "Are you having troubles this morning?"

I was intent on not looking at his face, but when I heard the raw amusement in his voice my eyes flew up to his angrily. "No. Before you made an appearance, I was perfectly content."

"If I am not mistaken, you toppled of your own accord," he said to his defense.

"You startled me!" I pulled my bonnet from his grasp. "And do you have any idea how horrid it is to wear a bonnet? They are horribly uncomfortable, and the only vision you can perceive must be straight in front of your eyes."

"And when the wind becomes involved, even that isn't so."

I let out an exasperated sigh, frustrated that he wouldn't offer even the slightest hint of empathy. "You . . . are . . . *atrocious*."

He laughed and cast me a look that hinted at a challenge. "You called me that yesterday. It seems that your vocabulary would consist of a bit more variety."

I couldn't help but rise to the challenge. "Oh, it does." My voice was bold, and I looked him straight in the eyes. "Would you like to hear?"

He leaned back on his hands with a satisfied smile. "I would love to."

I turned to him, feeling extremely bold for reasons I could not name. "You are awful, barbaric, heinous, nefarious, abhorrent, flagrant, wicked, and *entirely* atrocious." I regretted the words as soon as they escaped my daring mouth. What was he doing to me? I was never this outspoken.

But Owen only laughed again, seemingly pleased with the insult. "Now, Annette, is that an appropriate way to speak to a friend?"

"Is teasing and belittling any way to treat a friend? Or a lady for that matter?" I felt extremely relieved that he had taken my insults so lightly. He must have known I didn't mean them. At least not all of them. In times of embarrassment, I tended to turn a bit atrocious myself.

"No, it's not," he answered seriously. He ran a hand through his hair as if frustrated about something. "I apologize."

I was surprised by his sudden change of mood. Attempting to swallow my pride, I said, "I'm sorry too. I really didn't mean all those things . . ."

He lifted an eyebrow in heavy skepticism.

"I didn't!" I protested.

"You did."

"I did not!" I suddenly felt the strongest urge to punch him, square in the chest, but something told me that more harm would come to my hand than to him, for the strain of his jacket against the muscle in his shoulders, arms, and chest warned me . . . and strangely captivated me. I looked away quickly, remembering that I was supposed to be angry with him right now.

He stood, laughing, and extended his hand in an offer to help me up. "You did mean it, and I deserved each and every word."

I ignored his hand. "I don't wish for your gallant assistance. I am quite capable of standing on my own, thank you."

"Are you?"

I stood up rather dramatically and looked at him with defiance. "I am."

"What an accomplishment."

I gasped. His lips were twitching at the corners, which I now knew meant that he was trying to hold back laughter. I then realized that I too was trying not to laugh, for the absurdity of what I had done dawned on me suddenly. Laughter burst from within me, and once it broke free, it didn't want to stop.

Owen tipped his head back in laughter of his own. I was reminded of last night at dinner, how easily we had laughed, and how heartily. His chuckling subsided and he looked at me with a broad grin. "You have the most unique and infectious laugh."

"What? I do not." I shook my head sharply.

"You do. It is unlike any laugh I have ever heard. Haven't many people told you that?"

I shrugged, suddenly feeling very self-conscious. "Not many people have heard it."

He stared at me in silence for a long moment. "Then I must be among the most privileged."

I dropped my gaze to the grass. The dimple was back, and it was paired much too handsomely with the warm, admiring look in his countenance. I didn't know how to respond.

His voice recalled my eyes, carrying a much lighter tone. "Would you like me to give you a tour?"

I waved off his offer and said, "I don't wish to rob you of your time any longer."

"It would be my pleasure. Please." His cajoling smile made the offer nearly impossible to refuse. I had planned on asking Mrs. Kellaway, but Owen probably knew the home just as well.

"Very well," I accepted, trying to hide just how glad I was that he had offered.

"Would you like to start with the grounds?"

I nodded, sweeping my gaze over the surrounding land. There was so much to see!

Owen beckoned me forward with a smile and a wave of his hand. "Come. We'll start with the gardens."

We set off together, snaking our way through the beautiful gardens; he allowed me time to admire each. My favorite was the rose garden. We stopped in front of a tall bush, adorned with miniature white roses. They looked like little flakes of beautiful snow.

Its neighboring bush, covered with soft pink roses, caught my admiring eye more than once. I quickly banished the admiration, telling myself that pink was an awful color, and that I wasn't allowed to admire it anymore. Melancholy pooled in my heart as I remembered all the things I tried everyday to forget. Pink did that in a way that nothing else could.

Owen reached forward and broke off a pink rose. "For you." He smiled knowingly. "I noticed you admiring them."

Unrest surged within me. "Oh, um . . . ," I didn't know what to say. Something inside me was begging me to accept it, to put it in my hair just as I always used to do. It was beautiful. The gentleness of it, the way the sun illuminated its most attractive hues . . .

I quickly stopped myself. No. It was not beautiful. It was ugly. "It must have been the white roses you saw me admiring."

He held up the rose in his hand, glancing at it from different angles. "Are you not fond of this color?"

"No, I'm not." Remembering my manners, I added, "But thank you."

"Don't thank me for a rose you find unsightly." He chuckled. "Would you like a white one?"

"That would be much better."

He reached down to pluck off a rose near the base of the bush, smiling over his shoulder. A movement flashed in my vision from the right. I turned my head and looked twice. A robust, angry-looking woman was bounding swiftly across the grass.

I was stunned by the resemblance she bore to an animal I had read about. I believe it was called an elephant. By the way she bounded with hefty footfalls, and carried herself with such powerful authority, it seemed to me that she was the very personification of an elephant.

I jerked my gaze to Owen. I was surprised to see that he was watching her approach with a calm, if not amused, expression.

"Owen Kellaway, don't you dare take a rose!" The elephant woman yelled, shaking a finger. "How many times must I tell you?" Her face was ruddy and her voice sounded gruff and quite terrifying.

Owen turned his head around to flash me a mischievous smile.

I knew mischievous smiles better than most, so from his I knew that he intended to pick the rose anyway. He grasped it by its stem and pulled up sharply, releasing it from the bush. Then he stood up straight and looked at me with wide eyes brimming with laughter. "Run!"

He grasped my hand and we took off, racing across the grass. The wind flew at my face, muffling my laughter along with my breathlessness. I glanced back at the woman, holding my bonnet against my head with my free hand so it wouldn't blow onto my face again. She was advancing with great haste, pumping her arms far too high to look natural.

We reached the broad stables on the northwest lawn and Owen pulled me inside, laughing and trying to catch his breath. Two grooms, busy feeding the horses, glanced up lazily at our entrance.

I leaned against the wall, laughing between my quick breaths. "Who was that?"

He grinned with amusement, his breathing heavy. "The groundskeeper's wife, Mrs. Berney. The woman of my nightmares."

"And now mine."

He laughed and leaned toward me as if to tell me a secret. "When I was a young boy, I was quite like your brothers. Nothing pleased me more than good mischief. But you have experienced that firsthand, haven't you?" He shook his head slightly as if he had forgotten.

I raised an eyebrow. "It seems that is still the case."

He chuckled. "That may be true, but I used to pick roses everyday. I told Mrs. Berney that I picked them as a gift for my mother, when really I picked them solely to make her angry."

"Well, she certainly seems angry now."

Owen nodded in agreement and smiled down at me. Under his penetrating gaze, I felt as though his eyes were taking in every feature of my face—every flaw. I was suddenly very aware of how unbecoming I must have looked, for I had spent less than two minutes getting ready. My face grew hot.

It was then that the door flew open and Mrs. Berney entered, still upholding her scolding finger. She was even more terrifying at closer range. "Owen Kellaway, you give me that rose this instant." She narrowed her eyes in deep malice.

Owen quickly threw his hands behind his back. "What rose?" His mischievous grin had returned.

Without hesitation, Mrs. Berney raced behind him and snatched the white rose from his hand. She glowered at him, the expression making her lower teeth jut out in front of her lip and her eyes shine venomously. Perhaps it wasn't an elephant that she personified, but a very hefty snake. She held this terrifying expression for several seconds before turning on her heel and storming out the door.

Owen turned to me with a wry grin. "Can't you see why she would haunt my dreams?"

My wide-eyed gaze still held on the door from which she had just departed. "Yes, I most definitely can." I turned to him with a smile. I was surprised to see that in his hand he held the pink rose he had first removed from the garden.

"This one will have to suffice." He extended the rose to me.

I didn't move. "How did you—"

"I held it in this hand the entire time," he explained. "Mrs. Berney didn't even notice."

I eyed the rose with careful scrutiny. It sat so innocently in his hand, and I could have sworn I heard it begging me to accept it. But surely nothing so beautiful could be so innocent. It was trying to trick me.

Owen tilted his head to look more directly into my eyes. "I can assure you that it isn't poisoned."

I glanced up at him from under my lashes, a small smile creeping onto my lips. But I said nothing.

"Annette, what do you have against this color?" He asked, apparently sensing my resentment.

"Nothing."

"Then take it. Please. And you will learn to love it." His smile felt like a gift in itself.

I accepted it, only because I knew he wouldn't relent until I did. I held it far away from me, making a note to dispose of it later.

His gaze flickered from the rose to my face, confusion written on his features. Thankfully, he moved his eyes from mine without asking for an explanation. He nodded to the stalls. "Would you like to meet the horses?"

Excitement surged within me. There had always been a special place in my heart for animals. "I would love to."

I followed him down the aisle to the nearest stall where a tall, dark horse stood, shifting restlessly. "This is Cosmo," Owen said. "He belongs to my elder brother, Edmond."

I rubbed the horse's muzzle and ran my finger along the space between his eyes. My father once told me that a horse would become your best friend if you did that. Cosmo's fur was short and coarse, and the fuzzy skin on his snout was slightly wet. Owen moved down the row, naming off each horse. I paused at every stall to greet each, being sure to stroke them between the eyes.

Owen stopped at the stall second to the end to rub the muzzle of a copper-colored horse. "This one is mine. I received him from my father when he was only a foal."

"What is his name?" I asked, leaning toward the horse in curiosity.

"First, you need to understand that I was very young when I named him." I could hear the smile in his voice.

I turned around to face him. "Now I'm really curious."

Owen dropped his gaze and scuffed his boot across the floor. He glanced at me with a small smile. "Horsey."

I laughed. "Horsey? You're lying."

"I'm not."

I looked at the horse again. He had large, round eyes and a playful expression. "He certainly looks like a Horsey."

"That is precisely what I thought." Owen laughed and gestured to the last stall. "And this lovely mare's name is Eve."

I walked up to Eve's stall and stroked her head. She had a black, shiny coat with friendly, delicate features. She whinnied heartily and it almost looked like she was smiling. I rubbed between her eyes and down her muzzle, her short whiskers tickling my hand.

"I think she likes you," Owen said, leaning against the wall.

I smiled at her. "She's beautiful."

"I agree." There was something about the way he said it that made me glance up at him. He was staring at me with an expression that made my heart skip. I moved my gaze away quickly and cleared my throat. I had never been looked at the way Owen was looking at me. I found it painfully unsettling. The heat in the stables was suddenly too much.

"I should go check on my brothers." I turned for the door quickly, eager to escape that unnerving look in his eyes.

"Wait—" Owen grasped my arm before I could escape. "I cannot allow you to leave until you have seen the orchard. Trust me, you do not want to deny yourself the opportunity."

I turned around. Thankfully, his light expression had resurfaced. This I was more comfortable with. "Fine. But we need to hurry."

Owen led me across the lawn to the iron gate at the entrance of the orchard. It was situated on the east side of the property. He pushed open the gate and extended his hand in a gesture for me to precede him. Inside the gate was a small set of stone stairs, and walking down the steps, I stopped in awe at the beauty of the little orchard around me.

Tall apple trees flanked a pathway of sun-golden stone, each tree standing wide and in full bloom, extending a broad canopy of shade across the path.

Owen walked to a carved wooden bench that was positioned under a tree halfway down the path. "Would you like to sit down?"

I nodded and took a seat beside him on the bench, looking around at the magnificent beauty of the place. "I have never seen an orchard."

He looked at me, half his face in sunlight, half in shadow. "You haven't?"

"No."

He stood and walked to the nearest tree. "Then you must taste a fresh orchard apple." He plucked two apples from the tree and returned to his seat beside me.

I took an apple from his extended hand and returned his warm smile. "Thank you." The apple felt like a gift of the most thoughtful kind. How had Owen changed so quickly? Only a short time had passed since I had been tempted to inflict serious damage on his much-too-handsome face.

We ate our apples in silence—not uncomfortable silence, but the relaxing kind. The kind that settles all nerves and banishes all doubt. I listened to the birds chirping and the breeze rustling the leaves in the trees. I had no desire to break the silence, but Owen's voice snapped it right in two. "Tell me about your aunt."

The question unsettled the relaxation that I had felt from the warm silence. I really didn't want to lie to him too, but I didn't want his pity. "Well, she is kind, accommodating—"

"Don't try that with me, Annette," he interrupted. "You may have convinced my mother, but it won't work on me."

"What do you mean?" I asked sheepishly.

"What kind, accommodating woman threatens two little boys for being imperfect?" His eyes housed a fire that I hadn't seen before. "And sends them off with their sister to change their entire disposition in only a few weeks? Please tell me the truth about her."

He held my gaze with determination that demanded an honest answer. He had behaved decently today; perhaps I could confide in him. I fixed my sights on an apple in the tallest tree across the path. It sat far apart from the rest, on the highest branch. It rested singular and defiant, alone and unreachable—just as I was supposed to be.

I stared at the apple with determination in my own gaze that I wouldn't look at Owen, for fear of seeing pity in his eyes. "She is horrible," I began in a hushed voice. "She spends most of the day out of the house, visiting friends, traveling. When she is home, she . . . well, she threatens to throw us out, or starve us." I swallowed, fighting an unwelcome memory and continued quickly, trying to dispel the unrest that I could feel rising in Owen.

"Sometimes I fancied the idea of being thrown out. I was certain that we could fare well on our own, without a penny to our name." I laughed lightly, though I did not feel it. "But it's all right. We have what we need, and she doesn't beat us anymore." I regretted the words as soon as they escaped me. I had said too much. It was as if I could feel Owen's anger break free and rise into the breeze.

"She beat you?" His voice was quiet and dangerous.

"I can usually prevent it now that I am older," I stammered. "She rarely attempts to strike the boys."

"Rarely?" He got up quickly and stood in front of me, obstructing my view of the apple, forcing me to look at him. "You can't go back to her. You can't." He paced in front of me, fists clenched at his sides. I didn't like seeing this side of him, not one bit. "How long has it been since she hurt you?"

My gaze flickered to the new bruises on my arms. For a moment I thought my movement went unnoticed, but Owen's sharp blue eyes caught everything. He leaned forward and set his fingers on the bruise so gently I hardly felt it. But I certainly felt the shiver that his touch sent down my spine.

"It's nothing." I pulled my arm away, trying to reassure him with my eyes.

He must have noticed my discomfort, because the intensity of his gaze softened and he took his seat beside me on the bench. I was a little shaken. From what I had seen of him, I wouldn't have guessed that he had this side to him.

In a softer voice, he asked, "How long has it been since your parents passed away?"

My heart lurched at the question. Why did he have to ask me so many questions? It was only another way for him to make me vulnerable. I replaced my sights on the apple. The combination of his piercing gaze and the ache in my heart would be too much. "Nearly five years."

He didn't speak for several seconds. "They were always very kind to me. I am sure they were kind to everyone." His voice was so gentle it made my heart ache deeper.

"They were."

"How old are your brothers?" I could hear his curiosity.

"Peter is seven and Charles is five."

He was silent for a moment, then said, "So Peter was two years old, and Charles was only an infant?"

I nodded, being sure to keep my gaze fixed on the apple.

"And you have looked after and taught them all on your own." He stated it as a fact and I couldn't detect any pity in his voice. Something else lingered in his voice, though—something that I couldn't find a name for. He fell silent for several heartbeats until I could feel the heat of his gaze on the side of my face. It felt as though his eyes were boring a hole into it. What was he doing? Why was he trying to make me uncomfortable?

Without warning, he moved his fingers to the side of my face and turned my head so that I was forced to look at him. My heart jumped furiously and my cheek burned under his touch. He took hold of a loose strand of hair and tucked it behind my ear. His fingers brushed my jaw so softly it sent fleeting chills down my neck and spine.

"You are so brave," he said in a hushed voice.

The unexpected tenderness of the gesture struck my heart forcefully and I realized that I had been very wrong in my first appraisal of him—he most certainly could be serious. I would prefer his atrocious teasing over . . . *this* any day. I knew that whatever *this* was, I didn't like it. It tugged at the tender parts of my heart and made me feel completely defenseless in a way that I never remembered feeling before. In fact, I felt strangely close to crying, which would not do.

But I could feel battling forces within me, one ordering me to pull away, the other tempting me to lean closer . . .

I immediately pushed away the unwarranted desires of that other force. I had learned which one I could trust and which one would deceive me.

So I turned my head away from Owen and stood to walk in front of the tree with the unreachable apple. Away from him as I was, I could take hold of my emotions again, I could think clearly. I placed my hand on the ragged bark of the trunk and listened carefully to the beating of my heart as it sought ceaselessly to regain its normal rhythm. I didn't dare turn around, so I just stood there, waiting for Owen to break the agonizing silence. When he did, however, I wished he hadn't.

"Is that why you insist on doing everything on your own?" Although his voice was gentle, his words struck me with the panic-ridden feeling of being unarmed. He was uncovering buried truths from the deepest recesses of my heart, and I felt completely exposed by it. I heard him walk up behind me. "Because you've had to? Because, for the past five years you've had no one to depend on, and no one to trust?"

I squeezed my eyes shut, hoping that doing so would drive away the tremor that was spreading through me. He was unearthing my pain too easily. Pouring salt on the oldest wounds of my heart, making them sting anew. I wanted to run away. I wanted to run as far away as possible from this man who was too skilled at finding my weaknesses—the weaknesses that I liked to deny I even had. I wasn't going to speak. I couldn't speak.

Owen's hand fell gently to my shoulder and he leaned from behind to speak softly near my ear. "Please know that you can depend on me. And that you can always trust me."

I was grateful that he didn't try to make me look at him, for if he had, I don't know what I would have done. All my strength deserted me and my hand slid down the tree and fell to my side. That other force was at work again, tempting me to lean into him, to bury my face in his shoulder and cry like I hadn't for years. To let him wrap his arms around me and hold me. To allow myself to depend on him, to trust him.

This was Owen Kellaway I was thinking about. I must have been going mad.

"I will be waiting inside, if you wish to continue your tour." His hand fell from my shoulder and I heard him walk away in silence, shutting the iron gate behind him.

My shoulder tingled from where his hand had rested and my heart reeled at his departure. He must have known that I needed to be left to myself, that he had severely disheveled my emotions. I needed to be alone to realign them.

I had begun to doubt the wisdom of spending any portion of time with Owen. If in the short hours of the day he managed to already discover this piece of my heart, it terrified me to think of how much yet he could learn of it. Or steal of it.

There hadn't been a man to exist in the world that could flutter my heart the way Owen did with a mere smile, and it was not something that I could allow any longer. I had made promises, and in my experience with life, promises were not made to be broken.

I steeled myself and closeted my emotions, rubbing my hand against the trunk of the tree, tracing my finger in an indiscriminate shape. Memories filled my mind and, in an effort to stop them from coming, I closed my eyes.

But life would be far too simple if memories could be as easily dismissed as visions could.

# Chapter 7

*Five Years Before*

*T*he dry autumn leaves crunched beneath my boots, making tiny flecks of dead, broken leaves billow up and cling to the hem of my gown. The sun had barely risen and was casting deep peach and orange rays over the dew-covered grass. I clutched Charles in my arms, trying to keep him warm, keeping his small round cheek pressed against the warmth of my chest. Peter tottered along beside me, one hand grasped in mine. His fingers were nearly as cold as mine were, and his cheeks and the tip of his nose were rosy from the bite of the crisp morning air.

We were approaching the edge of the lawn where our phaeton was prepared to convey Mama and Papa to Kellaway Manor, the home of their closest friends. It had been quite a long time since they had made the trip, and I was now old enough to look after my brothers on my own. My parents had only five servants, all of which they trusted to help care for us in their absence.

I smiled as Papa scooped Peter up and placed a kiss on his rosy cheek. Peter giggled and squirmed from his arms, eager to return to the entertainment of the dry, crunching leaves. Papa's warm, green eyes shifted to me with a smile dancing around them. I moved into his outstretched arms, leaning my head against his chest, Charles encased between us. "I will miss you," I said softly. And I meant it, even though I knew he would only be away for two days.

"I will certainly miss you too, Anne," he said with a hearty chuckle, reaching down to tweak my nose.

I batted his hand away, laughing, and moved to Mama. She wrapped her arms around me in a tight hug. I buried my face in her shoulder, inhaling the floral smell of her rose perfume. Her blond curls fell on Charles's face, making him giggle. He grabbed a strand with his tiny hands, trying to stuff it in his mouth.

Mama pulled away and laughed, a quiet bubbling sound, and smoothed a hand over his peach fuzz hair. Then she waved Peter away from his leaf crunching and pulled him into a hug. "We will see you tomorrow night," she said, looking at me now. "Look after the boys while we are gone. Do not become distracted with unimportant matters. While we are away, the boys are to be your only concern. Your papa and I are trusting you with a great task."

I lifted my chin. "I will take perfect care them. I promise."

She smiled then, giving me a quick kiss on the cheek, and stepped toward the phaeton. "I have no doubts that you will keep that promise in one perfect piece."

Papa winked at me. "Not a crack?"

"Not a crack."

He grinned and gave Mama a hand up into the phaeton, then followed into the seat beside her. He looked down at me from his high seat above the two tall, fast wheels. "We love you very much. Be good." Another wink followed his words.

He and Mama waved and I waved back, wishing they would stay. Then Papa led the pair of young horses loose into a quick trot, and I watched the rickety wheels of the phaeton fly past me in a streak of bright yellow. My eyes followed after them down the road until the phaeton was nothing but a dot in the distance.

Charles was shivering now, and I was too, so I took Peter's hand and together we walked through the dead, dry leaves again, until we entered the house.

The rest of the day passed slowly. I hadn't realized how difficult it would be to keep Peter and his constant movement under control, and to keep careful watch of Charles at the same time. I wondered how Mama managed to do it every day with only a little assistance from me. The servants kept out of our way, as instructed, so I was left to all these duties alone. It was exhausting.

My arms and back were sore from holding Charles, and I was reaching my end with chasing Peter around the house. So when sundown came the following day, I was entirely ready to pass my brothers off to more capable hands.

It had rained that afternoon, so we had stayed inside for most of the day. But with Mama and Papa arriving soon, I wanted to be waiting outside for them when they arrived. I put on my favorite pink muslin dress, Mama's favorite too, then we stepped outside and walked to the edge of the lawn where the leaves were now wet and soft from the recent rain. Peter scowled down at the wet leaves, stomping his feet on them, disappointed that they no longer made a sound.

As we waited in the chilly autumn air, the sun went down and the moon came out. The longer we waited, the more quiet everything became, as if the wet, soundless leaves had sent a message to the rest of the world to keep silent too. It wasn't until Peter's teeth started chattering that we turned back toward the house.

Once inside, I put my brothers to bed and sat in Papa's chair by the drawing room window, watching the dark, unoccupied road, hoping, waiting. It took only a few hours for worry to really set in. I thought I could never sleep, peering out the window every second as I was.

But eventually, I did fall asleep, with the skirts of my pink dress clutched into tight balls in my hands.

It wasn't until two days later that we received word of their death. It was unexpected, a result of carelessness. Returning home from Dover, they had traveled dangerously close to the white cliffs. Somehow that old phaeton had fallen over the edge. It could have been the horses' fault, it could have been the phaeton's fault. But I refused to believe that it was Mama and Papa's fault. They would never choose to leave us like that.

Papa's will was found and specifically stated that our guardian was to be Papa's sister, Ruth Filbee, and her husband. But she was a recent widow, and although it was rare for a woman alone to be our guardian, we were unarguably being sent to her tomorrow.

When one of our servants delivered the news to me, my heart lurched in my chest, threatening to break open with the sudden pain. I shook my head hard, hoping that doing so would make me forget what I had just heard. But it only made it worse, making the words throb in my skull, echo in my ears. They are dead.

Tightness rose to my throat, grasping at it, making my breath come in hard, heavy gasps. Hot tears sprang into my eyes, distorting my *vision. I swallowed, then swallowed again. I breathed in shallow gasps. And I stood with my fists clenched at my sides. "No. No. No." I shook my head again, and my voice broke into sobs. I was shaking.*

*Without listening to another word, I ran to my brothers' room, pressing my hand against my chest, struggling to somehow hold the broken bits of my heart together inside of me.*

*Charles lay awake in his bassinet and Peter was asleep in his tiny bed. Wiping tears from my eyes so I could see, I lifted Charles into my arms and pulled Peter up onto my lap as I sat on the edge of his bed. His eyes blinked open and he looked at my tear-streaked face, dazed and troubled at seeing me that way. I hugged him tightly, never wanting to let go. His mussed dark hair stuck to my cheek where my tears flowed freely.*

*Peter pulled back to look at my face again. Then, with a look beyond his years with concern, he lifted a small hand and rubbed the tears from my cheeks. He scowled at them, as if he thought they didn't belong. He raised his hand again and wiped, and wiped, and wiped my face again. His gentle swipes turned into soft slaps as he scowled at the steady flow of tears that refused to stop. But then he paused, and looking down at his wet fingers, and up at the new tears on my face, and he started to cry too.*

*He didn't know, of course, what had happened. And he surely wouldn't understand. He was only crying out of confusion and frustration over the fact that he couldn't stop my tears from coming. And he was all the more precious for it.*

*Then Charles, apparently sensing the discord around him, burst into tears of his own. His soft whimpers sounded deafening. His tears left tiny droplets clinging to his lashes. So together we sat, all of us crying, and I was the only one who actually knew why. How long we stayed like that, I didn't know, but eventually the flow of tears lessened a bit, and I could breathe and think a bit clearer.*

*So in that grief-filled moment, looking at Peter's wobbling chin and round, watering eyes, and Charles's little mouth opening in a quiet yawn, I realized something very important: My brothers needed me. I couldn't allow myself to cry, to be weak. They were so young, so innocent, so precious, and dependent. On me. They depended on me now, and me alone. I needed to be strong and unbreakable, so they could be too. My moment of weakness was over.*

*I grasped Peter's wrist as he reached up to my face again, stopping his hand. I wiped my own tears from my face and drew a shaky breath. Then I wiped away his. And then I spoke to my heart for the very first time. A tiny voice inside my head told it:* You are invulnerable. You are unbreakable. You shall give all your love to Peter and Charles. You shall always listen to what I tell you to do. You shall love the boys and care for them all your life. And you shall never make me cry again.

*The words granted me some form of unearthly strength, and I knew my heart would obey me. In the deepest coves of my mind I heard it whisper back. It promised.*

*So I sat there on the edge of Peter's bed, two little boys in my arms, shaking limbs and unsteady breathing, and no idea of what would become of us. But my eyes were bone dry, and that was what made me strong.*

# Chapter 8

*Present Day*

*Not a crack.*
Mama and Papa hadn't known just how long they would be away, just how long I would keep my promise from breaking. Forever does not know minutes, hours, or days.

Feeling a sharp poke on my finger, I realized that I still clutched the pink rose in my hand. I would certainly have to dispose of it. With one last composing breath, I turned my back to the tree and started toward the gate, anxious to get to the library, to return to my brothers and their lighthearted spirits.

When I opened the door to the house, I found Owen waiting by the drawing room. He greeted me with a cheery smile. "What would you like to see next?"

I was relieved that he was back to his old and strangely new self; that he wasn't going to try to make me feel things I didn't want to feel. "My brothers are in the library, so perhaps we can start there."

"Perfect," he said.

When we stepped into the library, I was instantly greeted by the smell of wood and old leather. I saw my brothers each sitting on one of Grandfather's knees. He was reading them a book, altering his voice for each character that spoke. Peter and Charles were so engulfed in the story that they didn't notice my entrance.

Grandmother did, though. She looked up from her embroidery and her eyes flew open wide with delight. "Miss Downing! There you are! Oh, these boys have been perfect little angels." She eyed

Owen with a scolding frown. "Owen, dear. You cannot be spending so much time with Miss Annette. You may anger her fiancé."

My eyes widened. *Fiancé?*

Grandmother let out a very loud, hooting laugh. I looked up at Owen just in time to see his jaw tense.

"Oh, I joke, I joke." Grandmother appeared much more amused that Owen.

I felt my face warm. Peter and Charles looked up from Grandfather's book and gave me two very wide smiles, as if just noticing my presence in the room. Charles slid off of Grandfather's lap and ran over to me. He grabbed my arm and started dragging me to a seat beside him. "Grandfather is reading us a very funny story. Come listen!"

I laughed, grateful for his rescue, and allowed him to pull me to the chair. Owen brought his own chair up beside me and sat down. "I have an idea," he said, leaning forward to speak to my brothers. "Why don't I take you two outside to ride horses?"

Peter and Charles turned their heads briskly to look at one another. "Horses?" Peter said with awe.

"Yes, horses. Ponies too. Would you like to join me?"

They nodded with perfectly round eyes and gaping mouths, then jumped from Grandfather's lap and ran toward the door. "Are you coming, Annette?" Charles asked with a nervous look.

Owen grinned at me in his teasing way. "I suppose you are invited."

Charles's uneasy expression was enough. "Of course," I said, stepping forward to take Charles's hand. I was a little nervous too—it had been a very long time since I had ridden a horse. But the thought of riding again made my stomach flutter.

Owen held the door open as I walked by and said, "We'll have to explore the library another day."

I stopped by my bedchamber before we set off to the stables. Grandmother had sent Lizzie to fetch me a riding habit that belonged to Owen's sister, and I needed to change into it quickly. While I was there, I handed the pink rose to Lizzie. "While I am gone, will you dispose of this, please?"

She gave me a puzzled look. "Why dispose of it?"

She was right to be confused, it was a silly thing to ask, and I really didn't feel up to offering an explanation. "Nevermind," I dropped the rose down on my bed and wiped my hands on the skirts of the deep green riding habit I now wore. I would have to get rid of it myself later.

I raced down the stairs and met Owen, Peter, and Charles outside. By the time we arrived outside the stables, my brothers were absolutely mad with excitement. They had never ridden a horse and it seemed that the idea was even more riveting than any mischief that they had ever caused, all put together. They tugged on my arm and pulled on my skirts for me to walk faster, and they even sneaked behind Owen to push him through the door.

Once inside, Owen introduced them to each horse, and let them choose which they would like to ride. Peter chose a dark brown filly, and Charles chose a biscuit-colored pony.

Owen turned to me. "And for you?"

I looked over all the horses. Eve stood in the last stall and when I walked up beside her, she looked at me expectantly. I thought I could see a bright smile shining in her eyes. I had to choose her. "I'll ride Eve."

He grinned as if he had known I would pick her. "Of course."

With a groom saddling up our horses, I stood back, nervously rubbing my palms down the skirt of the riding habit. It fit me well enough, but was a bit loose in some areas, which I had expected, considering my petite figure.

I felt my nerves go taut because of the last time I had ridden a horse. The experience had left me with a small patch of fear. It was when I was eleven years old, and I had made the mistake of going for a ride by myself—on a new, poorly trained filly. The ride started out fine, but as we went on, she became restless, and before I could return to the stables, I had been thrown off. All I could remember was seeing the ground as it rushed up at me, and waking in my bed a few hours later with a broken arm.

I tried to distract myself by turning my attention to my brothers, who stood beside me bouncing up and down on their legs, eager to mount their horses. I hadn't noticed that Owen had walked beside us until he spoke. "It seems that you boys are ready to go." He chuckled. "Now we need only to convince your sister."

I shot him a subtle glare. He must have noticed how nervous I was. I certainly couldn't have anyone assuming that I was nervous to ride a horse. "Convince me of what?" I asked a little too innocently.

He raised an eyebrow and gestured to the mounting block resting beside Eve, then began helping my brothers onto theirs. I swallowed and walked tentatively toward Eve. I stroked between her eyes and spoke softly in her ear. "My name is Annette, and we are going for a ride."

Her ears twitched and she turned her head slightly toward me as I spoke.

"Is that fine with you? If not, please acknowledge so." I waited for a few seconds, but Eve sat still and straight, like a well-trained horse was supposed to do. I felt like I could trust her. After stepping onto the mounting block, I carefully eased my way onto the saddle. I grasped the reins in my gloved hands. They felt old and familiar and somehow they settled my nerves. I smiled back at Peter and Charles. They were grasping their pommels tightly and giggling uncontrollably. Two grooms were standing beside them, reins in hand, prepared to help them along on their ride.

Owen approached beside me, astride his copper horse. "Off we go."

I smiled, trying hard not to let it reveal my anxiety. Taking in a deep breath, I loosened my hold on the reins slightly and set off at a nice slow pace.

After a few minutes of this, I grew more comfortable, and let the reins a little looser. Eve sped up to a trot, the brisk midday air picking up speed as it flew past my ears. It sounded like old memories of time spent with my father.

Owen turned his head and flashed me a smile. "Are you enjoying yourself?"

"Very much," I said.

One side of his lips curved upward in a daring smile and he looked at me out of narrowed eyes. "Would you dare go faster?"

My heart fluttered with a mix of emotions. Excitement, fear, anxiety, bravery, and boldness all waged for supremacy within me. Together, they reached a stalemate. The resulting action was me dropping the reins and letting Eve have her head. She sprang into a furious gallop and we streaked past Owen in a blur of green on black. And I was fairly certain that I shot him a mischievous grin before I did.

I heard his laugh and the brisk hoofbeats of his horse as they picked up speed. Exhilaration took over my senses and I threw my head back, letting the wind fly past my face, through my hair. This time, it sounded like freedom.

The sound of hoofbeats grew nearer behind me, and so did Owen's laugh. Something flared inside of me. With him approaching close behind me, this suddenly felt like a race. And if it was, then I *had* to win. We were heading straight for the woods at the edge of the property, which I assumed was the decided finish line. Eve was giving it her all, her head borne down in acceleration, her black hooves barely skimming the grass as she ran. I couldn't remember a time that I had ridden so quickly, or been so daring.

The woods were within our grasp now, and although Owen was close behind, I could tell that Eve would win. She showed no signs of exertion and flew onward with the same determination that I felt within myself. With a final, unexpected surge of speed, we slipped past the grass and into the trees.

I pulled back on the reins, slowing to a gradual stop. My breath came quickly and my heart was racing, as if I had been the one running. I couldn't stop the laughter that I felt rising in my chest from bursting out of my mouth.

Owen and his horse bolted through the trees and came to a stop beside me. He wore an expression that was half bewilderment and half admiration. "I have never seen a lady ride so fearlessly."

I patted Eve's neck. "She is amazing."

"She is." He nodded in agreement. "Horsey isn't as quick as he was in his younger years. I knew he would be unable to compete with her."

"I would be inclined to blame the rider," I said in a light voice.

Owen raised both eyebrows at me with a laugh. I threw him a smirk and turned Eve toward the lawn. I could hear him laughing behind me as he caught up to me on the grass. He was probably as surprised as I was by my choice of words.

Peter and Charles came into view, and despite our distance, I could hear their giggles clearly.

"It seems they are enjoying themselves," Owen said with a chuckle.

"Indeed." I laughed. "Anything that will keep them out of trouble."

His smile grew. "No young boy is truly a young boy if he doesn't get into some trouble." His words rang with familiarity.

"You sound like your grandmother," I said, rolling my eyes.

"My grandmother is a very wise woman."

I fixed my gaze forward, watching the delighted expressions on the faces of my darling brothers. Grandmother and Owen were completely right. No matter what could be done to improve my brothers' behavior, Aunt Ruth's wicked intentions wouldn't be satisfied. It was impossible to alter the natural inclinations of a young boy to the extent that Aunt Ruth desired. Their behavior could be adjusted, yes, but they couldn't lose their mischievous spirits entirely. And quite frankly, I didn't want them to.

Owen's voice broke into my thoughts. "I don't wish to neglect my responsibility any longer. I will start by teaching them the basic rules of being a gentleman."

I was puzzled for a brief moment, but then remembered that Mrs. Kellaway had charged him with the responsibility of training my brothers—something that I had not been very happy with. But now that Owen had proved himself to be a bit less horrid, I felt guilty that this responsibility had been thrust upon him.

"You really don't have to. I can handle it," I said in a brisk voice.

He flashed his warm, easy smile. "I have no doubts as to whether you can handle it. I am sure that you can. But I want to help."

I maintained the direction of my gaze at my brothers straight ahead. I didn't like receiving favors from people without being able to repay them somehow. It made me feel like some kind of thief. And with accepting help came feelings of inferiority and helplessness. "You must be very busy with your profession. I don't want to intrude on your time."

I caught a glimpse of him out of the corner of my eye. It looked like he was shaking his head. "No, Annette, you are completely missing my incentive. I don't think my spare time could be spent in greater pleasure than if I could spend it with you. Helping your brothers will only give me greater reason to claim your time more often."

My face grew warm and I dared a small glance at him. He was looking at me through friendly, persuasive eyes. I had to admit to myself that I enjoyed his company too. Although he could be very teasing and somewhat flirtatious (as I was beginning to discover), I had seen that he could still be kind, thoughtful, and friendly.

I sighed, aiming for nonchalance in my voice. "Very well. But please, tell me how I can repay you."

He cast me a look of exasperation. "I don't desire payment."

"Please." I waited, considering the thoughtful expression emerging onto his face. After a few moments of silence, Owen turned his head to me with a triumphant grin. His expression surprised me. What had I just committed to?

"Fine," he said. "I will tell you how you can repay me." He grinned mischievously and his voice dropped to a whisper. "With knowledge."

My brow contracted in confusion. "Knowledge about what?"

"You."

My heart sunk. He already knew far too much about me. But I had asked him for his payment request, so I couldn't turn back now. I would just have to lie about whatever knowledge he wanted. "What about me?"

Owen studied my face for a brief moment, his eyes squinting in thought. "For every improvement I help make on Peter and Charles, I get to ask you a question of my choosing. And you must answer honestly."

I started sweating. This was *not* good. Why did I insist that I repay him? Why had I not seen this coming? He had already discovered some things about me in the orchard that I didn't want anyone to know, and now he had this deceitful way of discovering even more. I tried to look the least bit unsettled. "We have a deal, then." I was proud of how steady my voice sounded.

He grinned in his triumphant way. I really needed to stop letting him win at so many things. It wasn't something I enjoyed.

We met my brothers near the rose garden where we all dismounted. Owen tried to show Peter and Charles the rose bushes, but their eyes strayed to the horses more than was discreet, so we decided to take our ride a little longer.

While my brothers were talking and giggling, Owen and I talked and laughed as well. It was strange to me how much I enjoyed seeing his smile, and how easily he could make me laugh. It was different and exciting and completely rejuvenating. *Perhaps he isn't as atrocious as I thought*, I reasoned to myself. I knew for a fact that I hadn't laughed so much in my entire life as I had in the last few hours, and I could hardly believe how much time had passed when we were called in to change for dinner.

Owen held the door open, and as I passed him, he said, "Meet me by the water gardens tomorrow afternoon. And bring the boys."

The evening was spent much the same, in smiles and laughter and, thankfully, a lack of mischief. I spent hours talking with Grandmother and Grandfather, and found that both had traveled all over the world. I enjoyed listening as they told me of all their adventures.

I spoke more with Owen too, and when I retired to my room that night, I could hardly remember what we had even spoken about. I could recall a few stories about his patients and childhood memories, but it all seemed to pass so quickly. I remembered more about how easy it was to continue our conversation, and how it felt like he had been my friend for much longer than a single day.

When I saw the pink rose in a vase on my writing desk, it seemed different. It seemed almost . . . harmless. I walked beside it and dared myself to touch one of its velvet petals. It was soft and gentle, not dangerous and hurtful. I was amazed at how much it had changed in such a short time.

Exhaustion began to set in and I crawled into bed with a smile that felt as unwaveringly wide as Grandmother's eyes. I had no desire to dismiss it, so I let it melt slowly into my face as I relaxed. And just as I was falling asleep, I remembered having another lazy thought about Owen's rose, how lovely it was, and how I might just keep it.

# Chapter 9

The next afternoon, when we met Owen by the water gardens, the sky looked very likely to rain, stirring black and grey clouds. Owen consented to show us the library instead, and I was more than happy with the agreement. Aunt Ruth didn't have a library in her home, and she had scarcely any books, so exploring the library would be most exciting. Owen showed me the dozens of shelves that were home to the largest and most grand collection of books that I had ever seen. A table was set up next to the fireplace and I couldn't help but sit down in one of the cushioned chairs beside it.

I asked Owen to show me some of his favorite books, so he found Peter and Charles a few entertaining books to occupy their time, and took a seat beside me.

I listened as he read some of his favorite passages and poems from his favorite volumes. He had the sort of voice that is impossible to become bored listening to. He spoke with such expression and passion for the things he read about that I could tell that he valued his education immensely. He moved on to show me some of his father's sketches from the many places he had traveled, including Italy, France, and Germany. He also showed me sketches of many different prospects of Kellaway Manor.

One sketch of a gorgeous estate caught my eye. "What's this?" I asked.

"That is Willowbourne." A long pause followed before he said, "My uncle's."

I studied the picture more closely. It was absolutely stunning. "Is it far from here?"

He glanced up from the sketch. "Actually, it's quite close. Only fifteen miles away. I used to visit there often as a boy." Something flashed in his countenance. Something sad and troubling that threatened to melt my heart. It surprised me, for I hadn't imagined Owen could ever look so . . . broken.

"Have you not visited in a long while?"

He shook his head. "Not since I was seventeen."

There was clearly something personal and painful associated with the place and I needed to know what it was. He had delved into my personal affairs yesterday in the orchard, so now it was my turn. "What happened?"

He fixed his gaze on the sketch for several moments. The library was silent except for the crackle of the fireplace and the quiet patter of rain on the window. Owen was silent for so long that I was almost convinced that he hadn't heard me. But then he drew a heavy breath and traced his finger along the outside of the picture of Willowbourne. "It was my favorite place in the world. I spent every summer there, and as a young boy, it seemed that there was never enough time to explore the entire place." He lifted his gaze to me, and I thought I could see a sort of sad longing in his eyes.

"I had a cousin who lived there. Theodore was his name. He was five years older than me, my brother Edmond's age. But Edmond preferred to stay home, rather than come to Willowbourne. He had plenty of friends here, but I had none. Theodore was my best and only friend, and I looked up to him as the example of everything I wanted to be. He was so many things: a role model, a confidant, and the most trustworthy, kind, generous, and humble person I ever knew."

Owen turned his gaze to the fireplace. "That last year I visited was when he died. Only a week after I arrived he fell terribly ill. But the physician that was called treated it as nothing. He might as well have pronounced Theo dead before he even made his lazy attempt to heal him."

I watched with alarm the signs of bitter anger rising in Owen. His jaw was clenched and his hands were curled into fists on the table. "I had to watch my best friend die under the inept care of this indolent man who called himself a physician." His words were clipped and harsh. He took a heavy breath. "Perhaps he could not have helped him. But if he had only tried harder . . . ,"

My mind spun. I knew that being a younger son, Owen would not inherit Kellaway Manor, so I assumed that was why he pursued a medical profession. But his reasoning seemed to run deeper than that. "If this man was so awful, what then drove you to become a physician?" I asked.

He was silent for a moment. "I suppose I felt the need to be what that man wasn't. I needed to be the one that would have saved Theo. The one that wouldn't have given up so easily and treated his responsibility with such flippancy. I would be the doctor that people could count on to truly care about their loved ones. A doctor that they could trust to try his hardest to save them." When he finally looked away from the fire and at me, I saw everything. Everything from the pain in his heart to the determination in his eyes. "If I can do anything of importance with my life, it would be to become the man that Theodore was, and the physician that man wasn't."

There was something about the nobility of his words that made my heart skitter with admiration. And something about the sad twist to his smile that made my heart break in two. He understood the sorrow of real loss. He had lost someone he loved too.

There was no need for me to say anything. It would have somehow ruined whatever understanding was passing between us. So I sat back, content with the silence, and flipped through all the remaining sketches.

Peter's voice from across the room made me jump. "Annette, will you read this story to me?"

I turned in my chair with a soft smile. "Of course."

He grinned and hurried over to sit on my lap.

Charles jumped to his feet and stopped, disappointed, right in front of Peter and me. "Peter!" he exclaimed. "I wanted to sit there."

Owen laughed and patted his leg. "What a blessing it is that I also possess a very comfortable lap."

Charles walked over to him with a shy smile, and Owen hoisted him up onto his knee. Charles giggled and looked at Peter with such a smug grin that I had to laugh. "This lap is much more comfortable."

Peter frowned. "It is not!"

"It is," Charles said cooly.

Owen and I were laughing so hard at this point that I could hardly get the words out. "That's enough, boys."

Peter cast Charles one last scowl before I began reading. But when Peter pointed out that he had a closer view of the book, Charles wouldn't stand for it. So Owen took the book and read for a while. Something melted within me as I watched Charles's head nestled against Owen, and watched his eyelids flutter closed. There was finally someone else in the world that he could trust. And if Charles could trust Owen, maybe I could too.

At dinner, I could tell that Peter's and Charles's table manners were improving, and I was relieved (and shocked) again to see that another day had passed without any mischief from them. Certainly they had something up their sleeves, but at the moment, that didn't matter to me. What mattered was the warm, buzzing feeling inside my chest—happiness. Something that I realized that I hadn't felt for far too long. It was a feeling that I hadn't thought that I had missed much. But I was wrong, and even willing to admit it to myself. I hadn't realized that I had been unhappy, until I felt again what it was like to be truly *happy*. The feeling was foreign and renewing, and I never wanted it to leave me.

During the next days that passed, that happiness carried with me like feathers on a bird's wings. Each day I met Owen by the stables, or by the gardens, or in the library where we talked and laughed for hours. The passage of time continued to shock me, and I hardly noticed my brothers who picked roses and rode horses alongside Owen, or sat in the library with books while we sat and talked and sketched by the fireplace. I had been at Kellaway Manor for a week now, and it felt as if I had known Owen my entire life.

One night in the drawing room after dinner, Owen apologized again for neglecting his responsibility to the boys. I had nearly forgotten about the entire thing, but he insisted on giving them their first official lesson. He gathered my brothers over to the settee where we sat, and told them, "Meet me by the water gardens tomorrow afternoon." He threw me a smile. "I suppose you may bring your sister."

I was suddenly very nervous. The portion where Owen would teach my brothers was harmless, but the thought of my payment— his having free reign over my secrets, I certainly did not like. I didn't even know if I had secrets, but if I did, I was sure that Owen could uncover any truths he wanted. He was good at things like that.

So to ease my worries, I told myself that I would just have to be better at hiding things about myself and telling lies if necessary; I was very good at things like that.

I awoke before the sun the next morning, hoping to have a chance to spend a portion of time in the library before my brothers awoke. I hurriedly dressed and made my way quietly to my favorite chair in the library. The entire house was silent except for the sounds of birds singing outside the windows. I curled my legs under me and picked up the sketchbook I had looked at a few days before. I couldn't help but turn to the page covered in the beautiful sketch of Willowbourne.

Why wouldn't Owen go back? It was a question that had bothered me for several days now. I could tell that he loved the home very much, and I could see that he longed to visit again. But part of me understood. His cousin, a large part of why he enjoyed visiting, would not be there. Perhaps he was afraid to go back and face that void. I tried to imagine myself visiting my old home without seeing my parents inside. It would not be even nearly the same.

I closed the book and walked to the nearest shelf to scour it for something of entertainment to read. Nothing on that shelf caught my interest, so I moved to the shelf beside the window. I picked up a book that looked promising and read a few lines. The writing was tedious and unimaginative, so I placed it back on the shelf. As I was turning away, something caught my attention out the window.

I promptly stepped forward for a closer look. A man dressed in a foppish yellow waistcoat and very tall top hat was speaking to a young woman by the rose garden. She was facing away from me, so I couldn't see her face, but she wore the apron of a serving girl.

I could see signs of struggle as she tried to pull away, but the man held her tight around the arm and it looked like he was speaking very harshly, for his face was only inches from hers and his grip tightened more by the second. I pulled away from the window, heart pounding. She needed help! I was about to hurry outside to the young woman's aid, when she kicked him hard in the leg and jerked her arm away. I watched with alarm as she ran toward the house. Her round brown eyes and shining dark hair flashed into view. It was Lizzie!

My gaze darted frantically to the man but he made no attempt to pursue her. He rubbed his leg where she had kicked him, adjusted his cravat, and sauntered lazily toward the woods.

I raced out the door of the library and intercepted Lizzie on her way to the kitchen. "Lizzie!" I said in a loud whisper. "Are you all right?"

She looked at me as I approached, her eyes brimming with tears and her breathing ragged. She slid her hands down the waist of her dress and huffed with a too-innocent look. "Why would I not be all right, miss?"

"I saw you outside with that man. Did he hurt you?"

Her eyes shifted around the room at everything but me. "What man?"

I exhaled sharply. "Lizzie. I *saw* you from the window in the library. Who was he?"

She pressed her lips together and slumped her shoulders in defeat. "I don't know who he was."

"He didn't give you a name?"

"Heavens, no. He caught me by the arm as I was walking through the garden." She looked around the room frantically. "I really shouldn't be talking to you, miss. If he knew another person saw him—"

"What did he want?" I interrupted.

Her gaze darted to me and then away as quickly as it came. "Nothing." She tried to hurry past me but I caught her by the wrist.

"Lizzie—"

She whirled on me fiercely. A single tear glistened on her cheek. "Please. I don't wish to speak about it." Then she pulled her hand away and darted down the hall and out of sight.

I was frozen in shock where I stood for a few moments. Strange men didn't just wander onto someone else's property at sunrise and harass their servants for no reason. Lizzie seemed very affected by whatever had happened, and I needed to find out what that man wanted. She could be in danger!

I headed back to the library and glanced out the window again. The man was gone along with any traces of his visit. He had apparently come on foot and brought nothing with him. I sighed with frustration and sat down with the book I had found before I had looked out the window. I tried to read it, but my mind wandered too readily and I couldn't concentrate. I needed to know who that man was, and I needed to know what he said to Lizzie. Perhaps tonight I could ask her again, once she has time to relax. I was eager to tell Owen too, for I was sure that he could find a way to help. Or at least convince Lizzie to tell him what the man said to her.

With these thoughts to sedate me, I spent the rest of the early morning in my room. Grandmother had given me a short lesson on embroidery two days before, and I felt that I should use this free time to practice. I was never very good at embroidery when I was a young girl, and I very well despised it, but Grandmother expected me to finish the piece I had started before I left. I was most likely the very least accomplished young lady on the planet; Mr. Coburn and Aunt Ruth had certainly made that known on many occasions.

I gasped. The needle had stuck me right in the thumb. I cursed Grandmother silently for insisting that I do this. The mess I had created of the embroidery was enough to prove that it would never be a skill of mine. I threw the hoop onto my bed and, glancing at the clock, realized that it was about time for breakfast.

I left my room and found my brothers in their bedchamber bouncing on their beds. They told me that they couldn't help themselves and that they wouldn't do it again. I seriously doubted it, but they gave me such darling smiles that I couldn't possibly be angry with them.

We made our way to the dining room and I reminded myself that I needed to tell Owen about the man I had seen, but Mrs.

Kellaway told me that he was with a patient and wouldn't return until the afternoon. So when I stood by the water gardens with Peter and Charles that afternoon, I had the firm intention to tell Owen about the strange man as soon as I had the chance.

We waited for several minutes, and I was beginning to grow impatient. I had started fidgeting with the fabric of my gown and tapping my foot. Owen hadn't met us yet, and Mrs. Kellaway had said he would be back by now. I passed the time by looking around at the beautiful fountains and stones and the large, impressive miniature waterfall at the center. I was about to venture to the stables to visit the horses, when I saw Owen step out the back door of the house.

A minute later, he walked up beside us. "Good afternoon," he said in a friendly voice. I noticed that he had a freshly shaved jaw. Why was I noticing his jaw? He turned to me with his wide, familiar grin. "I have decided upon the first lesson."

I raised my eyebrows in curiosity. "What is it?"

He answered by speaking to my brothers. He turned to face them, bending over to be closer to their height. "I am going to teach you boys the first and most important lesson that you can learn. If you wish to be a gentleman, it is absolutely essential. I am going to teach you the proper way to treat a lady."

I scoffed unintentionally.

Owen turned to me with a look of surprise. "What? Have I not redeemed myself?"

I shrugged, willing myself to have a teasing glint in my eye. "Partially, I suppose."

He stepped closer to me, and I couldn't help but notice the stark contrast between his eyes and their brows and lashes illuminated by the sun as they were. While his blue eyes looked even more deep and vast than usual, his lashes and brows remained every bit as dark. They seemed to be the perfect frame for the picture of the sea that his eyes made me imagine. He tipped his head down to look more directly at me. His voice sounded low and determined when he said, "Then allow me to finish the job."

I tried to look unaffected by his closeness and the tone of his voice. He stepped away from me and I caught my breath. Then he told my brothers to take a seat. They sat down on the grass and

Owen stood in front of them. "What do you suppose a gentleman ought to do if a lady needs his help with something?" His voice sounded so professional that I had to bite back laughter. This was so ridiculous!

"He should help her?" Peter guessed.

Owen nodded. "Good."

"What if she doesn't want him to help her?" I cut in.

Owen looked at me with a half smile. "Then she will be sure to let him know."

A small grin crept onto my lips.

"A true gentleman will drop whatever he is doing to assist her," he continued. "No matter how important the task may seem." He walked over to me. "Annette, will you climb up there for a moment?" He pointed to the top of a large stack of stones that spanned the miniature waterfall. The top stone must have been fifteen feet high and was covered in slick moss.

I looked at him in disbelief. "What?"

"I arranged a staircase out of the flat stones beside it. You can use that to climb up." He smiled crookedly. "Unless you don't think you are able." His voice carried that challenging note that made my pride flare.

I narrowed my eyes. "Are you truly telling me to climb something *again*?"

"Indeed," he said. "But this time there is a factor that will drastically alter the outcome."

"Oh? What is that?"

A grin touched his lips. "This time I'm strong enough to catch you."

He probably expected a blush, and I may have blushed, but I took an appraising glance at his arms and said, "I doubt that." But truly, I didn't doubt it at all.

I didn't wait for his response, but I could hear his low, amused laugh as I hurried over to the stack of stones and spied the flat stones beside it. Calling them a "staircase" was a bit of a stretch, but by the looks of them I thought I could get to the top unscathed. Taking a deep breath, I began climbing.

I gripped the highest stone within my reach and looked down at the stone near my feet. It was the largest of the group, serving as a platform for all the rest. Once I had my feet in place, I moved my hands up and stepped higher at the same time, testing my weight on one of the balancing, less stable stones. I didn't sense an immediate change in stability, so I continued upward the same way. It was a slow, tentative process, but I was approaching the top without mishap. A little smile curled my lips as I stepped up onto another stone, smaller than the last.

Pausing to look down, I saw that Owen was standing right below me, watching me closely. I shot him a smirk. "Owen, I'm not going to fall, you know." I turned around and started climbing faster.

His voice carried up to me through the soft rushing of the water. "I never imagined it."

As I grew higher above the ground, nervousness began fluttering in my stomach. A sharp thought struck me as I was approaching the top: why was I doing this? And a more disturbing thought: why did *Owen* want me to do this? I cursed myself for my lack of wisdom. I hadn't even stopped to consider his reasoning until now! But it was too late. I needed to prove that I could scale to the top myself.

The "staircase" ended several feet below the top, so from where I stood, balancing on the smallest stone, I placed my hands on the highest, broadest stone and hoisted myself up. Moss coated the outer edges, and it was slimy and disgusting under my fingers. I pushed myself into sitting position and crossed my legs casually.

I looked down at Owen triumphantly, expecting to see a look of defeat on his face for doubting me. Instead, he looked up with a congratulatory smile—and something else. Something else was twinkling in his eyes . . .

My mouth fell open and I gasped. It was the same mischievous twinkle that I had seen in Peter's eyes so many times. But I had noticed it too late. Owen had already begun disassembling his stone staircase.

I leaned forward in outrage. "What are you doing?"

Peter and Charles were giggling as if they had known about Owen's evil plan. I shot them a berating scowl.

Owen glanced up innocently. "I like to teach by example. So I am going to demonstrate how a gentleman should rescue and assist a lady in distress."

I shook my head. "No. No. No. You most certainly are not. I am getting down by myself." I realized how childish I sounded, but I didn't care. If Owen thought he could trick me into going along with his little "demonstration," then he was horribly mistaken. I cursed myself for not expecting this. I knew Owen well enough now that I should have foreseen a trick.

He tipped his head to the side and raised his eyebrows. "Annette—"

I lifted a hand to stop his words. "That's enough from you, thank you." I glanced over the edge of the stone. The rocks sloped straight downward with hardly any visible places for stable footing. If I could slide down, I would at least be able to get down quickly. Or, if I climbed down, I could stay against the stones firmly enough to keep myself from falling.

I had already hesitated for too long. I was losing my nerve. So before I could consider any other options, I turned around onto my stomach and slid down to where I hung just above my chin. I searched frantically for a niche in the rocks in which to place my foot. I found one, thankfully, and moved my hands further down the stone.

My foot slipped.

I let out a small screech and slammed my hands against the rocks, grasping for any handhold I could possibly find. My fingers caught in a small crevice between two stones. I struggled to steady my breath. Why had I been so daft? I hadn't proved anything but my stubbornness by trying to climb down. And now, I was hanging helplessly, letting Owen win again.

"Just let go!" he said from beneath me. "I'll catch you, I promise."

I peeked at him from under my arm. His arms were outstretched in front of him and his eyes were begging me to trust him.

My hands were already aching with the effort of maintaining my grip, so I didn't have much of a choice in the matter. So I squeezed my eyes shut and let go. The brief moment that I was falling reminded me in a moment of panic of the time that I fell from the tree. I had shut my eyes then too.

But the pain didn't come this time. I didn't open my eyes hours later to see a doctor busily checking for injuries. Instead, I opened my eyes to see a doctor, a much more familiar one, holding me in his arms, smiling warmly into my eyes.

"I told you that you could trust me." His voice was quiet and reassuring, and it made me forget why I was so upset with him. The warm summer air around me seemed dull and lifeless compared to the warm way Owen was looking at me—the way his smile made me smile instantly, as if I were his reflection in a mirror.

I realized to my embarrassment that I had been grasping his lapels—quite tightly. I released my grip and, intending to smooth out the wrinkles I had put in his jacket, ran my hand firmly over the lapels. It was a mistake. My hand froze over his chest and my heart picked up speed. My eyes flew up to Owen's face. Another mistake. The smile in his eyes had been pushed into the background by something else, something that I didn't know what to call. It was suddenly more intense than warm and much heavier. No one had ever looked at me like that before, and I felt deeply unsettled by it.

I frantically hurried my gaze away from his eyes, hoping to find something less unnerving to look at. But my gaze froze on his charming smile, the way his lips curled up more on one side, making that dimple dent his cheek. This was worse. This was much worse for I noticed with a leap of my heart just how close his smile was . . . how easily I could kiss it.

I quickly tore my gaze away and looked down, so flustered with myself that I didn't know what to do. What was wrong with me? This man had just tricked me into being trapped on top of a fifteen-foot-high stack of stones and now I thought about kissing him? Something was seriously wrong with me. Something was seriously wrong with this entire situation.

I looked up at Owen with a glare, hoping that by doing so I could dispel whatever was lurking in his eyes. It did, thankfully, and in fact, it seemed to take him completely by surprise. He set me down quickly and backed a few steps away. I felt relieved and strangely disappointed at the same time. His mischievous smile reappeared as if it had never left.

I hardened my scowl and planted my hands on my hips. "You tricked me!"

He backed away and looked at my brothers with a terrified expression that made them laugh. "I assure you, on most occasions a lady will show gratitude."

I let out a frustrated sigh. "I would not have even been trapped up there if you hadn't tricked me into doing it!"

"Oh, I don't believe I tricked you. I merely gave you a challenge that you were unable to resist."

He was right, and both of us knew it. But I really didn't like it when he was right. Anger bubbled inside of me and broke free from its confinement. The result was most pathetic. I stomped toward him with the darkest glare I could manage and instinctively raised my fist.

He lifted his eyebrows and the corners of his lips twitched. "Are you going to *hit* me?"

I looked back and forth between my fist and Owen's twitching lips. A small laugh escaped from me, and Owen's shoulders began to shake. We both burst into laughter and I dropped my pathetic fist. Peter and Charles burst into giggles too, and the four of us laughed and laughed until I was sure that whatever Owen had done that made me upset wasn't at all important.

When my laughter was finally diminishing, I looked up at Owen weakly. "Why are you so good at that?"

He looked confused for a moment. "At what?"

"Making me laugh when I'm upset with you."

He chuckled and shook his head. "No, I think you laugh at yourself first."

"I do not!"

"I think you do." He tipped his head down to look at me more directly. "And something I have come to know about you, Miss Annette, is that you cannot stay angry with anyone. A strength of character that I wish I had."

"More of a weakness as I see it," I muttered.

He shook his head again. "No, because if you were able to stay angry with me, we wouldn't still be friends, now would we?" He raised his eyebrows in question.

I looked up at him from under my lashes, a small smile curving my lips. "We most certainly would not."

He sighed and put both his hands on my shoulders. I tipped my head back to look into his friendly eyes. No matter how much he liked to tease me, I didn't want to stay angry with him. I enjoyed his company too much. And I needed a friend.

"I'm sorry for tricking you. It won't happen again," he said.

I arched an eyebrow and smiled. "So you are finally admitting that you tricked me?"

"If it will make you accept my apology, then yes, I am."

I pressed my lips together to hide my smile and forced a thoughtful expression onto my face. I couldn't let him think that I was so willing to accept. "You give yourself far too many reasons to apologize."

He gave a solemn half smile. "Another one of my faults. But a fairly new one. I don't think my manners have ever been in such disarray as they are when I'm with you. But still, I have no plausible excuse for my behavior." He looked at me intently, seeking forgiveness in my eyes.

I hesitated for several seconds. "Fine. I forgive you." It would have been impossible not to.

His half smile grew into a full smile. "Thank you." Then he turned and walked over to my brothers who were busy splashing their fingers in a fountain. He caught their attention by sitting down on the edge of the fountain beside them.

"Now. Part two of your lesson: what do you suppose a lady likes more than anything in the world?"

Charles looked up, the sunlight reflecting off his golden curls. "Her brothers?" he guessed, earning a chuckle from Owen.

"In the circumstance of your sister, then I believe you are right." He winked and folded his arms. "But your sister isn't like most ladies in that regard."

Unable to prevent myself from inquiring what exactly he meant, I walked over to the fountain and took a seat beside Peter. I leaned forward and cast Owen a puzzled look. "What do you mean?"

"You know what is truly important," he said. "You don't obsess over beauty, fashion, money, or titles. You care about your family, the well-being of others. In the few days that I have known you, I haven't once seen you worry about yourself. I haven't once seen you try too hard to be elegant and refined. You know who you are, and you won't let anyone distort that. I have never met a young lady like you, Annette." He drew a breath. "And I can't imagine that I ever will."

He was looking at me with such a strange expression that I had to look down. It bothered me how easily he could make me blush. I had found pride in my ability to brush off any kind words from any gentleman without any response but a curt "thank you." But Owen wasn't just any gentleman. I couldn't deny it.

I shrugged and dared myself to look at him. "I have never had a desire to be like other young ladies. In fact, I find most of them very annoying."

He threw his head back and laughed his infectious laugh. "And there we have another way you differ from them. You speak your mind."

I scowled half-heartedly. "Not always."

"Oh? Then is there something you wish to say to me?" The insinuating tone in his voice made another blush creep up my cheeks.

"Hmm. It appears that there is. Charles, Peter, cover your ears for a moment." He leaned forward and winked at me.

I gasped in outrage and he laughed, seemingly very pleased with my reaction to his teasing or flirting or whatever it was. "You're awful," I said with a scowl.

His eyes widened and a grin lifted his lips. "Oh, I see you have graduated from *atrocious*."

A small laugh escaped me and I sat back in surrender. He was immune to my insults by now.

Owen turned his attention to my brothers again, resuming his tutorial tone of voice. "Anyhow, the answer I was looking for, when I asked you what a lady likes more than anything in the world, is . . . compliments."

Peter's brow furrowed. "What is a compliment?"

"To compliment someone is to flatter them with kind words. To tell them of something that you like about them, whether it be of their appearance or conduct. But don't be mistaken into thinking that you should pay a compliment to every pretty girl that passes by. Give compliments only to those who truly deserve them."

He stood up and walked in front of me where I sat on the edge of the fountain. His body acted as a shield from the sunlight, trapping me in his shadow. I looked up at him. Nervousness fluttered in my stomach for a reason I couldn't name.

"Now, I know your sister doesn't particularly like compliments," he paused to shoot me a relentless smile, "but she is certainly one who deserves them." He waved my brothers over. "So, come here and practice your compliments. You may say something about her beauty, her kindness, or whatever it is you like about her."

I watched with amusement as Charles trudged to his feet and stifled a giggle. There was no possible way that he would take this seriously. He stopped beside Owen in front of me and flashed me a gap-toothed smile. "Your eyes are green." He giggled and looked at Owen for approval.

Owen laughed and knelt beside Charles on the grass. He was facing me, his line of sight directly even with mine. He looked back at Charles briefly. "Almost. But you must tell her more about her eyes." He took a slow breath and moved his gaze to me. "Tell her how beautiful they are, and how they make the rest of the world disappear. How any man would have to be blind not to lose himself within them."

I scolded my heart for how wildly it was jumping around in my chest. *This is only another demonstration. Surely he is not serious*, I told my heart.

Charles giggled again. "I don't want to say that!"

Owen didn't move his gaze from my face. "Don't worry. That one was from me."

As much as I willed myself not to blush, I couldn't control it. How did one respond to that? *Thank you*? I certainly couldn't let him assume that I welcomed his flirting—for I was now quite sure that was what he was doing. I clasped my hands together tightly in my lap and pretended to be deeply interested in them.

Owen finally looked away from me and I could stop holding my breath. He patted Charles on his back. "Give it another try."

I forced a smile to my face to hopefully diminish my blush. Charles looked up and chewed on his lip, apparently struggling to find another kind thing to say. After a few moments, his face lit up and he said quickly, "You are the kindest sister I ever met."

My smile grew and I pinched his chubby cheek as I had done so many times. "Thank you, Charles."

Owen nodded approvingly. "Well done." Then he waved a hand for Peter to stand.

Once in front of me, Peter grinned and, with much less of a struggle than Charles, said, "You are very funny, and you have a pretty smile."

Owen slapped him on the back. "Two compliments at once, well done. You are a natural." He paused. "Although . . . you might add more detail to your description of her smile."

My stomach lurched. Now the teasing would begin in earnest.

He moved even closer to me, kneeling on the grass as he was, until he was so close that I could smell the fresh scent of his jacket and all the masculine smells I remembered of my father—the woods, fresh air, and that familiar smell that I called sunshine.

"But first, you must take her hand," he said. His eyes were locked on mine as he spoke. He reached out and uncurled my right hand from my left, and held it between both of his.

My heart very nearly escaped my chest.

"The simple touch of a hand will help convey the earnestness of your words." His gaze flickered back to Peter quickly before settling on my face again. "But the true task lies with your words. For your words must convey the earnestness of your heart."

I felt my cheeks grow warm. My hand was starting to sweat in his.

He slowly drew a breath and released it. "As for Annette's smile, you might add that it is one of the rarest and most beautiful kind. It is the kind that can lift any spirit and erase any doubt. One glance at a smile like that and any reason had for sorrow is forgotten. It can charm, it can tease, it can tempt. It can compete for a man's heart unknowingly. And it will always win."

My blush was too hot for him not to have noticed it by now. If he was going to continue speaking, he would have to do it without looking at my face. I quickly dropped my gaze to my lap and held perfectly still. Why wouldn't he stop? Couldn't he see that his words were very unnerving to me? And good heavens, what were Peter and Charles thinking of all this? Surely they didn't understand as I did that Owen was not serious. Silence stretched for longer than I expected. I definitely could not think of a time that I had felt more awkward than I did in this moment. Or rather, these *moments*.

When he spoke again, his voice sent a ripple through the air so tangible I thought I could reach out and touch it. "A humble lady," he began, "may still doubt the truth of your words. She may require further assurance of your earnestness. In such a case . . . ,"

I glanced up just as he shifted my hand in his. Then he lifted it slowly and pressed his lips against the back of it. My breath refused to come. Chills spread through my entire arm.

His lips lingered there for a second longer and then he raised his head, looking into my eyes again. "In such a case she may need a kiss to finally convince her."

I wanted to glare at Owen, but my defenses were uncharacteristically weak. All I could do was sit in the proceeding quiet, willing my heartbeat to slow and my cheeks to cool. Owen's eyes were serious, but slowly a ghost of a smile built on his lips, working to belie his eyes. Surely he was not serious. Certainly.

To my relief, Peter released a giggle that sounded deafening as it pierced the taut silence. "I will never do that!" he exclaimed between giggles.

I exhaled sharply in what sounded like a failed attempt at a laugh. My hands were shaking and my heart refused to calm itself. I couldn't let Owen have such an effect on me! He wanted a reaction, so I needed to give him the opposite.

Slipping my hand from his, I glanced at Peter, who was giggling wildly. At least somebody thought Owen's remarks were amusing. I smiled and took a steadying breath before saying, "So Peter, all you ought to do is tell Aunt Ruth what a lovely smile she has, and she will be so flattered that she won't even imagine punishing you."

He jerked back in disgust. "But her smile is not lovely!"

"Charles? Perhaps you should tell her, then."

He widened his eyes and shook his head. "Never."

I laughed and was surprised that I didn't hear a laugh from Owen. With a lighter mood in the air, I sneaked a glance at him. He was still looking at me in his penetrating way, but it was only for a second longer.

He drew a deep breath and flashed his familiar smile and when he laughed it seemed like a delayed reaction. "Annette is right. Flatter your aunt, and she will love you so much that she will give you a big, wet kiss on your head every night." The teasing gleam in his eye was back.

A loud laugh bubbled from me as I watched Peter and Charles's reaction. They reared back in disgust and shook their heads, absolutely revolted.

Owen stood and put a hand on each of their shoulders. "Very well," he sighed. "Just a small kiss."

Charles stepped away from Owen, giggling and shaking his head vigorously. Peter threw Owen's hand off his shoulder and said, "No, no, no. Disgusting."

Owen laughed. "Don't worry, I'm teasing. Although, I do not know your aunt, so I suppose it could happen."

I shook my head along with my brothers. "No. Our aunt wouldn't willingly go near any of us with affection. No matter what kind things are said to her."

I meant it as a lighthearted comment, but I saw a flash of sadness in Owen's eyes as he looked at my brothers, then at me. But he didn't say anything about it. Instead, he cleared his throat and said, "Do you boys have any questions?"

They shook their heads.

"Good. Now I want you to listen carefully. If there is one thing that I want you to remember from this lesson, it is this: Never mistreat a lady. Ever."

My brothers stared at him in awe, surely committing every single word to memory.

"Not with insults, not with physical harm. Do you understand?" Owen's voice was soft, but had a firmness that could not be argued.

Peter and Charles each gave a dignified nod that seemed to satisfy him.

"Now for your assignment. I want each of you to give a compliment to Grandmother, and my mother, Mrs. Kellaway, today."

Peter and Charles nodded in agreement. I was somewhat surprised to see how excited they seemed to be, as if it were an exciting secret mission that they were allowed to be a part of, instead of what they would have usually seen as a boring assignment.

"Can we do it now?" Charles asked.

Owen waved a hand toward the house. "Go on."

Their smiles grew and they raced off across the lawn. I turned toward Owen, who was now sitting beside me on the fountain. He was grinning as he watched them run, and my heart warmed a little to see it.

"Thank you for doing that," I said. "They obviously enjoyed every moment."

He returned my smile. "I enjoyed myself too." His gaze went back to Peter and Charles who were already halfway to the house. He was watching them with a look that cried out affection in every feature of his face. "They are good boys," he said. "Amazing boys. You are raising them better than anyone else could have, and I hope you know that."

Something inside me lifted at his words. Something heavy and painful that had been aching for so long. "Do you really think so?"

"Without a doubt. Don't listen to anyone that tells you otherwise."

I thought of the pie man, Mr. Coburn, and Aunt Ruth. Had I listened to them? A small lump made its way up to my throat and I had to swallow hard to get rid of the feeling. "Thank you." My voice cracked.

He gave me a look so gentle that it felt as if he had wiped away the tears I felt within me, all with that one look. I wondered if I actually cried, if he would wipe away the real tears too. I hoped he would.

I promptly stopped myself. That could and would never happen. I had promised myself long ago that I wouldn't cry again. And I intended to keep that promise. So I stuffed the emotions down into my heart, as deeply as I could. But it felt as though everything that I had buried deep within my heart was coming too close to the surface—dangerously close. And I wondered suddenly with a strike of fear if anything else would even be able to fit.

"Would you like to take a walk?" Owen's voice broke into my thoughts.

I gave him a grateful smile and nodded. A walk would be a nice distraction. So I stood and took his arm without hesitation.

We stepped out of the water gardens and started toward the west side of the grounds. It was a hot day, but the soft breeze was enough to keep cool. By now, my bonnet had driven me completely mad, so I slipped it off and held it instead, enjoying the warm feeling of the sun on my face. The last signs of my sunburn had finally faded, and I was grateful to be able to comfortably enjoy the sun again.

"Are you ready for my first question?" Owen asked with a crooked smile.

Oh, no. I had nearly forgotten about my "payment." Actually, *I* remembered quite clearly, but was hoping that he had forgotten. I should have known he wouldn't forget something like that. My stomach fluttered, but I tried to sound calm.

"I suppose," I said. I was proud of how normal my voice sounded.

He looked heavenward and mused, "Hmm . . . what shall I ask you?"

I stopped walking and turned to him with a look of surprise. "You haven't already planned a question?"

"Oh, I have. I was only attempting to build suspense." He flashed his teasing smile.

I shot him a scowl, making him chuckle. My stomach was fluttering even more now that I knew he had planned the question. That meant it must have been a personal one that I wouldn't want to answer. I swallowed my worries. *It will be fine. I don't have to tell him anything I don't want to.*

We started walking again, my heart beating faster with every step. Finally Owen said, "Very well, I will ask my question. Don't worry, it is an easy one. I want to know, Annette, why do you despise the color pink?"

My stomach dropped. This was certainly not an easy question. I turned to him with the most convincing look I could muster. "It simply isn't pleasing to my eye."

He lifted an eyebrow in deep skepticism.

I cringed. I should not have entertained the idea that he would accept an evasive answer like that.

"I can see it's much more than that," he said. "You seemed repulsed by it. You looked almost . . . afraid of that rose I gave you."

Oh, yes. The rose. I drew a deep breath and looked at the rose garden up ahead. Could he read my mind? Is that how he always knew the most personal questions to ask me? I cleared my throat. "It is my least favorite color, and it always has been. Nothing more."

I looked up at him, hoping to convince him with the false sincerity in my eyes. It didn't work.

He tipped his head and gazed into my eyes for a long moment. "You're lying."

"What?" I asked, momentarily taken aback. "No, I'm not."

He smiled knowingly. "You are. And you are terrible at it, by the way."

"I am not!"

"Most people are. It's simple to see once you discover how to sort out their lies."

"And how do you sort out their lies?" My voice came out heavy with doubt.

"Everyone does something that gives them away." He said it as if he wanted to end the subject right there. Perhaps that would have been best, but my curiosity tugged at me, forcing me to inquire further.

"Well, what do I do?" I tried to keep my voice casual.

He turned to me with an amused expression. "Are you admitting that you've lied to me?"

"If you're the expert you claim to be, then you should know if I have."

He let out a sound that was a mixture of a sigh and a laugh. "If I tell you, then I won't be able to discern when you're lying anymore."

I sighed. I needed to know. It would bother me all night. This called for extreme measures. "Fine. Tell me, and on my word of honor, I won't lie to you ever again."

He eyed me carefully, and paused for several seconds before saying, "Very well. We have a deal." Then he turned his head, trying to hide his growing smile. "It's your nose."

I gaped in surprise. "What about my nose?"

"Your nostrils flare as soon as you finish speaking."

"They do not!"

He threw his head back with a laugh. "You wanted me to tell you, so I told you. I find it very adorable, actually." He winked at me in a way that I could only interpret as flirtatious.

I shot him a look of consternation and looked away from his charming smile. "Well, in that case, I will try never to do it again."

He laughed again then looked at me seriously. "*Now*, you must answer my question honestly. What do you have against the color?"

I swallowed and wiped my sweaty palms on the skirt of my gown. These sort of things hurt to speak about. I think that was what was making me so nervous. I didn't like to feel the pains of past losses that I had so carefully tucked away. I took a deep breath to begin.

"When I was a little girl, I adored pink. I made sure to wear it every day. Whether as my dress, gloves, boots, the trim on my bonnet, or a bow in my hair." I glanced up at Owen to see his reaction. He looked mildly surprised, but deeply interested.

"I wanted to surprise my mother when she returned from her visit here, so I wore her favorite pink dress of mine. And when she didn't return to see it . . . " I looked down, suddenly feeling very self conscious. "I don't know, I suppose the color just wasn't so pretty anymore. Nothing was pretty anymore. The color transformed in my eyes to something that meant hurt, and disappointment, and that my mother wasn't coming back. And I hated it for that."

I felt a lump in my throat again and I found myself wishing that Owen would just laugh at me. Then I could be angry instead of sad. I was waiting for him to say something, but he seemed to be waiting for me to look at him. I laughed softly at myself. "I know. It's ridiculous."

I peeked up at his face. But I didn't see amusement or even a smile in his eyes. I saw solemn understanding and the same warmth I had seen so many times now. Except it didn't surprise me anymore. "No, I don't think it's ridiculous at all," he said.

I took a breath as relief flooded through me. He understood. And he didn't look at me with pity either. He never did. I gave him a small grateful smile that he returned.

"I'm sorry for insisting that you take that pink rose. I wouldn't have, had I known how much it hurt you."

I brushed off his words. "The rose is just fine. I . . . I like it now." I smiled up at him reassuringly, and gasped.

He was staring at my nose.

"Owen!" I quickly used my hand to cover it. "I am not lying!"

He tipped his head back in a roar of laughter. "I'm sorry, but I had to be sure."

# Chapter 10

Grandmother was rambling on about Peter's and Charles's compliments with undying ecstasy at dinner.

"He told me I had beautiful hair! Oh, my, I haven't been told my hair was beautiful since it turned grey over twenty years ago! And little Charles kissed my hand! Can you believe it?" She paused to release a hoot of laughter. "I am flattered, to be sure!"

Owen winked at the boys and whispered, "Well done."

After the men joined us in the drawing room, I listened as Grandfather told us of the events of his day, and to my surprise, he stood and performed a song while Mrs. Kellaway played the pianoforte. His voice came out gruffer in song, and was not, I must admit, the most pleasant sound. Owen and I locked eyes in the middle of his performance and the laughter I had been harnessing suddenly threatened to break loose. I had to bite my lip to keep it at bay. Owen's mouth was clamped shut, but his eyes pooled with tears and his shoulders shook.

After the agony of Grandfather's performance, Mrs. Kellaway cleared her throat and asked for everybody's attention. Once all eyes were on her, she began, "I have decided, soon after Alice, Edmond, and my husband arrive, we are going to host a ball! Won't that be splendid? It has been far too long since we have, and I believe it is long overdue. And, of course, we have Miss Annette staying with us, and what better way to celebrate than to introduce her to all the unmarried gentlemen in town? She can dance with each one, all night!"

My stomach lurched with a sudden surge of panic. I had never had a season, and had certainly never been to a ball. Before moving to Oak Cottage, my parents had employed a dance instructor, but I doubted I would remember many of the steps. Most of my practicing came from my father. Country dances in the sitting room had been prevalent in our house. I smiled a little at the memory.

"Yes, yes, yes! Perfect idea, Catherine!" Grandmother yelped giddily. "What was the name of the gentleman we met at the Thornton's ball last year? Oh, yes, Mr. Baines! He is a handsome gentleman if I ever saw one, and so agreeable! We must introduce him to Miss Downing! He will be proposing marriage before he even finishes one dance." She was so giddy by now, that she was rubbing her hands together with excitement. Then her eyes widened to an impossible size. "Unless, of course, all the other gentlemen duel Mr. Baines before he has the chance! My, my, wouldn't that be a sight to behold?"

My face burned. I forced a small laugh. "I certainly cannot imagine that happening."

Grandmother gave me a sneaky look and glanced over my shoulder. "Why ever not? It seems we already have one gentleman prepared for that very duel." She threw her head back and released a hooting laugh. With a curious look I followed her gaze over my shoulder. I was so taken back by what I saw that all I could do was stare. Owen's eyes were narrowed and his mouth was set hard and firm. A muscle leapt in his clenched jaw.

"Will it be swords or pistols, Owen? You could, of course, resort to fisticuffs if the situation becomes dire." Grandmother could barely be understood through her laughter.

I quickly whirled back around, flustered and embarrassed beyond words. What did she mean? Owen wouldn't care if her ridiculous scenario happened (which it wouldn't, I was sure of it). My cheeks burned hotter as I wondered if it was possible that Owen might care. He had been spending a significant amount of time with me, and something told me it wasn't just for my brothers. And then there was the flirting . . .

I shushed my thoughts, too afraid to acknowledge what they meant. Grandmother was still hooting, but the rest of the room was filled with an awkwardness that was so centered around me that I needed to leave. Now. As much as I tried to prevent it, my voice came out shaky when I said, "Charles, Peter, I think it is time I take you to bed."

I stood from my chair and thankfully, as if he were playing along, Charles yawned as I took his hand. "Please excuse us." I couldn't pull them to the door fast enough.

Against my will, my curiosity forced me to peek at Owen again just as I was leaving the room. He was watching me with a look so foreign to me that I didn't know what to think of it. But it was also familiar somehow. My gaze froze on that look until I placed it: It was the same way he had looked at me in the water gardens today after he caught me—when I had thought about kissing him. I hurried through the door, shaking my head in an effort to clear it. I must be imagining things now.

I tucked my brothers into their beds and walked swiftly down the hall to my own bedchamber where I plopped down on my bed, exhausted, confused, and completely terrified. I had never been to a ball! I hardly knew how to dance! How could I go to a ball without knowing how to dance? The very thought was ridiculous, and the image even more so. I didn't know what Owen's unnerving look meant, but I didn't want to think about that at the moment.

*It is all in your imagination*, I told myself. But I felt something poking within me, sharp and insistent, trying to convince me that it wasn't my imagination at all. But that "something" had to be wrong. Didn't it?

I couldn't think clearly any longer. The dull pain in my head had now buzzed into a full, throbbing headache, and I was afraid my skull would burst from an overdose of thought. So I settled into my nightdress, blew out the candles, and drifted into a restless sleep, unable to answer even my own questions.

On my way to breakfast, I passed Lizzie in the hall, and seeing her reminded me that I had forgotten to tell Owen about the strange man yesterday. How had I forgotten such an important thing? I noted that I would certainly tell him today. But I worried that everything would be awkward between us after what Grandmother had said the previous night. I felt terrible about how I had left in such a hurry, but the embarrassment of the situation still burned my cheeks at the thought.

I flashed Lizzie a smile as I passed her. "Good morning."

She smiled back, but I could tell it was forced. Whatever that strange man had said to her was still troubling her immensely. When I had first met Lizzie, it had seemed impossible that she could ever appear so upset.

I sat down beside Peter and Charles in the dining room and searched for Owen at the table. As usual, he wasn't there.

Mrs. Kellaway greeted me with a warm smile. "I trust you slept well?"

"I did, thank you."

She leaned forward across the table. "Now, I would like to speak with you a bit more about the ball. My daughter, my son, and my husband will be returning three days from today, and I would like to hold the ball four days after their arrival, so they have sufficient time to settle in. I sent the invitations a fortnight ago, so everything seems to be in order."

I looked down at my plate and my stomach pooled with dread. The ball was a week away. "I don't have a suitable gown, so perhaps I could just stay in my room with my brothers."

She threw out her hand. "Not a problem. We will take you to Madame Fareweather to have a gown made for you. I have seen miracles worked by her hands before. She will have a beautiful gown finished, boxed, and delivered by the day of the ball. I am sure of it."

"I think that is a perfect idea, Catherine," Grandmother piped in from across the table.

I shifted uncomfortably in my chair. Aunt Ruth had finally succumbed to purchasing a small number of inexpensive gowns for me when securing the buttons on my old gowns had become nearly impossible. But there was no sense in hoping that she would find it in her heart to send a portion of her money to Kellaway Manor to purchase a ball gown for me. And I certainly didn't have money to spend on such a fine thing.

I swallowed and looked down at my plate. "I can't afford a gown."

"I will provide the funds, not to worry," Mrs. Kellaway said.

I shook my head. "No, I—"

"Yes. We shall leave in one hour. Did you have anything else planned?"

These women were relentless. I sighed. Besides telling Owen about the strange man, nothing came to mind. "No."

"Wonderful!" she exclaimed almost as giddily as her mother. "One hour it is."

"That sounds perfect," I said, forcing myself to accept their kindness despite the struggle within me. A ride to the nearby village did sound very nice, and I had never worn a ball gown before. The thought caused a ripple of excitement to fly through me.

Grandfather looked up from his plate. I had almost forgotten he was there. "I'll take care of the boys while you are gone," he volunteered.

I smiled at him. "That is very kind of you." Then I cast Peter and Charles each a sideways glance. "Be on your best behavior."

"We will!" Peter vowed. "I've been practicing Grandfather's trick very much, so I can show him how I've improved!"

I laughed as I remembered Grandfather's invisible needle and thread. "I'm sure Grandfather would love to see it."

"I most certainly would," he confirmed with a smile.

After I finished eating, I hurried to my room to make myself somewhat presentable. My hair was being uncooperative as usual, so I combed through it and pulled it back into a bun of sorts. It was the best I could do. Just as I was about to leave my bedchamber, the door swung open and Lizzie walked in, avoiding my eyes as best she could. "May I offer assistance?"

I studied her for a moment. She was fiddling with the fabric of her apron and seemed to be extremely nervous. My hair did look absurd, and if Lizzie was to begin arranging it for me, I could offer a gentle inquiry about the strange man. Hopefully I could discover more about what he was doing here.

"Well, I could certainly use some assistance with this mess." I pointed at my head. "If you would be so kind."

She looked shocked that I had asked, but nodded sharply. "Y-yes, of course, miss." Her usual cheerful smile was missing.

I took a seat in front of the mirror and Lizzie stepped behind me with a hairbrush and pins, setting to work methodically on my hair. I could feel her hands shaking. I watched her carefully in the mirror, trying to decide the best moment to speak. But she worked in consistent silence, brushing and pinning, and never taking even a second to glance up. This was so unlike her.

Deciding any time was as good as another, in a careful voice, I said, "Lizzie, I do not want you to be in danger." The hairbrush froze on my head and her eyes flew up to meet mine in the mirror. "Please tell me what that man wanted from you."

She looked down again, and I could tell my words had upset her even more. "Can we please not speak about this?" Her voice shook.

"No. I need to know what he was doing here. You were accosted by a stranger. That is no small thing. I haven't informed anyone of it yet, but I will unless you tell me what he said to you." I held her gaze in the mirror.

She swallowed and her chin started quivering. She was silent for a long moment, and I started wondering if she had even heard me. Finally she said, "I am sorry, miss. I can't tell you."

"Why not?"

"He made it quite clear." A tear slid down her cheek. She quickly swiped it away.

Dread filled my stomach. "Did he threaten you?"

Little sniffs and whimpers were the only response I received. It was enough to know the answer. I lowered my voice and made it as gentle as I could. "Lizzie, you will be safe. I will tell Owen, and—"

"No! No. Please don't tell Dr. Kellaway. Please."

"I must. If this man really threatened you, he needs to know. Mrs. Kellaway should also be told. They will be able to help you."

She was silent for a long moment, shaking her head and wiping her tears. Finally she said, "He wanted information. But I didn't give it to him. I beg you, please don't tell anyone."

I sighed, torn about what I should do. What information did he want? As much as I scoured my mind for ideas, I came up blank. I decided to pry a little further. "Will you tell me what information he asked for?"

She took a deep, quaking breath, then started on my hair again. Her hands still shook, but her tears and sobs were gone. "No, I can't. But will you give me your word that you won't tell anyone about this?"

"On the condition that you inform me if he returns."

She considered my offer with a faint look of fear in her eyes. "I promise."

I didn't know why I was doing this, but I knew Lizzie would be stricken dead with betrayal if I told a soul. I didn't know why that was so either. But it frightened me to see such raw fear in her eyes. So I said, "Then I promise too."

Her face flashed with relief and she finished my hair, pinning and brushing until it looked as it had my first day here. I almost thought she would cheer up again, and that she would be the same as she had always been. But as I watched her reflection in the mirror, I could see fear ease back into her eyes and affect the way she held her head, the way her words shook, and the way her gaze scattered.

I thanked her for her help and stood from my chair. Then Lizzie gave a stiff nod and hurried toward the door. I walked over to my trunk to find a gown, and was facing away from the door when I heard her, in a voice as quiet as a whisper.

"I wasn't the only one he threatened."

Chills raced up my neck and arms and I whipped around as fast as I could. But Lizzie was already through the door.

I rubbed my arms to hopefully stop the chill I felt. Dread pooled in my stomach and made my chest feel tight and constrained. *Did she mean me?* I dismissed the thought as quickly as I could. I didn't even know that man, what possible reason could he have to threaten me? I tried to shake off the tremor that was coursing through my limbs. What had I done? I had agreed not to share this with anyone, and now there could be multiple people in danger! I pressed a hand to my forehead, feeling my headache returning. I needed time to relax and think, but I was leaving to visit the dressmaker soon, and something told me that that would not be relaxing at all.

# Chapter 11

In the carriage, I sat next to the window with Mrs. Kellaway beside me and Grandmother across from me. It was a short drive to the village, and Grandmother had gone into raptures over how quaint and darling it was. While she spoke, she nearly bounced in her seat. Her eyes, of course, were as wide as saucers. I had certainly never seen a woman of her age so full of life.

"Are you excited, my dear?" she asked.

"Very much," I said with a smile I didn't feel. My thoughts were still caught on Lizzie and what she had revealed to me. I gazed out the window, seeking something to distract me from my worries. A distant estate caught my eye and triggered something in my mind. I had seen it somewhere before. I stared at it until it was nearly out of view. Tall and wide, the stretching lawn and hexagonal pond, the beauty of the gardens and the rolling hills around it—it had to be Willowbourne! Owen had said it was nearby.

To be sure, I tapped Mrs. Kellaway on the arm. "What is the name of that house?"

She squinted out the window. "Oh, that is Willowbourne. Isn't it lovely? My sister and her young daughters are in residence."

I took another glance out the window. Lovely didn't even begin to describe it. The sketch Owen's uncle had done did nothing but injustices to its perfect architecture and colorful gardens. The way it was built on the peak of a hill made it stand like a grand castle and emulate beauty in every sense of the word. I wanted to go inside. How had Owen condemned visiting a place like that? "It's breathtaking," I said. "I'm sure you've been inside?"

"I have, many times." She gazed a little wistfully out the window. "But it has been a long while since the last."

"Owen told me what happened to your nephew. I am very sorry."

She turned her gaze to me, a sad twist to her smile. "Yes, he and Owen were very close. Owen nearly died when Theodore did. He was lost in anger and resentment for so long." She shut her eyes and shook her head, as if trying to forget an already banished memory. "He knew from a young age that he would need to find a profession, having an elder brother. So it was only one year later when he began medical school, determined to be an honorable physician and a great man. I think he has come to be both."

Grandmother perked up with round eyes and pursed lips, giving me her full attention. "And quite handsome too, no doubt." She winked. "Don't you agree?"

I laughed and looked down, feeling my face warm. "I suppose."

A few minutes later, around the time Grandmother had finished her hooting laughter, we arrived at the village. I stepped out of the carriage, amazed at the amount of shops lining the streets, many more than the village near Oak Cottage. Grandmother led the way, pointing out her favorite bakeries, jewelers, and bookshops. On occasion, she peeked her head into the door of a shop and greeted the owner—all of whom instantly recognized her. It did not require much perception to gather that she came here often.

I watched as young children flocked to the windows of sweet shops, nearly drooling as they pressed their faces against the windows. I smiled as I watched them, thinking of Peter and Charles and how much they would love it here.

"Here we are," Grandmother said, stopping in front of a little dress shop at the curve of the road. She threw the door open and marched inside. "Gertrude!"

I eased my way through the door, surprised and amused again at Grandmother's familiarity with this village. A woman appeared from around the corner wearing a smile so large and open-mouthed, that I imagined, had she been closer, I would have seen the back of her throat. "Harriet! Oh, it has been nearly a week since I have seen you! Much too long!" Grandmother met her halfway across the room with a hug. She began saying something else to her, but I couldn't decipher the words.

Then the mantua maker hurried across the room to me, making the floorboards creak beneath her feet. Seeing her more closely, I noticed that she seemed to be a bit younger than Grandmother, but not much. Her eyebrows were extremely arched and thin, and she had a large, dark mole at the corner of her mouth. "I hear you need a gown. My name is Madame Fareweather. Come, come, we will get started."

She grasped me by the arm and led me to the center of the shop. "First, I will need to do a fitting. If you become nervous, just fix your eyes on my beauty mark. Count the hairs if you like. Customers have claimed it works wonders."

Oh, my. As much as I tried, I couldn't hide my shock.

She and Grandmother burst into hooting laughter. I laughed too, relieved that she wasn't serious. "I'm teasing! Although, I cannot imagine who wouldn't adore looking at this lovely little thing." She stroked a finger over her "beauty mark." I laughed awkwardly, wondering if she had actually been serious after all.

Still chuckling, she set to work on my fitting, measuring and pinning and taking notes as she went. As much as I tried to prevent it, my gaze was drawn to the mole much more than I would have liked. And, feeling the boredom she anticipated, rather than counting the hairs, I decided to come up with a name that was a little more fitting than "beauty mark." After much thought, I decided that "beast mark" would be sufficient.

"There. I'm finished." She beamed at me. This time, I actually could see the back of her throat. "Now, how many gowns would you like made?" she asked, turning to Mrs. Kellaway.

"Just one today. Something suitable for a ball."

"Very well." She raised a very thin eyebrow and eyed me from head to toe, circling around me. Then she stopped at my face and I watched her brown eyes carefully studying every one of my features. "Not the longest neck, tolerable nose, nicely colored lips, rosy complexion, very handsome eyes . . . ,"

She rubbed her beast mark and looked up, clearly deep in thought. I had no idea what she was doing, but it certainly made me uncomfortable. "I have it!" she screeched, making me jump. "Pink! Oh, yes, pink is the color for her."

Dread dropped through me. "I don't wear pink."

The dressmaker gave me a look that said, *you will wear what I say you'll wear.* But instead, she asked, "Why ever not, my dear?"

My heart sunk. I had no plausible answer. She tapped her foot impatiently. "Um . . . well, I—"

"You will look stunning in it."

"Wait—"

She turned around to face Grandmother and said, "Harriet, I will have the gown delivered six days from now, as you requested. Thank you very much for coming!" Then she pressed a hand to my back and led me to the door, prattling on about how lovely I would look in the pink gown.

Once out of the shop and away from that frightening woman, I was able to fully comprehend what had just happened: I had no choice but to wear a pink gown to the ball! I took a deep breath to steady my nerves. Yes, the rose didn't seem so awful anymore, sitting on my writing desk nicely as it was, but wearing pink was much different than seeing it, and I did not know if I could bring myself to do it. My list of worries and questions was reaching a length that inspired madness.

Despite my feelings about the gown, I thanked Mrs. Kellaway and Grandmother for being so kind as to purchase it for me. And on the carriage ride home, I missed the excitement I had felt about wearing a ball gown. It had now deserted me entirely, making me empty and dull inside. My newfound worries and questions from the past day would have to suffice to fill the emptiness within me. There were so many, after all, so I had no doubt that they could.

I gave Peter and Charles each a hug when we arrived back at the house late that afternoon. They told me of the enjoyment they had with Grandfather, reading books, learning tricks, and learning to play whist. They were so energetic and lively that I had to laugh when I saw Grandfather asleep on the sofa. They had clearly worn him out.

"And look what he gave us!" Charles held out his little palm, revealing two shiny pennies. "Two for me, and two for Peter."

Peter showed me his hand where two identical pennies lay.

I smiled down at them. "That was very kind of him. Keep those pennies safe until you can use them to pay for something you want. No need for stealing."

"We must pay for what we want," Charles said, repeating the line I had tried to commit to his memory. "Can we use them to pay for some sweets at the bakery or a pie from Mr. Co-worm?"

I laughed lightly. Mr. Co-worm was a much more fitting name for that odious man. "Of course. Just be sure it is something you really want. We do not want to waste money either."

They nodded, clutching the pennies in their fists. I had a feeling they would keep them very safe.

I stole a glance around for Owen, but didn't see him. I thought about asking Mrs. Kellaway where he was, but with Grandmother in the room, I didn't dare. But as if my thoughts controlled it, Owen walked through the door immediately after I noticed that he was gone. His eyes landed on me and he flashed his easy smile. I instantly smiled back. Thankfully, it didn't feel awkward at all.

After Owen had greeted each of us, I watched as a footman approached him with a letter on a salver. Owen opened it promptly, not waiting to read it privately. His eyes ran smoothly down the page, then stopped suddenly. His jaw clenched and his grip tightened on the paper.

Something was wrong, I could tell. I glanced around at the others in the room, but no one seemed to notice what I did.

My gaze jumped back to the rapid rise and fall of Owen's chest, and the distress that cried out in every line of his face. I watched with alarm as he crumpled the letter in his hand and strode from the room, closing the door behind him.

It startled me to see him like that. I scanned the room for any similar reactions, but still no one else acknowledged his departure. Whatever was in that letter had certainly troubled him immensely. I needed to find out what it was.

Trusting that Peter and Charles would behave for a few minutes longer, I sneaked out the door, endeavoring to find Owen and discover what that letter entailed. I hadn't seen the entire home yet, but I had seen most of the main floor and the second floor where my bedchamber was.

After scouring the first two floors, I found no sign of him. The staircase to the third floor awaited me, so I started carefully upward. At the top, I felt an odd sensation that I was trespassing—that I wasn't meant to be up here. But my curiosity carried me forward into the long hallway, not allowing me any control.

My footsteps echoed on the marble floors as I looked all around me, taking in the beautiful arched windows and the portrait gallery across from them. I stopped in front of a portrait of a young boy. He looked to be close to Charles's age. Stepping closer, I recognized his deep blue eyes and golden hair, and the little dent in his cheek. Owen.

I smiled at how endearing he looked as a young boy. I stood on my toes and looked even closer. The artist had captured his countenance perfectly. I gasped, and then laughed, identifying the expression in his eyes. It had the same mischievous twinkle as Peter's and Charles's eyes.

Walking down the line, I saw the portraits that I assumed must be of Owen's brother, Edmond, and sister, Alice. As children, the three of them looked very alike, but as I walked, I found recent portraits of the entire family, and the resemblance was slight. Edmond, the eldest, had Owen's same striking blue eyes, but his hair was much lighter. Alice had the same auburn hair as her mother, and a faint mischievous twinkle in her eye as well. I smiled, suddenly looking forward to meeting her again.

Remembering why I had ventured here in the first place, I continued down the hall and turned right. Just as I did, the sound of a pianoforte reached my ears. It played a soft, simple tune, and stopped. I paused where I was, waiting to hear more, but the sound never came. It was enough, though, for me to follow.

I hurried on soft feet to the end of the hall and peeked through the doorway from which the sound had come. The room was dim and large, with a lofty ceiling and one small window. And sitting on the bench of a pianoforte, with his head bent over a letter, was Owen.

He couldn't see me from his angle, but I could see him clearly. My heart twisted at seeing his face. Whatever frustration he had exhibited when he first read the letter, was now raw sadness. I watched his eyes skimming the wrinkled paper again, and what looked like guilt flashed in his eyes. He ran a hand through his hair, then slammed it down onto the bench.

I was startled. I had never seen Owen so uncollected, and I never could have pictured it in my mind. But here it was, right in front of me, and I had no idea of what I should do.

I felt awful, standing here watching him, for I was sure that he wouldn't want to be seen this way. I cursed myself silently. I shouldn't have come up here. He needed to be alone. I tried to put myself in his situation, and I knew that I would have certainly preferred to be alone, rather than have someone sneak up on me wanting an explanation for something that was obviously very upsetting.

My decision was clear: I needed to leave. But before I knew what I was doing, my disobedient feet carried me past the doorway and across the room. My heart pounded in my ears. My mind censured my movements as I inched closer to Owen. His head was still bent over the letter, and I was so quiet that he didn't notice me until I was five feet away.

His head jerked up and I spoke too quickly. "Owen, I know I should not have followed you up here, but I wondered what was the matter."

He didn't say anything, but looked at me with such heavy pain in his eyes that I wanted to reach out and comfort him somehow.

"You can speak with me about it. If . . . if you would like." I was horrible at this.

He held my gaze for several seconds in silence before he released a sigh and set the letter down on his lap. Hardly aware of my own movements, I sat down beside him on the bench. He rubbed the back of his neck and looked down at the letter again. Taking a deep breath, he turned his head to look at me.

I realized with a rush of hot embarrassment how close I had sat to him. I shifted a few inches away discreetly, which caused an unwelcome sense of disappointment to drop through me. I ignored it and waited a little longer, until Owen finally spoke.

"A patient of mine . . . she—" His voice was throaty and quiet, and he struggled to finish the sentence. He looked down at the letter again. "I just received word that she died three days ago. I couldn't save her."

My heart cried out for him. I remembered what he had told me in the library, about the doctor that could not save his cousin. "Owen, it is not your fault."

He looked up sharply. "Of course it's my fault! Her family trusted me. She was even engaged! I know that feeling of disappointment and anger. And now, I'm the physician I swore I would never be."

I studied his profile as he stared at the letter. He was completely distraught. I needed to choose my words carefully. "Did you do everything you could to save her?" I asked gently.

He turned his gaze back to me and breathed heavily. "Everything." His voice cracked as he said the word.

I turned so I faced him completely. "Then if you believe you're like the physician who treated your cousin, you are wrong. Because you told me that he was lazy and uncaring. You told me that he did the minimal amount of work and treated the illness like nothing. Yes, the outcome was the same for you, but the difference between yourself and that physician is significant."

I tried to convince him with my eyes when I said, "You didn't give up, and you did everything you could to save her. He did not. That is what matters, and you cannot blame yourself after you've done all you are capable of. I am sure her family sees that, and if they don't, then they are to blame for their false accusations."

Owen dropped his gaze. I waited, hoping my words had done something to lessen his pain. The room was silent for a long moment except for the sound of his breathing. I waited even longer, and I could sense a sort of struggle within Owen as he stared at the letter again. Then he drew a deep breath and held it, and when he exhaled it sounded like a heavy sigh.

When he looked at me, the guilt I had seen before was gone. "Thank you, Annette," he whispered.

Then he moved, shrinking the space between us. And by the end of that one swift motion, he had his arms wrapped around my waist, his face buried in my shoulder, his cheek against my neck. I caught my breath, and as if completely independent, my arms wrapped around him too. He held me tight, and I was consumed by warmth, and I could feel the beat of his heart against me. His breath brushed the back of my neck as he thanked me again.

I hardly knew how long he held me like that, or how fast my heart was racing until his arms loosened and he pulled away. I felt a cold chill as soon as the warmth of his closeness was gone, but the look in his eyes nearly matched it.

He gave me a small smile just as I felt something melt and catch fire inside me. There was nothing more to be said, and something about this moment made me think that any more words would only trivialize everything else.

So I stood and walked from the room. For some reason, it didn't feel like walking at all. I was convinced that my feet never touched the ground. I stopped at the top of the staircase and took a moment to steady my breathing. I pressed a hand to my chest, feeling the steady beat of my heart, when seconds ago I had felt Owen's, so close to my own. I couldn't identify what my heart was feeling at that moment, but it was very unique and intense.

And suddenly, for the first time, it felt like my heart was trying to tell *me* something. It surprised me so much that I quickly blocked it out before I heard it. I couldn't listen to my heart! My heart listened to me—I was in charge. My heart had always known that.

So why did I feel like that was bound to change?

# Chapter 12

When I took Peter and Charles to the north lawn the following day, Owen was waiting to meet us for his next lesson.
After I had left him on the third floor the day before, I hadn't seen
him much all evening. But when he did come down for dinner, he
told us to meet him here. It worried me, after his first lesson, that I
would be a major key to another "demonstration."

But thankfully, when we arrived, I noticed targets set up across
the lawn. The only way I could imagine being used in a demonstration of archery, would be *as* a target. Even that was extreme for
Owen, so I allowed myself a sigh of relief.

Owen greeted us with a wide smile. "Are you ready to learn how
to shoot?" I was grateful that he was back to his cheerful self again.

Peter and Charles looked across the lawn in awe and hurried
to Owen's side, nodding and giggling as they went. I smiled as I
watched them. This was certainly an activity that most young boys
enjoyed, and one that they had been deprived of.

Owen walked toward me and placed a bow in my hand. "Do
you know how to shoot?"

I shook my head. It was something I had always wanted to learn,
but never had.

"Then you must join us." He gave me such a cajoling smile, that
I couldn't possibly say no.

"Very well." I said, studying the bow I now held. I had no idea
how to use it.

Owen motioned for me to stand in front of a target, and he
stood in front of his own. Beginning with a demonstration, he

removed his jacket and raised his bow. I had never seen him without his jacket before, and it made him seem more like himself—casual and free. He released the arrow and hit the target perfectly. He turned toward me with a winning smile, then bowed swiftly. I rolled my eyes.

He then shot three more arrows, and I watched with quiet awe the way his muscles strained against his shirt. I had known he was strong, but without his jacket, it was completely obvious, and I couldn't take my gaze off the steady, graceful slope of the muscles in his arms and shoulders. He hadn't lived an idle life; that was certainly evident.

My brothers were eager to try, so Owen helped them next. After several attempts, Peter finally hit the target from a closer range. After he had hit it once, he rarely missed.

"Well done!" Owen said. "You are a natural."

I could tell Peter was trying to keep his smile moderate when he said, "I know."

When Charles tried, though, he struggled to come even close to the target. Owen gave him plenty of advice, but nothing seemed to do the trick. Charles shot arrow after arrow with no success. While Owen was working with Charles, I decided to try myself. I watched carefully as Owen adjusted Charles, and tried to replicate his stance. I was proud of how accurate it felt, until I released the arrow.

The moment I let it fly, I lowered my bow and watched with alarm as my arrow flew into a tree at least twenty feet behind the target. The arrow embedded itself in a branch near the top. I gasped and covered my mouth, embarrassed, trying to hide my smile.

I could feel the shock of Owen's gaze on me, so I turned to him nonchalantly. "I was aiming for the branch just above that one."

An amused smile teased his lips. "Were you?"

"I was. I came awfully close, didn't I?" I had to bite my lip to keep from smiling.

He lifted a hand to shade his face from the sun, and squinted at the tree thoughtfully. "Perhaps you should try again. Certainly you will hit it this time."

"I could hit it with my eyes closed, to be sure," I said in a faint voice.

"Really? Is that so? You must demonstrate." His face was perfectly smooth and in character, but his eyes betrayed amusement. I knew he was playing with me, but I was far too good at this game.

"Very well. Fetch me an arrow. But before I shoot, you must know that I prefer to choose my target *after* I have released my arrow." I grinned to myself. Now I had won for certain.

His act faltered for a quick moment in a look of surprise, but his cool demeanor quickly recovered. "I have never heard of such a technique. You must be a true master."

"I confess, I am."

"And a true master of archery prefers to use the same arrow when aiming for the same target each time she attempts it, does she not?"

Momentarily taken off guard, and having no idea of what he meant, I replied, "Well, of course."

A grin lifted one side of his mouth, making his dimple appear in his cheek. The mischievous twinkle flashed in his eyes.

Oh, no.

"Then you must recover that arrow if you hope to ever hit your target."

I knew I was good at this game, but I had forgotten just how skilled a competitor Owen was. He knew as well as I did that I couldn't back down from a challenge. I took a deep breath.

The time those years ago when I had climbed a tree with Owen flashed in my mind. It was not an experience that settled among my fondest. I had spent so long wondering how it would feel to fly, to soar out of the branches above and touch the clouds. But the ground was where I belonged, and it was still where I belonged.

Now he was going to make me climb a tree again. It took all my concentration just to retain my calm, cool expression.

"Oh, how perfect this is. I forgot to mention that I am also a master tree climber," I said as I walked past him with a lifted chin, and started toward the tree. I caught a look of amusement on his face as I passed.

My brothers giggled behind me as I stopped in front of the tree. I stole a glance backward at them, and found Owen standing directly behind me. His resolve had crumbled, for he was smiling without reservation now. "Annette, don't do it," he warned.

"I have to recover my arrow, of course. You reminded me yourself."

He looked at me in disbelief. "You are really going to climb a tree again?"

"Yes," a smile crept onto my face, "but this time there is a factor that will drastically alter the outcome."

His lips twitched. "What is that?" he asked, echoing my words from the water garden.

"This time I'm skilled enough to descend it."

I turned swiftly to face the tree again, grinning at my wit. I could hear Owen laughing behind me with disbelief and amusement. My eyes traveled up and up. The tree was very tall. But, to maintain my act, I pushed aside my nerves and started climbing. The trunk was too wide for me to wrap my arms around, so I jumped and grabbed the lowest branch, and swung my foot onto a knot in the bark. The movement jostled my ribs on my right side and I winced, pausing to painstakingly collect my breath.

Recovered momentarily, I continued climbing, gripping each branch above me, and stepping onto the branch below. I stepped onto a crevice between two branches, and hoisted myself up repeatedly, until I could see the arrow wedged deeply into the base of a thick branch only a few feet above me. One more step up would do it.

I clung tightly to the trunk and studied the position of the branches above me. The nearest branch was a bit too high for me to reach, and I could see no stable place for footing. I paused my climbing to catch my breath and consider the options before me.

That was when the rain started.

I hadn't noticed the sky turn grey or the clouds grow dark, but there it was above me.

I felt a single, fat drop on my arm. Then a second, and a third. I looked up to see the rain intensifying, drops landing on my face and in my hair. It was warm rain, and it took me completely by surprise. The leaves of the tree seemed to shield me partially, but once the rain intensified, it tore through the leaves effortlessly, until it fell down on me in heavy, wet sheets.

I shifted my grip on the trunk to wipe the water from my face, and looked down through the rain. Owen was absolutely drenched.

He was holding his jacket over Peter's and Charles's heads, blocking the rain from them. I wanted to laugh, but realized that this was not a laughing matter at all. I was trapped in this tree, and my boots had become very slick. How had I let Owen trick me into climbing something *again*? I couldn't blame him this time, though. I had gotten myself into this, and I needed to get myself out of it. I would not go falling out of a tree again, that I was sure of.

Without thinking, I hugged the trunk as tightly as I could, and began inching my way downward, moving my arms under the branches that came in my way. The descent felt painfully slow, and I could feel the ragged bark of the tree scratching through my gown. I dug my fingers into the trunk, and pressed the side of my face against it. By now, I was completely soaked, and I could only hope that my gown hadn't become transparent. My hair was dripping and plastered over my eyes, so I could scarcely see a thing. I was beginning to wonder if I would slip.

Just then, I felt two strong hands grip my waist and heard Owen say, "Let go!"

I was startled enough already that I dropped my grip on the trunk instantly and felt myself being pulled backward. I must have been closer to the bottom than I thought. My eyes caught a quick glimpse of Owen through the hair over my eyes and the sheets of rain that blurred everything.

He was laughing as he lifted me from the tree and spun me around to face him. I landed softly on my feet and before I knew what had just happened, I was laughing too. His hands fell from my waist and he grasped my hand. Charles took Owen's other hand and Peter took mine, and we raced blindly to the house. I laughed until my stomach ached and ran as fast as I could, nearly tripping over my wet gown.

We burst through the door and stopped in the hall, our gasping breaths and laughter echoing off the walls. Owen released a sigh and raked his hand through his hair, releasing drops of water. "Well, that was . . . sudden."

I nodded, trying to stop laughing. The laughter alone was making my ribs ache. Climbing that tree had not been an intelligent move, for more reasons than one.

Owen tipped his head to look at me. His lips quivered. "'Master tree climber'?"

"Well, I couldn't allow you to win!"

He chuckled. "It seems that we need to call this match a draw."

I shook my head, refusing to secede. "I didn't climb that tree only to end with 'a draw'." A realization made me gasp. "And why is it that every time you teach Peter and Charles, I am forced into climbing something?"

"You can't blame me this time. You started it. I was only playing along."

"At least admit that I won," I said with a pleading look.

His eyes were shining with amusement as he stepped toward me. Then, placing his hand against the wall behind my shoulder, he leaned his head even closer and whispered, "Never."

I gasped in outrage, ducked under his arm, and whirled to face him again. He was unbelievable. I was the clear winner. I was about to protest, but he was already laughing at me, so I let the subject drop. At least, for now. "Fine. A draw."

Just then, the sound of humming reached my ears. Owen and I stopped and looked toward the end of the short hall. It was a strange, high sound, and I couldn't decipher a tune at all.

"That sounds like my Grandmother," Owen whispered.

Just after he spoke, she appeared, walking past the end of the hall. She glanced lazily down it, and took another step. Then her gaze jerked down the hall again. Her eyes lit up like she had just struck gold. Her lips pursed into a tiny heart.

I held my breath.

"Boys!" Grandmother yelled down the hall to my brothers. "Come along with me to dry off." She waved them forward, and took their hands once they reached her. Her lips were still pursed and her eyes were fresh with mischief. She turned and shuffled away from the hall, pulling my brothers along with her.

I released my breath slowly, carefully, thinking she was gone. But then in a swift motion, she peeked only her head around the corner, put a hand to her pursed lips, gave a low, hooting chuckle, and disappeared from sight.

I grimaced. How embarrassing! She must be thinking all sorts of things right now that weren't true. She obviously took Peter and

Charles just to leave me alone with Owen. I glanced up at him tentatively, hoping that he didn't realize Grandmother's scheme.

He was smiling down at me, and it made my heart skitter a bit, for I noticed that the rain was having a very unfair effect on his appearance. The water was doing nothing but favors for him, soaking his hair, and dripping down his face, and catching in his lashes, and landing on his lips . . .

I stopped myself, realizing how long I had been staring at him, and how unbecoming my own appearance must have been, for I was sure the water was having the absolute opposite effect on me. I could feel that my hair was hanging loose and was plastered to my face. I suddenly felt extremely self-conscious and excruciatingly awkward.

He lifted his jacket and shook the water from it, then draped it over my shoulders.

I looked down at a puddle near my feet. "You don't have to."

He waved off my protest. "Take it. Would you like to sit down? We can light the fire in the sitting room and dry off. Besides, you now owe me a question."

Oh, yes. Another question. My stomach fluttered, but I flashed him a smile anyway. "That sounds nice. Thank you."

After Owen lit the fire, he positioned two chairs closely across from each other, and we sat down in front of the fireplace. I wrapped Owen's jacket snug around my shoulders and sat back, sinking into the comfortable chair. I could already feel the radiating warmth of the fire wicking away the water from my gown and skin and hair. It felt wonderful.

Owen was leaning forward in his chair, watching me intently. I tried to ignore it, looking at the flames dancing in the fireplace, but each time I peeked at him again, he was still staring at me.

"What?"

He scrunched his brow and narrowed his eyes. "I'm thinking of a question."

I nodded in understanding and looked back to the fire for a while, but I could still feel his gaze on my face. I looked at him again. He was still watching me. And in my current state, it made me feel especially self-conscious.

"Do you have to stare at me while you think?" I blurted.

He looked down with a soft laugh, then up again. "There is nothing I would rather look at. Why would I choose to gaze elsewhere when there is so much beauty before me?"

I looked down, feeling my face burn, regretting that I had even asked. Beauty? I had just nearly drowned in rain. I could not even begin to think of how to respond, so thankfully, Owen spoke again to rescue me from my distress.

"I have chosen a question," he said.

My eyes shot up to meet his. My heart pounded hard in my chest.

"What are you most afraid of?"

The question rang in my ears. What was I most afraid of? It was something that I hadn't ever really thought about. Perhaps Owen could choose a different question, one that I actually had an answer for. My mind threw a thought in front of me suddenly. The thought made my heart race even more and I realized that I was afraid of something. Very afraid.

I closed my eyes for a moment, then took a deep breath and opened them. Owen watched me patiently, waiting for an answer. Why did he want to know this? I gathered the fabric of my skirts into tight balls in my hands, hoping that it would provide me with some stability—that it would give me something to hold onto.

I began in a taut voice, "When my brothers and I first went to live with my aunt, I was very afraid of her. I feared her voice, and her demands, and her expectations of me. Everything she told me was . . . belittling. Never kind, never caring. I feared that she would hurt me if I did something wrong. And sometimes she did. But her words always hurt more than anything else."

Owen was leaning forward now, and in his eyes I could see that fiery anger that I had seen in the orchard when I talked of Aunt Ruth before.

"I longed to have someone that would protect me from her harm. But with no one to rely on, I realized that the only person that could do that for me was myself. *I* could choose what to do with her words. Once I discovered that, everything changed. I was free from her and everything else. I felt . . . unbreakable."

It seemed odd to be saying these things aloud, but it filled me with a power that spread throughout my entire body. I actually did feel the things I was saying, and to declare them aloud was incredibly satisfying. My voice lowered and my spirits dropped as fear and worry caught up with me again. I tightened my grip on my skirts and moved my gaze to the fire.

"But the thing I fear now, more than anything, is that my brothers will suffer from her as I did, and that they will believe the things she says to them. That she will hurt them the way she hurt me. I've already seen it beginning, and I can't bear to imagine them so defeated."

I looked away from the fire and back at Owen. His eyes held heavy sorrow and hot anger all at once. I found myself wishing again that he would just laugh at me. But instead, he reached forward and uncurled my hand from my wad of skirts, and held it between both of his. The gesture itself surprised me, and the warmth of his hands against my cold hand sent sudden chills up my arms. He rubbed his thumb over the top of my hand in a circle, watching it carefully.

"I cannot imagine how they could be defeated with someone as brave as you watching over them." He looked up then, and I felt oddly shy in the moment, with my hand in his by the warm fire, and looking into his smiling eyes. My heart was beating hard, and I tried to calm it, telling it, *Owen is only a friend, nothing more.*

I repeated those words to my heart until I was sure it was true. But for some reason, my heart refused to listen. It thudded quickly in my chest and I felt, suddenly, as I did the day before—that it was trying to speak back to me. It frightened me, and made me feel completely defenseless. I needed to find something to laugh about before I could hear what my heart was trying to reveal to me.

"Considering how fearlessly they hid my bonnet with her underthings, I doubt that they are extremely afraid of her, at least."

Owen tipped his head back with a laugh, and I took the opportunity to slip my hand away. There. My heart became silent then, and my thoughts were rejuvenated.

"We may need to save that story for another day," I said, answering to the curious look he cast me. "Thank you for teaching them to shoot. They seemed to be enjoying themselves, until the rain started, anyway."

He shook his head with a wry smile. "The real enjoyment began after the rain started."

I rolled my eyes. "I changed my mind. I certainly won."

"We agreed on a draw," he said with a teasing grin.

I gave an exasperated sigh. "No, because that means you are still a partial winner. And you always win." I hated admitting that to him, but we both knew it was true.

"Not always."

I cast him a skeptical look. "Oh? Then what have I won?"

He drew a breath, held it, and looked at me with deep thought evident throughout his expression. "More than you realize," he said in a quiet voice. His mouth was curled in a smile, but his eyes were solemn and they held both a statement and a secret, strategically leaving me bereft. He was digging into my heart with his questions, but I realized that I had no idea of what was in his. I wished I hadn't agreed to his terms. It didn't feel like a fair arrangement at all.

All I could do was raise an eyebrow at him, and wonder what it was that he was hiding from me. But from the depth of his gaze and the careful ease of his facade, I feared I would never know.

When I stood from my chair to leave, a severe pang struck my side suddenly, making me gasp. My hand flew to my right side instinctively.

Owen's brow furrowed and he stepped toward me. "Are you hurt?"

I shook my head dismissively. "It is just an old injury. I broke some ribs a few years ago that never healed sufficiently. I'm afraid scaling that tree may have awakened the pain a bit."

His concern only intensified. "What caused the injury?"

My heart pounded hard. I did not want to talk about this. I swallowed. "It was nothing important."

Owen caught my arm as I turned to leave. "Annette. Did your aunt have anything to do with it?"

I took a deep breath and faced him. His eyes were looking into mine so deeply I felt as though he knew my answer before I said it. "Yes," I whispered. "But it was a long time ago."

"Please tell me what happened."

My hands shook as I rubbed them over my skirts as a distraction. I had never told another person about this. I had been trying to forget for a very long time.

I cleared my voice of the lump in my throat. "When we first went to live with our aunt, she was furious. She met with her solicitor ceaselessly, trying to find a loophole in my father's will. She later saw that the benefit of taking us in was admiration from her acquaintances, but at the beginning, she wanted nothing but to be rid of us." I didn't dare look at Owen's face as I continued to the worst part of the story.

"During that time, she instructed her servants to deprive us of food for several days at a time, but I usually managed to sneak something for my brothers. As a result, I . . . well, I grew rather thin and she caught me smuggling food from the kitchen one day and threw me to the ground. Because I was so frail, my ribs easily broke, and she never called for a doctor."

I glanced up for a brief moment. Owen was shaking his head, his eyes flashing with anger. "If she were a man, I would call her out," he mumbled.

"Owen—"

He drew closer, stopping my words. I looked down at the wooden floor, but he took my chin between his thumb and forefinger gently, lifting my face to look at his. "She will not hurt you or your brothers again. I promise. I will *not* let that happen."

I felt the threat of tears stinging my eyes. I quickly blinked them away. Why was my heart behaving so wildly? Perhaps my ribs had been the last and final cage that could contain it, and whatever happened today had damaged my only remaining defense.

"I will not let that happen," he repeated in a softer voice. There was something in his piercing eyes that convinced me to believe him. If only for the moment.

But when I left the sitting room, I still believed him. And when I ate dinner, I still believed him. And I went to bed that night, still believing him.

# Chapter 13

On my way to breakfast the next morning, a footman stopped me at the base of the staircase with a letter. I was astonished, and confused, for I hadn't received a letter in years, other than the invitation from Mrs. Kellaway to visit here. I stopped where I was and hurried abruptly back to my room to open it. The only person I imagined it could be from was Aunt Ruth, so I shushed my confusion and tore open the letter.

It was much longer than I had expected, and my suspicions were confirmed upon seeing the narrow, stiff writing covering the page.

*Niece,*

*I know I made it quite clear that you were to stay at Kellaway Manor for the remainder of the summer, but I have fallen victim to quite the snub from all of my dearest friends. Can you believe this? They are under the impression that I sent you dreadful little orphans off just to be rid of you. They think me a great barbarian! It is absurd! I have since been receiving not half the calling invitations as before, and I have not dined at Plumgrove once!*

I rolled my eyes. Aunt Ruth had obsessed over the magnificent Plumgrove for years. She was often invited to dine there with her idol, Lady Rosanna St. James. I smiled at the distress she must be having over it.

*My reputable hospitality is being viewed as naught now that you little monsters are gone. It sickens me. Therefore, I would like you to return a full report of the progress of the boys. I remain firm on my wishes in their regard. I will not have you returning with those ill-behaved, poorly educated scoundrels only to recover my admired image in society. It is worth the wait to see them improved as they need to be. Understand, though, that you may return at any time now, as long as the boys are behaving as they ought. Her Ladyship, Lady Rosanna St. James, is most disdainful about the suspected truth of your absence, and without dining at Plumgrove, I fear I shall wither away to nothing.*

*I hope that this excursion has allowed you some exposure to eligible gentlemen, for the greatest victory would be to have you married off and caring for those little devils on your own. My excuse for ridding myself of you would then be completely plausible and even more advantageous than the previous arrangement. Keep your nasty freckled face hidden beneath your bonnet and you could perhaps have a chance at a tolerable match.*

*Mrs. Ruth Filbee*

I threw the letter down on the writing desk, disgusted. What I wanted to do was tear the letter to shreds. But I chose to control myself and took a seat instead. We had been here at Kellaway Manor for nearly two weeks now, and imagining returning to live with my aunt sickened me. It would happen eventually, but I hoped that eventually wouldn't be for a very long time.

But this change was temporary, and the letter reminded me of that fact. I imagined staying here forever, living in comfort, with people who wanted me here, who made me laugh and feel happy every day of my life.

I tore my mind away from its pensive hopes. I couldn't stay here forever, and that fact was irrevocable. But I would try my best to make "eventually" last as long as I could possibly manage.

I was overcome with a feeling of unwarranted excitement as I picked up a quill and placed a sheet of parchment in front of me.

Owen was not going to allow Aunt Ruth to pester us any longer, and neither was I.

I chewed my lip, trying to decide the best way to begin. A sardonic smile curled my lips as I wrote.

*My dear aunt,*

*It is a shame indeed that you have been unable to dine at Plumgrove, but perhaps it will be a thing of positive consequence. You may be able to button your emerald gown again! I assure you that would be a true wonder. Anyhow, you have requested that I inform you of the developments of Peter and Charles. Here is what we have accomplished: Nothing. Absolutely nothing at all. But of course, they have terrorized the Kellaway's cook and sneaked a mouse into the dining room. Indeed, it appears that they are worse off than before. We will need as much time as possible to reach your expectations.*

*Yours,*

*Annette*

*P.S. I have very exciting news! I have counted four new freckles across my nose. Isn't that delightful? I adore them all, and have even named one after you.*

I bit back a laugh and set the quill down on the desk. That should do the trick. I sealed my letter, my movements stiff and hard, and picked up the one from Aunt Ruth. I held it in front of my face and stared at it, wishing I could burn a hole in it with the hot anger of my gaze. Tearing it to shreds was still a possibility, but a better idea came to my mind in a jolt of spite. I folded the letter and placed it on the desk. Then I sat back in my chair and imagined myself tearing Aunt Ruth to shreds instead. It was much more enjoyable.

After breakfast, I sat in the morning room with Mrs. Kellaway while my brothers read in the library with Grandfather. She was working on an intricate piece of embroidery while she spoke with me about upcoming plans.

"You will absolutely love my daughter, Alice. I just received a letter from her this morning saying that she is bringing a friend along as well. Miss Charlotte Lyons. Both are very amiable, elegant young ladies." As if remembering something very important, she looked up from her embroidery with a sharp jerk of her head. "Speaking of elegant ladies, I am expecting three of my dearest friends to come for tea this afternoon, and I would be delighted if you would join us. The baroness of Pembury, Charlotte's mother, will be among the party."

I cleared my throat. "I would love to." I hardly knew what I had just agreed to, for my thoughts were still stuck on Aunt Ruth's letter, and my heart was pinching with sadness since I had been reminded that we would have to go back to her again.

Mrs. Kellaway cast me a warm look and set to work contentedly on her embroidery again. I watched the needle she held between two poised fingers. I was so incredibly bored that my vision began to lose focus as I stared at the sharp needle. I counted her stitches, slowly, and the activity was so monotonous that I was sure I would fall asleep with my eyes open. I was jostled back to my wits by the sound of muffled speech.

"What?" I asked, blinking hard.

"The ball is now only three days away." Mrs. Kellaway beamed, looking at me as if she expected a certain reaction. "Are you not excited?"

I swallowed. "I am, very much." The words granted me a sunken feeling, but my lips curved upward in a forced smile anyway.

One side of her smile quirked up, reminding me of an expression I had seen on Owen's face so many times. "Please remind me, have you had a season in town?"

I shook my head, suddenly feeling the shame of it. I had, as a young girl, desired a season one day. But as I grew older, and my responsibilities grew with me, I decided that the fantasies London had to offer were no longer paramount. Besides, there was no possible way that my aunt would have allowed it. Husband hunting was the aim of the come-out festivities, and I had long since decided my spinster fate.

"Do you know how to dance?" she asked.

I nodded. "I know well enough, I think."

"The minuet, quadrille, waltz?"

I nodded again, although the steps were very faint in my mind.

"Ah." She smiled at me and set to work on her embroidery once more.

I could not find the strength to stare at that needle for another second. "I should find my brothers," I said, standing from my chair. "I wouldn't want them to tire your father again."

A look of understanding flickered across her face. "Very well, dear."

I backed toward the door. "Thank you." Then I gripped the handle and slid past the frame, enjoying the fresh smell of the hallway, and leaned against the wall.

The morning room was stifling, and my worry about the ball was too much to bear confined in that little, quiet room. I was dreading the afternoon tea now for so many reasons: I would have to sit in that room *again*, be surrounded by elegant ladies, and worst of all, I would have to act like an elegant lady myself, which was not my finest ability.

I spent the next few hours in the library with my brothers and Grandfather. I was pleased to hear that Peter and Charles had been practicing their reading and were actually enjoying it. Whenever I attempted to persuade them to read, there were always dozens of complaints to be expected. But, of course, at Aunt Ruth's home there were a very limited number of books to choose from, and here at the Kellaway's library there were hundreds of books of all different subjects. The passage of time soared quickly with my nose in an entertaining book, so I had to grimace with distaste when I looked at the clock. It read three, which was when Mrs. Kellaway liked to take her tea.

I moved with slow steps to the morning room on the east side of the home. It was quiet—I could hear every click of my boots against the marble floor, until a shrill laugh cut into the air like the call of a bird.

I stopped at the door of the morning room, took a deep breath, preparing myself, and entered with a wide smile.

Grandmother sat on a chair in direct view of the door and returned my smile. Surprisingly, I was relieved to see her. My eyes then took in three unfamiliar women, each with an aloof glance to dart my way.

My smile was pressed down to nothing by the weighted disdain on one woman's face as she swept her gaze over me. She seemed to be appraising me with that one look, and I thought I saw a hint of a challenge in her eyes. My attempt at a confident entry was completely halted. I lifted my lips again for Mrs. Kellaway's sake and curtsied politely.

Mrs. Kellaway motioned to the seat beside her and introduced the women to me.

The first two names were insignificant to me, but when she introduced the third woman—the one with the haughty, disdainful eye, she said, "Might I make known to you Lady Pembury. She is the mistress of Eshersed Park just north of the village. As I told you, her daughter, Miss Charlotte Lyons, is the young lady that is coming here to visit with Alice tomorrow."

I placed a glance on Lady Pembury, and even included a smile, but her eyes were still fixed on me with such scrutiny that I dashed my gaze away as quickly as I could.

Then in a faint voice, she said, "My daughter is . . . ," she clicked her fingernails together and grinned sedately, "most delighted to have the opportunity of visiting. After all, she has come before, and adored your home immensely. And at any rate, the members of your family are so agreeable and charming that I cannot see how that is not also a large reason for her anticipation to arrive."

"I am glad to hear it," Mrs. Kellaway said. "She is very welcome to visit whenever she would like. She and Alice are nearly like sisters it seems." Her smile flashed and she sipped her tea.

I saw a hint of impatience in Lady Pembury's eyes, and in the way she pinched her lips together and clicked her fingernails faster. "Your son," she blurted, then recoiled at the brevity of her words. "I mean, are your other . . . children staying here as well?

Mrs. Kellaway's brows wrinkled a bit as she stared at Lady Pembury. "Owen is currently living here, and Edmond will be returning with my husband tomorrow as well. They have been on a hunting excursion for nearly a month now." Her tone turned wistful. "I am greatly looking forward to their arrival."

Lady Pembury appeared to only have ears for the first portion of Mrs. Kellaway's remarks, and her fingernails began clicking even faster until Mrs. Kellaway finished speaking. Then she smiled like she knew a secret, and the clicking stopped. "Charlotte has met your son, has she not?"

Mrs. Kellaway squinted. "Yes, yes, she has met them both. Each time Alice has brought her to visit."

"Ah. That is right. And your sons were at the last season in London, yes?

"Yes."

Lady Pembury's smile was making a slow creep upward until she looked like a cat before a wounded bird. Stealthy, patient. But she wasn't planning to pounce yet; I could tell by the way she sneaked around the subject with careful ease. I wasn't sure what the subject was, exactly, but in the short few minutes since I had met this woman I guessed that she was very skilled at getting what she wanted.

"The younger of the two, I understand, has quite the attachment to my daughter." She threw a glance at me with a lifted eyebrow.

The other ladies in the room whispered at this and I saw Grandmother's eyes widen.

Mrs. Kellaway choked on her tea, then set it down, her eyes lit up with sudden interest. "Owen? Does he, now? How can you be certain?"

"Seeing them dance together in London was testimony enough."

My heart was twisting with so many emotions that I nearly dropped my teacup. An intense burning had filled me, consumed me, and brought me to the will of this clever, disdainful woman. I tried to appear nonchalant when I noticed the satisfied smile on her lipsticked lips, aimed at me.

Did she suspect that I was here trying to secure Owen? The thought was absurd. But her catlike features held every sign of suspicion as she watched me over my teacup. She lowered her voice and leaned toward Mrs. Kellaway, as if the words were meant only for her ears, but I heard them perfectly. "With Charlotte coming to visit, I daresay we have an engagement on the horizon."

Mrs. Kellaway looked stunned, and for some reason, she shot me a concerned glance. My heart was thumping so hard I could hear the blood rushing in my ears. My hand shook as I sipped my tea. Why was this conversation so painful to witness? Why did I feel unable to sit in this chair any longer without bursting to pieces? I tried to remain as normal as possible, but the feeling in my heart and in the pit of my stomach was not normal at all.

It was a different feeling than earlier, sitting in this stifling room. It was much different, and from the deliberate glance Lady Pembury cast my way, and from the slow smile that contorted her lips, and from the glow of accomplishment and satisfaction in her deep green eyes, I realized with a start that I was the wounded bird, and she had just somehow caught me.

While the conversation turned to fashion and lace and collars with "inexpressibly fashionable Vandyke points," I sat restlessly, sipping my tea endlessly, and trying to puzzle out why I was feeling the way I was.

Owen was only a friend! Why should it matter that he had a previous attachment to someone I have never even met? It didn't matter. So why did I feel like something within me was being torn slowly apart? Why did I feel so deceived and upset? My heart pounded as I realized how very wrong I had been to learn so much of Owen, to come so close to him. Whether I liked to admit it or not, my heart was in great danger. Owen would be far too easy to fall in love with, and I was already halfway there at least.

I sipped my tea again, and again, but it did nothing to steady me. In fact, I was convinced that with each sip a new surge of piercing emotion dropped through me, like the tea was a poison making me weaker and weaker with each drink.

So I set down the cup, and closed my ears from the talk of lace, and attempted to close my eyes from the sight of Lady Pembury and her wicked, stealthy claws, but most of all, I tried my best to close my heart from everything else.

When the conversation finally died off, and the women pranced from the room, I stood as quickly as I could. My legs shook. Just before I left the room, I caught a glimpse of Grandmother, who looked nearly as disheveled as I felt inside. She shook her head just as I tore through the door.

As fast as my trembling legs could carry me, I went up the staircase, and into my room, closing the door tightly behind me. I leaned my back against the wall, using it as the support I needed. It was cool and stabilizing against my back, but it wasn't enough. I needed fresh air and sunshine and fierce breezes to untether this feeling from me.

The bright warmth of the sun's rays awaited me as if they knew I was coming. I began across the lawn in a brisk walk, but my legs carried me into a run before I could control them. The clouds were sparse today, dispersed across the wide sky in tiny wisps, like the sky was a clear blue canvas, and the clouds were sporadic brushstrokes of white paint, meant only to break up the expanse of nothingness that spread above the land as endlessly as the burning within me.

I stopped at the edge of the woods, caught my breath, and found a broad tree stump for a chair. Tiny rays of sunshine filtered through the trees above and around me, dotting my gown and the dirt and the bushes with pockets of light, fighting against the blankets of shadow being cast by the lumbering maples all around me. My gaze settled on the flickering rays of sunshine. I wished I could somehow grab hold of one and implant it inside of me so I could recover the warm, peaceful feeling I had enjoyed for such a short time.

Crossing my legs with a sigh, I bent over and picked up a leaf that had fallen near my feet. I rested my face on my hand and twirled the stem between my fingers, thinking, trying to count the emotions that battled within me. I gave up immediately, throwing the leaf to the ground. I didn't even know what to call what I was feeling, and it frustrated me, because it was somehow familiar.

Amid my puzzling, a memory entered my mind from years before. *It was Grace's puppy.* My upper lip curled in distaste as I recalled that day.

*Seven Years Before*

"May I please have a puppy?" I asked Mama for what felt like the thousandth time.

She looked up from her reading with a frown. "Annette. What did I tell you yesterday concerning this very thing?"

I dropped my gaze to my lap. Drat. I had even found her favorite novel from the library and brought her a cup of steaming tea with cream. Surely a puppy was a small price to be paid for my kindness today. At least, that was what I thought before.

"But Mama, I will take perfect care of it, and I will play with it and comb its fur and feed it—"

"We have no use for a dog, and until you stop neglecting your studies, we will not even consider having one. Do you understand?" She looked at me with a small scowl, an expression that I rarely saw on her face.

My hopes dropped. "A cat would be just fine too," I mumbled.

She shook her head. "Peter is far too small to have any animals in the house. I have told you this many times. Now, remember, and there will be no need for this conversation again." She lifted her teacup to her lips.

I scowled. Why had I let my hopes scale so high? It was always nothing but disappointment that followed. And if I hadn't let myself hope for a puppy, then I wouldn't have felt nearly as disappointed as I did now. I was certain of it.

"I am going outside," I said around the lump in my throat. Then I ran to the door and stepped out under the sun that was sure and consistent. Just like Mama and Papa's refusals. I ran to the edge of our small patch of land and stared across the path that separated my house from Grace's.

Grace and I were polite enemies. In my mind, at least. She had perfect honey-golden curls. I had always wanted golden curls. My hair was plain and straight. She had dozens of pretty dresses that she used to pretend she was at a ball. And all the gentlemen danced with her at that pretend ball, because all the boys liked her. She only spoke to me when she knew her words would make me angry. That was certainly what she did, because I was never happy speaking with Grace Dawkins.

*And there she was, walking down the path, curls bouncing with her steps. I squinted to see what she held in her arms. It was small and black. I squinted harder. It moved.*

*"Netty, Netty, Netty!" she yelled, waving her hand with a smile.*

*I did not like to be called Netty.*

*"Look what my papa brought home for me!" She was closer now, and with a few more excited steps she was two feet away.*

*I looked down at her hand that was holding a little black puppy against her collarbone. My stomach twisted.*

*"Isn't she pretty? Oh, she is so very pretty. I have chosen to call her Coal. You see? Because she is black just like coal."*

*Coal was the most absurd name I had ever heard. My heart pounded as I watched the little puppy lick Grace's hand and nestle its tiny head into her shoulder. She even had a little bow tied around her neck.*

*"Would you like to hold her?" Grace asked, extending the puppy in my direction.*

*My eyes filled with tears that I blinked away. "No, I do not want to hold her."*

*Grace looked shocked and covered Coal's ears as if the dog understood my rejection. "Netty! Do you not think she is pretty? She is soft too, very soft. Feel her soft fur. Feel it. It is so very soft."*

*I folded my arms to keep my emotions in their proper place. "Her fur looks quite sharp to me, actually, so I do not wish to feel it."*

*Grace hugged her puppy to her chest and looked at me with outrage. "Her fur is not sharp!" She shook her head and turned to leave. "Coal is the greatest puppy in the world and you are just jealous that I have her."*

*I angrily wiped the tears from my lashes as I sat down on the grass. I watched Grace walk away, whispering and singing to her new, perfect little puppy as she went. I had wanted a pet far longer than Grace had! It was not fair. It was not fair at all.*

*Present Day*

Jealousy. The feeling that the hateful reverie evoked in me matched the emotion that had been tearing through me since I had learned of Owen's anticipated engagement to that Miss Lyons.

I was startled, and quickly dismissed the idea. I was not jealous! What possible reason could I have to be jealous of this girl whom I had never met in my entire life? Why would I be jealous of her marrying a completely atrocious man who teased too much, and whose eyes were much too blue, and who had far too infectious a laugh, and who gave me far too many reasons to smile?

Yes. That is right. I stood and brushed the bits of leaf I had torn apart from my lap. That is entirely right. I was not jealous at all. Not one bit.

So I walked back to the house, stuffing everything inside my heart as I always had, and using the vigor of my steps, I squeezed it in as deeply as I could. There. Everything was back to its proper place. Then I slid through the door, and headed back to the library.

I thirsted for conversation that wouldn't include the word *lace*, and if that could be found anywhere in this world, I was confident that it would be with my little brothers.

# Chapter 14

*A*nnette! Look what Owen gave us!" Charles ran toward me with a grin that stretched impossibly wide as I entered the library. Peter dashed up beside him and held out his hand for me to see. They each held a small berry pie cradled in their bent fingers.

"He bought them at the village." Peter's eyes fell on the pie again, and he tipped his head back to look at me with wide, astonished eyes. It was as if he had been waiting for this his entire life. Then he and Charles ran over to the far table to admire their pies some more.

It was then that I noticed Owen lounging in one of the cushioned leather chairs by the fireplace. My heart quaked upon seeing him again, seeing his playful grin and dark, framed eyes. I wondered if he knew that I knew about his attachment.

"Oh, yes," he said. "And I heard from your brothers a little tale about a man with a large belly who doesn't like to share his pies." He stood and walked toward me, a smile full of question on his lips. "Is this true?" His eyes were on the brink of laughter. "And they also told me what their sister said to this man about his leaking, revolting eyes."

I scowled at him, suddenly feeling very defensive. "So?" I planted my hands on my hips and challenged him with a look.

He looked taken aback, and his smile fell into a scolding frown. "What have I done now?"

I shrugged, not knowing how else to respond.

He stepped toward me cautiously, and in a quiet voice, asked, "Are you disappointed that I didn't bring a pie for you?"

My mouth dropped open and I shook my head in quick protest. "No, I—"

Owen placed a bag in my hands to stop my words. "You are most graciously welcome."

I peeked inside, giving him a hesitant glance. There in the bottom of the paper bag sat a little pie identical to the ones that Peter and Charles had.

I lifted my gaze slowly, back up to his face. "Thank you. But that is not why I glared at you," I added, making sure he didn't still think that.

He raised an eyebrow. "Oh, I think it is."

"It is not. I have had the pleasure of taking tea with your mother and three of her friends today, and I am just a bit . . . ," I searched for the right word, but Owen filled the space himself.

"Annoyed? Feeling on the brink of death?" He spoke with such plainness that I had to laugh.

"Something like that."

He chuckled, giving me a little smile that fluttered my heart. "I want to hear more about this man with the leaking eyes."

I held up a hand and squeezed my eyes shut, trying to shake that odious man from my head. "I do not want to talk of or think of or see him ever again. That is all you need to know."

When I opened my eyes again, I found Owen wearing an amused expression. "Tell me exactly what he looks like. What color are these famed eyes? Just how large is his belly?"

I slapped my hands over my ears. "No. No. No. Stop!" But I could still hear him, and my smile stretched wide before I could recall it. My laugh bubbled loud from me before I could contain it. I uncovered my ears and folded my arms, pressing down my laugh. "He is a repugnant man who sells pies near the village by my aunt's house. He does nothing but insult us and so I insulted him right back for a change. That is all."

Owen's smile slackened. "He insults you?"

"Well," I shrugged one shoulder, "he tells me that I'm inelegant and . . . other things, and scorns my brothers for how they look and behave. But he is so very arrogant, that is why he says the things

153

he says. And he has an ill daughter, which I know has caused him much grief, so I believe that he drowns out his sorrow with spiteful words like some kind of . . . big, smelly, revolting bully."

Owen's lips twitched. "'Big, smelly, revolting bully'?"

"Yes," I asserted. "A big, smelly, revolting bully. That is exactly what he is."

Owen dropped his chin and laughed under his breath, looking down at his boots. "Will you promise me something?" He looked up again and I greeted his gaze with a suspicious look.

"What?"

"Promise me that, if you see him again, you will call him that very thing."

Had I heard him right? "A big, smelly, revolting bully?"

"Yes."

I contemplated the idea for a moment, hiding my grin under compressed lips. "Very well. I will."

Then, imagining the look of shock on Mr. Coburn's face if I called him that, I let loose a sound that was a mixture of a laugh and a snort. Owen's eyes widened and he reared his head back in laughter. My laughter followed his without a trace of delay, but something within me stung when I realized that after today, it would be Miss Charlotte Lyons that Owen would laugh with, and talk with, and sit in this very room with. Not me.

The sting cut my laughter down in an instant, building some sort of barrier between us. I needed to leave before he made me laugh again, I decided firmly. But my will was diminished when Owen reached his hand out and brushed a piece of my hair off my forehead. His fingertips grazed my ear and cheek, sending a tingle and a hot blush up my face.

"I never properly thanked you for what you said to me, two days ago. On the third floor." His voice was hushed, serious, and his eyes were full of so much warmth that I was sure I had melted. The melting and blushing continued when I recalled that night, how he had wrapped me up in his arms, and how his whispered breath had brushed my neck when he thanked me . . .

"You did thank me," I said quickly.

He shook his head. "Not properly." His lips quirked into a little smile that betrayed mischief. "Not properly at all."

I couldn't help but gasp. I shot him a look of consternation that only made him laugh. It was only a quick laugh, though, before he became serious again. He was standing so close. I could smell the fresh soap and clean fabric and warm sunshine on him. I could see clearly the slow rise and fall of his chest, and the stubble on his jaw, and the lopsided curve of his mouth, and the dimple denting his cheek.

"I cannot tell you what your words meant to me." His voice was hushed again, still, unwavering. "But I mean to thank you—really thank you for what you said. And for the strength you gave me. I don't know how I could ever repay you."

Had he moved closer? I couldn't be sure. But what I was sure of was that he was not repaying me at this moment—standing so close to me, robbing me of my strength and weakening my resolve to leave, making me feel rooted where I stood.

"Well," I took a step back, away from him, and smiled, hiding my galloping heart, "I'm glad I was able to help. After all, you have done so much for my brothers and me while we've been here. You certainly don't have to repay me." I forced my smile to widen for my own sake, to somehow convince myself that this was normal, that I wasn't unraveling—that my heart wasn't threatening to burst. But Owen stepped toward me again, filling the space I had opened. He was looking down at me with a hint of a grin on his lips, but with such a mystery in his eyes that I couldn't even begin to solve it.

"Tell me how I can repay you. Please." His voice sent a wave plummeting through me.

I couldn't. I could not think clearly with him standing this close. It was impossible. But his eyes were insistent, beckoning, and they wouldn't let me escape. I stepped back again, a half step, and found myself against a bookcase. And apparently Owen still felt the need to torment me, because he filled the space again with a slow step. My heart picked up speed. I was trapped in every way possible. I was trapped against this bookcase, I was trapped in Owen's gaze, and I was helplessly trapped by my legs, which I was sure couldn't move no matter how much I willed them to.

He tipped his head closer and his gaze dropped slowly from my eyes to my mouth.

I couldn't breathe.

"Would a kiss suffice?" he asked in a low voice.

Chills spread all over me and my heart skipped what felt like several beats. My face was consumed by heat. My eyes flickered to his lips, missing their usual smile. "What?" I stammered.

He made a sound—a deep, quiet laugh. "I can guess by the color of your cheeks that you heard me perfectly the first time."

His lips were grinning now.

I tore my gaze up to his eyes with a scowl that was meant to berate him. My face burned hotter and my heart skittered wildly. My throat was suddenly very dry, and I was left completely incapable of speech.

Then I remembered that my brothers were sitting in the corner near the door, and I felt a fresh wave of embarrassment. I moved my gaze around Owen to my brothers across the room. To my relief, they were still completely engrossed with their pies.

Owen turned his head ever so slightly backward, in my brothers' direction, as if he had read my mind. Then he looked at me again and drew a slow breath that was mixed with a low chuckle. "Oh, yes. I forgot that we had an audience. Perhaps you ought to settle for your second choice of payment then. Or we can reserve the kiss for another time."

I swallowed hard and shot him the sharpest glare I could manage. I was certain that I had never felt this unsettled in my entire life.

He laughed lightly. "I should expect to be called atrocious at any moment now."

It was impossible not to smile at that. And that smile may have been what stopped Owen from hearing how loudly my heart was beating. I couldn't let him hear it and know how severely he affected my normally quiet heart.

He took a deep breath and quickly became serious again. "Your second choice then. Tell me what you want."

My mind raced. The question was absurd. I didn't need anything from him, and I didn't want anything from him. I couldn't gather a single thought into words, so I decided that I needed to look away from his penetrating eyes. It was the only available solution I could think of. So I sneaked my gaze off of his face and looked around his shoulder, searching frantically for an idea. My eyes caught on the little table near the fire, and the sketchbook that rested on top of it.

"Willowbourne," I blurted, darting my gaze back to Owen. His eyes widened in surprise, then his brow contracted. Realizing how that sounded, I tried to recover and said, "I mean . . . you."

He raised his eyebrows. A grin pulled on his lips.

My face burned again, and my thoughts were whirling around in my skull so fast that I could hardly grasp onto one. "I mean . . . ," Taking advantage of the opportunity, I slid around him and walked to the table and picked up the sketchbook. My hands shook as I quickly flipped through the sketches and found the one of Willowbourne and its many windows and hexagonal pond. I held it up and pointed at the page. "*You* go back to Willowbourne. You can repay me by going back to visit Willowbourne."

I didn't know what I was saying, but it seemed to take Owen completely by surprise. He stayed where he was and looked at me, a twinge of regret in his expression.

"You told me that it was like home to you," I said. "And you haven't been there for years. I saw it, you know. I saw it on my way to the village."

His expression was suddenly all curiosity. "What did you think of it?"

"It was beautiful. Breathtaking, even."

His face lit up at my words and he walked over to me. He took the book in his hands and stared at the sketch. His eyes flashed with sadness and regret and fear all at once. Was I asking too much of him? I promptly dismissed the worry. If he agreed, this payment would not be easy for him, but I was sure he would be glad afterward. And I couldn't deny that there was something malicious inside of me that looked at this situation as an opportunity for revenge. Answering his questions for his payment was certainly not easy for me. So asking this of him would only level the game a bit.

When he looked at me again, there was a spark of suspicion. "Why do you want me to do this?"

I smiled a little. "Because I can see how much you love it. And if the past is what is keeping you away, then go. Because the past is powerless unless you grant it power. And it can do so much harm with that power. It can haunt and frighten and deceive. But the past is completely insignificant next to the present. And if you continue giving it power to haunt you, it always will."

When I finished speaking, I was overwhelmed with a sense of melancholy. I didn't know where that speech came from, but it cut me straight to the core. And Owen was looking at me with such a strange expression that I had to look down. Then, in a sudden jolt, I knew I couldn't stay in here any longer. I needed to leave. So I forced a smile and said, "Just consider it." Then I turned and left the library, feeling like the biggest hypocrite alive.

When I got to my room, I sat down on my bed, a pinch of ache in my heart. What was happening to me? Why were my emotions running so wildly today? With a sigh, I lay down, and stared at the ceiling—stared at nothing. I wished I could also feel nothing, but my wishes would not prevail. My wishes never prevailed. I could sense a change occurring within me, and it was strong and persistent, like the bite of a broken promise. No matter what I tried, it wouldn't leave me alone.

Taking a deep breath, I tried to clear my head. Surely I could think of nothing and feel nothing if I really focused. I gave up after a few seconds. To focus on nothing was nearly as impossible as it was to reverse this change within me.

*No.* I sat up, halting my thoughts. *No.* I could and would and must reverse this change. I was master over my emotions, over my heart. It was not a question. And if being around Owen had given my heart this false sense of independence, then I was glad Miss Lyons was arriving tomorrow. Because then he could toy with her heart, not mine. I could easily stay away from him. *Yes.* That is what needed to happen. I needed to stay away from him. No more laughing to the point of tears, no more games. If I had to lose Owen in order to properly manage my heart, then that is what I would do.

I stopped myself. I wasn't losing Owen. He was never mine. And he couldn't be mine. I had made a promise to my parents and to myself, and I didn't intend to break it. I could not allow myself to be distracted from my responsibility toward my brothers. They had nothing—no one—but me, and already I had allowed my heart to slip, to focus on something besides my sweet little brothers and what they needed. How would Mama and Papa see me now? How greatly would they disapprove? The thought sickened me. Owen could not replace my brothers in my affections. His time could not become more important than theirs. I could not love him and love them properly all at once. I feared my heart wasn't capable of such a thing.

I wanted to sit in this room and stare at nothing. Because this was a place of order, of rightness. Not that warm library with that secretive, teasing man and his piercing eyes and golden hair. If I was going to leash my heart properly, it would have to be as far away as possible from Owen Kellaway. And that is precisely where I intended to put it. My wishes may have never prevailed, but my intentions always did.

I hardly slept that night, and restlessness pulled me from my bed the moment the sun touched my window. Today was the day that everyone would arrive. Today was the day I would reclaim control over my heart. *And today was the day I would begin staying away from Owen.* The firm thought sent a heavy stone of ache to thud in my chest. It beat at my ribs like a thousand barbed fists. But I held onto it, hoping that maybe it could replace my heart all together, hoping that it could whisk away every emotion into its hard, stony walls before I could discover a way to feel them.

Lizzie came in early to help me get ready, and I couldn't help but notice how distant she still seemed, as if she was still afraid of something. I could tell by the way her eyes darted and how her voice shook. I watched her carefully, trying to decipher something—anything from her movements. But it was impossible. And I knew she wouldn't tell me anything, so I didn't even bother asking. And at any rate, my throat was much too tight for words. There were too many other matters on my mind.

After Lizzie left the room, I lingered a moment in the ivory chair before the mirror and listened to the birds outside my window. Their chirps held notes—high, resonating sounds—but when they merged together, they held no melody. They were like lonely pieces of sound searching for a place to belong among the bushes and trees and endless grey morning sky. Their noises entered my ears, scratching at my soul with fear and wonder. I was weak, and I hated myself for it. I wished that I could stay in this chair forever and not have to see what awaited me on the main floor.

My gaze was pulled to the mirror, to my face and my wavy hair, lost between light and dark. There was a glint in my eyes as unmistakable as the breath I held in my lungs. Determination and unwavering resolve cried out in that glint, and seeing it gave me the last burst of strength I needed. So taking a slow exhale, I began mentally assembling my defenses, piece by piece, layer after layer, from my head to my toe to my heart. Until I was sure that even the deepest pair of blue eyes couldn't pierce it.

"Blasted boy!" I heard exclaimed as I stepped onto the cold marble of the main floor. I stopped, bewildered. Mrs. Kellaway was running in an almost violent fashion from the drawing room, still in her nightdress, with tight curlers wrapped atop her head. "He ran off without a care about seeing his own brother, sister, and father welcomed?" She stopped running abruptly and pressed the back of a hand against her forehead.

Grandmother stood near, and placed an austere glance on her daughter. "Now, Catherine. In my opinion, mind you, the boy may have finally come to his senses. And I might add, given the newfound circumstances, he should have visited a long while ago, if only to keep himself acquainted with the place."

I felt a keen urge to turn around before I was seen watching and listening. I felt that the conversation was not meant for my ears. And the sight of Mrs. Kellaway running around in her nightdress was certainly not meant for my eyes. My thoughts were confirmed by the sharp glance Mrs. Kellaway threw to silence Grandmother when she spotted me at the base of the staircase. I hurriedly put on an apologetic expression, but Grandmother welcomed it with a smile that was meant to dismiss the situation as ordinary.

"Good morning, my dear. Aren't you up early? You look lovely. Let us take a turn around the house to the morning room, shall we?" Her words came very quickly, and her arm was looped around mine before I could say a word.

She nearly dragged me around the corner and down the hall before I finally asked, "What is wrong?"

She didn't answer until she had steered me through the door of that cursed morning room. She was surprisingly strong. She let go of my arm and sat down with a sigh. A huffed breath began her words. "Owen ran off to Willowbourne late last night." She threw her hands in the air. "Heaven knows why."

I couldn't hide my disbelief. Or my smile. I quickly dashed it away, but not before Grandmother noticed it. "Well, it is very nice to see that someone agrees with me. I have been hoping he would return for years. He didn't choose the greatest time to leave, to be sure, but whatever it was that pushed him out the door must have been sent by angels."

I barely caught her sly smile and wink.

She placed a wrinkled, bony hand around mine and looked up at me. I thought I saw tears in her eyes. "Thank you, my dear."

I opened my mouth to deny my involvement, but she stopped my words by looking down at her hand on mine and shaking it gently. "You are a truly magnificent person, and have been a sure blessing to everyone in this home. To everyone within the realm of your life, of that I am most certain." She glanced up at me then, and a little smile tugged her heart-shaped lips into their telltale purse. She clucked her tongue and shook her head. "I have never seen a boy so helplessly smitten."

I shot her a questioning look, but before I could inquire as to her meaning, the door burst open and Mrs. Kellaway stood panting, combing her hair with her fingers. "A carriage just pulled up the drive! Mother, go to the door and greet them, if you would, please. Thank you kindly."

She was about to turn around when she flashed me a wide smile. "And congratulations, Annette, I was most pleased to hear the news! We all knew it was only a matter of time." Then she disappeared around the doorframe in a swish of white gown and auburn hair.

What news? I was beyond confused. I blinked, swallowed my nerves, and followed Grandmother from the room, trying to comprehend what I had just learned: Owen is at Willowbourne. Miss Lyons is waiting in the carriage, and Owen is away at Willowbourne. A strong surge of relief galloped through my chest.

We stopped behind the butler in the entry hall, just as a group of footmen descended upon the carriage. I felt strange, waiting to greet others into their own home, but Mrs. Kellaway was busily being made ready, and she was the hostess. I adjusted my gown and smoothed my hair. Nervousness fluttered violently in my stomach. I straightened my posture, and peered out one of the front windows.

Through the warped glass, between the metal frames, I could see two ladies being escorted up the drive on the arms of two footmen. One I recognized as Alice from the portrait gallery. She had the same auburn hair as her mother, and it reflected copper in the morning sun like a new penny. I remembered her faintly from my short visit ten years ago, but Owen tended to be a bit more memorable. The other, I knew, must be Miss Lyons, but I didn't get a complete look at her until the door swung open.

My ears were instantly greeted by the sound of shrill laughter. Sunlight and floral scents wafted through the door, then a head crowned with pale, golden hair, and a set of large, thoughtful eyes came into view. Miss Lyons had her arm looped through Alice's and they laughed together as if sharing a secret joke.

My stomach dropped. Her skin was a milky, clear, white, without a blemish to be seen. Her hair was thick and smooth and fair. Her eyes were an icy blue. A sharp pang of inferiority stabbed me like a knife. It was no longer a question why Owen had fallen in love with her. *Owen had fallen in love with her.* The thought sent a cold, bitter string of ache to wrap around me. I had nothing to do but stare, and wait to be awkwardly noticed.

Alice saw her grandmother first, and ran toward her for a hug. After she pulled away, her eyes caught on me for the first time, and her brow scrunched together in confusion. I mustered up a bleak smile. Awkward silence hung in the air, making my face warm.

"This is Miss Annette Downing," Grandmother said, coming to my rescue, "a dear friend. She and her young brothers are visiting for the summer."

Alice's face dawned with understanding and her lips curved into a smile. But not before I saw her exchange a quick look with Miss Lyons. "It is wonderful to meet you! We don't often have visitors. My name is Miss Alice Kellaway, the daughter of your hostess, but you may call me Alice."

I smiled at her familiarity. "And you may call me Annette. I visited here once ten years ago. We met as children."

"Hmm. I don't seem to remember . . . ,"

"I was the girl that fell from the tree," I said, smiling.

She laughed. "Oh, yes! How droll you are!" I noticed that her eyes were warm and friendly just like her mother's and were the color of burnt honey. She turned and looped her arm through Miss Lyons's arm again, and pulled her forward. "Grandmother, Annette, this is my dearest friend, Miss Charlotte Lyons."

Miss Lyons dropped an elegant nod. "A pleasure," she said, her voice as milky smooth as her skin. When she raised her head, I was met by her icy blue eyes and a close-lipped smile. "How long have you been staying here?" It was a simple question, but her eyes betrayed deep interest. I wondered why.

"Nearly a fortnight."

Her lips still held their smile, but her eyes flashed with surprise. "Mmm . . . how delightful."

She turned toward Grandmother and greeted her with a bit more enthusiasm, and I watched, feeling that knife of inferiority digging deeper into my skin. Her posture didn't slouch for even a second, and her voice was steady, smooth, and convincing. And when she laughed, it wasn't shrill and cutting like her mother's. It was soft and tinkling like a bell.

She clasped her hands together in front of her and looked from side to side, then beckoned Alice forward with a look. "Where are the others?" she questioned, raising a delicate eyebrow.

She asked the question with no particular address, and for some reason, I felt inclined to answer. "Mrs. Kellaway will be with us in a moment, Mr. Everard is in the library, I believe, my brothers are in their room, and Ow—er—Dr. Kellaway is away for the time being." I watched with suppressed amusement as the smile fell from Miss Lyons's lips.

She jerked her gaze to Alice, who raised her own eyebrow. "Where is he?" she asked, looking at her grandmother.

"He is away at an estate . . . one that he has not visited for a long while." Grandmother said, throwing her a look full of hints. Apparently Alice understood, because her face lifted with disbelief and delight at once.

"When did he leave?" The disbelief was displayed in her voice.

"Late last night."

Alice's jaw dropped and she exhaled sharply. She shook her head. "I just cannot comprehend it!" She smiled, looked heavenward, and closed her eyes, as if absorbing everything she had just heard. "I never would have expected that. At least not until . . . ," Her voice trailed off, and she looked at Miss Lyons with raised brows. Then they both erupted into tinkling laughter. I thought it must have been that secret joke again.

Miss Lyons's face turned wistful with longing. "I am very anxious to see him. Will he return soon?"

The look on her face and the tone of her voice gave me a strong urge to roll my eyes.

Grandmother scowled briefly, then tipped her head to the side and flashed a smile. "No. We haven't any idea when he will be returning. It could be as much as a fortnight." Her brow contracted. "Or was it a month?"

Miss Lyons and Alice shared a dismayed look. Grandmother shrugged, and I could see a little grin breaking through her act. "Why so distraught, dears?"

Miss Lyons smoothed a perfect hand over her hair. She cleared her throat. Even that sounded elegant. "Oh, I am grand, do not worry. I have only missed him terribly, and hoped to see him sooner than that." She released a dramatic sigh that would put Lizzie to shame.

Grandmother shook her head slowly, as if deeply upset. "I am sorry to hear that." She placed a hand lightly on my shoulder, and gave me a look of long-suffering. I caught a twinkle in her eyes before she turned her head back to Miss Lyons. I was sure it was a mischievous one. It terrified me.

"Because," she said with wide eyes, "if you are expecting an offer of marriage, you must know that Owen has already offered for Miss Annette, here."

# Chapter 15

A fierce wave of shock rolled through my stomach. I jerked my head to Grandmother. She was grinning at me, and gave me a quick nod, as if encouraging me to play along with her ridiculous charade. I was completely dumbfounded. What was the matter with her? She was clearly losing her mind. I was sure of it now. I remembered how she had been present in the morning room for tea the day before, when Lady Pembury had spoken of Owen's attachment to her daughter.

When I moved my gaze to the two elegant ladies in front of me, I saw Alice staring at me with round eyes and a hand over her mouth. Miss Lyons watched me with downturned brows and compressed lips. And a challenge.

"I—um . . . ," I struggled for words that would deny what Grandmother had said, but I was hopelessly mute, and could not think clearly for my life.

"She is very sorry for the misunderstanding," Grandmother inserted with quick precision. "She has a thing . . . a bit of memory loss. Bless her." She turned her gaze to me and placed her other hand on my other shoulder. "Remember? Owen offered for you and you accepted nearly a week ago?"

I was completely appalled. I was certain that Grandmother was the only one struggling with memory loss. She winked. I scowled with a look that said *have you lost your mind?*

Apparently she had. "Oh, yes, of course you remember!" She patted my cheek, then grasped my arm and pulled me away, while yelling over her shoulder, "We are going to fetch your mother, Alice!"

I tried to wrench my arm free, but was again completely surprised by how strong Grandmother was. And perhaps I was weakened by the shock of what had just happened.

She let go of my arm once we were out of earshot. I found myself able to speak again, and in a voice just above a whisper, said, "I am not engaged to Owen!"

"Yes, yes, I know that." She waved a hand in the air as if swatting unseen flies.

I jerked back. "Then why—"

"Because," she interrupted, "I thoroughly despise Georgiana Lyons, that is why." A little hoot escaped her pursed lips. "You must play along. Please."

I was still confused. "What does your dislike of Lady Pembury have to do with me being . . . ," I lowered my voice, "'engaged to Owen'?"

Grandmother huffed then looked at me as if I was the most daft person in the world. "If we can convince Miss Lyons that you are engaged to Owen, then she will surely leave immediately, and her mother may not have the satisfaction of having a daughter married to one of the wealthiest men in town."

I was now even more confused. "Owen is a doctor!" I reminded her, my voice leaping above my strained whisper. "He is not wealthy. His elder brother will inherit everything."

She sighed, and after a prolonged moment of silence, said, "I should not be telling you this, but I believe you should know if you are going to go along with my plan."

I scowled. "But I—"

Grandmother raised a hand to stop my words. I folded my arms, trying to hold my anger inside. "Owen had a cousin," she said. "Theodore. They were the dearest of friends. Did Owen tell you about him?"

I nodded.

"He passed away, as you must already know, and Owen stopped returning to Willowbourne. Well, Owen's uncle, master of Willowbourne, has passed away recently. It was a terrible shock.

But with no other sons, who do you suppose he left his living to in his will?"

Realization crashed over me. It all made so much sense! How could I have missed it?

"Owen," I said. Saying his name aloud sounded like complete truth to my ears, and I scolded myself for not realizing it sooner. A feeling of resentment settled between my hot anger and confusion. Why hadn't Owen told me? I had convinced him to revisit the place and he hadn't even told me the truth.

Grandmother gave a tight-lipped nod. "Indeed. And that is why Miss Charlotte Lyons cannot have him. Her mother discovered the truth about Owen's inheritance when Alice let the news slip while she was dining with the family at Eshersed Park."

I raised an eyebrow. "Much like you just let the news slip to me?"

"Ah, but it is different. You will not spread the gossip around town or try to ensnare the poor boy." She grinned, reassured.

"But if Owen arrives and sees that everyone is under the impression that I am engaged to marry him, that is exactly what he will think. He will think that I am trying to ensnare him!" The truth of my words hit me hard with potent fear. That *could not* happen.

"Nonsense. I will take care of everything. Please play along. I beg you."

I shook my head, holding my stance. "No. I'm sorry. But you must tell them the truth."

"I cannot." Her voice was firm, losing its giddy tone.

"Then I will." I held her gaze with defiance that I didn't feel. "The truth will come out no matter how long you delay it. Willowbourne isn't far from here. Owen could be back as soon as tonight." The fear in my stomach punched at me. I swallowed and wiped my sweaty palms down my skirts. "What about your daughter?"

Grandmother grinned, not the least bit distressed. "I have already informed her."

"Of what?"

"Your engagement, of course."

My jaw dropped. That was the "news" Mrs. Kellaway had congratulated me for! Shaking my head, I put my face in my hands, trying to somehow hide from my predicament.

"Now, now, no need to despair. As soon as Miss Lyons leaves, I shall confess to my scheme."

I parted my hands. "What if, perchance, Owen arrives prior to Miss Lyons's leave?" I said, reminding her of the most glaring issue.

Grandmother threw out a hand, scrunching up her face. "Nonsense. She will be out the door before we know it."

I couldn't believe this was happening. My legs had begun shaking, and my hands were still sweating against my face. "No. I am not doing this. It's completely absurd. I'm going to tell them the truth right now."

Then I planted my hands on my hips, turned around, and walked away, promising myself to never trust an old woman ever again. Especially one with a mischievous side.

I may have told Grandmother a bit of a lie. I was not going to tell everyone the truth straight away. I was actually heading straight to my bedchamber to curl up in my bed and try to calm myself and try to disappear. My thoughts were running far too wildly for me to trust them, and I didn't trust myself to speak. It would only make the situation worse in my current state.

Walking with hurried steps, I stepped back into the entry hall, now empty, and started up the spiral staircase. Anger vented through my huffed breaths, quickening my pulse, and clouding my mind with heat. How dare Grandmother put me in this situation? How dare she expect me to play along without any remorse? I shook my head and cursed Grandmother under my breath.

When I reached the second floor, I nearly collided with Mrs. Kellaway who stood just around the corner at the top of the staircase, talking with Alice and Miss Lyons. I let out a little shriek as I tried to avoid them. Thankfully I skirted around all three before anyone could be knocked to the ground by the force of my steps.

Mrs. Kellaway's eyes flew open wide and she gasped, placing a hand to her chest. "Good heavens, you gave me a fright!" Then she laughed, chest heaving as she caught her breath.

"I'm sorry," I said in a glum voice. My little escape plan was now completely foiled. I was standing right before the three misinformed people that needed to know I wasn't truly engaged to Owen. And I had to be the one to tell them. There was no delaying it now. My jaw set as I locked eyes with Miss Lyons, who looked as frightened as Mrs. Kellaway, her cool blue eyes round, her perfect lips parted.

I wished I could shoot her a glare that would make her even more frightened, but I stopped myself. She had given me no reason to dislike her, but for some reason, I already knew we would not be close friends. Ever. And I knew the truth would do nothing but please her, so a tiny part of me didn't want to tell it.

I scolded myself for thinking that way, and pushed aside the nervousness and fear within me. There really was nothing to worry about. I could easily make certain they knew it was Grandmother who was responsible for all this.

When I took my next deep breath, it came out as a shudder. I wiped my sweaty palms on my skirts. *Go! Say it!* I encouraged myself. I tried to plan my words in my head before I spoke, something I was never very good at.

*I am not engaged to your son,* I rehearsed. *I am sorry for the misunderstanding. Your mother is an old, mischievous dolt who finds pleasure in torturing me.*

I was pulled from my thoughts when Mrs. Kellaway grasped my hands in hers. I hadn't even noticed her step closer, or seen her expression change. Her blue eyes were misty and her voice cracked when she said, "I am just so happy to know that you will be my daughter-in-law. I couldn't have dreamed Owen would choose someone as wonderful as you, Annette. I have never seen him happier than he has been since you arrived here."

Her words sounded genuine, and they burned me from within. Something else must have made Owen happy, because there was no chance that it could have been me.

But still, her words lingered in the air between us and I just stood there, staring at her tears of joy, staring at my hands that shook in hers, at Alice and her unreadable expression, and at Miss Lyons with her bristled stare.

I felt sick. I felt deceived and trapped and despised. Owen did not propose to me! He did not want me! He didn't love me. He loved Miss Lyons. And every accusatory, loathsome look she wanted to cast my way was completely justified. I tried to imagine myself in her situation. If I were in love with someone, only to find that he was being taken away by someone else, would I glare at that person? Probably.

Mrs. Kellaway squeezed my hands, stopping their shaking and pulling me from my rambling thoughts yet again. "Thank you," she said in an airy voice. "As soon as Owen returns, we shall begin wedding preparations." She released my hands then, and gave her eyes a final wipe.

I wanted to scream, but I didn't get the chance. Mrs. Kellaway's mouth broke into a huge smile, and she motioned toward Alice and Miss Lyons. "Have you met my daughter and her friend?"

"Yes," I said curtly, managing a stiff smile.

She seemed to recognize the awkwardness of the situation between Miss Lyons and me, because her smile dropped suddenly. Silence hung in the air again, so I made a firm decision that I needed to act before I was interrupted. My heart was racing and I was sure it was only a matter of seconds before I vomited or fainted. Or perhaps both, so I needed to get the words out as quickly as possible.

"I didn't mean for this to happen," I blurted.

Mrs. Kellaway looked a question at me.

I took a deep breath and tried not to look at Miss Lyons. "I'm not—"

My words were halted by the echo of hurried feet along with the sound of Peter's panicked voice. "Annette! Charles is stuck!"

I whirled around just in time for Peter to grab my arm. His face was wet where tears had smeared across his freckled cheeks. He sniffed and tugged me in the direction of their room.

I quickly excused myself with a fleeting glance at Mrs. Kellaway, who looked stricken with shock and worry, and ran after Peter down the hall. As we approached my brothers' room, the soft, dull sound of muffled cries reached my ears. When I stepped through the door, with the sobbing Peter behind me, I looked around the room frantically, trying to follow the sound with my eyes.

"Where is he?" I asked.

Peter raised a shaking finger in the direction of a short, wooden cabinet with two cupboards and a Charles-sized drawer at the bottom. "W-we just wanted to s-see if he would fit, but the drawer g-got stuck," Peter sobbed.

"Charles is in *there*?" I asked in disbelief, running toward the cabinet. I squatted down in front of the little drawer, whimpers and sobs reaching my ears from inside it.

Wasting no time, I grabbed the handle and pulled back with a jerk. But the drawer was, indeed, stuck. I tried the same method, again, and again, each time with renewed vigor. I dug my fingers behind the corners of the drawer and attempted to pry it open. It wouldn't budge.

Panic set in wholly, making my heart thud in my chest and blood rush past my ears. A sick feeling of dread sent chills tingling down my neck. There was no entrance for air in that drawer. Charles could suffocate within minutes.

My breath came in shallow gasps, and I tried the handle again, pulling with all my strength. It didn't succumb. I pulled again on the handle, prying with my fingers, wishing desperately for strength beyond my own weak arms and tired fingers. I repeated these futile attempts for several minutes, hating the sound of Charles's desperate cries, but I wasn't strong enough.

My mind reeled, struggling for an idea. The air was surely expiring in that drawer and I didn't know how to open it. I paced in front of the drawer, tugging on the handle vigorously each time I passed it. My rattled breathing and galloping heart were the only sounds I could hear.

*The only sounds I could hear.* I stopped, panic and cold, raw terror scratching over me with icy fingers.

The crying had stopped.

My breath caught in my chest. Never before had silence had its own sound—its own deafening, sickening sound.

"Charles! Charles!" I yelled, shaking the cabinet now, kicking it, doing anything I could to loosen the drawer. My hands shook, my legs shook, everything shook. The room seemed to be shaking too. "Charles!" My voice shook.

I racked my brain for options, but there was no place for rational thought. I threw myself against the cabinet, grasping the handle in desperation. I got a firm hold, and jerked backward with all my might. A sharp *bang* cut through the air as the drawer jarred open. Scrambling forward, I looked inside—even though I was afraid of what I would see. Of what I would know. I saw his blond curls first, strewn across his forehead. He lay curled more tightly than I would have thought possible, his hands twisted beneath him, his knees tucked to his chin. I saw his long lashes, curling up from his eyelids that lay closed. His lips were parted slightly, an illusion of breathing. But he did not breathe. He did not make a sound.

A lump tightened my throat, and my chest constricted. I tried to draw breath, but it was like pulling a single thread from an intricate piece of embroidery—taxing and extensive, and not worth the struggle. I was helplessly paralyzed before the sight of my little Charles, white, motionless, and quiet.

But I needed to move. Now.

So reaching inside the drawer, I pulled him out, hooking my trembling hands under his arms. Then I fell back, hugging his limp form to my body. I held him in my arms, cradling his head. He was so small. So young. Too young to die. Something inside of me was crumbling, and it hurt me like a physical blow.

"Charles! Charles!" It was all I could say. I shook him, as if hoping to wake him. My voice cracked, my heart broke, and I almost cried. My fingers found their way to his neck, to the spot just beneath his jaw where a doctor had once checked me. Pressing two fingers against his neck, I froze.

A powerful surge of hope pounded through me. I felt a pulse. A slow, soft pulse almost too discreet to notice. I kept my fingers there, not wanting to abandon the feeling of his heartbeat. Then I saw his chest rise with a broken breath. I gasped with delight.

His eyelids fluttered, twitched, and opened. He gulped for breath, and a new tear leaked from his eye.

I slumped with relief, convinced that I had never truly known relief until this day, and kissed his round cheek, his little nose. I wiped the tear from his temple and took his face in my hands. His eyes were wide, dazed, and alive. That was all I cared about.

"Do not ever do that again." I gasped, still shaking.

"But—but Peter didn't think I could fit, and I knew I could fit, so I had to prove it." His voice was quick, soft, and slightly raspy. And it was my favorite sound in the world.

"Promise me right now that you will never try to prove you can fit in anything ever again. Even if you are certain that you can."

He looked worried, as if noticing my distress for the first time. "I promise."

I pulled his head onto my shoulder and rocked him in my lap, squeezing him tightly to make sure he was still there, and that he could still breathe.

From behind me, I heard Peter step up beside me, worry crossing his face for a brief moment as his gaze found his brother. I had nearly forgotten he was here. "Charles?" he said in a tentative voice.

Charles lifted his head from my shoulder and twisted to look at Peter. A smug grin lifted his lips. "I told you I could fit."

A little laugh escaped from me, transforming into hysterical laughter as it went. I couldn't control it. And I wasn't allowed to cry, after all. Laughter was the only way to achieve a sense of release. Peter and Charles stared at me blankly for several seconds before erupting into their own familiar giggles. I felt so much relief and joy that all other dilemmas were pushed aside. I didn't have to think about Owen or Miss Lyons or the mischievous Grandmother. I could focus on my little brothers, and how grateful I was to have them. To love them, and to be loved by them. It was all my heart wanted.

I didn't hear Mrs. Kellaway enter the room until she was directly behind me. Her voice was laced with a hint of panic. "Is he all right?"

I turned my head in her general direction, but was too drained of energy to rotate completely around. Smoothing my hand over Charles's sweat-dampened curls, I nodded.

When I heard no response, I forced myself to turn around. Miss Lyons and Alice stood in the doorway, Miss Lyons chewing a dainty fingernail.

As I looked up at Mrs. Kellaway, she met my gaze with furrows of concern in her brow. She knelt down beside me, and the only sound heard was the fabric of her gown brushing the marble.

"What happened?" she asked, apparently sensing the weight of the situation.

I relayed the details to her briefly, which led to many gasps and heavy exhalations. Saying everything aloud made my previous urge to laugh disperse to nothingness. It was real. I had almost lost Charles. Again, a river of relief cascaded through me as I squeezed him even tighter. He was alive! And to try to comprehend the alternative was unbearable.

After a few minutes, Mrs. Kellaway, her daughter, and Miss Lyons left the room, leaving me to my thoughts and the giggles of my brothers. A tightness gripped my stomach as I remembered everything.

I was still helplessly trapped in Grandmother's scheme. I had missed the perfect chance to set things straight.

But right now, my opportunity was gone. The only way to console my nerves was to find something else to do, somewhere else to be—something else to think about. And I knew the perfect distraction, the perfect thing.

# Chapter 16

The stables smelled of wood and animals and every scent that comes with them. After I made certain that Peter and Charles were entertained in Grandfather's company, I sneaked out to the stables to see the horses and maybe even ride one. Eve stood in her stall, her black coat gleaming like a lake in moonlight.

She whinnied heartily as I approached; her playful eyes and almost-smile turned my way. Dust motes floated visibly above me, seen only as rays of sunshine lit them through the two small windows. Scraps of discarded hay littered the ground around my feet.

I rubbed two of my fingers between Eve's eyes, thinking, trying to relax.

Scanning my surroundings for grooms or other people, thankfully, I found none. I needed to talk to someone, freely, without reservation. My gaze found Eve's dark eyes. That someone might as well be a horse. I scanned the stable one last time for anyone that may have a propensity for eavesdropping, then began talking.

I felt like a dolt pouring out my concerns and questions and fears to a horse. But it felt comfortable and relieving; I didn't have to worry about being judged. I told her about my aunt, and her requirements of my brothers. I told her about Kellaway Manor, and how at home I felt with these people and how I would soon have to leave. I told her about Owen, and how in love he was with Miss Lyons. My voice and heart felt heavy when I said that part. I considered asking her why, but I knew she wouldn't know the answer; not as clearly as I knew it now. The realization had been sneaking up on me, and now there was nothing left to hide it.

Owen was much more than a friend. I feared I had fallen in love with him.

But oh, how dearly I had tried not to. I leaned my elbow on the gate of Eve's stall and rubbed my forehead. Perhaps it wasn't too late. Perhaps I could forget him. There was still time before Owen returned. I could still turn my heart in the right direction. But the most pressing issue, the false engagement, led me to ramble on to the horse for another five minutes. I asked her what I should do about it. She didn't answer.

When I finished talking, the stable was thick with the silence that I had dispelled with my prattle. I felt a small sense of release, but not enough to be comfortable. The idea of a ride didn't sound quite as appealing as it had earlier, so I gave Eve one last stroke between her eyes and decided on a brisk walk instead.

The sun had its usual effect on me, warming my body and mind and clearing my head. The breeze ruffled my hair and whipped gently on my gown. *What was I going to do?* I repeated that question to myself, hoping that after so much repetition I could find an answer. What was I going to do? I wished the wind could speak to me. Surely the wind had the answer but its whispers were too hushed to be heard above the roar in my mind. It was an absurd thought, but it frustrated me nonetheless.

I was just passing the boundary of the lawn and stepping into the woods when he sneaked up on me.

His cold, sweat-slicked hand grasped my wrist with a firm hold. I cried out, lurched backward in the direction of the nearest tree, and was whipped around. Before I could cry out again, his hand was pressed firmly over my mouth.

"Hush," he snarled. "Be silent and I won't have to hurt you." His voice was rough, deep, and eerily calm, and I didn't recognize it. But his face I *did* recognize. It was the face of the strange man who had threatened Lizzie. And now he had come for me.

Thinking in a jolt, I twisted my face away from his hand and spit out its taste. His grip still held firm on my wrist, but I jerked my elbow backward, hitting his ribs with a direct blow. On impact he let out a small moan, bending at the waist, but his hold on my wrist remained steady. His dark eyes fell on my face and I was shocked to see they held amusement. He was laughing at me.

Wasting no time, his other hand tightened around my other arm, just above the elbow. In a swift motion he pulled me closer, so close that he could whisper in my ear.

"If I were you, mademoiselle, I wouldn't try that again."

Disgusted, I pulled backward, away from the wet breath of his words against my ear. I could see his face completely now—the angry glint in his eyes, the deep lines around his mouth, the sharpness of his cheekbones. Panic tightened a cord around my stomach. My heart beat so hard it hurt. I needed to get away before something terrible happened. There was something about him that screamed *terrible* in every sense of the word, and I didn't want to find out what it was.

My arms weren't free, but my feet were readily available. Using all my strength, I swung my leg forward, aimed at his knee. My foot made perfect contact. He instantly loosened his grip and reached for his knee, swearing under his breath.

Taking the split-second opportunity, I jumped backward and turned, nearly tripping on a tree root. I had only made it two steps before my arm was in his grasp again. This time his fingernails dug into my skin. His hands were cold and slick with sweat, but his grip was unfailing. He jerked me backward, toward him again, until I was looking into those terrible near-black eyes. But this time there was no laughter.

I was trapped. My mind reeled, but terror overtook too many of my senses to allow me any clear thought. "Owen!" I screamed just before the man had his hand over my mouth again.

What was I thinking? Owen wasn't here; he couldn't hear me. No one could hear me. I was completely alone.

"So you know Dr. Kellaway, hmm?" he asked. The hushed, careful tone of his voice hinted at hatred, and that same terrible thing that I didn't want to discover.

A feeling of dread dropped through my stomach. This man was no friend of Owen's. A sharp instinct told me to shake my head.

He dropped his hand from my mouth and used it to grip my other arm. He leaned his head down closer, twisted sideways, studying my face. "You know him," he said with a low chuckle. "You care for him."

The chuckling increased in volume until it verged on insane. My arms burned and stung in his unyielding grip. What did he want? The question burned in my skull with raw foreboding. I needed to get away. Now.

I quickly surveyed my surroundings—the thick mottled tree behind the strange man, the rocks at my feet, chunks of flat and round stone. I was a mere five feet from the edge of the woods, so I wouldn't have to run far to reach safer territory. I frantically searched for options, considering the idea of hitting him with a stone. It seemed to be the most promising thought yet, so I grasped on to it. I only needed a way to pick up a stone . . .

The laughter stopped so abruptly my heart jumped, severing my trail of thought.

A crazed smile spread his lips, showing his yellow teeth. "But does *he* care for you?" he asked. "Does he care for you like you care for him?"

The question was no longer intended to humor him. His eyes showed real curiosity. Which scared me even more than the actual question. My gaze darted to an oblong stone near my left foot. Without thinking, I stomped on his foot and ripped one arm free, reaching downward. He grabbed it again without wasting a second. With a sneer, he kicked the stones away from my feet, sending them at least ten feet deeper into the woods.

My heart sunk, then picked up speed. My only plan was ruined.

I glared at him through a loose strand of hair on my face. "What do you want?" I yelled as close to his ear as possible, hoping that the loud sound would give me an opportunity to jar my arms free.

He cringed, taking a step backward, but never loosening his solid grip. Anger was displayed all over the lines in his face, but surprisingly, he continued with the same question. "Does . . . he . . . care for you?"

My vision blurred as he squeezed my arm tighter. His question seemed irrelevant in so many ways. "Why do you want to know?" My voice was fierce, which I was quite proud of.

"Tell me. Now." He let one of my arms loose for a quick moment, pulling aside his jacket. A flash of menacing silver caught my eye.

A dagger.

Impossibly, my heart beat faster. "No."

"No?"

"No," I confirmed, feeling an unwarranted prick in my heart as I said the word.

He clenched his jaw, kicking the dirt with the toe of his boot, apparently frustrated. "Then who?" His voice rose. "Who does the monsieur love? What is the name of the lady that he is mad for, that he would give anything for? That he would die for?" Everything about his words screamed mockery, and I almost thought the crazed laughter would begin again.

Miss Lyons came to my mind immediately, but his intentions pertaining to her filled my mind with apprehension. Why did he want to know? He was mad. That was the reason, and I could see it in the gleam of his bloodshot eyes.

"Tell me! Or those you love will face the consequences."

My heart raced. Escape was my first priority, and I needed a way to distract him. "I think I know," I said.

He froze, willing me to proceed with a nod of his head. "Who is it?" I cringed as he tugged me closer. His rancid breath filled my nose but I resisted the urge to retch.

"What?" I asked, only half my thoughts on the conversation, the other half on escape possibilities. "Oh, yes, I know."

His face contorted with impatience, obviously leashing masses of anger. "Who?"

My heart beat loudly as I formulated a plan in my mind. His hands slid down my arms and tightened around my wrists. My hands quickly lost sensation.

"Tell me!" he repeated in a growl.

"Milba Durbin," I blurted without thinking, my eyes wide.

He froze. "Milba Durbin?"

"Yes. Miss Milba Durbin of Canterbury." I willed my nostrils not to flare as I repeated the lie.

He glanced upward at the trees with a look of victory on his face. This was the distraction, my split-second opportunity. Leaning back with all my weight, and trusting his tight grip on my wrists, I swung my legs upward and forward, slamming my feet into his torso.

I heard the sudden exhalation of air knocked out of his lungs, and the sound of his back crashing against the tree behind him. I fell as his hands slipped from my arms. Scrambling to my feet, I dove forward and ran.

I had never run so fast in my entire life. My feet slapped hard against the grass and I didn't look back until I reached the house. When I did, there was no sight of the man at the edge of the woods. I imagined him standing behind that tree that he slammed against, watching me. There was no way I could know if he was. The thought placed an icy shiver between my shoulders.

I did not go inside. I couldn't, not while I was so confused and scared and disheveled. I needed to make some sense of what had just happened. So I sat down with my back against the door, tucked my knees to my chest, and focused on my breathing. Who was that man? Why did he want to know who Owen loved? It was an absurd question, and to puzzle out its meaning was nearly impossible.

I put my face in my hands, wishing desperately for answers, for rest from this day that was so warm and beautiful. So deceitful. Too much had happened to me today. It was far too much to handle all at once and I felt at the edge of madness. Already a fierce headache buzzed against the back of my skull, begging me for answers that I didn't have. Those answers were what I wished for most desperately now, and I knew a person who could hopefully grant that wish.

Lizzie was walking out of the kitchen with another maid when I found her. I saw in her eyes a flash of worry that told me she knew why I had stopped her. Without protest, she followed me into the empty dining room where I planned to relay the entire story.

"What happened, miss?" Her eyes flashed with apprehension.

"The man that threatened you. He found me at the edge of the woods." I promised myself not to break eye contact. I needed her to feel an obligation to reveal what had truly happened that morning.

Lizzie's face paled. Silence filled the air for a long moment. "Are you hurt?" Her eyes darted to my upper arms, the color lingering pink, where his fingernails had left tiny red marks in a curved line.

"I am fine. But I need you to tell me what information he wanted from you. Please." I tried my best to plead with my eyes as well as my words.

Tears sprang instantly into her eyes, surprising me. "I didn't tell him, I swear it! I did not tell him anything."

"What? What did he want to know?"

She looked down and clasped her hands together, squeezing them tightly. I could hear her slow, careful breathing. It was as if she was still afraid to speak about it. I was about to repeat my question when she finally answered, in a hushed voice, "He wanted to know who Dr. Kellaway loved." She looked up then, a look of fear on her tear-streaked face. "He told me that he would abduct me, or—or murder me if I told anyone what he said. I'm sorry," she sobbed, putting her hands to her face, "I should have told you before."

My heart pounded. "Is that all he said?" I knew I sounded unsympathetic, but my curiosity couldn't be helped.

She dropped her hands. "Well, he said something about the look on Dr. Kellaway's face when he does it. The revenge. But I don't know what he meant."

"What? Does what?" My mind was pulling me from all different directions, leaving me unbalanced.

Lizzie shook her head with small movements. "I don't know."

The word *revenge* burned in my ears. "Lizzie, we need to tell someone about this. We need to warn Owen."

The thought of something terrible happening to Owen filled me with a renewed sense of urgency. But he was at Willowbourne, and no one knew when he would be returning! I felt conflicted, lost between wanting him to hurry back so I could warn him about the man, and hoping that I would never have to face him again to explain why his entire family believed that we were engaged.

I leaned against a chair for support, feeling a sudden lightness in my head. Black splotches filled my vision in angry bursts.

"Miss? Miss, are you all right?" The words swam like water in my ears. The room spun, a blurry swarm of wood and glass and fine decorations and a girl with dark hair. I didn't want to faint. Fainting was for people that were weak, and I was not weak. Was I? My hand slipped from my support, and thankfully all consciousness fled before I hit the ground.

I awoke to the smell of rosemary and a pair of icy blue eyes. It took several seconds and dozens of blinks against the sudden light to wholly absorb my surroundings. I was laying on the recamier in the drawing room next to the window. The new sense of warmth from the late afternoon sun dispelled the prick of cold on my arms, giving me a strange feeling that I was wrapped in a blanket. A dainty hand held the potent rosemary smelling salts beneath my nose. The dainty hand and the icy blue eyes belonged to Miss Lyons.

"She's awake!" The exclamation brought the sound of hurried steps to my ears. Mrs. Kellaway, Alice, Grandmother, Grandfather, and two men I did not fully recognize came into view above me. Then Charles's dimpled grin and Peter's twinkling eyes appeared above me like two precious gifts.

"You fell down."

"And then you slept for a very long, long, long time."

"And then your eyes just opened."

I knew it was my brothers talking, so I laughed, even though I could hardly decipher their words. Slowly inching my arms to each side of me, I pressed myself into a sitting position, wincing from the unexpected pain. My head throbbed, filling my ears with the sound of my heartbeat with every movement.

"How are you feeling?" This came from Mrs. Kellaway.

I found her face among the many peering down at me. I mustered a smile. "I have felt better." I was struck with a wave of embarrassment at the amount of attention that was focused on me, especially in my current state. "But I will be all right. Thank you," I added in a hurried voice.

Mrs. Kellaway put a gentle hand on my arm, then looked back at the others. "We had quite the scare this morning with Charles, here," she offered as explanation for my fainting. She went on to tell the entire story, filling me with an odd sense of dread—but for something that had already happened.

The older man I recognized as Mrs. Kellaway's husband, smiled down at Peter and Charles with a distance in his gaze that looked like old memories. Perhaps they were memories of his own sons as children causing mischief. His face was kind, wrinkled from years of laughter.

The younger man, Edmond, I recognized mostly from the portrait gallery. His eyes were striking, much like Owen's, and when he reached down to pat Charles's shoulder with a congratulatory grin, it reminded me of something Owen would do. The gesture made me want to scowl, tell him that Charles should not be encouraged, but I realized that since I had come here, smiling had become a much easier alternative.

"But little Charles is well now, thank heavens. That is what is important," Mrs. Kellaway finished.

A series of agreeing nods followed. "Let us get to introductions, then." She turned toward her husband and son with a broad, almost proud smile. Her eyes lit up like gems as she spoke. "Henry, Edmond, this is Miss Annette Downing, a dear friend and future daughter in-law, as I have already shared with you, and these are her precious brothers, Peter and Charles."

I wanted to faint again. I wanted to scream, *I am not engaged to your son!* But mostly I wanted to slap the smile off Grandmother's face. I felt guilty for the thought, but it made me happy all the same. How much longer could this carry on? How could I tell the truth now? Grandmother needed to do it. I shot her a begging look, but she greeted it with a sly wink.

I had no idea how to react to that. My head hurt too much. All I could muster for words was, "A pleasure to meet you."

Then, remembering why I was here—what had led me to faint, I was filled with a sense of urgency. No matter what Lizzie wanted, it was past time to inform these people of their trespasser. But I didn't want anyone to fret over me. I glanced quickly at my arms and was relieved to see the redness was almost entirely faded already. Taking a breath, I chose my words carefully.

"I need to warn you of a potential threat." I said, focusing on the elder Mr. Kellaway in particular. "I have seen the same man twice wandering on your property. He threatened a maid and he questioned me about Owen, but I don't know for certain of his intentions. But they aren't good, to be sure."

This caused a ripple of worried glances. "What do you suspect of his intentions?" Mr. Kellaway asked with no remnants of his warm smile.

I didn't know how to respond. But by the man's dagger and evil sneer and hatred in his voice when he spoke of Owen, I had a suspicion.

"I think . . . well, he had a weapon, so he could be intending to harm Owen or . . . or something worse." I had to swallow back the words that were too blunt for my own ears. *Could the man be intending to kill Owen?* I shook the thought from my head. It was poison to my already frail consciousness.

Mr. Kellaway stood, turning abruptly from his chair. "I am going to inform the servants of this. They must be watching for any unfamiliar person who steps onto my property and report the news to me." With a quick smile, he added, "And thank you, Miss Downing, for the wise precaution."

After Mr. Kellaway left, I felt strangely satisfied and relieved, which gave me permission to feel exhausted. Alice helped me to my room where I curled up between my cool, crisp blankets and fell asleep the moment my eyes closed. I had never slept so well in my entire life.

The heavy sheet of slumber didn't split for even a moment until the bright sunlight of morning shone through my eyelids, bringing my mind to attention. How many hours had I slept? It seemed to be late morning, and I had fallen asleep late the previous afternoon. That was a long time without checking in on Peter and Charles.

After dressing quickly, I raced downstairs and found them sitting on the bottom step, their giggles bouncing off the surrounding walls.

I sat down on the step just above them and leaned my head forward. "What would you like to do today, Mr. Atrocious and Mr. Mischievous?"

Charles seemed to respond more quickly than if I had called him by name, turning sharply and flashing me a grin. "Which one am I?"

"Hmm," I mused, feigning deep thought. "You are certainly Mr. Atrocious."

He scooted up a step so he sat beside me, then leaned back with a pensive expression. Then he smiled broadly, as if I had just flattered him beyond words.

"So I am Mr. Mischievous?" Peter asked, scooting up as well.

"Well, of course you are, Mr. Mischievous." I ruffled his hair. "And I would like to spend the entirety of this day with my two favorite little gentlemen."

The giggles resumed, and I almost audibly sighed. It was just what I needed. I needed everything to be the way it used to be. I needed to spend all day with my precious brothers and them alone. No wicked grandmothers, or elegant, haughty young ladies, or too-handsome gentlemen. My life was in control before I came here to Kellaway Manor. I knew who I was and what my sole purpose was—to care for my brothers. My heart understood its duties and obeyed me. It was strong.

But now, it was becoming frail and yielding and I needed to change that. I needed to make it understand what it must contain and what it can and cannot feel.

So today, I was to start by reminding my heart of what was important. And that was Peter and Charles, because they occupied the only two seats in my heart and they always would. My attention had been too scattered; I had been neglecting them. Never mind Aunt Ruth and her punishments; never mind that we were going back within a month. Peter and Charles had changed since we arrived here. They were becoming well-behaved little by little, but were still the same boys that I loved.

"When is Owen coming back?" Charles asked as I tucked him into bed that night.

I lifted the blanket over him and tucked it under his chin. "Probably soon." My stomach gave a rather hard plunge at the thought. But something inside me lifted at the same time. I didn't have the alertness to puzzle out what it meant.

"How soon? Will it be very soon?" Peter asked from his bed across the room.

I shrugged my shoulders. "I don't know."

They settled into their blankets with looks of disappointment. My heart melted a little. They missed him. And although I told myself not to, I missed him too. "Do you enjoy spending time with him?"

Charles nodded up at me, his head sinking into his pillow until just his round face peeked out from the plume. His eyelids drooped and his mouth stretched open in a quiet yawn. He smacked his lips and turned his head to the side. "It's like having a papa, I think."

My heart fell and I felt suddenly adrift and broken. We were going to have to leave this place eventually—my brothers were going to have to leave Owen. I didn't want to imagine how that would fragment their tiny hearts. They had grown too close to him. My heart thumped loudly as I remembered that I had too.

I let my gaze linger on their curled lashes and youthful faces and soft smiles waiting to dream. They deserved a life full of dreams that were not only dreamed, but also realized. I leaned over and placed a kiss on each of their foreheads. "Goodnight."

# Chapter 17

$\mathcal{I}$ was invited to practice embroidery in the drawing room with Alice and Miss Lyons the following afternoon, which was something that I had been trying determinedly to avoid. But for politeness's sake, I found myself outside the drawing room door at precisely two of the clock. I checked my warped reflection in the curve of the door handle and took a breath. Entering the room should not have required so much fortitude, but the prospect of polite conversation never failed to make me uneasy. Polite conversation with someone who didn't seem to like me much would be extremely difficult. And I had an inkling that Miss Lyons didn't like me above half.

I pushed open the door and entered hesitantly. Alice greeted me with a wide smile. "Annette! I was just telling Charlotte how you should be here soon, and now here you are! Come, sit and have some tea." She used the needle from her embroidery to point at the empty cushion of the sofa beside Miss Lyons. "Oh! And you must try one of these cakes. They have been a favorite of mine since my nursery days."

I smiled, relieved by her kindness, and moved toward the sofa.

"I have heard so much about you but have not spoken to you hardly at all," Miss Lyons said, turning to me as I sat down. "I must own that I would have been vastly disappointed had you not come to visit with us." Her smile never reached her eyes.

"I thank you both for thinking of me."

Miss Lyons reached for the cream pot on the tea table. She added three slow drops of cream to her cup and took a miniscule sip. "You must be so very lonely. It would seem that you don't have many friends, given your hapless situation." She lowered her voice. "I have heard a tale or two about your aunt. She sounds positively wicked! You poor, poor thing."

Something about the tone of her voice settled uncomfortably in my ears. I cleared my throat. "You shouldn't pity me, truly, I—"

"And you have not even been to town! To be deprived of such an experience would render me utterly heartbroken! I cannot comprehend the longing you must have for a season."

I pressed my lips together until she finished speaking. "Country life has always been my preference."

Her eyes rounded and she looked at me in the way a teacher might look at a pupil. "Town is full of many more wonders than you can imagine. But I don't expect you to understand its superiority over *country life* given your inexperience."

My mouth was very near hanging open. My cheeks tingled with a hint of shame.

"When I am married, all my pin money is going straight to London," Miss Lyons continued excitedly. "Parasols, fans, shawls, and all the lace and silken gowns I can afford. What do you think, Alice? Do you think my husband will allow me all these pretty things?"

Alice tapped her finger on her lap. "Perhaps." They shared a smile that looked like it held a secret. Then Alice looked at me and her expression turned inquisitive. "I'm curious about how your engagement to my brother came to be."

My stomach flipped. "Oh?"

"Was it love at first sight? I do adore anything romantic."

My eyes shifted to Miss Lyons, who was listening intently. Heat spread on my cheeks. An opportunity to reveal Grandmother's scheme was hovering over me. Heart pounding, I tried to plan my confession in my mind.

"Alice! You've made the poor thing blush!" Miss Lyons appeared to be barely concealing a catlike grin that could rival even her mother's. "Just tell us . . . how much time have you spent with him? I understand perfectly well how charming he can be. Those minutes can blend into hours without the passage of time being felt."

Why did I feel as though she already suspected the truth? My pride may have been bruised for a moment, but being called "poor thing" twice in one conversation was enough to cool my cheeks. I raised my chin and said, "From the moment I arrived we have spent nearly every hour of each day together. He insisted so."

Miss Lyons and Alice both seemed mildly surprised by my calm response. I was only relieved that it was actually honest.

"Politics and horses were surely common topics of conversation during those hours." Miss Lyons straightened the pendant at her neck, creating a disinterested pause. "You must have been acutely bored."

I shook my head and gave a theatrical sigh. "I cannot imagine ever being bored in Owen's company. I haven't yet, I assure you." It was another true statement that produced an amusing expression on Miss Lyons's face. I held back a grin.

She appeared to be searching her mind for another comment. "But you must have been rather starved for feminine conversation."

"Not at all. Owen is actually quite entertaining when he speaks of the latest rage in female fashion."

Both ladies raised their brows. I smiled contentedly and took a lemon cake from the tea tray. "Bonnets are of particular interest to him. Trims, ribbons, lace, we have discussed it all."

Alice released a girlish giggle. "Truly?"

My smile widened at the sound of her contagious laugh and I nodded. Owen and I had, in fact, discussed such things while riding one morning. My heart ached a little at the memory. There were few memories remaining that didn't hurt my heart in one way or another. It seemed that the memories that hurt the most were of moments I could never have again. And they were cruel, because those were the kind of memories that were impossible to forget.

Miss Lyons was very near glaring at me when I glanced her way again. Quickly, she cast me a smile. But I had seen the daggers. "I wonder," she said in a quiet voice, trailing off.

"Pardon me?"

She cleared her throat and arched an eyebrow as she stared at her cup. "I was just thinking . . . what have you to trade for the living Owen is providing you with at Willowbourne? I do not wish to offend, but your family is practically unheard of. Do you have a dowry?"

I sensed the makings of a trap. Tentatively, I answered, "I don't."

"Remarkable, isn't it, Alice?" She exhaled heavily and her eyes darted in my direction. "That he should choose to marry her for lack of all that."

My cheeks tingled with heat once again. Alice was beginning to look uncomfortable.

"I never thought him to be a romantic of any sorts. It is astonishing that he should overlook *so much* for the sake of his heart." Miss Lyons shook her head in false awe. She was very skilled at making one aware of one's flaws. But I did not need assistance to recognize how inept I was.

I pressed my lips together and stood. "This has been delightful, but I must see to my brothers."

Alice acknowledged me with a nod. I thought I saw an unspoken apology in her eyes. Stepping away from the sofa, I took two additional lemon cakes from the tray to save for Peter and Charles. There was one cake remaining, and Miss Lyons was staring quite possessively at it. So, in a sudden impulse, I swiped it off the tray from under her longing eyes.

Her cake-trance broke and she cast me a pointed look. Then it softened until there was only amusement and something like pity in her eyes. She already knew she had won the greater prize.

*Where did that come from?* I berated myself. I was not a contender for Owen's affections. I was falsely engaged to him—a very reliable friend. Yes. A trustworthy, kind, honest, fun, and charming *friend*. I stopped myself short. Listing his positive traits was not wise.

I released a tense sigh as I stepped out of the room. Anxious didn't even begin to describe how I felt. The thought of Miss Lyons discovering the truth about the counterfeit engagement was enough to make my stomach heave.

After I located my brothers, I wandered. Then I wandered again. Sitting still was not an option. I hadn't seen Grandmother at a time I could speak with her alone, so I kept one eye on the drive where Owen would arrive, pleading the heavens to keep him at Willowbourne just a bit longer, while at the same time wishing he would hurry back. The contradiction confused me, making me even more anxious. My hope was that Grandmother would confess before he arrived, but I suspected that her plan did not entail any sort of confession. Consternation quickened my pulse by the second.

When evening arrived, and everyone gathered in the drawing room, Grandmother dropped her piece of embroidery in her lap and proclaimed, "I miss my dear grandson. He must return soon or I shall topple over in this chair and die. Right here on the floor."

"Mother!" Mrs. Kellaway exclaimed.

"And what about poor Miss Annette? She must be out of her wits without him here!" Murmured agreements and light laughter followed.

I imagined myself stealing her needle and using it to embroider her mouth closed. But instead I just blinked and stared, numb to the mortification.

"Well, he should be home soon enough," she finished with a sigh.

After a few short minutes of light conversation, my heart leapt at the sound of locks clicking and boots scuffing and wind sliding through the doorway of a quiet house. The butler's voice boomed through the door and Owen's voice followed.

"Oh! That must be him!" Grandmother exclaimed, eyes wide and unaware of my distress. Or enjoying it.

Miss Lyons shifted her position on the settee. She smoothed her curls with one hand and pinched her cheeks discreetly with the other, leaving them rosy and perfect.

My stomach tied itself into a heavy knot and my heart felt on the brink of combustion. Quick footsteps turned and gained volume, matching the rate of my racing heart. I wiped my sweaty palms on my skirts, trying to invent an impossible plan.

Then I saw him, the first glimpse of his black coat and boots and his dark golden hair and easy smile. His eyes slid over the room and fell on me with a weight I couldn't explain. Then his smile grew and my breath stopped like a candle flame between wet fingers. I realized it had been three days since I had seen him, but it felt like a lifetime. My heart screamed at me, but I couldn't understand it.

Surely it was reminding me of what I already knew: that I was no match for Owen Kellaway.

Peter and Charles ran to him first, speaking over each other in an attempt to be the first to narrate the past three days. I stared at the ground beneath my chair and wished it would swallow me whole. Voices of greeting filled the air around me, but I didn't look up. I couldn't look up.

"How have I gone an entire month without seeing you, my fair-haired beauty?" Laughter accompanied Owen's words. Miss Lyons *was* a fair-haired beauty. *Owen's fair-haired beauty.* My heart pounded as I slowly lifted my gaze.

"I see you haven't lost your droll attempt at humor, brother." Edmond rolled his eyes.

Owen laughed deeply, slapping him on the shoulder. "I see you haven't learned to appreciate it."

Edmond smiled. "But I have learned to ignore it."

"What a show of humility, denying my compliments."

I quickly dropped my gaze again, relieved that Owen was addressing his brother.

"Miss Lyons?" A pause. It was Owen's voice. He sounded surprised. "Good to see you."

I held my breath.

"And it is a pleasure to see you," Miss Lyons answered, her voice alluring and coy—vomit inducing.

A few words passed between Owen and his father, and although I wasn't looking, I could feel the pressure of many gazes resting on me. I picked up the nearest book I could find and flipped through the pages, pretending that I was deeply interested in Greek mythology.

Then Miss Lyons's smooth voice cut through the air in a shard of exaggerated surprise. "Are you not planning to greet Dr. Kellaway?"

So the ground had not swallowed me whole. Heart galloping, I put the book down and slowly raised my head, desperately hoping that I was not the *you* Miss Lyons spoke of.

I was.

Anticipating my reaction, Miss Lyons was standing very close to Owen, grinning at me with a catlike resemblance to her mother. She was close to catching me in her claws too. My gaze shifted to

Owen, who looked at me with a question in his eyes. A question that I could neither name nor answer.

I stood, not even attempting a false smile. The effort wouldn't do any good. The truth was coming out tonight whether I liked it or not, and that was certainly not something to smile about. I stopped a few feet too far in front of Owen and tipped my head in subtle acknowledgment, trying not to look at his confused expression and fallen smile. The room was painfully quiet.

"Well, I should expect a bit more affection from you two! You are engaged, after all." Miss Lyons looked between us, her eyes round with shock.

There. She said it. My face burned with humiliation. I couldn't look at Owen, so instead I looked at Grandmother. She stood far to the left near the fireplace, and I was surprised to see a twinge of guilt in her expression. I wanted to run away. I could feel the heat from my face tingling on the tips of my ears. How could I have let this happen? I should have contradicted Grandmother the moment she told this lie. Instead, I had spent three days living it.

But it was time to stop prolonging the inevitable. So taking a shuddered breath, I dared myself to glance at Owen. He was looking at Miss Lyons, his brow knit in confusion, but only a second after I moved my gaze to him, he was looking at me again.

His expression was impossible to read. *Why isn't he saying it? Why won't he just tell everyone that we are not engaged?* The silence in the room was too thick; I was suffocating in it. So without permission, my feet carried me forward, around Owen, and out the door where the air was fresh and I could drown in my humiliation alone.

I didn't stop walking. Not when I heard the creak of a door opening, not when I heard footsteps falling behind me, and not even when I heard Owen call my name. I didn't stop walking until I was outside and Owen's hand was closed around my elbow. He didn't speak, he only breathed and waited for me to turn around.

The quiet had reached a complete new level. It seemed greater somehow, filling a larger space than just a small room. The black, star-speckled sky hung like a monster above me, like it could easily swallow me whole. But I had learned that it surely would not, so I didn't even bother hoping. Sweeping every last bit of nerve I could muster, I turned to face Owen, grateful for the dim moon as our only light.

"It was your grandmother," I said, my voice too quick. "The moment everyone arrived, she—she told them that you . . . proposed to me, and every opportunity I had to contradict that was interrupted in some way, so it carried on for far too long." I paused to breathe. "I told her to confess, but apparently she finds pleasure in torturing me, because she refused. But don't worry, I am going back in there to set everything right."

I realized I had been staring at the buttons on his jacket, so I glanced up briefly, afraid of what his face would show. I wasn't sure what I was expecting, perhaps a small grin, or astonishment, or even anger. But what I saw was not any of those things.

His expression resembled something like . . . hurt. But it was only for a moment. A teasing grin lifted his lips, but it seemed half-hearted, blended together with the flash of hurt I had seen in his eyes. "Was it truly such torture to be engaged to me?"

His question took me off guard, burning my face and making me increasingly flustered. I let out a loud laugh. "I—no, it was the fact that your grandmother continued to lie about it. Everyone was put under false pretense, and that was what tortured me. You did not, in fact, offer a proposal, and everyone assumed that you had."

I hated the way my heart raced talking to Owen about this. Standing so close to him in the dark, with only the tiny stars as companions. I hated the way he was standing, with his arms folded tightly, looking down at his boots with a scowl on his face. When he looked up, he stepped toward me at the same time, making my breath stop in my throat.

"Well, suppose I did?" His voice was careful, quiet enough to match the silence around us.

My heart flipped in my chest and I stepped backward almost frantically. As I did, my feet stumbled over themselves and I lost my balance. Owen stepped forward smoothly and caught me by the waist before I fell. My face burned with embarrassment and the small of my back tingled where Owen's hand held me righted.

Then he stepped closer again, and I felt my unstable balance falter even more. I heard his breath quicken the moment mine did.

But his hand did not leave my waist, and his eyes didn't abandon their softness and determination as they searched my face.

He repeated himself, slowly, and in a lower pitch that made chills travel down my arms. "Suppose I had proposed to you. What would it have been?"

My heart fluttered painfully. My gaze dropped to his buttons again. It was impossible to look at his eyes, not with his closeness and that question lingering in the small space between us. How could he ask such an absurd question? He must know how uncomfortable it would make me. He loved to make me uncomfortable. It was a question that I had never asked myself, and hearing it made my heart scream louder. But I blocked out its words. I couldn't afford to hear it. My armor was supposed to be strong enough to defend me from anything—even Owen. So why did I feel so vulnerable?

Without warning, Owen slipped a bent finger under my chin and nudged it up, forcing me to look into his eyes, the very thing I knew would unarm me entirely. The moonlight cast his face dark in shadow, his jaw was clenched tight in anticipation, his eyes narrowed slightly, searching every inch of my face. This needed to stop. The empty space between us glared at me, begging me to fill it, if not with myself, then with words.

"Why do you want to know?" I croaked.

Owen shook his head almost imperceptibly and the hand that was resting under my chin lifted slowly to my face. He watched his hand carefully as he gently traced the outline of my jaw with two knuckles. This was too much. My breath trembled on the way out.

When his eyes moved to mine again, my warmed heart caught fire. "I need to know," he whispered.

Then the silence thrummed between us, heavy and insistent, and my mind threw an answer to my lips before I could let my heart have a say. My voice cracked as I spoke, and I felt the foreign threat of tears as a knot in my throat. "No." I swallowed. "It would have been *no*."

Owen's hand fell to his side, and he took a step back. He swallowed and a muscle jumped in his jaw. I couldn't understand what his eyes held, but it shattered my armor into millions of tiny shards.

And so I stood completely vulnerable in front of the man that was far too skilled at uncovering the truths of my heart. Panic filled me as I stared into Owen's eyes. They lacked their usual playfulness, but harbored an anguish that silenced my roaring mind, leaving only the voice of my heart to be heard. In desperation, I tried in vain not to hear it. Because I was afraid, very afraid of what it would reveal to me. But the night was too dark and silent, and Owen was standing too close, and the pull of his gaze was much too strong for me to fight the screams of my heart any longer.

So in that moment of undefended barriers and vulnerability and dark silence, my heart whispered to me the truth that I had been refusing to hear, the reason I felt so broken and confused—I loved him. I still loved him, and I knew, deep inside, that that would never change.

I fell back a step, feeling a now-familiar lightness in my head. I had known—surely I had known all along, but it had been too frightening, too contradictory to everything my mind told me. My heart refused to be silenced any longer. It scared me.

I was looking down, but I felt Owen step toward me again, heard him say my name. That was the last straw. So I ran. I ran away from the tiny stars that seemed to laugh at me for my foolish heart. Away from the dark, silent night. And away from that atrocious man who I just knew would try to follow me. But he didn't. And somehow I loved him more for it.

It wasn't until I reached my bedchamber that I stopped running. My feet echoed through the hall and up the staircase, but I did not care. Only when the blankets of my bed plumed around me, and my eyes were positioned firmly at the ceiling did I allow myself to catch my breath and focus on keeping my composure.

*Suppose I had proposed to you. What would it have been?* The question burned in my mind, making me wonder if my response had been honest. And why did he need to know? Why did he look at me the way he did? Could it be possible that he loved me too? My heart leapt at the thought but I quickly shushed my ridiculous idea. There was no sense in hoping. I had decided long ago that hope was far too dangerous to trifle with.

I had glimpsed Owen's heart in his eyes tonight, but it was like peering through the window of an expensive shop. Within there was so much that I wanted, that I could convince myself I truly needed, but none of it I could possibly afford.

So I could not entertain the idea of him ever loving me for a second longer. My heart had place for my brothers only, and I could not replace them or disregard them in any way. I set my jaw and affirmed the message to my heart so it understood. But the ache in my chest that followed assured me that my heart would struggle for a very long time. So, suddenly, I was grateful for Miss Lyons, coming here to take Owen away. It was the only solution. Then perhaps my heart would finally understand. For it understood loss quite well.

Dread filled me at the thought of returning to the drawing room to collect Peter and Charles. I could only imagine what was happening right at this moment. Miss Lyons laughing her tinkling-bell laugh, and Mrs. Kellaway weeping into her husband's handkerchief, and Grandmother accusing me of fancying the thought of marrying Owen so ardently that I had manipulated the entire family.

An apprehensive sigh escaped me as I stood and headed down to the drawing room to fulfill the pending demise of my last shred of dignity. My only wish was that I would not have to face Owen again.

# Chapter 18

*I* awoke the next morning with a muddled mind but with clear intention of thanking Grandmother. After I had entered the drawing room the night before, I found her in tears as she was completing her belated confession. From what I knew, Grandmother had given every detail, excluding her reasoning, of how the lie began. Relieved, I spoke as little as possible before taking my brothers up to their room. Mrs. Kellaway had asked me where Owen had gone. I said I didn't know.

And now, as I walked down the staircase, I still didn't know. So counting myself fortunate, I made my way to the morning room where I assumed Grandmother would be. I didn't want to think about Owen for a second longer. The dull ache in my head testified that I had spent more than enough hours trying not to think about him while I should have been sleeping. They were wasted hours now and I regretted every one of them.

When I came to the large window framing the vast prospect of the back property, I found Alice leaning against it with a hand on the pane, her nose nearly pressed against the glass. Not wanting to draw attention to myself, I sneaked around her, but was stopped almost immediately.

"Oh! Annette, I did not see you there," Alice said, turning her face from the window. "How are you this morning?"

I turned around, only inches from escape. "I am well. And you?"

"Quite." She smiled, and after a pause, her brows turned down in pity. "You must have been so mortified. You poor thing. My

Grandmother dines on mischief and has quite a strong taste for the devious." She laughed, amusing herself.

"Yes, I have certainly learned that."

Alice laughed again, then turned to the window with a sigh. "I daresay it was even more excruciating for my dear Charlotte. It is certain that she will not let Owen out of her sight now, at least not until things are settled between them."

I stepped closer to the window, feeling a weighted stone of ache returning. Owen and Miss Lyons were walking arm in arm by the stables, having what looked like an enjoyable conversation. I wondered if he teased her and made her laugh like he so easily made me.

"Settled?" I asked.

Alice leaned toward me with a wicked smile, and her voice dropped to a whisper. "It is only speculation, of course, but it is more than likely that he will propose during the ball tonight."

Oh, yes. The ball. I had nearly forgotten about it and that dreadful pink dress. My stomach tied itself in a tight knot. I was not yet prepared to lose Owen. Less than one day was too short a time to properly train my heart. My gaze found Miss Lyons again, her dainty hand curled around his arm, her icy round eyes fixed on his face with such obvious adoration that I wanted to vomit. Even through the smudged glass I could see her batting lashes.

In that moment I realized that Miss Lyons was just like Grace Dawkins. But Owen was much more important than a puppy. There was no sense in being jealous. Even if Owen did love me, I could never take any of my heart from my brothers. They needed it more than Owen did. He didn't need it at all, in fact. He had plenty of hearts in his hands without even trying.

"I hope you haven't come to care for him," I heard Alice say.

I looked away sharply, turning toward her. "Of course not. He has been a great . . . acquaintance since I arrived here. That is all."

Her arched eyebrow softened. "I am glad to hear it. I would not want to you experience what poor Charlotte felt when she believed you to be engaged to him. It left her destitute of all imaginable happiness. It absolutely destroyed her. In all honesty, I doubted the truth of your engagement from the beginning. Owen and Charlotte have been perfectly compatible since the moment they met, and I could not comprehend the idea of his affections venturing elsewhere."

I watched them out the window. Pain dug itself deeper and deeper into my chest each time Owen smiled. So he never cared for me. I was merely a form of entertainment until Miss Lyons arrived. I had spent hours with him, playing along in his elaborate game.

Alice exhaled another sigh. "They truly are designed for one another, don't you think?"

I pressed my palms against the windowsill. I felt the sting of betrayal and anger threatening my strength. Every moment I'd spent with Owen, every bout of uncontrollable laughter and every secret I had entrusted him with, I regretted. Because in those moments, I had let it become more than just a game. Something I never intended to do. But for him, that was all it ever was. I was a plaything to amuse himself with while he had the chance.

I had spent my time listing his positive attributes instead of his faults. It was a weakness of mine to overlook faults for the sake of a few kind words or feelings of temporary security. I felt comfortable and secure with Owen. That was where I went wrong.

I tore my gaze from the window. "Undoubtedly," I said. And I believed it.

Alice offered a smile then leaned toward the window in the manner of someone who intended to stay a long time. I was about to turn to leave, but my eyes caught her smile just as it faltered. "Who is that?" she asked, pointing through the glass.

I squinted in the direction of her pointed finger. There, between the thick entwining branches of the woods, I could see a face. Chills started a long voyage over my skin. It was the strange man.

He could barely be recognized from our vantage point, but his top hat was as high as ever, and his hard gaze was fixed on Owen and Miss Lyons. I didn't waste a second. Leaving Alice gaping out the window, I ran for the door with panic buzzing through me. By the time I stepped onto the lawn, my heart was in my ears. I wasn't sure what I planned to do, but a closer, uninterrupted view of the situation was necessary.

I only made it a few steps unnoticed by Owen. He stared, confused, but I kept running. The man noticed me next, cocking his head then retreating into the trees with spine-chilling certainty.

I stopped abruptly, slumping with both relief and defeat. He got away again! And what was stopping him from returning? Absolutely nothing. He felt no threat from us here. I took a heavy breath and squinted at the trees. The man was surely gone and I could only hope that Alice was informing her father at this moment.

"Annette? Is something wrong?" It was Owen's voice. It dug deeply into my ears and fit perfectly. But it was softer, more careful, and it weakened me to the core.

I kept my gaze beyond him at the trees, and I kept my voice cold. "The man that has been trespassing. Did your father speak with you about him?"

"Yes, he did." A pause. "Did you see him?"

I nodded and forced myself to look at Owen. I wished I hadn't. His eyes were too searching, too full of questions, looking too deeply into mine. I feared that he could see my heart through them, manipulate it. I feared that any words passed between us now would be written on my heart forever, and I would never find a way to erase them.

"At the edge of the woods," I said. "I only thought I should warn you, but he is gone now."

I didn't wait for a response. I turned and headed back to the house. But I didn't run like I did the night before. I walked, strong and independent and untouched. Just like I was supposed to be. Coming here to Kellaway Manor had been a mistake. The fresh company and picturesque scenery had stolen my identity. I was not that happy, giggling girl that climbed trees and admired pink roses and dreamed. I was Annette Downing, a girl who knew her purpose and honored it—a girl who couldn't afford to dream.

I thought of the time I climbed that tree ten years ago. I had allowed myself to climb so high, not realizing that I would have to come down eventually. Not realizing that the boy that stood below was too weak to catch me—that I would have to come down alone.

Since arriving here, I had been climbing and climbing that same cursed tree. And now, much like before, I was falling, but it hurt much worse this time. And there was no one waiting to catch me at the bottom. Hope worked that way. It coaxed and encouraged people to climb, never caring to warn them of the fall that was coming.

When I got back to the house, I found Alice speaking frantically to her father, pulling him by the arm toward the doorway I was entering through.

"He's gone," I said. "I saw him just for a moment before he turned and departed."

Mr. Kellaway's eyes flickered out the window then back to me. He sighed and rubbed his jaw. "Thank you, Miss Downing." Then started toward the door and I stepped aside. With his hand on the handle, he turned toward me and asked, "How many times have you seen this man?"

"Three times now." I paused. "Perhaps you might assign a few servants to keep a specific watch on those woods. All three times I have seen him he came from the woods and departed through them also. If they were being guarded, entry would be nearly impossible. And if he did attempt it, he could be easily apprehended."

Mr. Kellaway's gaze softened in thought and he gave a quick nod. "Of course. I will do just that." He released the handle and returned in the direction he came, presumably heading to the servants' quarters.

Alice watched her father leave then placed a hand to her chest. She looked at me with genuine concern. "Good heavens, are they all right?"

"They seemed perfectly content." I hoped my voice didn't sound bitter. Thankfully she didn't seem to notice.

"What do you suppose that man's purpose is, coming here and frightening us all so?"

I remembered with a pang of dread that man's question: *Who does Owen love?* I had immediately known it was Miss Lyons, and now, so did he. My stomach pinched. If servants stood guard, there was no possible way that the man could return unseen. Whatever threat he posed was gone. I allowed myself to relax. "I don't know."

After I found Grandmother and thanked her for the previous night, she broke into a new bout of crying, refusing my gratitude. Once her tears were subdued, she cajoled me into sitting and working on embroidery for much longer than I would have liked. I managed a few stitches without creating a large knot. After visiting with her for some time, I remembered why I had liked her in the first place. Aside from her mischief, she was truly a wonderful woman.

When she finally let me go, I headed to the library, assuming I would find my brothers there. Their routine had, for several days now, consisted of spending hours playing in the library and listening to Grandfather's stories. But when I opened the heavy door, I was surprised to see Grandfather sitting alone in one of the leather chairs by the fireplace.

"Miss Downing?" He looked up from his book and blinked at me through his spectacles. "Where are your brothers today? I have missed their company."

I blanched. "They haven't been here with you?"

He closed his book. "No, but I just got here, so they could have stopped by earlier, I suppose.

My eyes widened and my heart dropped.

I was out the door, through the halls and outside before I could fully process my thoughts. *Tell me, or those you love will face the consequences.* The strange man's words pounded in my ears from days before. He was here! He could have abducted them! He could have hurt them . . . he could have . . .

"Charles! Peter!" I screamed. The sun beat down on me as I ran across the lawn for the second time today. I gasped for breath as I searched around the stables, then ran across to the rose garden. "Charles! Peter!" My throat ached from yelling and my lungs from running. This could not happen. Not Peter and Charles. He did not hurt Peter and Charles. I refused to believe such a thing.

"Annette?"

I spun around at the sound of Peter's voice. "Peter!" I knelt in front of him and threw both arms around him and Charles, who stood beside him snickering.

"Where were you?" I asked over their little shoulders. "I told you never to come out of doors alone . . . ," My words stopped as I caught sight of two leather boots stepping up on the grass beside us.

"Owen brought us out here. We were looking for you, actually," Peter said.

My heart jumped. Preparing my best scowl, I looked up. Owen smiled down at me, a sight that made my heart jump higher.

"I hope that is all right, I felt the need to give them another lesson."

I stood, ignoring his hand, rage pounding through me. "I thought they had been . . . ," I stopped myself, rethinking my words. "I mean . . . I didn't know where they were, and I have been looking for them." I put my hands on my hips without realizing it. "Why did you take them without my permission?"

I didn't care that Owen stepped closer and put his hands on my brothers' shoulders, or that his smile grew. "We wished to surprise you."

"Oh? Really? Surprise me with what?" My voice was hard and unfeeling. I liked the sound.

Owen's smile fell into a rueful frown. "I apologize, Annette, I thought you wouldn't mind."

I didn't answer. I did not wish to speak another word to that manipulative, much-too-handsome man. The awkwardness of last night still thrived in the air between us and he acted as if it was not there. I needed him to give my brothers back to me and return to Miss Lyons. Surely he was missing her violently at this point.

"I am sincerely sorry," he said. "Please forgive me."

I could feel his gaze on me; I could imagine the sincerity on his face.

"There was no climbing involved this time." I could hear the grin in his voice.

I stared at the ground.

Then to my dismay, he knelt down in front of me, entering my line of sight without warning. The teasing gleam was in his eyes. "Annette Downing, I beg you, forgive me for abducting your brothers without your consent. It will not happen again." One side of his mouth lifted higher than the other as he spoke, denting his cheek with that dimple.

I felt the threat of laughter in my chest, despite the anger and resentment that I felt only moments before. But somehow I managed to keep a straight face. "Very well. I forgive you. But you better have taught them something amazing."

Owen laughed, a sound I had missed so much. "Boys, present your masterpiece."

Peter withdrew a folded piece of parchment from his pocket and handed it to me in a neat square. He erupted into giggles as I raised an eyebrow in his direction. Charles joined in, stepping backward.

"They wrote it on their own," Owen said. "I only guided them in the right direction."

Not sure what to expect, I unfolded the "masterpiece" and read.

*Annette, O, Annette*
*Her hair is the color of the crust of bread*
*She makes us laugh every day*
*She tucks us into our little beds*
*Annette, O, Annette*

I resisted the urge to laugh, lifting the paper higher so I couldn't see Owen's shaking shoulders.

*We are her brothers, atrocious ones*
*She is our sister and is very kind*
*Even though she is a lady, she still runs*
*Annette, O, Annette*

My laughter escaped as I finished their poem, and Owen joined immediately. I stepped toward Peter and Charles and threw my arms around them again. "That was a wonderful poem! Which one of you is going to be as famous as Shakespeare?"

Peter pointed at himself, nodding emphatically. I laughed at Charles's scowl and pressed my thumbs to each side of his mouth, lifting his frown into a smile. He giggled, pulling his head away.

"I am sure that you will both be even greater than Shakespeare. Thank you. I do run quite a lot, don't I?"

This made them giggle, and I squeezed them tighter. I almost glanced at Owen, to thank him with a smile, or a few short words, but I stopped myself. My heart could not endure such torture any longer. And I didn't want my newfound ill opinion of Owen to be changed by his pretty words. I could not believe a single one of them.

"I think Grandfather is missing you two," I said, brushing a stray curl from Charles's forehead. "I had better take you to the library."

Peter's giggles halted. "I don't want to go to the library."

"I don't either," Charles added. "Owen said he would show us the orsher."

"Orchard," Owen corrected with a laugh. "And yes, I did make such a promise. Would you like to join us?"

"Yes, please come, Annette!" Charles said, tugging on my skirts.

I sighed inwardly, wishing my brothers were not so adorable, and wishing that Owen was not acting this way—that everything could be the same as before. It was completely false, and we both knew it. His smile was weakening my defenses as it always did, but at this moment I lacked the strength to rebuild them. I would speak cooly, avoid his eyes as much as possible, and keep my distance.

"Very well, I'll come," I said plainly.

Within seconds of my response, I was being pulled along by the arm toward the orchard on the northeast corner of the property. I had been there only once since I arrived here, and remembered the experience as very unnerving.

When we reached the iron gate at the entrance, Owen motioned us ahead of him. I was greeted by the sweet, sticky smell of fresh apples. The trees made a canopy of shade above and around me, their remaining flowers the color of new snow. Their branches and leaves grew so close that they stood as one wall on both sides, not allowing the light breeze to penetrate their barriers, robbing the air of all sound but the soft rustle of leaves. The small pockets of light that entered through the gaps between branches reflected off the path, creating the illusion of walking on gold.

I gazed at my surroundings in awe. I had forgotten the beauty of this place. Or perhaps I hadn't noticed it before.

The little bench where Owen and I had sat my second day here remained unmoved, nestled near the trunk of a tree halfway down the path.

"Would you like to sit down?" Owen asked, stepping up beside me.

My stomach flipped as I tried to predict the outcome in my mind. I would sit down, Owen would sit beside me and talk to me, and smile, and possibly even laugh. It was a perfect storm.

"No, thank you," I answered, focusing my gaze on Peter and Charles as they jumped, trying to touch the bottom branches of each tree. "I would rather stand."

"Then I will stand also," he said decidedly.

I could feel his gaze on the side of my face, watching every blink of my eye. The seconds stretched on and I was tempted to make light conversation, if only to dispel the silence, when Owen said, "Please let me know what I have done so I may apologize."

This brought my gaze to his face. His brow was furrowed with concern and his eyes showed regret.

"You have done nothing to warrant an apology. In fact, you deserve my gratitude. Peter and Charles's poem was darling." My voice was stiff.

Owen shook his head. "No, Annette," he walked in front of me, "something is wrong."

He was right. Something was very wrong. I had let myself fall in love with him. And every pound of my heart testified that it was true.

"Nothing is wrong," I repeated. I forced myself to hold his gaze, to create believability. It didn't work.

"Did you find out about Willowbourne?" he asked in a quiet voice.

I remembered what Grandmother had revealed to me about Owen's inheritance. I had been angry at the time, wishing he had trusted me enough to tell me. "Your Grandmother may have mentioned something."

He sighed and rubbed the back of his neck. "I wanted to tell you. And I almost did, I was just . . . afraid."

I felt as though he had just shared a deep secret. Owen afraid? I never would have thought it possible. "Afraid of what?"

He looked down, his uncertainty obvious. After several seconds he looked up again. "I was afraid that you would see me differently if you knew. That . . . my possessions would become who I was. Does that make sense?"

I nodded, feeling an unwelcome smile on my lips. "You are not a large house, Owen. And you are not dozens of acres of beautiful property either."

He laughed, making my smile grow. "And you, Annette, are not a pitied girl who lacks the accomplishments of most ladies because of her hapless circumstances." His voice softened, losing the traces of laughter. "You are so much more than that. You are strong and brave and selfless and unfailingly kind. You are optimistic and caring and lovely."

I knew I was blushing and I hated myself for it. Owen was only doing what he did best—deceiving me, trying to make me believe his words. But I knew better.

"That is not true, Owen. Most people do not see me in that way," I said, my voice defensive. "Most people see me as the unaccomplished, unfortunate girl that I am. My misfortune has defined the opinion most people have of me, including my aunt, who is admired only for her assumed charity toward my brothers and me. Only what is seen can truly exist."

Owen shook his head subtly, his eyes full of such softness that I felt crumbled. "I am afraid that sometimes what most people fail to see is what truly exists. They invent an opinion of someone and move along, not daring to discover the true character beneath the facade. And do you remember what we agreed we had in common, your first day here?"

I shook my head, although I did remember, and I predicted his words before he spoke them.

"We are not like most people," he said, smiling wider now. "And we would never try to be."

I couldn't help the smile that sneaked onto my face.

"And so the privilege is mine to have seen what truly exists within you, Annette. What most people have missed." His expression turned solemn, and a sadness settled in his gaze. "I will remember always."

My throat tightened with the unexpected threat of tears. Was this his way of saying farewell? Acknowledging that after today he would be engaged and everything would change more than it already had? I could no longer accept that Owen had always been insincere. He had been a great friend, and I could not deny that. It was not his fault that I fell for his charm. The fault was entirely my own.

"Well, then." It was all I could think to say.

Owen cleared his throat. "Thank you for giving me incentive to visit Willowbourne. I needed to go back and visit—for my aunt's sake as well as my own. My aunt and cousins were very distraught, and were put at peace to know that they could remain living there." He paused, smiling. "You would love my aunt. And Peter and Charles would have a wonderful time with the younger children there." He looked down at his feet. "Please come visit often."

The thought of visiting Owen and Miss Lyons in their beautiful home sickened me. No. After I left Kellaway Manor, seeing Owen again was not an option. But for politeness sake, I said, "We will see if . . . we can stop by. Eventually . . . maybe."

Owen was still looking down and I could see something of a battle in his features. Then he looked up, his expression far from relaxed. Something was bothering him. He hesitated for a second longer, staring at me with that same battle in his eyes. "You could live there," he said suddenly. "At Willowbourne."

My heart all but stopped. I was sure the shock showed on my face.

The look in his eyes was fragile, broken, and it plucked at my heartstrings without mercy. "Don't worry, Annette. I assure you, what you told me last night is perfectly understood." His jaw clenched after the words, but he continued, "You and your brothers can live there, and I will act as your guardian. I could not bear to know that you were living with your aunt again."

His mention of the previous night consumed me. It hadn't been a real proposal, but what if my answer had been different? Would he have proposed? Hope gripped me again. What if he did love me? I scolded myself. My conversation with Alice this morning was enough to know that he did not. He was going to marry Miss Lyons and they were going to live happily ever after at Willowbourne together. And I did not want to be a part of it. That would be suffering like I had never known.

"Thank you for the offer, but I cannot accept," I said, a lump in my throat. "My aunt needs us to return." I started toward my brothers, intending to leave with them immediately, regretting that I had even come.

Owen was walking after me. "Annette—"

"No, Owen." I said, turning around quickly, then facing my brothers again. My chin was trembling. "No." I took them each by the hand and led them through the gate, ignoring their protests. I didn't look at Owen as I passed, afraid of what I would see.

Something within me broke as I stepped out of the orchard. And then the one promise I had managed to keep broke just as quickly. A tear leaked from my eye, sliding down my cheek, on territory it hadn't seen for years. A second immediately followed, and my body shuddered with a silent sob. I bit my lip, begging myself to stop. I was stronger than this.

But the tears kept coming. I didn't have a free hand to wipe them, so I let them fall, praying that Peter and Charles would not look up—that they wouldn't see the weak thing their sister had become.

But they were already looking up, watching me with eyebrows drawn together and questions in their eyes. "Why are you sad?" Peter asked.

I forced a smile onto my face and released his hand to dry my cheeks. "Not to worry. I will be just fine." I wished the words were true. I took a deep, shaky breath. "Now run along to the library. Grandfather has been missing you all day."

With a final concerned peek at my face, they hurried to the house. I followed them slowly, trying to regain my composure. I was not a watering pot. I did not cry over a man! It had been a five-year struggle to meet what was required of me, but I had somehow managed.

Now, all that was required of me was to make my heart understand and forget. It seemed a simple task, but my heart was even more independent than I was these days, and it didn't want to forget. So I walked over the grass to the house with my hand pressed to my chest, hoping to somehow keep the pieces of that broken thing together inside me.

It was around six of the clock when Grandmother hurried me up the stairs to begin getting ready for the ball. Lizzie was waiting for me in my room when I arrived, smiling again, which shocked me, but obviously anxious to begin, which didn't shock me at all. "You are going to look ravishing tonight, Miss. I am sure of it."

It was then that I spied the pink gown on my bed, hanging off the edge, its skirts flowing down like a fountain. It was intricately beaded on the neckline, and made of what I could judge to be very fine fabric. Mrs. Kellaway must have paid a substantial amount of money for it.

I couldn't stop staring. Was I really going to wear that? It was beautiful to say the least. And I hated it. In some way, the color was not only connected to my mother anymore. It was also connected to Owen. The pink rose he had given me. And I had lost him too.

But that did not matter any longer. Tonight I had a goal in mind. Tonight I was to fall out of love with Owen, and to do that, I was to see that he carried out his proposal. *And after I see that he is truly gone forever, and that he truly does not care for me, and that he truly can never be mine, I will be content. I will take my brothers with me in the morning and return to Aunt Ruth. To the life we led before, and I will love them and only them for the rest of my life, and we will never visit Willowbourne.* It was a definitive plan, not to be brought to alteration by any charming words.

As Lizzie helped me into the gown, I didn't dwell on it. I repeated my plan in my mind, determination igniting in my soul like a torch. Tonight was not a night of weakness. Owen's blue eyes would have no effect on me tonight. I was blind to his charm.

"Miss Downing!" Lizzie gasped. "You already look stunning and I have not even done your hair!" She let out a sound resembling a yelp as she pulled me to the mirror. I tugged my gloves on as I sat down, refusing to look at my reflection.

Much later, she stepped back, clearly admiring her work. I glanced up, hoping to see the glint of determination in my eyes that I had seen only a few days ago. It was there, burning visibly, daring Owen to try to woo me. But tonight he was not going to succeed.

"Wait!" Lizzie exclaimed as I stood to leave.

I turned to her without expression.

She smiled, waving a box in the air. "You forgot the matching slippers."

# Chapter 19

The guests were already entering the ballroom when I arrived. I thought of my brothers secure with Grandfather in the library. I desperately wished I could be with them, but the ball was an essential part of my plan. And my plan could not be tampered with.

I searched the room for Mrs. Kellaway, or Alice, or even Miss Lyons in the various groups of chatting women that were not engaged in the dance. I found Alice with two other ladies standing in a triangle, whispering excitedly.

I moved toward them, and Alice looked up just as I was approaching. "Annette! Oh, you look lovely! Come, come, meet my friends."

She pulled me forward with a gloved hand and introduced me as if we were the dearest of friends. I smiled politely and took a steadying breath, preparing to deliver my first rehearsed line. In a whispered voice, I said, "Where is Miss Lyons tonight? We must ensure that your brother carries out his proposal." I smiled slyly, matching the look on Alice's face.

"Yes. We must. She is currently dancing with Edmond, and Owen is here somewhere . . . I saw him only a few short minutes ago."

I scanned the crowd, searching the mass of laughing faces for Owen. I did not see him. The song ended, and a gentleman invited Alice to the next dance. I stayed where I was, standing alone. Where was he? My eyes continued their search.

Across the room, I noticed a tall, dark-haired young man watching me as he sipped out of a large glass. He was leaning against the wall, speaking in hushed tones to a man standing beside him. The man glanced my way then threw a smile in the dark-haired man's direction.

I looked away quickly. Were they speaking about me? Turning and walking a few steps to the right, I sneaked a glance behind me to see if they were still staring. They certainly were.

I swallowed and scanned the room again, wishing desperately that I could find someone to speak to instead of standing here awkwardly. Alice's friends had disappeared to the dance floor, so I was helplessly alone when the dark-haired man started across the room, his steps and his gaze in my direction.

I looked down, tugging at my gloves as a distraction. I was not accustomed to speaking to unknown gentlemen, and I was certainly not accustomed to receiving attention from them. It was making me acutely uncomfortable to have one headed in my direction.

By the length of time I had been staring at my gloves, I deducted that he was only a few feet away now. I lifted my gaze to see him. He was smiling, which should have given me comfort, but his was not a comforting smile in the slightest. It put me ill at ease for a reason I did not know. He was moderately handsome with his dark hair and dark eyes, I noticed. But that smile . . .

"Good evening," he said in a purposely slurred voice as he took the last step toward me. He offered a slow bow, and glanced up at me.

I dropped a quick nod, feeling like a horse being appraised as his gaze not-so-discreetly swept over my figure.

"My name is Mr. Robert Baines. I could not help but notice such a lovely lady in such an eye-catching gown." He smiled that unsettling smile. "May I inquire the name of this lovely lady?"

His name sounded familiar, but I couldn't quite place where I had heard it before. I held my expression at a blank state and said, "Miss Annette Downing."

"Ah. A lovely name to suit a lovely lady."

I wished he would stop calling me that. I forced a small smile onto my face. "A pleasure to make your acquaintance, Mr. Baines." As I said it, I recalled the night Grandmother had spoken of the upcoming ball, embarrassing me by her talk of dueling. Mr. Baines was the name of the gentleman she had mentioned.

He grinned down at me and leaned closer. "The pleasure is mine, Miss Downing." The current song ended and the room cheered for the ensemble. "May I have the honor of the next set?"

I felt my face blanch, but I gave a polite nod. I had certainly not been expecting (or at all hoping) that I would have anyone soliciting for my hand. He extended his arm to me and I took it, heart pounding. What if I didn't remember the steps? I forced myself to remain calm as I stepped away to stand in line across from him in the center of the floor.

The song began and we stepped together. I shifted uncomfortably as his hand wrapped around my waist and lingered there. He was very close. And when he spoke I could smell heavy brandy on his breath.

"This is one of my favorite dances, you know."

I glanced up at him as we turned, willing my mind to focus on the steps and not on his much-too-searching eyes and unsettling smile. When I finally stepped away from him to move down the line, I took a deep breath. All the other gentlemen held me at a much more comfortable distance. Miss Lyons was among the women, smiling in an obviously well-rehearsed way, glancing up through her lashes with lips upturned demurely.

I was through the line and back in the arms of Mr. Baines before I had sufficient time to relax. He slid his hand over my back and pulled me much too close. I turned my head to the side, missing a step as I tried to move to a more appropriate distance.

He gave a low chuckle. "Am I distracting you?"

I shot him a look of dismay. I should not have agreed to dance with this man. Grandmother had described him as agreeable, but I found him to be quite the opposite.

"No. You are disgusting me, actually," I said as I pulled backward. My heart raced at my insult, but he laughed.

Just then, over Mr. Baines's collar, I spied Owen standing against the wall straight ahead. His gaze was fixed on Mr. Baines through narrowed eyes. His arms were crossed and his jaw was firm.

Mr. Baines tugged me closer, blocking Owen from my sight.

I endured the rest of the dance in silence, and I could not have been more grateful when the music came to a halt. What a presumptuous cad Mr. Baines was! I shot him a final scowl then removed myself from his hands and hurried to the side of the room where Owen was not standing.

Fortifying my heart and my resolve, I dared myself to look at him. My heart leapt at the unobscured sight of his formal jacket and cravat, his hair looking darker in the dim light. He wasn't smiling, though, and I found myself wishing that he would. It had been too long since I had seen his smile, and it strengthened me more that I cared to confess.

I stopped myself swiftly. Owen's smile was the absolute last thing I was supposed to be thinking about. Suddenly, as if he knew I'd been watching him, his eyes met mine across the room with a flash of admiration.

I hurried my gaze away as quickly as I could. *No*, I amended, *his eyes are the last thing I should be thinking about.*

Seeking a distraction, I found Grandmother standing alone only a few feet away near the wall. She was wearing a thoroughly frilled puce gown and headdress and was nibbling contentedly on a tart. I walked toward her and she greeted me with a rueful smile. "I am afraid Mr. Baines is not the gentleman I thought him to be. He certainly had me fooled at the Thornton's ball."

I nodded my agreement.

She shook her head and clucked her tongue. Her eyes ventured to the opposite side of the ballroom. "But Owen, he is a gentleman to the very core." She gave a hooting laugh. "Perhaps you ought to dance with him for the rest of the night."

"I would prefer to abstain from further dancing." I didn't think my composure could handle such a thing.

Grandmother gave a huffed breath and planted a hand on her hip. "There is nothing more I can do for you two. One can try to make a blind person walk, but they cannot make them see. And they cannot guide them indefinitely to all their destinations. They must learn to find the way on their own." She sipped from her champagne flute and sighed. "I suppose it's time I trusted fate to the task." Then she turned and walked away in the direction of the dessert table, leaving me alone and confused once more.

The thought crossed my mind to follow Grandmother and inquire what she meant by her philosophical speech, but with my nerves on edge, I did not feel at all equal to the endeavor. I promised myself that I would gather the courage to carry out my plan to ensure a proposal for Miss Lyons later. So, feeling excruciatingly awkward, I stood where I was, forcing my eyes away from where I knew Owen was, and praying that Mr. Baines would not find me again.

After a few moments of this, I felt the tap of a long fingernail on my shoulder. I turned to see that someone almost worse had found me.

"Lady Pembury," I said in a weak voice.

She greeted me with a condescending nod, staring at me with her disdainful eyes. "Miss Downing, is it?"

I nodded, feeling thoroughly scrutinized by her gaze.

"I see you have discovered how to wear a proper gown. I almost expected you to wear that inadequate thing you wore for tea."

She looked very much like her daughter. They had the same piercing eyes—though the color differed—and the same golden curls. The similarities didn't end there. They both used words as weapons. It was an arsenal that I knew to be the most afflicting. I stared at her with as much dignity as I could muster, making the decision in myself that this woman was not going to bring me down with her haughty words.

She turned her head slowly to the left and gave an amused sigh. "Look at them. They presume that they can steal him from my dear Charlotte."

I followed her gaze behind me. Owen was standing beside Edmond where a group of young women flocked, waving their fans in a way that was meant to be alluring, batting their eyes and laughing at every word Owen said. He wasn't smiling though. He shot Edmond what seemed like a pleading look, making him laugh.

"The gossip has spread about his inheritance, you see. Now every young lady is vying for his heart. *Every* young lady." She gave me a pointed look out of her sharp green eyes, then moved her gaze to Owen again. "I hope all those young ladies know that they are not designed to be mistress of such a magnificent home. I hope *all* those young ladies know that they are inferior to my Charlotte and that she has already stolen Dr. Kellaway's heart." She looked at me again, her expression all challenge and warning, then added, "But it is my hope that they will accept their defeat with grace."

I looked at Owen again, a heavy weight settling over me. Lady Pembury was watching the side of my face. I could imagine the slow smile curling her lips as I stared at the man that her daughter intended to marry. Owen would have an awful mother-in-law; there was no question. But my plan still needed to be carried out. He needed to propose to Miss Lyons tonight, and it needed to happen soon.

I realized I had been staring at him for far too long, because his eyes found mine. I dropped my gaze the moment it met his, but it was too late. I knew he was walking toward me, and I could only imagine his stride: quick, with purpose, the way it always was.

I repeated my plan in my mind as he approached, reminding myself of my intentions, securing my barriers. *Confidence*, I told myself. *Look him in the eye.*

But looking into his eyes was not an option while my heart was racing the way it was. So I turned my head to Lady Pembury. She looked slightly distressed, but concealed it well beneath a painted grin. "Oh. Here he comes now. What a surprise."

He was only twenty feet away, sliding past groups of people, making his way toward us. My heart quickened with each of his steps, knowing that the closer he came the stronger it needed to be. Only a few short seconds longer and he was there, standing directly in front of me. Too close. Too handsome.

"Lady Pembury." He gave her a stiff nod in greeting, then returned his gaze to me. "Annette, will you come with me for a moment?"

I was shocked, but there was no trace of argument within me. Lady Pembury looked daggers my way as I took Owen's arm. I felt him gazing down at me as we stepped away, but did not allow myself to look up into his eyes. But there was nothing that could have stopped me from hearing him whisper, "You look beautiful."

My heart jumped. I cleared my throat in the most detached manner possible. "Thank you."

He stopped walking once we were across the room and turned to face me. I could no longer avoid his eyes, so I glanced up. He looked confused, searching my face as if he expected to find clues there.

I cleared my throat again, grasping onto my plan in my mind. The first step was to make light conversation, then deliver my second rehearsed line of the evening. "Lady Pembury and I have met before. She came for tea only a few days ago," I said.

Owen's lips lifted in a small smile and he raised an eyebrow. "Do you enjoy her company?"

I glanced in her direction again, not surprised to see that she was watching me with a lifted chin and narrowed eyes. "Not particularly."

He laughed, sending a ripple through me, then said in a quiet voice, "Perhaps we should go fetch the acorns."

My head snapped in his direction of its own accord. "Was she—"

"Yes. She was." He chuckled lightly. "A common victim of my mischief. Something that I cannot say I'm ashamed of."

My mind raced. Lady Pembury was the woman walking beneath the tree that day, ten years ago. I couldn't help but laugh. I no longer regretted a single one of those acorns. But what did Owen have against Lady Pembury?

Amid my thoughts, I hadn't noticed Owen step closer. It was an almost indiscernible distance, but I felt it all the same. I took a passive glance around the room, and found Miss Lyons speaking with Alice.

I needed to find my voice, to deliver my next line. "Well, I see no significant faults in her daughter. Have you seen her tonight? She looks lovely. You must invite her to the next dance."

His gaze did not leave my face. "I'm afraid I had a different lady in mind."

I felt my eyes widen and my heart picked up speed. Did he mean me? I looked down, adjusting my gloves as a distraction. "Oh?"

He leaned his head closer, pulling my gaze to his effortlessly. "May I have the next dance, Miss Annette Downing?"

My breath caught in my throat. I had not prepared for this scenario. "No, thank you. I do not wish to dance with any gentlemen tonight. I came only for the company."

His eyes flashed with hurt. "Oh, yes. Robert Baines can't be considered a gentleman, so that was why you agreed to dance with him." His voice was nothing but a mutter.

"I—I couldn't think of a way to refuse him," I said as a guilty feeling spread in my stomach.

"You could have told him what you just so easily told me."

My heart pounded. I tried to put on an apologetic expression, but Owen brushed it off.

"Goodnight, Annette." Then he turned and walked away with that same hurt lingering in his eyes.

I felt as though I had been physically struck, as if my breath had been knocked from my lungs. Coming here had been a mistake. How did I assume that resisting Owen's charm was even possible? Why did Owen prefer to dance with me? If he was planning a proposal to Miss Lyons, wouldn't he be with her at every opportunity? It was too confusing, and my plan was beginning to sound unrealistic.

"Annette!" Alice hurried toward me. She gripped my arm and pulled me to the wall. "I have the perfect plan," she whispered. "Owen has always been a bit . . . timid about his affections, so Charlotte and I have concocted a way to ensure a proposal. After this next dance, Charlotte will become ill. Pretend, of course. Owen will surely follow her into the hall on physician instinct, or, perhaps, instinct of the heart." Alice's eyes twinkled with mischief. "And they will be alone. Then Charlotte will offer some encouragement, a bit of flirting, and Owen will finally propose!"

I wanted to feel excited, but instead I felt dull and empty. "That sounds like a successful plan, Alice."

"Oh, it is, to be sure." She nodded with wide eyes. "Charlotte is receiving even more than she hoped for. It is absolutely perfect."

I was confused. "More than she hoped for?"

Alice lowered her voice. "Well, originally she hoped for Kellaway Manor, but mistress of Willowbourne was a much greater achievement."

My stomach twisted in a tight knot. "But Owen was never to inherit Kellaway Manor."

"Yes, I know that." She waved her hand in the air. "I meant that originally Charlotte hoped to marry Edmond, but when she learned that Owen was to inherit a much greater prize, she decided that he was the superior catch. She always thought him to be more handsome anyway." Alice shrugged and smoothed a hand over her curls. "Oh! The song just ended!" She shuffled forward and stood on the tips of her toes, looking over the crowd.

A sickening feeling spread in my stomach. Miss Lyons was after Willowbourne. She didn't love Owen. And Alice had spoken about it without a hint of shame.

I listened with half an ear as Alice announced the developments of her plan. At the point where Owen followed Miss Lyons to the hall, I joined Alice where she stood, feeling quite ill myself. I tried to catch one last glimpse of Owen, to see him leaving, so my heart could fully understand its loss, but a man with a very tall top hat stood in my way, blocking my view.

Frustrated, I stepped back, feeling the threat of tears once again. What I had convinced myself was right was now wrong. Owen did not deserve such deceit. Miss Lyons only wanted to secure a good future for herself. Such things were not unheard of, but Owen didn't deserve to be tricked, no matter how much silly tricking he had done himself.

Trickery of the heart was a whole different matter.

I could feel the beginnings of an ache in my head, and watching the spinning gowns surrounding me only made it worse. This was not how I wanted to spend my last night at Kellaway Manor. I wanted to spend it alone in my room. From now on, avoidance was my only hope. If I could manage to avoid Owen until I left in the carriage with Peter and Charles in the morning, then everything would be fine. I would then never have to know if he married Miss Lyons. I would never again have to ignore his charm. He would be allowed to fade into memory, become distant, until I forget the shade of blue of his eyes and the sound of his laugh. My heart, like any wound, should heal if left untouched.

After I located Mrs. Kellaway, I told her I felt ill and walked myself to my room, taking the hallway on the opposite side of where I imagined Owen professing his love to Miss Charlotte Lyons.

I changed out of the horrid pink gown the moment I closed my door. I couldn't venture to the library now—I was presumed to be ill, so I decided sleep was my best option.

As I crawled under the blankets, I hoped that I would dream of Aunt Ruth's little cottage on the hill. Because that was where my dreams belonged. That was where I belonged. And no matter how much it frightened me, or how many tears it caused to wet my pillow, I was going back tomorrow.

# Chapter 20

By the time the sun showed its first sliver, I was up, packing my trunk. My brothers' trunks came next, so I sneaked down the hall to their room, hoping not to wake them with my echoing feet. Once all three trunks were full, I gently shook each of their shoulders.

Peter opened his eyes first, squinting and slowly sitting up.

"We need to leave soon," I said, smoothing his mussed hair.

"Are we going to the village?" His voice was still groggy from sleep.

"Yes! Please, please may we go?" Charles asked from behind me, nearly leaping from his bed. "Owen said we could go today if you let us."

My heart sunk, but the words needed to be said. "We are going back to Aunt Ruth's house today."

I wasn't fully prepared for the looks on their faces. Peter looked confused at first, then his eyes filled with tears almost instantly. Charles's lower lip quivered. "Why can't we stay?"

"We have already stayed for far too long."

They both sat quietly for several seconds, then Charles said, "But—but what if Aunt Roof still thinks we are bad?"

I pulled them both into a tight hug, partly to console them, partly to keep my heart in one piece. "You are the best boys in the world. Not to worry. You have behaved well almost the entire time we have been here." I pulled away, wiping the tears from their cheeks. "I won't let her hurt you. She will not send you away."

"Owen said that too," Peter said.

My throat tightened in its fight against tears. Of course Owen said that.

I took a deep breath. "Well, I have packed your trunks. The carriage will be here in one hour."

They nodded obediently and climbed out of bed, but I could still hear their sniffing. It was selfish of me to do this, to pull them away from the joy they had found here. And I felt that I was betraying myself by choosing to leave. But it had to be done.

When we got downstairs, I was disappointed to see that we were not the only ones awake. I could see Mrs. Kellaway sitting on the settee in the drawing room. My stomach dropped at the possibility of seeing Owen again. That certainly could not happen.

"Annette, is that you?"

I smiled through the archway and open door at Mrs. Kellaway. "Good morning." It was the most daft thing I could have said. "I—I didn't know anyone else was awake."

"Alice and Charlotte are taking a turn around the grounds, too."

I nodded slowly, expecting to be told at any moment that I was invited to Owen and Miss Lyons's wedding. "Oh."

She sighed, placing the book she was reading on the cushion beside her. "Come in. I know of your plans to return to Maidstone."

I had ordered the carriage the previous afternoon, informing only Mr. Kellaway. I should have known that he would pass the news to his wife.

With Peter and Charles following behind me, I stepped into the drawing room, taking a seat beside her. "I want to thank you and your husband for allowing my brothers and me to stay for such a prolonged amount of time."

She turned her eyes on me with a look of sadness. "You are very welcome to stay as long as you would like. Did your aunt request that you return?"

"Yes," I lied.

She watched me closely. "If you are sure. I have certainly seen an improvement in the boys' behavior." She smiled at my brothers then turned to me again, her eyes glistening with tears. "It has been wonderful coming to know you, Annette. You remind me so much of your mother."

In the weeks since I had arrived here she had hardly mentioned either of my parents. Perhaps the subject was too sensitive, or she was afraid of hurting me, but what she said now was the greatest compliment.

"Thank you."

Mrs. Kellaway nodded subtly, giving a half-smile. "Please come visit again soon."

"Of course."

Her eyes widened, as if she was remembering something important. "I must go wake Owen to bid you and the boys farewell! He would be devastated if he knew you had left without parting words."

I nearly collapsed as she hurried from the room. I looked out the front window, desperately hoping to see the carriage pulling up the drive. It was not there, of course, but that was not going to stop me from running outside. I grabbed my trunk and instructed Peter and Charles to do the same, then we rushed out the front door, my heart hammering in my chest.

The sky was grey, lacking light from the still rising sun. I could see the empty drive ahead of me, looming like a fateful truth that I couldn't escape. The carriage wasn't scheduled to arrive for another thirty minutes. It was useless to hope that Owen would spend thirty minutes getting out here.

In fact, it took him less than two.

Nervousness spread through my veins as I watched him step through the front door of the house and start running across the lawn. He wore only a shirt and breeches, his hair mussed from sleep. It wasn't fair that even now he looked as handsome as ever, especially with the nameless look burning in his eyes as he ran toward me. He stopped only a few feet in front of me, breathing heavily. "Annette . . ."

My heart leapt. It was cruel of him to do this, to come this close to me, to cleave my heart in two when it was so close to finding relief. To say my name the way he did, to look at me the way he was.

"You can't leave." He shook his head, drawing closer. His hand touched my face, unraveling my resolve in an instant. "You can't." His voice was hoarse, vulnerable.

"Yes, I can." I said, not expecting the tears that stung my eyes. I stepped back, and his hand fell from my face. I took Charles's hand and pulled Peter to my side. "It has been weeks, and our aunt needs us to return at once." I paused, deciding how to phrase my next thought. "Congratulations on your engagement."

His brows drew together. "What?"

My heart raced. "Did you not propose last night?"

"To whom?"

"Miss Lyons."

He exhaled a bitter sound that was almost a laugh. "No. That may have been what she wanted, but no, I did not."

Relief flooded through me despite my effort not to feel it.

"She wanted Willowbourne. That was why she came here at all. I could easily see straight through her game." He smiled slightly. "I thought you knew me well enough to expect that."

So he didn't love her. He knew of her intentions from the beginning. The news shouldn't have given me hope, but it did. *It doesn't matter*, I told myself. My mind couldn't be changed now. I was leaving this place. And no matter how much my heart wanted to stay, I was taking it with me.

He looked upward, exasperated. "Alice would stop at nothing to get the two of us together, as if allowing her brother to be used was completely acceptable." He shook his head, then his gaze settled on my face again. His tone changed, returning to the vulnerability from before. "Please don't leave."

"My aunt needs us," I repeated.

"For what reason does she need you?"

I kept my voice steady as I said, "She has missed us."

He gave a frustrated sigh. "I cannot believe that, Annette, and neither can you. Are you not happy here?"

"No, I was, we have been treated so well, but there is no reason for us to stay any longer." I waited, forcing my gaze to stay on his, to convince him as much as myself that I was making the right choice.

I could see apprehension in his eyes when he said, "There is nothing here that can make you stay?"

I breathed deeply and steeled myself. I forced the word from my throat. "No." It was a broken whisper, not the strong, unwavering tone I intended.

He folded his arms and watched his boot as he kicked the grass at his feet. After several heartbeats of silence, he lifted his gaze and stepped toward me again. I held my breath, clutching my brothers to keep my hands from reaching for him.

"If you refuse to stay, then I will follow you. If you step into that carriage and drive away, then I will follow on horseback."

I gasped and shook my head. "Owen—"

He stopped me. "Because no matter how much you pretend your aunt needs you . . . ," he reached out and brushed an errant strand of hair from my forehead, then said in a hoarse whisper, "I will always need you more."

It was a blow I couldn't take. The heartbreak in his eyes, the vulnerability in his voice. Hearing him say he needed me. He couldn't do that. Not if I wanted to leave here with a whole heart. What was I thinking? My heart hadn't been whole for a long time.

Charles was tugging on my skirts from behind. "I want to stay," he said. I could hear the tears in his voice. I turned around to see his little outstretched hand, holding the two pennies Grandfather had given him. His clear blue eyes were brimming with tears and his chin quivered. "I want to stay," he repeated, jerking the coins in my direction. Peter fumbled in his pocket and retrieved his pennies, extending his open palm as tears wet his freckled cheeks.

I shook my head quickly, fighting sudden sobs, and curled their fingers over the pennies in both trembling hands. The brink I was standing on was narrowing. Was my determination to love and protect my brothers resulting in their unhappiness? They were not happy with Aunt Ruth. They were happy here and I was trying to tear them away. I bent over and pulled Peter and Charles into my arms. Immediately after I did, the sound of screaming reached my ears from the left side of the house.

My head whipped in that direction the moment I heard it. I was alarmed to see Alice running toward us, her hair blowing wildly, her complexion ruddy. "Owen! Owen! Come quickly! The man— the man came back and he h-has Charlotte!" As she came closer I could see tears streaking down her cheeks. "You—you have to save her! He told me t-to send you."

Panic set in wholly as I realized what was happening. How had the man come onto the property again?

Owen was moving immediately, stepping toward Alice. "Where are they?"

"In the woods on the west side." She sniffed and wiped her nose with the sleeve of her gown.

He turned to me and said in a firm voice, "Stay here."

I shook my head deliberately. "No, I'm coming. I can find him!"

"No!" He stopped me. "He is dangerous. You will stay here with Alice and the boys." He gave me what looked like a pleading look then turned and started running in the direction Alice came.

I gave an outraged gasp and followed behind him, struggling to keep up with his long strides. "Owen! You may think me an incapable female, but let me assure you—"

He turned around and marched toward me, cutting off my words. To my complete astonishment, he hooked an arm around my waist and tucked the other under my knees and lifted me off the ground. "You . . . will . . . stay here," he said with exasperation, carrying me quickly toward the place where Alice and my brothers stood. My heart pounded. This was how he held me when he caught me from the waterfall. The warmth of him, the smell of him . . .

"Owen! I did not give you permission to carry me!" I attempted to say it in a bold voice, but my words came out rather breathless.

He glanced down at me with a rebuking look that bristled my pride. "And I did not give you permission to follow me. I cannot put you in danger." He set me down a few feet from Alice. His hand slipped from my waist and he looked down at me, his expression full of so many things I didn't understand, then he turned toward the woods without another word.

Anger bubbled in my chest. I was stubborn, it was a fault I possessed and completely recognized. But I wasn't fully aware of my own actions when I reached out and grabbed him by the back of his shirt, stopping him. "You cannot go alone! You don't even have a weapon! I will come and watch for trouble and then—"

He turned around with a groan. Something flashed in his eyes. Then in one swift motion he took my face in his hands, bent down, and kissed me.

It was unexpected and brief, but my mind escaped me all the same. His lips were pleading and unhesitant. I felt myself come completely unraveled in that moment—that sweet moment that could not have possibly lasted more than three seconds. Then he pulled away, too soon, his eyes burning through mine. "Stay here," he said in a hoarse voice. "Please."

Then his hands dropped from my face and he turned and ran toward the woods before I could catch my breath. I stood in shock, watching his back as he ran, trying to comprehend what just happened. Owen kissed me.

Owen. Kissed. *Me.*

How many times had I imagined that very thing? More times than I cared to admit. My face was thoroughly hot and I didn't dare look at Alice, but I could feel her surprise. But it was impossible that she could have been more surprised than I was.

I moved my gaze to the ground. My face and heart were on fire, but I forced my mind to collect itself and remember the most pressing issue. The strange man must have assumed that Owen loved Miss Lyons when he saw them together the day before. That was why he abducted her. I took a deep breath to steady myself, but my mind would not stop spinning and I could not stand still for a moment longer. I couldn't wait to know what happened. Impatience was a very dear friend to my stubborn quality.

"Peter, Charles, stay with Alice," I said briskly before I could change my mind. I guided them toward her with a gentle push, avoiding her expression, then set off after Owen, keeping a far enough distance between us so he wouldn't see that I had followed.

I could hear Alice calling my name, telling me to stop, but I didn't listen. I was halfway to the woods when Owen disappeared into the trees. My panic spread fire through my veins, propelling me faster. When I reached the edge of the lawn I plunged into the woods, skirting around and under loose branches that scratched at my face and caught in my hair as I ran. I realized how loud my steps were over the leaves and dead twigs, so I slowed to a walk. I strained my ears, trying to hear any sound that would indicate where Owen had gone. But I could scarcely hear a thing over my pounding heart, and I didn't dare yell his name, so I continued walking deeper into the woods.

After several minutes and many wrong turns, I reached a small clearing. Muffled voices reached my ears from the right and I cocked my head toward the sound. I followed it tentatively, sliding past trees and looking around them before proceeding. The voices grew louder, guiding me right, then right again. And then I stepped under a thick branch and I could see their owners.

It was another small clearing, with lofty trees surrounding it on all sides. The strange man stood with his back to me, wearing his tall top hat as usual. The sight was strangely familiar, but I couldn't quite place it. Owen stood facing me—facing the strange man. I stepped back, concealing myself behind the nearest tree, and squinted with surprise at Owen's face. His expression was . . . apologetic.

It confused me, and I was distracted for a long enough moment to fail to warn Owen. For in that moment someone else sneaked up behind him and hit him over the head with a thick branch.

I stifled a gasp, diving forward without thinking. My feet slapped against the leaves on the ground as I ran, and my knees hit the dirt painfully. "Owen!" My hands found his shoulders and I shook them. His head was slumped to the side, his eyes closed. He was not conscious. And I was kneeling on the ground between two very deadly men. I realized the weight of my mistake as I looked up at the man who had hit Owen, standing directly in front of me.

It was Mr. Coburn!

I stood, brushing the dirt from my gown. I was so shocked that words seemed to resist me. I stared at his balding head and bathwater eyes, opened wider than usual as he looked down at me. It was certainly him. And he had just seriously injured Owen. Fear and anger bounded through me. "What are you doing here?"

Mr. Coburn looked as surprised as I was. "I knew that Mrs. Filbee sent you away but I never imagined it would be here! Hah! What a monstrous coincidence this is."

"You didn't answer my question," I said, daring to step forward, keeping one eye on his branch.

"A feisty one, she is," the strange man said, sauntering up beside me. "With obvious unrequited affection for Dr. Kellaway." He chuckled, glancing down at Owen. "What a shame."

I didn't look at him. I kept my gaze on Mr. Coburn's grotesque equivalent. "What do you want with Owen? With Miss Lyons?"

At my words, a small whimper sounded from the right. I looked to see Miss Lyons, icy eyes wide, cheeks wet with tears, standing with her back against a tree. A rope was wrapped around the waist of her lavender gown, securing her to the tree with her hands tied behind her back.

"Revenge," came the strange man's voice.

I jerked my head to look at him, terror plunging through me as I recalled the feeling of his cold grip on my arms and his threats whispered in my ears. I swallowed and encouraged myself to sound brave. "What deed has Owen done that requires vengeance?"

He sighed and looked up, annoyed. "Coburn, bind her to a tree."

My jaw dropped. After a moment of hesitation, Mr. Coburn stepped over Owen and seized my upper arm, pulling me toward a tree near Miss Lyons. I kicked at his legs, thrashing, and even dug my heels into the dirt, but still he was able to drag me to the tree. He gripped my other arm and pressed my wrists together. Then he wrapped a piece of thick, rough rope around them, and just as quickly, took a much longer piece and strapped me to the tree around my middle, a confinement matching Miss Lyons.

The rope scratched at my wrists as I tried to withdraw my hands from it. "You are a big, smelly, revolting bully," I mumbled, fulfilling my promise to Owen. As Mr. Coburn stepped away, I caught a look of anger on his face, which gave me a strange bit of satisfaction despite my current circumstances.

The strange man watched me sedately. "Now, to answer your question . . . ," he said, adjusting the ridiculous amount of fobs hanging from his waistcoat. "Oh, I nearly forgot . . . ," he nodded at Mr. Coburn, "Tie up our dear Dr. Kellaway as well."

Mr. Coburn's gaze shifted to Owen and back to the strange man. "But, Jasper . . . what if he . . . awakens?"

"Then simply hit him over the head again."

I glared at the strange man—Jasper, as Mr. Coburn had called him—as his face spread into a wicked grin. My heart hammered in my chest. Surely Alice was informing her father at this moment, possibly even sending Edmond. I had seen the stable hands, they were certainly large and strong. Perhaps they were being sent also. They could be here in five minutes, perhaps even less. But would it be soon enough?

"There, yes, now make it a bit tighter, we don't want him escaping," Jasper returned his gaze to me once Owen was secured to a tree on the opposite side of the clearing. "You wish to know why I seek retribution? Oh, you must think very ill of me, but let me assure you, I only desire that Kellaway suffers as I did. That he experiences the same pain that he inflicted upon myself."

"Don't hurt him," I blurted, straining against the ropes confining me.

"Oh, no," he chuckled, "I do not intend to injure *him* any further. Eventually he would recover, and we cannot have that. Unless of course, I killed him, which is not my intention either." He walked toward me slowly, then stopped only two paces away. His eyes glinted like steel. "I shall hurt him where pain never heals." He jabbed at his own chest with a finger. "The heart."

Then he turned and walked swiftly to the center of the clearing once more, and faced me again, extending a hand in Miss Lyons's direction. "As you see, that is the purpose of the lady. When he awakens, he will have the honor of watching his love die before him. It is only fair, is it not? For when he failed to heal my Ariana of her illness, I was forced to do just that. And now he will pay the same price."

My mind swarmed. The letter. The letter that had troubled Owen so severely. The story of the woman he had failed to save, and her fiancé's resentment. And her mourning father . . .

My gaze turned to Mr. Coburn. "Your daughter."

He nodded curtly, avoiding my gaze. The coincidence was too wild to comprehend. Mr. Coburn's ill daughter was Owen's patient that died. Mr. Coburn had boasted that she was recently engaged. And her pending marriage was to be with Jasper. I stared at Mr. Coburn in shock and was surprised to see tears pooling in his eyes.

I never expected him to be so . . . softhearted. But all things considered, he was helping to plot a murder.

I could hear Miss Lyons sobbing at the tree beside me. I almost pitied her, but then, between sobs, she said, "He does not love me! He loves her!" A dainty finger pointed in my direction. I nearly audibly gasped. She turned her cold blue eyes on me, her accusation even colder. She desired a way of escape, and felt no qualms in convicting me in the process.

My eyes darted between her and Jasper. She was not backing down on her claim. It was a natural response, defending herself, but my situation was growing increasingly dire by the second. Her words, though somewhat understandable, shocked me nonetheless.

"Oh, do not look at me with that prodigious surprise!" she rasped. "I have seen the way he looks at you."

Jasper gave a low, husky laugh at this, leaning toward Miss Lyons with a smirk. "I applaud your attempt, Mademoiselle, but I witnessed you with him at the ball last night. I overheard the rumors of a proposal from his own sister."

"You were at the ball?" I asked sharply. My question was answered as I recalled the image of a man in a very tall top hat obscuring my view of Owen and Miss Lyons. A chill settled between my shoulder blades.

"Dr. Kellaway invited me himself. He hoped it would be a . . . token of apology. I took it as an opportunity to descend upon the property unnoticed."

It was a sure plan, for Lizzie and I were the only two who could have identified him. I looked across the clearing at Owen. He was tied to his tree sitting down, his head slumped forward, chin against chest. He was breathing, to my relief, and I thought I saw him moving.

"Help is coming soon," I stammered. "You will be outnumbered."

Instead of looking concerned, Jasper shrugged his shoulders. "Then we had best make this hasty." He peeked at Owen, who was stirring noticeably now. "What opportune timing."

Miss Lyons's sobbing grew to an excruciating volume.

Jasper reached Owen's tree an instant later and knelt down beside him with a sneer. "Good day. How was your slumber?"

I could see that Owen's eyes had opened. The sight caused a surge of unrest to rise within me. He was tied tightly to that tree, hindered from his blow to the head, and without anything in the way of weapons. I could envision no remedy to our situation, and it terrified me.

He blinked rapidly, releasing a soft moan. He was still unaware of his surroundings, I could tell. He looked oddly at ease, his scowling gaze shifting from Jasper to the rope at his hands. Then his eyes found mine, and the time for composure was gone.

"Annette?" he breathed. He looked as if the devil himself had landed between us, sheer terror crossing his face. He began vigorously pulling against his restraint. "Release her, now!" he yelled, his voice desperate. Jasper stared from Owen to me, looking perplexed as his smile faltered.

My throat tightened. "I'm sorry, Owen," I said, not expecting my strength to crumble so quickly. "I had to follow you." A tear slipped from my eye, something that was becoming an unwelcome habit.

Owen's jaw clenched as he momentarily gave up on his efforts of escape. His eyes lingered on me for a moment, flickering to the ropes around my wrists and waist. He then glanced up at Jasper. The look in his eyes could have sliced through a boulder. "Release her. Release them both, or I swear I will make you regret every blasted moment of your life."

Jasper's smile only grew, transforming into a fit of hysteria. "How *inattendu*! He does love this one." He gawked at Mr. Coburn, pointing a finger in my direction. "It was an unfair presumption on my part, I confess, but I cannot say that I'm disappointed. She has proven quite vexing. I shall delight in killing her."

I thought I had seen Owen uncollected before, but not to such an extent as this. Something within him snapped, the last and final straw laid. He pulled desperately against the ropes, yelling, pleading, as Jasper walked toward me. I bit down my tears, not willing to give him the satisfaction of seeing my fear. I watched Owen, his futile efforts unceasing, until Jasper stood between us. "Would you prefer pistol or dagger?"

Owen cursed at him from across the clearing.

My thoughts collected on Peter and Charles. What would they do without me? Where would they go? Back to live with Aunt Ruth? The idea stabbed at my heart. No. Owen would look after them, take them to live with him at Willowbourne.

"Very well, I will choose," Jasper said, pulling the shiny dagger from his jacket. He held it up, letting the blade catch light. "The pistol would have been far too loud, you see. I do not wish to alarm the neighbors."

"How considerate," I said with mock civility. I hadn't abandoned hope yet, surely help was on its way. We were no more than a mile from the house. What was taking so long?

Mr. Coburn piped in, his voice uneasy. "Jasper, perhaps—perhaps we might . . . reconsider whether it is entirely . . . necessary to commit the, um . . . the crime." He was standing near Owen, wringing his hands together uneasily.

Jasper whipped to face him, stepping away from me for an instant. I breathed a small sigh of relief. Every second of delay was precious. I locked eyes with Owen, trying to communicate somehow without words. His eyes held everything from anger to desperation to regret.

"Is this a coward that you are becoming, Coburn?" Jasper scoffed. "I never took you for a coward. We are avenging your daughter. Not to do so would be cowardice of the most unrespectable sort."

Mr. Coburn stared at the ground.

"And to murder a woman for the mistake of a man is respectable?" Owen said with disbelief. "That is dishonor of the most disgusting sort. If you must murder someone, then your business is with me. A duel. Release me and you will answer! Fair game. You choose the weapons."

Jasper gritted his teeth. "Enough of this. Time is wasting away!" Once in front of me again, he took his dagger slowly to my throat, pressing it there, not firmly enough to cause pain, but firmly enough for me to vividly imagine what this dagger—this man— was capable of. I felt its cold edge, a chilled breeze against my skin.

He faced me, holding my head against the tree with one hand. "I am going to enjoy this," he said, his eyes dark, lost of amusement.

My breath came rapidly, as if my body knew that soon it would take its last. "And afterward you will enjoy your hanging."

He pressed the blade against my throat, making me cry out. I couldn't see Owen, but I could hear him, desperately calling my name, pleading with Jasper not to kill me, thoroughly naming the consequences he would inflict if he did.

"Coburn, subdue him somehow!" Jasper screamed, returning his gaze to my face. "If a hanging is where this ends, then I will welcome it. My love and I will then have our marvelous reunion," he snarled.

*I don't believe such reunions exist where you are going*, I wanted to say. But I owed it to my brothers to hold my tongue. Making him angrier now would not be an intelligent move, no matter the satisfaction. "Would she wish you to do this?" I asked, my voice strained from the pressure at my neck. His eyes narrowed, but I continued, "Become a criminal for her sake, and blame her innocent physician for the cruel hand fate dealt her?" It was my last hope, plucking at his conscience with guilt.

He hesitated for the length of a blink. "Of course."

My stomach dropped.

In hysterics once more, he inched closer to my face, holding the dagger taut. "*Au revoir*," he whispered.

I squeezed my eyes shut, preferring my last sight to be of the back of my eyelids rather than this man's haunting countenance. The seconds stretched on and on. I counted to ten in my head. Nothing. Tears were slipping from my eyes despite my effort to control them. In my mind I said farewell to Peter, to Charles. To Owen. Owen, who I knew would look after my little brothers, repair their tiny hearts after they shatter. Raise them to be gentlemen. I paused my thoughts, silence filling my ears like a sound. Owen?

I could no longer hear him.

The same moment my eyes flew open, the dagger fell from my neck. I blinked away the tears clouding my vision and gaped at the scene before me. Jasper was being ground into the dirt, Owen on top of him, throwing his fists into his face, sounds of crunching accompanying each movement.

Miss Lyons gave a high-pitched scream.

All I could do was stare, absolutely shocked.

After several more strikes, and another for good measure, Owen took Jasper by the collar, jerking him to his feet. I watched his eyes dart around him, one already swelling. His nose was bent grotesquely and bleeding. Surely broken, explaining the repeated crunching.

"Coburn!" he screeched.

"Your coconspirator abandoned you!" Owen barked, thrusting him back by his collar. "He released me himself. Now, we can settle this like men, or you can follow him off this land while some of your face remains intact. Be assured that I will not hesitate to dismantle whatever body part necessary should you choose to return. Or if you fail to leave within the next two seconds."

The beating of horse hooves reached my ears just as Edmond and Mr. Kellaway burst into the clearing, pistols in hand. Their eyes fell upon the scene before them, surprise crossing their expressions before they dismounted and set to untying Miss Lyons and me. Owen clearly had control of the situation. Without a backward glance, Jasper retrieved his hat from the dirt and fled, holding a hand to his bleeding nose.

Edmond finished untying my ropes, concern on his face. "Are you hurt?"

I shook my head numbly, rubbing feeling back into my wrists. How was I alive?

Then Owen was there, pushing past Edmond, close enough to touch. Seeing his concern and fear tugged at the weak strings that were holding my emotions together. Needing stability, and acting on strange instinct, I threw myself into his arms, everything about the day's events catching up to me.

Without hesitation he slipped an arm around my waist, the other holding my head against his chest, as if he meant to keep me near his heart and never let me go. I could feel his hands shaking as he held me, and when he pulled away to look at my face I was surprised to see tears in his eyes. "You stubborn girl." He ran his hand over my hair and pulled my head to his chest again. "I'm sorry," he whispered, his voice husky with emotion. "I'm sorry."

Everything came pouring back to me—I had almost run away this morning. Owen had kissed me. I felt incredibly shy and confused as I recalled that particular event. It took a host of efforts, but

I pulled my head back to look at him and found my voice. "That man was mad. You couldn't have expected this to happen."

Owen drew an audible breath. "If the other man, my patient's father, hadn't released me . . . ," he shook his head, cutting off his own words.

For a strange reason I felt a smile tug at my lips.

"What?"

I pressed down a laugh, placing a hand over my mouth.

"Annette?" He looked confused, concerned by my sudden change of mood, no doubt.

"He is the man from my neighborhood. The one with the revolting eyes," I said. The wild coincidence of the situation now struck me as hilarious. Mr. Coburn, the man who I had despised, and still didn't particularly find agreeable, had quite possibly saved my life.

Owen still looked confused, so I explained the connection, lightening his expression to a smile. "To repay him for his deed today, we shall only refer to him as *slightly* revolting from now on."

My laugh came out as a snort. I knew the laughter was only coming as a replacement for crying, so I wasn't surprised when I ended up doing both. Owen wiped the tears from my cheeks and wrapped me in his arms again, cradling me as if I was the most precious thing in the world to him. I was enveloped with comfort and security, and at that moment I finally believed that he truly cared for me. That he loved me.

*But it doesn't matter*, I reminded myself. I had nearly left this morning, firm on my decision to remind my heart of its place. My brothers needed me to love them, and them alone, for I was the only one who did. I could not have Owen vying for my heart that already belonged to my brothers, who needed it so desperately.

*But are they happy? Are you happy?* I pushed the questions away, because I knew it was my heart that posed them.

I was suddenly very aware of where I stood, leaning against Owen the way I was, clutching his shirt in my hands like a child. It had been so long since I had felt comfort like this, or since I had felt so achingly loved. But it was an unfair, painful thing to prolong this moment. Because I was never going to feel it again.

I moved away from him too quickly. I could see by the flash of hurt in his eyes. I looked away immediately, but I knew in my bones that the pain in his eyes would haunt me always, and I felt my heart crack a little more. This crevice ran deep, and I doubted that I could ever find a way to fill it.

Gathering my resolve, I bit my lip to keep my tears inside and walked toward the trees where Edmond and Mr. Kellaway waited with Miss Lyons and the horses. Edmond was looking between Owen and me, a secretive smile touching lightly on his lips.

The men walked ahead, holding the reins as we started back to the house. Miss Lyons was riding on the horse beside me, deliberately avoiding my gaze. My head ached from thought, making my eyelids droop with the rhythmic motion of the ride.

By the time we reached the house, everything was hazy. Up the stairs, through the hall, into my room, Lizzie leading me by the elbow. My bed could not have been a more welcome sight. *I will only sleep for one hour*, I resolved.

But then my head hit my pillow and I slept for eight.

# Chapter 21

ou poor thing!" Mrs. Kellaway exclaimed as I told her the details of the morning. She had insisted that I take a meal with her in the sitting room as soon as I awoke. But she was certainly devouring my words faster than her food. She had already spoken with Owen and Miss Lyons, hearing their sides of the story, but mine was the piece of the puzzle missing.

"He held a dagger to your throat?" she said in quiet awe, a chunk of roasted duck hanging off the edge of her fork.

I nodded.

She gasped, shaking her head. The meat fell to her plate. "Thank the heavens that Owen was present to stop him."

I nodded again.

Her eyes were glued to my face, her expression unreadable. "You are not still planning to leave, are you?"

The question broke me from my thoughtless state. Was I going to leave? The idea was much less endearing now. For me to run off the land defiantly, besting my heart, being superior to its dreams. I was at an equilibrium, battling with myself over what decision to make over this very subject. And what about Peter and Charles? I had never seen the two of them so happy. Maybe the way to keep my promises was different than I had so narrow-mindedly determined before. But maybe it wasn't.

"Perhaps we will stay a few more days, if that is fine." It was the best response I could manage. I was afraid, and I didn't remember how to be brave.

Mrs. Kellaway smiled, her eyes bright. "It is my hope, and the hope of everyone in this house that you will stay even longer. But it is ultimately your choice, and I hope you make it correctly."

Make it correctly?

"I know for certain that one heart will break if you leave here." She leaned forward and hovered a finger above my chest. "If not another." Her smile turned secretive, matching the expression Edmond had displayed in the woods.

I had no idea of how to respond, and Mrs. Kellaway must have sensed as much, so she gave my hand a pat and suggested that I find my brothers who had been very worried about me.

I was grateful to leave, wanting to console my brothers as well as myself. I found them very close by, only a turn away from the room I exited, in apparent search for me. I extended my arms the moment I saw them, putting a smile on my face. They hurried to me with relief. Peter clutched my hand and Charles nestled against my side.

"I am just fine," I assured them in the softest tone possible. "Not to worry."

Charles lifted his gaze, small creases lining his forehead. Those creases I had seen so many times only now struck me forcibly. A little boy of five should never have so many reasons to frown, enough reasons to be worried and afraid. I had seen the same expression on Peter often. A realization came over me, filling me with guilt. Since arriving here, this was the first time I had seen that look on either of their faces. We had been here for weeks now, and not once had I seen those creases of worry. How could I possibly tear them away from this place?

"Were you afraid?" Peter asked, his eyes full of interest.

"Yes, but I am fine now."

"Owen said you were very brave," Charles remarked.

I looked down at him, eyebrows drawn. "You have been with Owen?"

"While you were sleeping? Yes."

A surge of gratitude erupted inside me. "What—how did you pass the time?"

Peter squeezed my hand eagerly. "He let us ride the horses! I got to ride the little black horse and Charles got to ride the brown one. I enjoyed it very much."

I laughed. "I'm glad you did."

"But I still missed you very much," Peter said with a little smile, melting my heart.

I pulled them both into my arms and gave the tops of their heads a light kiss. "I love you both very, *very* much."

Charles's voice was muffled against me as he said, "Owen said that he loves us too."

"What?" I pulled away so I could see his face, heart pounding.

His blue eyes gazed up into mine, not a hint of dishonesty there. "Uh huh." He nodded. "He told us that we were the best boys in the whole world and that we need to be good gentlemens to you our whole lives. And then he told us that he loves us."

My mind raced. I had seen the affection in Owen's eyes when he watched them, interacted with them. I could see that my brothers thought of him as their idol. But Owen truly cared for them, and I could see in both Peter's and Charles's eyes that it was the greatest gift. And it pained me to observe. How had being loved become such a rare novelty?

Charles pulled me from my thoughts by saying, "Oh! And then he said that he loves you too, very much, 'cept you don't love him back. Then he looked sad."

A breath caught in my throat.

"Why don't you love him?" Charles asked, concern plaguing his face again.

My emotions were held together by spider web strands. I swallowed, and tried to stop holding my breath. Both Peter and Charles looked up at me expectantly, clearly wondering the same thing I had wondered multiple times: how could anyone not love Owen?

"I do."

Charles's face lit up and he turned his gaze to Peter. "Let's go tell him!"

"No!" I exclaimed in panic. "I mean—no. You mustn't tell Owen that."

"Why not?"

"Because . . . because he can't know."

"Why not?" Charles repeated, his voice a whine.

"Because he just can't," I affirmed, searching my mind for a new subject. "Now, what would you two like to do? Would you like to visit the library and show me your favorite books?"

Peter's eyes flew open wide. "Grandfather could tell you a story! He tells the greatest stories!"

I slumped with relief. "Oh? That should be very nice. Hopefully Grandfather is there."

Charles nodded his agreement, then dropped his voice to a whisper. "I think Grandfather lives in the library. All the time."

I threw my head back with a laugh. "That sounds like a possibility. But where could he sleep?"

Charles's expression never strayed from serious. "Probably under the table."

I ruffled his hair, laughing, Peter joining me. "You may be right. If so, then we should have no doubts about his presence there right now."

Sure enough, as we stepped into the library, I spotted Grandfather sitting in a leather chair, book in hand, spectacles on nose. He glanced up as we entered, his wrinkled face lifting in a smile. "Good evening. I hoped to see you here."

Peter and Charles ran across the room to the chair beside him, pleading for him to tell a story.

"Very well, very well," he chuckled, standing to move a chair for me to sit in. "Owen told me all about the ordeal this morning," he said, ushering me into the chair. "Are you well?"

Had Owen been everywhere today? "Yes, I'm feeling much better."

"I am glad to hear it." His smile made his eyes twinkle. He took a deep breath that sounded like a sigh. "Yes . . . Owen spoke with me for a very long time this afternoon."

I wondered what he would say next, but instead of continuing that subject, he leaned forward in his chair, rubbing his hands together. "Now for the story. Hmm," he mused, looking from my brothers to me. Then he began, his voice smooth, easy to listen to.

"There once was a lovely young lady who carried with her a vessel full of water everywhere she went. She treasured this vessel, and cared for it deeply, but it had been scratched and worn over her life, and so the water within was what she so attentively nurtured. Never had she let a single drop of that precious water spill. In all her daily activities she held this vessel tightly against her, concealed beneath her thick coat, so none could see it or touch it, or, what she feared most—steal it."

Grandfather paused deliberately, looking between my brothers and me, lingering longer on my face, as if he could see my thoughts displayed there.

"She often visited the stream from which she had collected the water. It was the only stream she had ever known and this young woman found contentment in walking along its banks with her scarred vessel full of its treasured water. Never did she dream of other streams or other waters. Then one day, when this young lady ventured to the stream, she was astonished to find another stream running directly beside it. Unable to help herself, she walked along its banks too. As days passed, she grew attached to this stream and wished her vessel could give place for some of its water. But she knew her vessel was full, and still she infinitely valued the water from the first stream and knew it must not be replaced."

I felt my throat clench with emotion, feeling the truth behind this story nestle in my heart and remain, as if it intended to make a home there. My hand crept to my throat as I listened, intent on keeping myself in one piece.

"But as days turned into weeks, the young woman's longing for the new stream began to create fresh scars on her vessel, and soon, she feared, it would break and she would lose every drop of precious water within. So, if only to soothe the ache she felt, she dipped her hand into the new stream and scooped its water into her brimming vessel. Expecting the water would not fit, and overflow onto the rocks, the young woman was amazed to find that the water did not. Instead, the water entered the vessel and remained although it had appeared full. Unsure, the young woman took another scoop of water and poured it into her vessel. It too remained.

"Delighted, this young lady deposited scoop after scoop of water from the stream into her vessel and remarkably, she never spilled a drop from the first stream as she went. Her vessel, it seemed, could not become full. And as she poured water in, she saw the scratches fade from her vessel, and was filled with happiness like she had never before known. She had discovered a brilliant truth: that the water from both streams was infinite, and her vessel could contain it all."

Tears ran silently down my face as the poignant beauty of his story overwhelmed me. The message was clear, and it filled me with a new kind of strength.

Grandfather paused, finishing his story on a softer tone. "So, later in her life, as more streams appeared beside the two she now knew so well, she didn't hesitate to take water from each, for she now knew she did not have to lose a single drop to gain many."

When he finished speaking, the room fell into a silence too important to break. Every shattered piece of unknown had molded together, all my indecision brought to light. How had he known exactly what I needed to hear? Precisely what would tug at my heart more than anything else? The answer was simple. He was Owen's grandfather.

Grandfather smiled and nodded toward the door. "I believe he is in the orchard."

I smiled back, hoping my gratitude could be shown without words. And then I stood and left the room, letting my tears dry as I ran. I was afraid, but I also had hope, and somehow that was enough.

# Chapter 22

The sun was nothing but a dim glow in the sky, soon to set for the night. I had no plan, and soon after I stepped outside, my heart was pounding so hard I thought it might burst from my chest. What was I doing? What would I say when I saw him? Did I really want to tell him I loved him? No. I could not declare my feelings first. What if he didn't really love me? What if Peter and Charles had lied and the man in the woods was wrong? How could Owen possibly not have known already? I was a puddle every time he spoke with me, surely he already knew.

So what was I doing?

I was close to the gate now. The door lay open, inviting me in. Was Owen even there? My question was answered as I glimpsed him, standing with his back to me, arms folded across his chest.

My heart pounded. It was settled then. I was turning around. I ordered my feet to stop walking, to turn and never have to see what was in Owen's eyes tonight, but apparently, my feet did not seek my good opinion. They carried me forward, doggedly propelling me to the gate, through it, and then five paces more.

I stopped, tracing the slump of his shoulders with my gaze, wondering what it was that brought him here tonight. Did he need to be alone or did he wish me to come? There was still time to leave; he hadn't noticed me yet.

I took another unwilling step toward him.

A leaf must have crunched, or a twig must have broken under my boot, because he turned at that step, and then I knew I was finally paralyzed from taking another.

He didn't seem surprised to see me there, standing ten feet away. Doubt was cast on the path between us, leaving no room for surprise. "How are you feeling?" he asked.

"Much better." I had to force my mouth to form the words.

"Are you still leaving?" His voice was throaty and broken—full of doubt. It wrenched at my heart.

"No." I swallowed. "I think . . . I think we will stay a few days longer."

He seemed to relax at this, but there was something more that was tormenting him. He kept his arms crossed, as if it was the only way to hold himself together. The air was unmoving between us, not a breath of wind, yet there was a tension that could be snapped in two. I stood as still as I could, waiting for his words that I couldn't predict. The shadow of the sky fell over him, growing darker by the second, bringing the yellow of the sun to a deep gold.

"Do you remember the poetry lesson I taught the boys?" he asked.

I nodded, gripping my shaking hands on my skirts.

His eyes were careful, fear laced with anticipation. "If you will provide an honest answer, I would like to ask my question now."

I nodded my consent, nervousness closing my throat from words.

Drawing a ragged breath, he raked a hand through his hair. "Your honesty is crucial, Annette," he sighed. "Because I cannot go on without knowing this. Truly knowing this. I have been acutely tortured by this question for too long already and without an answer, I will be tortured always." He didn't move, speaking in a voice that was vulnerable, watching me as if I would run away any second.

My stomach tied itself in knots as I watched Owen growing dim with the sky. I could see him clearly in the waning light—I could see his eyes flashing with fear and carefulness, and his chest rising and falling with each broken breath. He hesitated for several seconds, each one containing an eternity.

"Do you love me?"

My heart pounded so hard it ached. Owen stood watching me, awaiting my answer, looking as if a word from me could shatter him apart. I did love him. I had loved him for what felt like a lifetime. So much within me insisted that I say no, that I run and hide like the weak thing I had become. But a part of me, the stronger, braver part of me refused to listen. I had balanced on these slender branches for far too long, and now I finally knew which way I wanted to fall.

"I do," I breathed.

It was as if the words threw Owen forward by some nameless force. He covered the space between us in four long strides, and before I had time to think, or take a single breath, he was kissing me.

One arm wrapped around my waist, the other holding my face, he pulled me close, his kisses beckoning, firm, full of nothing but aching emotion. His hand at my back was all that held me righted as he kissed me exactly the way he wanted. All my previous efforts to defend my heart and maintain its barriers were quickly unraveling, and the time for thinking was gone.

My hands clutched the lapels of his jacket, pulling him impossibly closer, kissing him in return. His fingers moved to my hair, guiding me into a kiss that was too perfect for words, my heart breaking apart at the aching emotion, and then being repaired flawlessly by the tender gentleness that increased as his lips slowed.

Everything was different about this kiss—there was knowledge and hope and understanding. Not a trace of heartbreak. And it did not take long for me to realize that this was not falling. Not at all. This was climbing higher than I had ever climbed before. I was at the top of the tree, standing beneath the clouds that seemed so close and away from the ground that now seemed so far. The sky was in my reach and there was at last nothing stopping me from taking flight.

By the time Owen pulled away I was nothing but a puddle at his feet, shaking in his arms as tears ran silently down my cheeks.

"Annette," he sighed in a hoarse whisper. His face was an inch from mine, his eyes shining with tears of his own. "I knew I couldn't let you go until I was certain that you didn't love me. I never dreamed that you did."

"What?" I asked as he swiped a tear from my cheek with his thumb. "You must have been entirely blind, then. Until today I hardly imagined that you loved me."

He gave an exasperated sigh. "I was not blind to your continuous glaring and fleeing from my presence. And I certainly was not deaf to being called atrocious repeatedly." His mouth curved into a small smile, his eyes roaming my face with such undisguised adoration that I was melted all over again. "I have been falling in love with you since that first lovely glare, the moment you arrived here wearing Charles's vomit like a champion."

I laughed, a choked sound in my throat.

He leaned down, pressing a kiss to my forehead, making a blossom of sweet warmth spread throughout my face. "You won my heart from me that day and I knew that I would never reclaim it. It has always been, and will always be yours, Annette. If you will accept it." His blue eyes gazed into mine, his very words inscribing themselves on my heart.

Beneath my hand pressed to Owen's chest, I could feel his heart pounding through his shirt, strong and sure. How was it that all this time it had belonged to me? It was too amazing to believe.

"But I have no money to give you, no dowry, no—no titles in my family, or any accomplishments to note . . . it is a lot to overlook." I remembered Miss Lyons's words, *That he should overlook so much for the sake of his heart.*

I was shaking my head, but Owen stopped me, holding my face in both his hands now. "Listen to me. There is nothing to overlook. I don't want to overlook anything about you, in fact. You are the most accomplished lady I know. You are accomplished in everything that truly matters, nothing that does not. You are accomplished in the art of taming mischievous boys, being unfailingly witty, selfless and devoted and brave." He wiped away another tear that slipped from my eye. "So brave," he whispered. "And there is nothing in this world that you could give me that is more precious than your heart, and I would treasure it forever—if you will allow me to have it."

My breath came in sputtering gasps as I nodded, the tears continuing to flow. I had become an official watering pot, but I no longer cared.

He wrapped me in his arms, encasing me in the warmth of him, his perfect scent that I had memorized but couldn't quite describe, and rested his forehead against mine. He quickly swiped away each new tear that slipped from my eyes. In that moment every trace of doubt was gone, whisked away by Owen's words and his smile and his love in my hands. With him, there would be no reason to doubt ever again. I knew it with a solid certainty that could not be denied.

I took a deep breath and smiled, bringing my hand up to his face, feeling the place where his dimple always showed. "You have had my heart for much longer than you think," I whispered.

His face split into a smile of disbelief and relief and then he kissed me again. All over my tear-covered face, my hair, my lips, until I was certain that I was completely, fervidly loved. And I didn't have to be afraid of anything. I was the girl with her vessel of water, full to the brim but never overflowing, I could love without end and be loved the same. It was the greatest gift under the sun.

When the last hint of daylight was gone and the sky was painted the navy and deep purple of evening, I finally pulled myself from Owen's arms and we started walking back to the house, hand in hand.

When we were approaching the rose garden near the back door, Owen turned to face me, his eyes soft, careful. "Wait here." Then he slipped his hand from mine without another sound and walked toward the rose garden. I watched as he removed a rose of indistinguishable color from the top of the nearest bush. He turned with a crooked smile and started toward me again.

As he moved closer, a patch of moonlight cut through the dimness, bathing the rose in silver, natural light. It was sloping gently, smoothly, and was the softest shade of pink. Owen stopped in front of me, holding the rose as if it was a fragile thing. I watched it, cradled in his hand, the stem broken off short near the head, not a thorn to be seen. It lay there like a secret that belonged only to us. And it didn't scare me at all.

"I daresay this would look enchanting in your hair," he said in a quiet voice, his lips quirked upward.

I smiled shyly and looked up into Owen's eyes. Nothing could dim the light I saw there.

He lifted his hands to my head, to the place where my hair was arranged in a loose twist. One of his hands curved around the back of my neck, the other fiddled with the rose and my untamable hair.

I kept my eyes focused on his cravat and the line of his jaw until he breathed in deeply, breaking the silence.

"Let this rose—this color, become something different tonight." His voice was hushed, and I felt him tuck the stem under my hair by my ear. "Don't have it haunt you for things that have been lost, but let it be a reminder of things that are new. Let it remind you, Annette, that I love you." He drew a breath and gave me a small smile, moving his gaze from the rose and down to my face. "But truly, that is not a new thing at all."

I found breathing incredibly difficult at that moment, with Owen looking at me the way he was, with that crooked grin and the dimple in his cheek. Then his hands fell from my head and he took a step back, his eyes roaming my face and my hair and the rose. I lifted my hand and touched the pink rose carefully, feeling its soft velvet petals that told me Owen loved me.

"You look beautiful." He drew closer again and took my hand, holding it as if it was just as fragile a thing as our rose. Then he lifted it to his chest and placed it where I could feel every beat of his heart. "Now that you know my heart is unalterably yours, I wish to ask you if you will have it forever, and if you will give yours to me—" he lifted my hand from his chest and brushed his lips across the back of it, then looked at me with a hopeful smile, "and if you will marry me."

My smile felt impossibly wide as fresh tears slipped from my eyes. I nodded. "Yes," I managed through my tight throat. Owen's smile grew with mine. I could imagine no other option for my life now than spending every last moment with him. I couldn't understand how I had been fully prepared to run away and never see him again. It seemed incomprehensible to me now.

The sound of giggles reached my ears and I turned my head in the direction they came. Peter and Charles ran out the door of the house, as if they had just spotted us out the library window. They ran to Owen with grins pulled to their ears.

"Annette does love you!" Charles told him, eyes wide. "So you don't have to be sad anymore."

Owen chuckled, throwing me a sideways glance. Then he scooped Charles up onto his shoulders, sending him into a fit of giggles. "That makes me very happy," he said, ruffling Peter's hair. "Do you remember the picture I showed you in the library?"

"The castle?" Charles asked from above.

Peter looked up at him, rolling his clear blue eyes. "It was called Will-a-thorn."

I stifled a laugh, sharing a smile with Owen. "Willowbourne," he corrected gently. "How would you like to live there?"

Peter looked confused for a moment, scowling up at Owen. "What about Aunt Ruth?" His voice was a nervous whisper.

Owen pulled Charles down from his shoulders and set him beside Peter. "You never have to see her again if you don't wish to. Do you remember my promise? She will never hurt either of you ever again." My brothers nodded, and Owen pulled them into his arms. The sight brought the sting of tears to my eyes. Owen reached for me, slipping his arm around my waist. "And she will never hurt you again either," he said in a whisper.

I felt the truth of his words nestle inside me like a precious gift.

"But will Annette get to come?" Peter asked.

Owen turned his smile on me, a sight that made my heart flutter, and I knew then that it always would. "Annette definitely gets to come."

Peter and Charles were giddy at this, jumping up and down, pulling on Owen's hand and dragging me by my skirts across the lawn and through the door of the house. "I get to live in a castle!" Charles yelled with unexpected volume as we stepped inside. I cringed at the echo it created, surely summoning every soul in the home.

Owen laughed heartily, taking my hand in his. "It seems we will have the entire house to tell of our engagement."

"Unless your grandmother has already spilled the news." I smiled up at him in the new light, memorizing every detail of his face over and over again.

His eyes filled with amusement and love and mischief all at once. "Annette . . . ," he raised an eyebrow in question, "did you do it again?"

"What?"

"Did you tell my entire family that I proposed to you before I actually did? I thought you learned your lesson from the first incident." His grin was all mischief now, his arms surrounding me, pulling me closer.

I was breathless; I could not manage a gasp. Instead I rose on my toes and kissed his grinning lips. There was nothing in the universe that I wanted more than what I had here in this room, and I knew it was all I would ever need.

I took a deep breath and smiled. "You're atrocious."

# Discussion Questions

1.  Throughout the story, Annette is burdened by a promise she made to her parents, and in turn, herself, to not allow anything to distract her from her responsibility toward Peter and Charles. How might she have interpreted this promise differently? How has it affected her decisions? Have you ever felt trapped by a promise? At what point can a promise be broken?

2.  In her society, Annette is considered unaccomplished because she doesn't draw, sing, or play an instrument. Because of this, she is deemed inferior. When considering her character, do you find any attributing accomplishment? What abilities and characteristics do you find more important to any society?

3.  Peter's and Charles's behavior improves gradually throughout the book. What circumstances influenced this change? How did Owen have a positive influence on their behavior and overall happiness? Do their roles have a large impact on the story?

4.  Securing an advantageous match was paramount in the regency period. When you consider Miss Lyons's deception, do you find any justification? Given her mother's behavior, what do you assume she was raised to believe? How does our upbringing affect our moral values?

5.  The pink rose is a continuous symbol throughout the story. What events led Annette to overcome her irrational fear of the color? How do you see this symbolism come full circle? Have you ever associated an object or sensation with an event? How did it affect you?

6. Owen conceals the truth about Willowbourne for most of the story. Why was this necessary? What was his intention for doing so? He had several opportunities to confide in Annette, but didn't. What does this tell us about his character?

7. Near the end of the book, Owen's grandfather tells a story. How do you interpret it? How and why is the message such a turning point for Annette? How does it apply to her views and reservations?

8. At the ball, Annette notes that Miss Lyons and her mother both use words as weapons. What other characters do we see acting similarly? How do the negative words from others affect Annette's self worth throughout the story? When used as weapons, how have words affected you?

9. After her parents' death, Annette adopted several different roles. How do we see each represented? How does she balance being a sister and motherly figure? What roles has Owen filled and will continue to fill in their future together?

10. Mr. Coburn, though a minor character, is portrayed as an antagonist. Were you surprised by his change of heart? What might have motivated him to turn against Jasper? What do we learn pertaining to revenge and regret?

# Acknowledgments

$\mathcal{T}$his story would still be inside my head without the help and support of so many people. I thought writing a book would make me patient, so first I must thank my family, who know that that is definitely not true, but love me anyway. I am so blessed to have had their encouragement every step of the way. Thank you for putting up with my laptop hogging, my many "just one second"s, and my overall craziness.

Thank you to Anna Rasmussen, my pretend agent and childhood mischief-making comrade, for being the kind of friend I could trust with the roughest of drafts and for enduring my ramblings about my characters while jogging. Thank you to Katelynn Bolen for her much needed feedback and for squealing over my story. Don't be surprised if you see her name on a book one of these days. Thank you, my reviewers. I love your books, your kind words, and you.

Thank you to my editors, Emma Parker, Emily Chambers, Hali Bird, and Jessica Romrell for believing in my story, answering my millions of questions, and fine-tuning this book to its best. To Priscilla Chaves, for the gorgeous cover design that I just can't stop staring at. I never will. Ever. To the rest of the team at Cedar Fort, you are so appreciated! So many people are involved in the final product, and I am so grateful for every single one of them.

I also must acknowledge the legacy of Jane Austen (including the amazingly cheesy movie adaptations), Georgette Heyer, and the many other inspirations that set me on this writing path that I love. And most importantly, my Heavenly Father, for the wonderful people and opportunities he has placed in my life, for letting me dream, and for guiding my hand.

# About the Author

Ashtyn Newbold discovered a love of writing early in high school. Inspired by regency period romance, she wrote her first novel at the age of sixteen. Because she can't vacation in her favorite historical time periods, she writes about them instead. When not crafting handsome historical heroes, she enjoys baking, sewing, music, and spoiling her dog. She dreams of traveling to England and Ireland. Ashtyn is currently studying English and creative writing at Utah Valley University. She lives in Lehi, Utah, with her family.

Scan to visit

ashtynnewbold.com